A THIRD KIND OF MADNESS

A Third Kind of Madness
Author: Christiane Knight

Published by:
Three Ravens Press
PO Box 502
White Marsh MD 21162
USA

www.christianeknight.com

Contact publisher for permission requests.

Photographer: https://unsplash.com/photos/person-holding-black-camera-2MYcbBBh9kE

Cover background image: https://unsplash.com/photos/a-close-up-of-a-red-and-black-substance-OOFSqPWjCt0

Cover design and interior book design & formatting by Leesa Ellis > 3ferns.com

Copyright © 2024 by Christiane Knight

All rights reserved. No part of this publication may be reproduced, distributed, or transmitted in any form or by any means, including photocopying, recording, or other electronic or mechanical methods, without the prior written permission of the publisher, except in the case of brief quotations embodied in critical reviews and certain other noncommercial uses permitted by copyright law.

Library of Congress Control Number: 2024908336

ISBN (paperback): 978-1-7368503-6-7
ISBN (e-Book): 978-1-7368503-7-4

A THIRD KIND OF MADNESS

CHRISTIANE KNIGHT

three ravens
PRESS

TABLE OF CONTENTS

CHAPTER 1	Panic Priest – Lonely City	1
CHAPTER 2	Talking To Shadows – Soma	12
CHAPTER 3	Second Still – Recover	20
CHAPTER 4	The Twilight Sad – There's a Girl in the Corner	29
CHAPTER 5	Them Are Us Too – Floor	38
CHAPTER 6	Public Memory – Heir	46
CHAPTER 7	Double Echo – The Position	54
CHAPTER 8	Bootblacks – Traveling Light	63
CHAPTER 9	Creux Lies – Misunderstanding	72
CHAPTER 10	The Foreign Resort – She Is Lost	79
CHAPTER 11	House of Harm – Control	87
CHAPTER 12	Body of Light – Don't Pretend	94
CHAPTER 13	Skeleton Hands – Unwanted	103
CHAPTER 14	Slowdive – alife	112
CHAPTER 15	Winter Severity Index – A Sudden Cold	121
CHAPTER 16	Box And The Twins – This Place Called Nowhere	131

CHAPTER 17	Tempers – Strange Harvest	140
CHAPTER 18	Hante. – Lies//Light	148
CHAPTER 19	WINGTIPS – The Eye That Follows Suit	158
CHAPTER 20	Fearing – Pictured Perfect	167
CHAPTER 21	Lush – Second Sight	177
CHAPTER 22	Twin Tribes – Shadows	187
CHAPTER 23	hemlocke springs - sever the blight	196
CHAPTER 24	Echoberyl – Swamp King	204
CHAPTER 25	Sword Tongue – Drowning	213
CHAPTER 26	Zanias – Unsaid	223
CHAPTER 27	Selofan – Give Me A Reason	233
CHAPTER 28	Drab Majesty – A Dialogue	243
CHAPTER 29	Lycia – A Failure	252
CHAPTER 30	Cranes – Inescapable	260
CHAPTER 31	Anaïs Mitchell – Bright Star	272

DEDICATION

To my muses, the ones who inspire me and give me the encouragement to shine. You know who you are.

Faron, you would have loved this one.

SPOTIFY PLAYLIST

https://spoti.fi/4d08wsF

CHAPTER 1
PANIC PRIEST – LONELY CITY

I live in a city known for eccentricity. Baltimore is a vivid place: a strange mix of Institutions of Art, trendy eateries, historic sites, and tourist traps versus hole-in-the-wall underground clubs and back alley art, and dirt bikers on city streets. We're known for Eubie Blake and John Waters, the Star-Spangled Banner and Edgar Allan Poe, for being both Charm City and Mobtown. It's full of hidden magic. And yet here I am, quiet and unremarkable, and with no idea of how I got this way.

I'd give a lot to have a touch of that magic in my life.

I guess some people might look at the fact that I was born Denise, but go by Denny and exclusively wear menswear or ungendered clothing (and sometimes a binder) and think I'm not that boring. But trust me, all that does is reinforce how uncomfortable I am with what life gave me, at least to start out with.

I'm a photographer, which is probably the most interesting thing about me. When I was small, I did nothing but draw and paint all the time. Every surface around me was covered in swirls of paint and scribbles. But when I was seven, my dad remarried. My step-mom, Lisa, did make some attempts to support me, but my dad became distant after the divorce. He eventually pushed me to go after a form of art that he considered acceptable. You know, something that I could "make a living" with. That's when I started calling him John instead of Dad.

He wasn't exactly mean, but he was never interested in me or what I might want. I learned to just do what I was told.

When Mom died, she left me an inheritance. I used it to go to art school, the Institute, which outraged John. He refused to give me any more assistance, and I've been on my own ever since. Lisa sometimes will mail me a card with some money.

She tries, at least.

I've lived here all my life, but I was never a real part of any social scene until I met the Ants. And once Joolie got her hands on me, I wasn't leaving the Ants any time soon. It's not like I had other options, anyway.

Lately, I've been looking to get some space from them, so I've been spending time at this coffee shop down the street from my studio. It's called The Frisky Bean, and it's frequented by the types of interesting people that I wish that I was. The Bean has really good coffee—better than those chain places offer.

I like the customers at the Bean. With their casual uniqueness, they seem more real than Joolie and the Ants. It's not upscale or trendy enough for Joolie anyway, therefore it isn't for the rest of the crew. They wouldn't be caught dead there. That gives me some breathing room from them, something I've really needed these days.

Oh, I should probably explain that the Ants are my art collective. I say my, but really, it's Joolie's, and I'd be more accurate if I said that I was her photographer. That's what I do; I follow the Ants around, documenting everything. We're called the Ants thanks to an art critic who referred to Joolie as a "pissant" in a blisteringly negative review. She took it as a badge of honor and dubbed our newly formed cabal "The Pissants." We promptly shortened it to the Ants. Either way, it's a ridiculous name but a pretty good story.

There are a couple of regulars at the Frisky Bean that I look for, who intrigue me or fascinate me; however you'd like to look at it. They're all the types that you can't look away from once you've noticed them—not necessarily beautiful people, but compelling ones. The kind you know will be making an indelible mark on the world. The ones we all wish we were, or maybe that's just me.

There's a stunning woman who works behind the counter. Vali, I think her name is. She's got short purple hair, a scruffy punk aesthetic, and a killer personality. She's a street artist who seems to know the name of every oddball or homeless person who comes in. She interests me, but she's not the reason I've been making sure to stop by on a regular basis to get coffee after working at the studio.

That reason would be a woman who sits in the same chair just about every afternoon, reading a book or writing in a journal and smiling to herself. It's a smile to die for, seriously—so brilliant, so genuine and warm, I feel like I might do anything to have it directed at me. She's not eye-catching in the same way that Vali is. Her build is more voluptuous, her hair more subtle, and her cards kept a touch closer to the chest.

I can't keep my eyes off of her. She seems like a deep thinker, quiet but with the capacity to light up a room. I've heard her laugh once or twice, and it made my heart jump in my chest. There's something magical in the way she captures my attention, I'm telling you.

I guess I have a crush on her. Pretty sad at the age of thirty-four, eh?

So what I do these days is finish up at the studio as fast as possible, then hastily walk to the coffee shop. I try to grab a seat somewhere where I can glance up at her often without being too obvious about it. Sometimes, that doesn't happen, and those nights are terrible for me. I leave in the most despondent mood, and the rest of the night is ruined. I don't know what's wrong with me that I get like this.

...that's not true. I do know. I have no life, not really. I spend my time following around my collective and taking photos of their work and their processes. I haven't created anything truly of my own in ages. Now I've seen something bright and shiny in the guise of a crush, and though I can't quite reach it, I sure as hell can look at it and dream. That's what's been getting me through my days. I feel pretty content with this routine, even though a part of me wishes there was more.

Because I have no life beyond work and mooning over someone who has no idea that I exist, I decide on the way over to the shop that my excuse for being there is editing photos on my laptop while I drink coffee. I've got a series of shots to piece together of Elise's newest choreography. Elise Shannon is the resident dancer of our group—massively talented but emotionally fragile. She went to the Peabody and had her hopes of being a professional dancer squashed by one of her teachers. She never really recovered from that. Joolie, of course, swept her up and worked on bolstering her confidence by encouraging her to perform her own solo choreography at our events.

I talk some shit about Joolie, but one thing she's got in abundance is the ability to find other's talents to prop her up. And we get plenty of opportunities to show off our work, thanks to her efforts. It's just that all our work ends up intertwined with hers.

I met Joolie in art school. She was already learning how to flex her charisma, slowly gathering her clique and followers. Her number one supporter has always been Xan Pang, her closest friend, her lover, and the only one of us able to give Joolie's work the legitimacy it needs. What I mean by that is that Xan's a writer, a poet and a creator of manifestos and essays. When he started attaching his words to Joolie's paintings, the art world began to pay attention. Before that, she was just another paint slapper in a city with lots of artists already competing for attention.

When I call Joolie a paint slapper, that's not an exaggeration. For a long time, she used to do these abstract portraits and still life works, which were nothing groundbreaking but still interesting. They had a spark of her energy in them, and that made them worth a look. That's how she painted when we were young, before…well, before the Ants became the main focus of her energy. Now, she literally slings big blocks of paint onto canvases, which isn't to knock that style of painting at all, but rather her intent in doing it. One night, when I was doing a series of shots documenting her process, she flat-out admitted to me that she does it because it's easier and faster. I remember just how that conversation went.

"It's about how many canvases I can get together for this show, right? You know how it is, Denny. The public expects a quick turnaround from me." After a moment of mixing a few colors with her palette knife and then smearing it across the field, she added, "Besides, I like watching Xan figure out how to make sense of all of these."

Elise, she's harder to understand. She's quieter than me, and that's saying something. I crushed on her for years, I'll admit. I met her when she was moonlighting as a model. That's how Joolie got to know her. Elise seems warm, even approachable. But she can snap into ice-queen mode if you get too close. She's got this glossy black, long hair that's so soft and silky. She's let me touch it, once or twice. The last time, she allowed me a kiss that burned for days, at least in my memory.

Then she went and slept with Xan. I think she slept with Joolie the next day.

The Bean is relatively empty at this time of day, especially on a Tuesday, and I like the feeling the place has when it's this deserted. It feels full of untapped energy. Vali is at the counter reading a book. It's really a casual atmosphere, can you tell? But she perks up when I come in.

"Hey there! How's it going, friend? What a gorgeous rainy day out there!"

She's so damn vivacious. It's hard not to feel like you're someone when she addresses you, but that's her special thing, and you can see it with everyone she interacts with. She's got a great way of making you feel important.

"Hey, Vali. I think this is my favorite kind of day, a perfect picture of autumn."

She grins and nods, effortlessly likable.

"So you know what? I think I want to live on the edge today. Will you make me something? A fancy drink? I have no idea what I'd like, so you have to guess." Why does saying this feel like a little rebellion?

She gives me a look of mock horror. "NO. You're going to try something other than black coffee? I am shocked, I tell you. Totally scandalized. This changes everything."

I think at this point, I might actually be blushing, and she gives me a break by making a big deal over picking out just the right syrup to put in my drink. "I think a good introduction would be a simple yet delicious vanilla latte." She looks up at me and tilts her head. "You know what? You've been coming in here a while, and I just now realized I don't know your name!"

This doesn't surprise me because I've never told her. No one ever knows my name; everyone but the Ants forgets it regularly.

"Um... I'm Denny." Nervous grin. Of course. That's what I do.

"Ah, that's a great name!"

Huh? No one's ever said that to me before.

"Denny, this one's on me. Here's to living dangerously! But I'll warn you, it's addictive." She cackles like a cartoon villain and steps over to help the next guy in line. I use that to escape to a seat on a couch that faces where I know my current object of obsession will be sitting and hope I'm not putting out a stalker vibe.

I'm barely settled in, laptop open when I hear the door bang open. I glance up to see the person I've been waiting for entering the shop. Vali greets her with a hearty, "Heyo, lady! What's going on? You look flustered."

When she pushes back some thick, curly hair from her face, I can tell she's irritated.

"Crappy day, and I didn't think I was going to make it here on time." She breaks into a big grin. "But I did! And oh gosh, do I need a latte. And that chocolate atrocity of a muffin there. And my throne!"

Vali laughs at this.

"You go claim it, and I'll bring you everything when it's ready. Go! Sit!"

I'm peeking over the laptop screen to spy on her interaction with Vali, but I quickly avert my eyes as she heads to the section where I'm sitting. When she gets to her usual spot—an armchair, grandly upholstered in red and purple velveteen—she flops down with a loud, happy sigh. And then she does something totally unexpected. She looks straight at me and flashes me a big smile.

"I'm glad that I didn't miss you, Denny. We have things to discuss, you and I."

Blink. Blink.

She just spoke to me, right? I heard that correctly, and she used my name? Should I go over there? I have no idea what to do in this situation.

After what feels like a million years, I manage a weak "Me? You wanted to talk?"

Smooth. Very smooth. This is why I get all the dates.

"Would you believe me if I said that not only am I talking to you, but that's the entire reason I'm here?" Her gaze shifts to the chair beside her, and she pats it. "This one's pretty comfy, or should I come over there?"

I guess my amazing inability to say the right thing has suddenly switched on because I can't manage to say anything at all. This doesn't improve when she laughs, grabs her bag and journal and plops herself down on the sofa.

Yes, the one I'm sitting on.

Next to me.

She's sitting next to me on purpose. If time stopped now, I'd be fine with this.

She laughs when Vali brings over her order and she's opposite where she should be, and instead, she's next to the most awkward person in the room. Vali just says, "Uh huh, okay." and sits everything down in front of us while trying to keep a smirk off of her face.

"So, hi." She takes a big sip of her latte, watching me over the edge of her cup.

I say nothing and try to manage a smile that I'm sure is ridiculous. I'm not really good at smiling.

She puts the cup down and then sticks her hand out. "I'm Peri, P-E-R-I Linden, like the tree. And it's about time that we meet, so I decided to do that now."

Oh shit, so this is actually happening.

I shake her hand as casually as I can possibly handle and take a breath first so I can keep my voice from wobbling. "I'm Denny Meyers. And I'll be totally honest, I have no idea why you'd want to meet me."

Yep. Smooth.

She cracks up, and I figure that's it, I've blown it. But it's like she can read me, or maybe I'm just obvious in my dismay that I'm screwing this up because she stops laughing and gets a concerned look on her face.

"Denny, I know that you're interested in me."

My face feels like it's on fire.

"I see you here regularly, and I know that you spend a lot of time looking at me. It's okay!" I must be looking panicked. "I look at you, too. I guess you didn't catch that."

She has such a sweet, reassuring smile.

I feel like I might pop. This is not a thing that I ever imagined happening, not her speaking to me or telling me that she was watching me, too. Maybe it goes to my head, because suddenly I feel brave.

"I... you know what? I have nothing to lose at this point." I take a deep breath and look at her expectant face. Her beautiful face. And everything pours out of me in a big jumble of words.

"I come here because I might see you. I'm sorry if that sounds like stalking. I just feel like the day is a better one when our paths cross, even if you don't know it. I've never even considered that you might have noticed me. I'm—I'm just this random person, you know? There's nothing special about me. Probably the only thing worth mentioning is that I'm observant, which is why I noticed you. And once I noticed you, I couldn't stop looking for you. And yeah, that doesn't make me sound creepy at all." Big sigh. I am so horrible at this.

She's shaking her head, like she disagrees with me, with a serious look on her face. "No, Denny, you have no idea how special you are. You think you're ordinary, but trust me, you're not. Do you know how I know that?"

"I... um... I have no clue. I didn't even know that you knew I existed until now, remember?" This entire conversation feels unreal to me, and I keep expecting someone to jump out and announce that they're filming a practical joke special starring my delicate ego.

"I started coming here in order to eventually meet you. I knew you and I were supposed to connect."

Wait, what?

She smiles, reassuringly. Which is a good thing because right about now, I'm sure that I've either hit my head and I'm hallucinating this whole exchange, or I really am being pranked. She seems to understand that I need a minute with this and takes her time sipping from her coffee. Finally, she sits her empty cup down on the table and turns her attention fully to me.

"This is probably going to sound weird, but I hope you hear me out. I actually was aware of you before our paths crossed here in this café."

"You were?"

There's a buzzing feeling in my head. How could this be? People don't notice me. It's something I can count on, moving through the world, mostly ignored by the people surrounding me.

"I saw your show at Under The Earth and couldn't stop looking at those photos. Each one was a perfect slice of time. I've never seen anything like it."

This was a long exposure series I did a few years back. It was before the

Ants started taking up most of my creative energy. Although there were some shots of each of the members, I took them in unguarded moments, not anything staged or designed to promote their projects. You would think that having a tripod set up taking long exposures would be noticeable, but not in our house. And there's no expectation of privacy there because it's all performance to them.

"My favorite ones were the ones with you in them and all the movement happening behind you. I know how hard it must have been to stand so still!"

That was a run of shots where I was the point of focus while traffic, pedestrians, or the night sky moved behind me. They were exceedingly difficult to get right, and I had been prouder of them than I'd been of any work I'd done before.

The fact that she liked those best loosens something in me. For the first time in a long time, I feel seen.

"I didn't put all of them in the show." I want to boldly share something of my secret self with this beautiful stranger. It's reckless, but maybe I need to be reckless for once.

I pick up my laptop and open a folder with the finished images from that show, expanding them into a gallery view so that she can scroll through them.

"No one's seen all of these but me."

As I start to turn the laptop screen to face her, she slides across the cushion between us so that she's next to me. I want to take a deep breath in, but I also want to not look like I'm freaking out, so I wordlessly place the laptop so that it's sitting half on my leg, half on hers. She's doing me a favor by not looking at me right now. I don't think I can hide how I'm feeling.

She starts scrolling through the photos, making little sounds of recognition or pleasure at the first ones in the queue. They're all shots that made it into the show, so I assume she's seen them before.

When she gets to the ones I didn't include, she slows down her scroll and starts to really examine them. I imagine her standing in the gallery, her eyebrows drawn tightly together, her focus tight, looking at each print hanging on the wall in the same way.

"This one. This shows why I've been drawn to you."

She's stopped at the photo that probably says the most about me, my career, and my place in my art collective. I'll describe it for you:

I'm in the foreground, off to the left in the shot, and the focus is on me. Behind me is the large, open space on the first floor of our collective's house, which we call the Compound. (It's the perfect name, really. Every meaning of the word applies.)

Behind me, there's a blur of activity from the other occupants of the house. Joolie is splattering paint across a huge sheet while Xan is jerking away from her to avoid getting caught in the spray. He's holding his notebook protectively against his chest. Elise is mid-pirouette, her hair in the process of loosening from a bun. Pod, the musician of our group, is turning to walk away from the others, his acoustic guitar slung across his back.

The way I've caught the action makes it difficult for a casual observer to pick out these details with a quick glance, but I know them intimately. I had told the Ants that I was working on a group photo idea for the collective, and they, of course, jumped on the idea. I took a series of shots that day, but only one or two were close to what the rest of the group had expected.

I hadn't dared to show them this image. They would have hated it, especially as they were blurred and I was in the forefront, a blow to their egos. But I loved everything this photograph said about them, about me, and about my place in the group.

"Your stare in this." Peri's voice is soft and intimate. "You're looking through the observer like you can see into our souls."

"I had to hold my eyes open for a while. You never know what you're going to get with a longer exposure like this, but I was really pleased with the outcome here."

She nods slowly, like she's thinking about something before she says it.

"You're out of place with them. But you're also the glue that holds them together."

"Naw, that's Joolie. I'm just usually in the background, which was why I liked this shot so much. It's such a reversal." I suddenly feel uncomfortable, like I've said too much.

"You don't see it? That makes sense, I guess." Her smile seems sad to me. "You are the only thing in that group that is calm and centered. You're the thread that links them all, whether any of you realize it or not. And I would put money on the fact that this image represents one of the only times you've ever put yourself before the rest of them."

I consider that for a minute before I answer.

"This show? It was the last show that was truly mine, with work that wasn't specifically tied to any of theirs. So… you're not wrong." I laugh, and I can hear the tinge of bitterness in it. "I always thought that if there were a retrospective of my work after I was gone, this photo would be the defining image of my career. How sad is that? Yet it's my favorite one."

"Aw, Denny. You deserve better than this." I glance over at her, and she looks like she's hesitating over something. I have no idea what, but I'm sure it's either pitying or calculated to cheer me up. Just great.

"I guarantee whatever you're thinking, I've either heard it or thought it already." It comes out harsher than I meant. She doesn't look fazed, though, to her credit.

"I want to know if you'll have dinner with me. Tonight."

I'm caught completely by surprise.

"Like—hang out?"

"Like a getting-to-know-each-other date, if that appeals. Or like two people becoming friends, if you prefer. Please say yes?"

"Um. Uh...Yes?" Seriously, I'd be an idiot to say anything else. Even though I don't believe this is actually happening, when the pretty girl asks you to dinner, *you say yes.*

After that, things start to blur. She smiles at me, and it's like the sun coming out from behind a cloud—it leaves me dazzled and feeling warm all over. Even if nothing else comes from this, I could live off that feeling for a long time to come.

"Do you know where The Maithe is? You can meet me there at eight if that's not too late?"

"That's the big old building down at the end of the street, right? I didn't think that people actually lived there."

"You must not have been by there lately." There's a look on her face, a sparkle in her eyes, that hints of a story to come. I am definitely intrigued. Nervous as hell, but intrigued. "Come to the front door, knock three times, and don't bring anything but yourself and your camera. Okay?"

"Uh, sure." Smooth, so smooth. "I'll be there!" I give her a weak attempt at a grin, and she leans over to kiss my cheek. And then she's gone.

I smell the scent she's left behind, apples and cloves and something earthy under it all, like amber. I'm sure I don't look creepy at all as I close my eyes and breathe in deeply, trying to get the last bits of it before it dissipates. It makes my head spin.

I wonder if that's a normal reaction to have when your crush asks you out. Everything feels off-kilter, but it's me we're talking about here. It's not like I know anything about what's normal when it comes to situations like this.

She said she's been drawn to me. I don't know how to process that. Nothing about this afternoon has felt normal. I've got this overwhelming sense of anticipation, and it scares me. Yet...

I have to admit to myself that I want more. Honestly, I feel like I can't resist seeing what possibilities tonight might hold, even though I'm afraid.

When did it get so dark out? The streetlights are shining through the big front window of the Bean. I need to hurry if I'm going to make it back to the Compound to pick up my camera and still make it to The Maithe in time.

As I walk out the door, I hear Vali call out to me. "See you later, Denny!" Little did I know how right she was.

CHAPTER 2
TALKING TO SHADOWS – SOMA

I manage to get in and out of the Compound without running into any of the Ants. I'm afraid that if I stop to talk to any of them, especially Joolie, I'll never make it to my date. It won't even be on purpose. They just have no concept of anyone's personal time requirements but their own.

I consider if I should attempt to dress up or if I'm reading too much into it and if I'll just make a fool of myself. I mean, that's always a possibility, no matter how things go down, right? I settle on picking out some clothes that make me feel most like myself.

I debate changing my pants, but they're fine. Black cargos rolled up at the ankles. When I step up or sit down, they pull up enough to show the brown and black striped socks I'm wearing with my Docs. Socks are one of the few articles of clothing that I use to show my personality, such as it is.

I need a fresh top. It's probably pretty chilly out there by now, so I trade out the white button-down shirt I'm wearing for a black one, and pull an oversized old man's cardigan on over that. It's a reddish brown color, which looks good with my eyes. At least, that's what Xan told me once. Of course, he was drunk, so what does he know? He would never say something like that to me when he was sober, or within earshot of Joolie.

Anyway, I look about as good as it gets, so now I need to decide what camera to bring. For anyone else, this would be a non-issue, but it's a big deal for me. I decide that medium format film is the right choice for tonight, and if I'm going to do that, I might as well go with a classic choice.

I've got one of those cheap plastic cameras that inherently creates dreamy shots, often with shallow depth of field and light leaks. It's the kind of camera that can give any inexperienced photographer shots worthy of being called art, and in the hands of someone experienced, the photos can be downright remarkable.

I enjoy using it when I don't want to overthink my art too much. It's freeing to just set up, point, and shoot. I can also do longer exposures or overlaid exposures on it, which can lead to complex outcomes. The thing is, I don't get to play with it much these days; I'm too busy taking "serious" photography, which is basically documenting life with the Ants.

Tonight, I hope to have some fun.

The Compound is on Calvert Street, not too far from the train station. It takes about fifteen minutes, tops, to walk over to the Mount Vernon neighborhood where The Maithe sits.

It would be fair to say that The Maithe dominates the block because the entire block is made up of The Maithe. It's a huge, triangular building made of red brick and sandstone–six stories of impressiveness, impossible to miss.

Yet somehow I haven't been paying attention, because the last time I saw this place it had looked abandoned. I knew that some band practiced there, but most of the building had been empty and closed up. Not now, though. Light is shining on the sidewalk from the windows on the first floor, and looking up, I can see that other rooms here and there have lights on, too. I can't see much through the big first-floor windows, but there is a spectacular chandelier visible. Pretty posh.

The door is dark wood, with a big pane of glass. I can't spy much through it; it's dark in the vestibule. There's no knocker, and I feel weird about knocking on the glass, so I guess I'm going to knock on the wood part of the door. It takes me a minute to get my courage up. I have no idea how she'll even hear me.

KNOCK. KNOCK. KNOCK.

To my surprise, the raps resound like they're amplified. I'm looking at my fist, perplexed, as Peri opens the door.

Oh fuck, she's gorgeous.

Where I'm drab, she's brilliant, the kind of beauty that catches your eyes without ever trying. She's changed into this deep red dress with a sweeping, flowing skirt, and on anyone else, it would probably look overdressed, if not ridiculous. Not on Peri, though. She looks like this is a perfectly normal outfit for her to wear to a first date. She's got a voluptuous build, and the dress plays it up perfectly, to my secret delight.

She's got a black shawl thrown around her bare shoulders, so I get glimpses of her olive-toned skin through the lace. Where the streetlights reflect off her hair, I catch hints of burgundy mixed in with the dark brown. She's smiling at me in a way that feels warmer than anything I've experienced in a long time.

"You are perfectly on time!" She reaches out for my hand, and I let her take it, in a daze. I am still having difficulty with the idea that she could be interested in me, but I'm doing my best to play it cool. More than likely, that means I'm being quiet and awkward, but she seems genuinely happy to see me.

"I hope you don't mind if we have dinner here? I thought about it, and I would rather just spend time talking to you over navigating interruptions from wait staff. Plus, I wanted to see if you would mind showing me how you work, at least a little. I can be your model, if you want?"

She's pulling me down a hallway as she tells me all of this, so it's not like I have time to disagree, even if I was inclined to do so. We stop in front of a small elevator with doors of shining brass inlaid into dark wood in an attractive pattern. We're reflected in the metal in a distorted sort of way, and all I can think is that it matches how I'm feeling.

"You live here?" I manage to blurt that out, then glance around the hallway nervously, anything not to feel more awkward than I already do. "Wow, this place is gorgeous!"

"Wait until you see my room." She squeezes my hand lightly. "The whole place is spectacular, though. I feel lucky to live here. If you end up sticking around, you'll get a tour." She winks at me as she steers me into the elevator, and the heat on my face is definitely not from the warmth of the small room.

She doesn't say anything else, but I'd swear she looks pleased with herself as she looks straight ahead at the closed doors. I should mention that she's still holding my hand. I don't think anyone's held my hand for this long since I was a kid. I'm acutely aware of my rough fingers, and I hope she doesn't notice.

We must have gone all the way to the top floor, and the layout here feels different than it did downstairs. The outer walls have windowed nooks with inset benches, perfect for reading or painting—of course, that's what I think of first. The inner wall has several doors, I guess, to private rooms. It occurs to me that the building is shaped like a triangle, and we're walking along one edge.

"My room is right down here." She indicates a door near the end of the hall. It takes me a minute to realize that it's the only room I've seen on the outside wall of the building.

"This one is different," I mumble, and she laughs, delighted.

"You see it because you're observant." She pauses at the door, and I can't stop my free hand from reaching out to touch the dark wood. It's smooth, perfectly finished, and feels slightly warm beneath my palm. "The towers are the only private chambers on the outside walls. The other outside rooms in the house are gathering spaces and have no doors."

She opens the door while she's talking and pulls me into her dimly lit space. I'm disoriented for a second—then she moves to turn on a lamp, and the room is flooded with warm, soft light.

The first thing I notice is the big, arched casement windows that have gauzy sheer curtains hung in front of them. I can imagine how the curtains billow into the room when the windows are open. It would make a great backdrop for a photo. She's not worried about anyone seeing in; obviously, we're high up enough, so that's not an issue. I can see city lights, softened by the sheers, glimpsed like stars on a hazy night.

The rest of the room is a clutter of belongings that cover almost every surface—jammed into bookshelves, hung haphazardly on the walls, scattered across tables in a jumble of colors and textures. Peri squeezes my hand, then lets it go so that she can take care of something or another, and I don't mind because I want to look at the art on the walls.

I recognize some of the artists as locals who have had moments of popularity over the past years. She's got an abstract from Raúl Morro, one of Joolie's rivals from our time at the Art Institute. It's a soothing wash of pinks and oranges with shocking lines of fluorescent green emerging and disappearing across the canvas. I've always liked his work.

Interestingly, he turned down Joolie's pitch to bring him into the Ants back when she was first trying to enlist members. For a while after that, she started using a lot of techniques similar to his but with less success.

"This is nice." I point to the painting. "Raúl was at school the same time that I was. I haven't seen his work around much lately, have you?"

She turns toward me to see which one I'm talking about. I realize that she's been clearing space on a table that already holds one of those big domed trays, the kind room service will bring you at a fancy hotel. I'm definitely curious what that's all about.

"Oh, right, that one. He painted it for me a while back. It's not my usual taste, but the energy in it is riveting, isn't it?" She seems nonchalant, like it's a normal state of affairs for a guy with a decent art career to paint for her. "I haven't seen him in ages; we had a falling out. I think he left Baltimore not long after that." She shrugs dismissively. Okay, I guess that's enough of an answer. I take the hint and change the subject.

"What's all this behind you?"

She grins at that, her face lighting up.

"This is our dinner whenever you are ready for it! As long as we keep it covered, it'll stay warm. Or would you rather continue exploring my room? I'll warn you, though, you'll definitely be hungry before you finish. There's a lot here to see."

I'm torn. My curiosity about possible hidden treasures is strong, but getting to know her over a mystery dinner concealed in a silver dome is also pretty compelling. I should decide for once not to be the awkward weirdo. And I should probably do it now because I won't be able to maintain it for long. Good impressions and all that.

"What if we eat, and then you show me your favorites in your collection?"

She seems happy with this plan and uncovers the tray to reveal a small feast of delicious-looking food. When I gasp at the array arranged there, she smiles and looks undeniably pleased with herself.

"I don't know what you like, so it's all a guess. We eat very well here at The Maithe, as you can see!"

She gestures that I should sit, and I obey, letting her take the lead. She seems to like that, as her smile gets bigger, and she makes a bit of a show while taking one of the plates and filling it with selections from the platter.

"You're okay with vegan? I wasn't sure, so I asked for what seemed safest."

"That's actually preferred, thanks—"

"Shhhh!" She cuts me off, a finger to her lips. "Not to be rude, I'm sorry. But around here, we don't use those words. I know, it's weird. But just humor me?" Her eyes are wide, earnest. I've been in enough gatherings with people from different backgrounds and customs at this point in my career to take it in stride, though this is the first time I've ever heard of something like this prohibition specifically.

"Um, no problem. Hopefully, I won't fuck up, but I'll do my best." I actually do worry that I'll mess up and say thank you at some point. Good manners have been one way for me to keep under the radar in social situations.

Her face turns sunny again when I agree, and I sigh in relief. That sigh changes to amazement when I look at what's on my plate. I've never seen food like this before, not outside of a fancy restaurant, anyway.

The center of the plate is some sort of roulade tart, made from a multitude of vegetables that have been sliced thin, then rolled tightly together and stood on end in rosettes that fill the tart. It has a crusty, flaky edge that makes me want to dig right in. The colors and textures remind me of a Klimt painting if a painting could be edible and delicious. Piled next to it is a serving of whole mushrooms of every color, gleaming with oil and decorated with herbs. Roasted vegetables on a bed of grains complete the plate. There's a scattering of pomegranate seeds, like tiny sparkling garnets, across them.

My mouth is watering. I've never wanted a meal so much in my life.

There's a voice in the back of my mind noting all of this with interest because I don't eat much as a rule. Food is usually something I deal with from necessity rather than indulge in with fancy fare. I guess everything is turned on its head today, including my appetite.

In the middle of the tray is a bottle of wine, but there's no label to tell me what kind it could be. Surrounding it is a generous pile of figs, apples, and pears. It's more than either of us could possibly eat in one sitting–too generous by far. They glisten as if they're dusted with fine glitter.

"This is too much!" Quickly, before she thinks I'm refusing it, I add, "This is magnificent, Peri; I'm overwhelmed." It's obvious that I've said the right thing because color spreads across her rounded cheeks.

Dining and conversing with Peri should be difficult for someone as introverted as I am, but she makes it easy. We sit across the table from each other, which would feel formal if we were in any other chairs but these velvety, overstuffed armchairs that don't really match the table and its trappings. She's actually turned sideways in hers, with her legs propped up on one of the arms. The skirt of her dress spills to one side, and her plate is on her lap, the picture of casualness. Me, I'm not quite that relaxed, but I'm showing more of myself with her than I usually do.

"Denny, why did you stop doing your own shows? Everything I see by you these days is always in conjunction with your collective."

"That's a good question."

I really don't want to answer it because I don't want to talk about the Ants right now when I'm finally enjoying myself away from them. But I'm beginning to realize that, for her, I'd answer any uncomfortable question.

"It's like this," I continue, "Being with the Ants is—it's like being in the midst of a hurricane. There's so much energy, but there's also some drama. Things happen, but you don't control how they happen. You find that there's one of two ways to be a part of the group. You let the wind push you where it will and hope that it's all good outcomes, or you waste a lot of juice trying to fight against the forces in hopes that they'll go where you want. If you're really lucky, you find your way to the eye, and you can let the storm whirl around you and move you places while you manage to stay untouched. That's where I try to be."

She frowns, her eyebrows creasing together as she considers what I've said.

"But is what you get out of this worth it? Everything you do is focused

CHAPTER 3
SECOND STILL – RECOVER

The sun's blinding light, unfiltered by curtains or shades, is what wakes me. For a minute, I feel bereft because I was in the middle of a dream, and everything was perfect. Until I opened my eyes, I wasn't alone anymore.

But no, I'm lying on a sofa in a room that takes me a few moments to recognize, and I'm definitely alone. What the hell? I sit up and look around, and my head does this tilt-a-whirl thing that tells me that I drank too much last night.

The sunlight hits a bunch of crystal-cut prisms that hang across the top of the window. The rainbows they create bounce and reflect all around the room, across books and art and the piled-up belongings of my missing host. Normally, I'd find that annoying, but for some reason, it feels charming here, a visible representation of Peri's energy or something. I wish it would conjure her up. Where did she go, anyway? I can't imagine leaving someone I just met to sleep unattended in my room. It's unfathomable.

Thinking about Peri makes me take a moment to mull over what happened last night because I honestly can't remember choosing to sleep here on this sofa or what happened after we kissed—oh god, she kissed me. My heart is pounding again just thinking about it, but why can't I remember past that point?

I'm starting to panic a little when I spot a piece of paper tucked under my camera over on the table where we had dinner. I try hard not to let my heart fall into my guts while I force myself to get up and read the note she left for me.

Dearest Denny,

I had places to be this morning, and I didn't want to wake you; forgive me. I left you some breakfast. If I don't return in a few hours, don't wait for me. I'll catch up with you as soon as I can.

Last night was lovely, and so are you.

– Peri

The paper is creamy and thick, the kind of paper for correspondence that's impossible to find these days, and costs a fortune when you do come across it. Her handwriting is a little messy and full of flourishes, and it's obvious that she uses a fountain pen, which I love. Those sorts of almost-anachronisms are close to my heart, but of course, you probably guessed that. I mean, I shoot with an analog camera and real film, for fuck's sake.

I tuck the note in my bag with the camera, then turn back to the table to see if I missed anything. The big silver dome from last night that covered our dinner is still there, although all our plates and leftovers have been cleared away. When I lift the dome, my curiosity is rewarded with the rich smell of fresh coffee and warm biscuits.

It's a simple meal, but the most delicious breakfast I've had in ages. I deviate again from my usual black joe by pouring some thick cream in the coffee and add butter and a drizzle of honey to the biscuits. I eat in silence while I consider my next move.

I want Peri to return, but I'm a little scared of what that will be like in the light of day. And my brain is being inconsiderate and withholding my memories of the night before from me. I truly can't remember a thing after that dazzling kiss. Did I embarrass myself? Did she decide I'm too confusing for her—too feminine, too masculine, not enough of anything to hold onto?

That's been a problem for me before, you see. So I tend to either keep everyone at arm's length or beat myself up mercilessly over it, or both at once if I'm feeling particularly masochistic. On reflection, though, Peri hasn't said anything that refers to how I do or don't perform or express gender. I realize that I feel a profound sense of relief.

"She said she came there specifically to see me," I muse out loud to the empty room. "She knew who I was before she met me. Don't be a dumbass, Myers."

No wonder I'm so messed up, considering the pep talks I give myself, eh?

I check my phone and realize that I've been lingering here over my breakfast for an hour. I'm itching to go develop these rolls of film, to see what kind of magic might have happened in the time I can't remember.

Should I leave my phone number or a note that says where I'll be later? It feels like a big assumption on my part. I guess if nothing else, she knows that she can catch me at the coffee shop. I don't really know how any of this works, if you haven't figured that out by now. Pathetic for someone my age, but there you have it.

I'm a little nervous that I'll run into someone on my way out of The Maithe because a building this big must have a lot of people living here, but the hallways are deserted. I manage to find my way without getting turned around, but before I leave, I take a moment to stand in the vestibule with my eyes closed.

I have this ritual that I do when I don't want to forget something that happened. I started doing it when I was young, when the good things were few and far between. I take a beat to savor the scents, sounds, and feelings of that moment, letting it all sink in while I pay close attention to how I feel. I call it creating core memories, something that I hope I'll be able to access for the rest of my life. Maybe it's dumb, but to me, it drives home a reverence for the times that feel the most meaningful to me.

So, I do that little ritual, and lucky for me, no one comes through the door before I finish. Maybe I should have done it while I was in Peri's room, but for some reason, this space and this moment—right before leaving—feel like the ones I need to remember. The background anxiety that I've been feeling about walking out without leaving a note settles once I do it, like I've somehow confirmed that I'll be back.

I know, it's weird. But I feel much calmer now.

Walking out into the sunlight after standing in the dim light of the vestibule leaves me blinking, blinded by the brightness of the day. I'm glad that I've already had coffee, because that means that I can skip going to the Frisky Bean and go directly to my studio. Anyway, I'm a little afraid that I'll run into Vali and she'll ask me about what happened with Peri.

Right, like she cares about my weird little life. I'm just a regular, not even a memorable one.

I keep replaying what I remember about last night while I'm on the way, but nothing new comes up in my mind. The climb up the stairs to the third floor, where I rent a small room, stops me from going over it endlessly. Even though I'm in decent shape, the ascent is strenuous enough to make me pay attention to my feet, not my brain. At least I'm in a legit space, not one of those illegal warehouses that aren't up to code. I don't need to worry about the electric or heat going out here, or worse. It's one of the things that I'm able to afford thanks to being part of the Ants, and I'll admit that I'm grateful for it. I can pay for rent here because I live at the Compound for free. Joolie's parents gave her a whole damn building for her twenty-fifth birthday, and Joolie immediately moved us all in.

It's a relief to get to work on developing the rolls of film. I think that I'm going to distract myself from endless overthinking by sinking myself into the task, but there are a lot more rolls of 120 film here than I remember bringing with me.

This is weird.

I won't be able to scan the negatives until they're dry, so I hang them up in my drying cabinet and take note there are twelve long strips hanging down. How is it that I don't recall shooting twelve rolls of film? Not only that, it's 120 film, and I can't see how I had that many rolls of film in my bag. It's expensive, and I haven't used it in a while. I think I haven't worked with it since the solo show I'd done that had caught Peri's attention.

I do a quick calculation in my head. If all those shots are decent, that's 180 photos. Now chances are good that plenty of those are tossers, but that is still going to be a great number of potential keepers to go through. I'm excited. And maybe they'll give me some insight into the parts of the night that I'm missing.

I have to kill time so that my negatives can dry, so I get the idea to walk to Mount Vernon Place, which is a park within walking distance from the studio. I can find a place to sit and take random photos and—if I'm lucky—talk my brain into remembering more about last night. I make some tea in a travel mug and grab the bag with my digital camera before I barrel down the two flights of stairs and out the door.

That's where I almost run headlong into Vali on the sidewalk.

We both do these ridiculous little shrieks, which I'm sure is hilarious for anyone who happens to see us in action. She backs up a little and starts laughing. Surprisingly, that makes me crack up, too.

"Denny! That was almost a first-rate impact!" She's still laughing as she glances up at the building that I've just burst from like my ass was on fire. "Is this where you live? No wonder you're at the Bean so often; you're just down the street!"

"Um, no. This is my studio, up on the third floor." She doesn't care about this, I'm sure. But Vali's looking at me like I should go on, so I keep babbling. "My photography studio. Though mostly, I just develop and edit up there. I like to do shoots in the real world." I pat my camera bag, as if that should answer everything.

"You sometimes edit them while you're at the Bean, right? On your laptop?" She grins when I nod an affirmative. "So, I've got a question for you. I can ask while you're walking if you're headed this way." She indicates in the direction of the Frisky Bean, which is close enough to where I'm going for me to nod again. "Cool, cool. Do you ever shoot concerts or shows? Straight up—if you don't, tell me no, and you won't hurt my feelings."

"Hmm." We start walking while I ponder it. "I have before, usually when I need extra cash. It's not my favorite gig, but if it's for the right people and circumstances, I'll do it. Do you know someone who's looking for a photographer?"

Leave it to you, Myers. Shy to the point of withdrawn unless someone asks you to get behind the lens. Then you get downright chatty. If I could roll my eyes at myself, I would.

"Actually, it's for a gig happening at The Maithe with The Drawback. That's the house band, so to speak, and we're doing a private party this weekend. They wanna get some promo photos done, and you've been to the house. And Peri likes you, and she recommended that I ask you about it." I swear that I catch Vali winking at that last bit.

"Did she now? When was this?"

"Just this morning! I was going to try and catch you before you left, but I guess I missed you."

Wait, how much about last night does Vali know? There's definitely a look on her face that implies she knows more than she's letting on. Or maybe I'm just imagining what I want to see. I can't tell anymore. I am my own unreliable narrator at this point.

"I guess so. I was in a hurry to get down here and work on the shoot that Peri and I did last night." I know that it sounds like I was just there to take photos. I'm curious if that'll get me any more info from Vali.

"She's super photogenic. I bet those turn out stunning." There's that wink again. I feel myself inexplicably starting to blush. Luckily, the wind is chilly enough that I can convince myself that's the cause of it.

"If she agrees, I'll show you them when they're finished. Oh hey, this is where we part ways," I say as we get to the Frisky Bean. She smiles, and I can imagine what it would be like if we ended up being friends. She's easy to talk to and genuinely warm. I like her a lot.

"I'd offer you a coffee for the road, but I see you've already got something. Want a muffin?" I shake my head no, and she nods like she expected that answer. "So, are you interested in the gig, or do you need more time to think it over? Don't feel pressured; I've got time to get back to Merrick about it."

"No, it's good. I don't have anything happening this weekend. I'd love to do the show. When do you need me there?" I'm feeling unusually wild and reckless, and I'll tell you the truth: deep down—much to my surprise—I'm loving it.

"Party starts at eight on Friday night, but if you could get there earlier and take some still shots of the band before they get sweaty as they do their thing, that would be awesome. And if you want extra credit, pics of the guests and the crowd are welcome." She turns to open the door to the Bean but pauses on the threshold. "You won't have to knock or ring the bell to be let in. Just come in and head to the ballroom. The house already knows you and likes you, so it shouldn't be a problem. See ya!"

I stand there like a big dope, staring at the closed door. The house... what? She must mean whoever owns the house, right? Or...fuck, I have no idea. I had to have misheard that.

It takes someone pointing out that I'm blocking the entrance for me to start moving along—after a mumbled apology, of course. If you're an introvert, you need to be a champion at apologizing.

After that interaction, going to the park feels anticlimactic, but I still have time to kill. I walk the rest of the way deep in thought, dissecting what just happened. I decide that, with the state of mind that I'm in, it would be smart to stay away from people. I walk past the tall, white marble Doric column of the Washington Monument. The street changes from being paved with granite sett to brick when I cross to Mount Vernon Place. I'm thankful for the shift because although the granite is pretty and makes for amazing photos, it's a bitch on the feet and ankles. I'm headed for a section of the park I particularly like, where a graceful statue of a naiad sits in the center of a marble fountain. The fountain is shaped in an elongated oval with a wall of marble banking the west end, and I like to sit or rest on it when I am spending time in the park. Today, I use it as a place to lean against while I look around for photographic subjects. The marble is cold, and I can feel where I'm leaning against it through my jacket sleeves.

The fountain still has water in it, even though it's past the season that it should be running. I drop to my knees, with my camera propped on the wall, and cast my gaze toward the naiad statue in the middle of the water. I almost always start with her when I shoot here; she's like a good luck charm for me, I guess. I'm focusing on the statue when I catch something beyond it, an unexpected movement that makes me look up, startled.

There's nothing there. Maybe I saw a bird fly by?

I look through the viewfinder again, lining up my shot, and I spy it again. I look away and blink, trying to clear my eyes. I don't notice anything unusual, and my eyes feel fine. I'm starting to feel confused, but also curious. I decide to take a couple of shots and see if there's something I'm missing, or if I'm just losing it.

The shutter closes and opens several times in rapid succession. When I look at the first image, an involuntary gasp escapes me.

The naiad, caught in her sculptural pose in the fountain, is in perfect focus in the center of the frame. What made me gasp is beyond and to my right of the sculpture—a blur of movement that confuses me as I try to make sense of what I'm seeing. There are two figures dancing, frolicking, or maybe fighting? I can't be sure because the camera has caught them in motion, a blur of swirling colors.

I look up from the camera, expecting to see them across the fountain from me, but there's nothing there but trees and birds, with cars moving in the background at the bottom of the hill. No people dancing, or whatever I saw those beings doing.

I want to freak out. I really do. This feels like some weird flashback that I can probably blame on whatever I last took at one of the Ants' parties. But as a photographer, I've got instincts that kick in when shit is happening, and they're telling me to freak out later and just shoot whatever I'm seeing right now. Or, more properly, what the camera's seeing, because my eyes aren't having any of it. I let them take over and fire off a bunch of shots, and then I capture some video just for the hell of it. I don't look at the screen while I'm doing it because I'm afraid I'll jinx whatever's happening.

I only stop because there's an intense flash of pain across my forehead, like a tension headache. The pain is blinding, and I'm rocked back onto my ass with a thud, my eyes closed. The sudden meeting of my body and the ground seems to short-circuit whatever was happening in my head, and the pain lifts like it was never there.

"That was fucking weird," I mumble out loud, half expecting someone in the park to see me and come running over. But no, thankfully, there's no one else around but me, so unless someone was watching from the Peabody, no one saw that exercise in grace. I make sure my camera is still okay because even though it was in my hands the entire time, I hit the ground pretty hard. Don't need anything jarred out of place right before a paid gig.

Wait. Vali never mentioned money. Well, shit. Hopefully, since I mentioned getting paid for other events, that'll stick in her mind. Though, I guess if this goes well, it might bring me other jobs, and that would be a bonus. Face it, Myers, you'd do this job just to see the inside of that building again, not to mention getting in good with Peri's friends.

The camera's fine, but I've got this almost superstitious compulsion not to look at what the camera captured until I get back to the studio, so I pack it back in my bag. Before I leave, I glance over to where I'd glimpsed the mysterious movements through my camera. Still nothing to be seen by my unaided eyes. Maybe my imagination is running away with me. Everything's been so *odd* lately.

Once I'm back at the studio, I check the film that's hanging up. It's solidly dry, which means that I can scan it and look it over. Before I get to work on that, I start uploading the images from the park onto my laptop, not even daring to watch while they transfer.

I can't do that as easily while I scan my negatives. The images flash on the screen and I try not to invest too much time into catching any of their details as I finish scanning. I want to look all of them over at once, and maybe confirm that the world has been hiding something from me. Right now, I'm starting to feel like someone who's been left out of important conversations while they happen all around them.

My head is starting to hurt again, and that's when I realize that it's almost dark. What the hell? I've been at this all day long, and I barely remember the time going by. I hate to admit it, but I need a break. I'm starving and beginning to feel out of it. Not like that's difficult, as strange as everything's been lately. I pack up the laptop, grab my camera bag and walk from the studio to the Compound. It doesn't take too long, especially as I'm walking quickly because it's cold now.

As I come up to the Compound, I see someone I don't know going through the front door. That's never a good sign, at least in my opinion. Walking in, I see that I'm right; Joolie's throwing a party. I need to get upstairs to my room right away before she spots me and tries to rope me into taking photos of a bunch of pretentious people she wants to impress.

Before I can make it to the stairs, I hear her call out my name. I can't stop a deep sigh from escaping.

"Denny! There's someone you just *have* to meet!"

I turn reluctantly, silently cursing my shitty fortune, and come face to face with Joolie. She gives me this crooked sort of grin and steps aside to reveal a wide-eyed Peri.

"Isn't she just delightful? I think she'd be the perfect model for my next canvas!"

Peri purses her lips as if she's tasted something sour, but of course, Joolie doesn't catch that. She never sees anything she doesn't want to see.

"I thought you were doing non-objective abstracts these days?" My voice is soft, and it barely carries past the loud music playing in the room—some experimental musician, and the tune can barely be called that.

"You know I'm called to follow my inspirations." She laughs in a way that I recognize, which means that she's nervous and doesn't want anyone to know it. "Maybe you could document the process for me? Just think, a switch like that could mark the next step in my career! You could witness it for the world!"

Oh wow, she's laying it on thick. Is she wasted already, this early in the evening? I glance over to Peri, who has said nothing at this point to either agree to or reject Joolie's proposal. She's staring at Joolie with this intense, unreadable look on her face, and suddenly something inside me snaps.

"That's what I'm here for, right?" I have to get out of here right now; I can feel my control starting to go. "Need to put this stuff away, excuse me." I can feel the tears welling up in my eyes as I break away from them and head up the stairs as fast as I can without looking like I'm running away. I'm enough of an idiot to have let myself be vulnerable, but I'll be damned if I'll let either one of them know that they hurt me.

CHAPTER 4
THE TWILIGHT SAD – THERE'S A GIRL IN THE CORNER

I hold it together on the way to my room, navigating the clumps of people, mostly strangers, who are grouped in inconvenient little clusters all throughout the house. Why do people at our parties always manage to block the stairs?

My room is on the third floor. The only other person who lives up here is Pod, and he's often not home, so it's usually the quietest part of the Compound. He also doesn't care about aesthetics much, so he took the rooms that faced Calvert Street and left me with the big room at the back that looks over the much-less-busy Preston Street. I mention aesthetics because my room has the distinction of being the single one in the house with both a balcony and a small deck. Even Joolie and Xan's floor only has a deck, though they have a bay window instead of a balcony.

I like to open the double doors to the balcony in all kinds of weather. That's the first thing I do when I get safely inside my room and close the door to the hallway. Maybe the fresh air will sweep away all the feelings I'm having. It's also a good excuse for starting a fire in the fireplace, so I do that after I drop my bags on my worktable. Breathing the smell of wood and oakmoss helps to calm me down. So does imagining myself throwing all my frustrations and pain into the blaze while I watch them burn up.

Once I have nothing else to do with my hands, the tears start in earnest.

I spend about ten minutes indulging in quiet sobbing before I hear a soft tap at the door. I don't think I can take more of this, but my heart still does a flip-flop when I hear Peri's voice call my name.

"Denny? Can I please come in? I really need to talk to you. I have so much to explain."

Ain't that the truth, but that's not what I say out loud.

"You don't have to explain yourself to me, Peri. I get it." My voice is shaking. "Joolie is very persuasive."

"Not enough to betray you." Her voice is steeped in sadness, and my stupid heart floods with the most dangerous feeling: hope. "Let me in, and I'll tell you everything. You can decide how you feel about me after that. Please, Denny?"

Fuck.

I want to angrily send her away, then punch every wall until my fists bleed. I want to beg her to hold me while I bawl my eyes out on her shoulder. More than anything, I want to shrink down so small that I become invisible, taking all the hurt and confusion I'm feeling with me.

Instead, I meekly tell her to come in. I mean, why not, right? I already feel crushed. I'm busy wiping the tears off my face when I hear the door's hinges softly squeak as it opens and then closes. I don't look up, not yet. I'm not ready to look at Peri or let her see the pain in my eyes that I know is on full display.

I see the movement of her skirt as she sits down gracefully on the floor next to me, so close that our knees almost touch. I sense that she's being careful to avoid making contact, which I appreciate. I'm seething over with emotions like a pot left on the stove too long; the last thing I need is to add more stimulation and confusing feelings.

"I came here to see you." Her voice is soft and tinged with emotion. "I didn't expect there to be a party, and I walked in with a group of other people. I was looking around for you, and Joolie found me and cornered me."

"I know how she is," I reply, and I fail to keep my bitterness out of my voice. "She probably tripped all over herself trying to get to you when she spotted you in the crowd. A beautiful stranger, untapped by any of her rivals? Couldn't have kept her away from you."

"Sure, but there's another reason for that, and you need to know about it, Denny. I wanted to explain this to you last night, but things got, um, sidetracked." She laughs, but I think I hear an undertone of bitterness. "It was wonderful, but I'm realizing the error of that decision now."

"Error?" Oh shit, it's worse than I thought. Everything inside me twists.

"Not like you're thinking! I rushed being close with you when I should have explained what I am first." I can't see her face, but I think she's assessing my reaction to her words. I'm confused, and I'm sure that's obvious.

"Joolie, being the kind of person she is, couldn't help but be drawn to me, just as you noted. But there's more to it than what you know."

"Can you explain it to me? Because nothing you've said so far is making me feel any better, to be honest."

"Of course. But would you please look at me? What I'm going to tell you is going to feel unbelievable, and I want you to see my face and know that I'm telling you the truth."

"I'm listening." Reluctantly, I move so that I'm facing her, and I mentally steel myself for whatever heartbreaking thing she's going to tell me. She waits until I meet her gaze, and I find that staring into those big green eyes of hers is making my heart pound in my chest.

"First thing: did you look at the photos you took last night?"

"I only saw the negatives. Not enough to see details, just enough to see hints of strangeness. Things I don't remember, not at all. And I don't think I drank that much?"

"You weren't drunk—not on alcohol, at least. More properly, you were drunk on me." She makes a face that plainly conveys that she knows she sounds ridiculous. "It's part of the effect I have on certain people, those who are receptive and who have talents that I can connect with. You picked up on that energy right away, which is why you were watching for me every day. Tell me, how did you feel after you would see me at the Frisky Bean?"

"Um...happy? Probably disproportionately happy for just seeing a crush, if I'm being fair, but it's not like I get a lot of pretty distractions in my life. Not ones that seem worth the effort, anyway." I'm starting to feel uncomfortable, and I don't know what to make of what she's telling me.

"Has anything changed for you since you first noticed me?" Her head tilts and her big eyes are focused on me intently. I can feel the unspoken challenge; she wants me to really think before I answer this question. I decide that's not a bad idea, but I don't like what floats to the surface when I do.

"I'm unhappy here." That admission makes me swallow hard. I've never said it aloud before. "I know that I'm really lucky to have all the benefits of being part of this collective, even if Joolie's got a chokehold on it. She's got money and power that I'll never have, and I basically get to ride on her coattails for the price of taking some photos of her and the group."

"But?" Peri won't stop with that probing stare.

"But I'm afraid that I'll never get to put my own work in front of an audience again. I'm scared that my name will forever and always be linked with the Ants, and any merit my art has will be obscured by that." I stop because the next words fill me with dread. But you know what? Fuck it. It's the truth. "I'm terrified that I'm nothing without them."

"How is that a change for you, Denny?" She's asking me in such a gentle way, but I feel almost compelled to answer honestly.

"I would never have owned up to that before I first saw you. I would have just stuffed all those thoughts down inside because I didn't think it mattered before. I wasn't worth spending that kind of time worrying about. I'm nobody, from a nothing family, with no connections or clout beyond what I've got in this house." I shrug, trying to find that dull acceptance that I had before by falling back on a gesture of indifference. She's not buying it, though. She leans towards me, waiting for me to say the rest of it. "Fine. Seeing you every day woke up some stupid semblance of hope and self-worth in me. Even though I knew there was no way a woman like you would or could be interested in the quiet, uninteresting weirdo that I am, deep inside me, there was a fucking ember of hope that it could happen. And that opened up the door for me to look at my life and realize how dissatisfied I am about parts of it. Is that what you wanted to hear?"

I don't know why I'm angry.

No, I do. She's making me admit things I don't want to think about. No, that's not fair, either—she's not making me do anything. She has a point; my whole outlook shifted when I started noticing her around. Now, I can't make myself forget the things I used to shove to the back of my head.

"I don't mean to stir these feelings in you, Denny. It's part of the process, and I don't have any control over how it happens. I'm just a catalyst." She starts fussing with the hem of her skirt, running the lace edging back and forth through her fingers nervously.

"No, don't apologize. I'm angry, but not at you. And I guess I'm embarrassed, too. I should be so much more than what I've settled for, right?" I take a deep, calming breath before I go on. "So, how does this tie in with what you've been trying to tell me?"

"What do you know about muses?" She's back to giving me the big green eyes stare. I'm so thrown by the apparent switch in topic I stumble over my words at first.

"I—um—I know the classical lore, I guess? Nine women who personified and inspired different creative arts, daughters of Zeus?"

"Those are the ones who are most famous, but in ancient Greece and Rome, there were known to be more. And beyond that, even more whose names have been lost to the ages, forgotten or hidden. Some of the muses keep to one art form, like music or poetry. Others, considered to be lesser muses, gravitate to any creative art and lend inspiration."

"What does that have to do with what we're discussing?" I'm suddenly sure that I know what she's going to say. I've got a sick, shifting feeling inside, like the way I feel when I first get on a boat. Seasick, set adrift.

"That's me. That's what I do." She's clutching handfuls of her skirt at this point, I notice, as the seasick feeling tries to take me over. "That's my function, my job in the world. Most people don't notice me unless they're a certain kind of creative sort. If I went back downstairs and spent more time at the party, half the room would find me utterly forgettable. The other half—maybe more, knowing the type of people who come to these kinds of parties—might climb all over themselves to get near me and get a piece of what I have to offer. You saw it with Joolie."

"I don't understand." I'm afraid to look her in the face. Either I've misunderstood, or she's trying to fuck with me. Or she's mentally ill; I guess that's an option. I knew this was too good to be true.

"Denny, please don't freak out? Just give me a little more time, and I'll show you." Her voice quivers, and the seasick feeling moves into my chest.

"How are you going to show me whatever this is that you're trying to sell me on? Make it make sense."

She sighs deeply like she's bone-weary. I'm exhausted by it, too, and I'm not even the one trying to explain something utterly unbelievable.

"How difficult is it for you to pull up the photos from last night?"

"Not at all. I'll need to invert the images for us to be able to see them properly, but I can do that fairly quickly." I don't expect her question, but a part of me is happy to jump on a topic that doesn't make me feel like the floor is falling away from under me.

"Can we look at those now? I think you'll be surprised."

I'm skeptical, but as I said, I'm thrilled to back away from this weirdness for a minute. Maybe it's too easy to fall into that mode, but I'll fully admit that I'm desperate to hold onto the feeling that she gives me without having to examine it closely, at least for a little while longer.

I get up and get out my laptop from the bag on the worktable. When I sit down on my old Victorian-style couch, Peri gets up and comes to sit beside me, her shoulder touching mine. I feel a flash of attraction flare up, and I bite the inside of my cheek just hard enough to make myself snap out of it. After I run the preset that inverts the images, I pull the first one up. I gasp when I open it because nothing in the image is as expected.

Peri is at the center, perfectly framed, surrounded by her art collection. The air sparkles around her, like crackling energy, though the practical part of my brain insists that it's got to be dust motes. Her hands are clasped together at her chest, one nestled inside the other. The pose feels both vulnerable and secretive. She's staring directly into the camera with those big eyes of hers like she can see into your soul—or my soul, as I'm the one behind the camera. I know that anyone who sees this photograph is going to feel an immediate connection to Peri, thanks to that intense gaze. I've somehow managed to get an incredible amount of crispness in the focus on her, even though I used a crude plastic camera. I can practically count each strand of her hair.

As I shift my attention around the image to focus on the pieces of art surrounding her, they seem to float up to the forefront of the image, one by one, and everything else—except Peri—fades back. I can feel my nose wrinkle as I try to figure out what's happening. It feels a lot like those 3D postcards and designs that were popular in the 70s, the kind where you could tilt it and see the image shift perspectives inside. Lenticular images, that's what they were called. I look up from staring at the photo and glance over at Peri. She's watching me intently.

"You're beginning to get it now." Her voice is pitched low, soft, and lulling. "Enlarge where Raúl's painting is in the picture. Tell me what you see."

I raise an eyebrow but do what I'm told. As I enlarge that section of the scan, I realize that not only is there no loss of clarity—I can see every paint stroke and color blend—the painting itself has that same lenticular effect happening to it. I feel like I can almost see beyond the sweeps of color to the canvas behind the paint. No, wait. The electric green ribbons that appear and disappear across the painting? I would swear on everything I own that those ribbons of paint come out on the other side, then weave back around to the front.

What?

"How is it doing that? How did I manage to capture it in this photo? This is freaking me out, Peri." That's an understatement. I am *extremely* freaked out, though I'll admit that I'm pushing that to the back of my mind in favor of the fascination I've got going on, looking at the image.

"Your photo captured the reality of things, their true images. Each of those pieces of art has the same quality as your photos, Denny, and that's why they're so vivid and multi-dimensional in your shots. Only a photographer with the same gifts can capture it on film. That's the true test, although I knew it without having to see this." She looks…proud? Impressed? I don't get it.

No, that's not true. I'm beginning to get it, deep down inside, and what she's saying both thrills me and terrifies me in equal measure.

"Can you please, in the interest of keeping my anxiety from skyrocketing, just tell me what you're trying to say? As plainly as possible, if you don't mind. I promise I'll listen and won't make a judgment until you're finished."

"After we look through a few more. I'll tell you everything then, and you can ask me to leave if you don't believe me." She juts her chin out, trying to look brave, I guess. The idea that I'll believe whatever she says to me, no matter how outlandish, has definitely crossed my mind.

"Okay." I sigh and click through a few more photos, adjusting them as I go.

There are a couple of shots in front of her art collection, taken in succession, and I love watching her face go from serious to laughing in the series. I realize that although I changed nothing about the lighting and didn't add filters, the colors in those shots slowly warm and deepen as Peri loosens up and begins to smile. It's so pronounced that it almost feels like they are shifting from greyscale to full color.

I glance at Peri after I catch on to this, and she is sitting there with an expectant look on her face, like she's enjoying watching me discover all the unforeseen outcomes in the photos from our shoot.

The next couple of shots all capture Peri in motion. She's twirling in the middle of the room, an expression of delight on her face, head thrown back. Her red dress spins away from her body in a fluid motion that I've managed to capture perfectly. Again, that sparkling energy—or dust motes, disturbed by her spin—is surrounding her. It almost feels like the image is vibrating; there's so much energy embodied in it. As I look at it, I can feel a rush of joy overcome me, and I gasp at that. It's so sudden and unexpected, and I feel a flush of warmth spread across my cheeks in response.

That warmth takes over my entire body as I hurriedly flip to the next shot. I must have clicked too many times because I find myself staring at the moment that Peri and I kissed, captured forever in an awkward angle that only seems to add to the charm of the photo. It's obvious that it was taken like a selfie, but somehow, that doesn't make the shot look amateurish. I guess that owes a lot to—once again—the crispness of focus in the photo. Printed out at the right size, it would look like you could reach into it and pull us out fully formed.

"This is exactly as I see you," Peri murmured. I realize that we're holding hands, and I have no idea when that happened. She's leaning against me, and I suddenly feel lightheaded.

She's right, though. I look in the image just like how I see myself in my head, how I want others to see me: a pretty femme boy, a handsome boyish girl, an androgyne so comfortable in their skin that they don't care about what anyone else thinks. I just am, in that moment. And that comfort, which is something quite new to me—that was Peri's doing. From the second Peri first spoke to me, she made it quite clear that she not only accepted who I am but also *liked* it. She liked *me*.

In the photo, all her attention is focused on me, not just her lips pressed to mine, but her hand on my face, her body turned in that cramped space to face me fully. Yet again, the sparkling energy is visible, but this time it seems to surround both of us and if I look at the image in the right way, I'd swear it was originating from the point where we were touching. I look at Peri, and I know my eyes must be filled with questions because she nods solemnly.

"There it is, the proof that we were meant to connect." She takes the hand that isn't holding mine and kind of waves it over the screen, and I swear that the sparkles bounce around on the image and follow her hand like iron filings jumping at the pull from a magnet. "That spark only happens with those who are of the right mind and heart, as well as talent. Many aspire, but few have all three requirements."

"I really don't understand what you're telling me, Peri." I'm floundering at this point because, in the back of my mind, I know damn well what she's trying to tell me, and I don't know if I want to believe it. Even though I've seen plenty of weirdness already, and you'd think that would be enough to convince me.

"Yes, you do. But you want me to say it, not you. If you say it, I have the leeway to deny it later and pretend that you misunderstood, that I played along with you to make you feel a certain way. If I say it, at least you know where we both stand."

"I—I wouldn't say that, exactly. I don't think I'll ever truly know that. But you are right, I want you to be clear and just tell me what you're saying." I'm trembling, and she squeezes my hand gently, a soft reassurance.

"Will you look at me, Denny?"

I hesitantly turn to meet her gaze, and those green eyes of hers lock onto mine. I realize that I'm going to believe whatever she tells me, and maybe that's because she's gorgeous and she seems to be into me for inexplicable reasons… or maybe it's because I'm a sucker, and I want this so badly.

You know what?

Fuck it, I'm in.

"Just tell me. You're right; I think I know what you're going to say. And I'm going to accept it because I want to believe in you. Maybe I need to believe in you." Wow, the relief that comes from this declaration feels like a weight that's been slowly crushing me has suddenly disappeared.

It must show on my face because her eyes light up in a way that I've never seen directed at me before, not from anyone.

"I'm not just a muse, Denny. I think I'm meant to be *your* muse."

She pauses, I guess to search my face for a flinch, a rejection. But I don't react at all. Nothing she's saying is surprising; she'd already implied as much. As weird as that is, I roll with it.

"I can always help others, inspire them, or imbue them with creative energy. But sometimes, there's a special connection, one that is destined to create greater change in some way. It's rare and powerful." She stops and glances away. She looks unsure of herself. It's incredibly endearing, coming from one as self-assured as she usually seems to be. "Honestly, all I know about it is what others have told me. I've never had it happen to me before now."

"But you know that we are connected in this way." I don't deliver it as a question, but she knows that it's there.

"I've never felt driven to seek out a specific person to connect with before. When I saw your photos in that show at Under The Earth—when I saw you in the images—I felt an inexorable pull towards you, something I've never experienced in all my time." She squeezes my hand when she says that, and her thumb strokes across my palm. It's the smallest gesture, yet something about it makes my cheeks blush, and my heart start beating faster.

"So...now what? What do we do now?"

Her fingers interlace with mine, and she leans against me and rests her head against my shoulder with a soft sigh. "I don't know. We figure it out as we go, I suppose. We let the connection between us grow. But for tonight, I'd like it if you showed me the rest of our photos. And if you kissed me."

How can I refuse a request like that? When the pretty girl asks you to kiss her, you say yes.

CHAPTER 5
THEM ARE US TOO – FLOOR

We don't get back to the photos for quite a while. I like that she doesn't rush anything with me. Maybe she understands that I don't really know what I'm doing. It's not that I haven't been with people. It's just that it wasn't ever reciprocated like this, in a way that makes me feel more than me just going through the motions of what I thought I was supposed to do. I don't feel like a conquest or someone pursued only to make the other person feel important. Peri makes me feel like there's no one else she'd rather be with at that moment or any other.

She finally pulls back a bit from my lips and murmurs, "I could do this all night. I want to do this all night. But is it wrong that I want to see the rest of the photos, too?" She's so close to me. I can hardly think clearly.

"Uh…" I take a deep breath. One of her hands has slipped from where she was cupping my face to grip my arm gently, supporting me as I regroup myself. That makes a surge of warmth wash across my cheeks, and I realize her suggestion makes sense. I need to get myself together, at least a little bit. I'm not used to these kinds of intense feelings!

Instead of saying anything else, I reach behind me, blindly groping for the laptop I'd carelessly shoved back there. She gently pushes me back and reaches to grab the laptop, sits it on my lap, then curls up next to me and leans her head against my shoulder as if it's the most natural thing in the world to do. I guess maybe if you're someone like her, it is.

I distract myself from my burning cheeks by scrolling through the rest of the photos. They surprise me, mostly because I don't clearly remember anything that happened after our kiss last night. I recognize the photos in the same way that I might remember a movie half-watched years ago—through a soft blur, one that makes me question if I'm just building false memories triggered by the photos. Peri makes little sounds of recognition or approval as they go by, though, so obviously, she isn't suffering from the same loss of memory that I am.

"Why can't I recall any of this, Peri? According to my brain, we kissed, then there was a big smudge of something I can't remember, and then I woke up alone."

"Oh." I can't see her face well, but I can hear a wobble in her voice that makes me think her confidence has slipped just a little. "I guess it was too much for you to take in all at once. That happens sometimes, I think. If you keep looking at the photos, it might come back?" She doesn't sound sure.

"You haven't seen this before now?"

"I-I don't know? You and I are connecting in a way that's different from what I'm experienced with, like I told you. I don't usually get this deep with the people I influence, especially not this fast." There's an awkward pause, and instinctively, I wait for what she hasn't said yet. After a moment that feels like an eternity, she twitches nervously, then continues on. "People sometimes have strong reactions to involvement with my kind. Obsessive, even. Because I'm on the wrong side of the interaction, I don't know if it'll happen until it does. They don't usually share the details of how I affect them like we are right now."

"So you're saying what, exactly?" I hope I don't sound as on edge as I'm feeling right now. Peri sits up and takes a deep breath, almost as if it's involuntary, like she's gasping for air. I get that. I feel like I'm drowning too.

"I'm saying that not only is this uncharted territory for both of us, but that I don't want you to get swept under in your involvement with me. Will you keep telling me what you're feeling and experiencing? I think that avoiding being fully honest won't play out well for either of us." She's staring intently at her fingers as she twists them in her lap. I can feel the tension coming off her in waves.

"What about you? Will you be honest with me, too? You know more about what to expect than I do. All of this, every bit of it, is unfamiliar and a bit terrifying. I don't know how to be in a relationship, much less one with someone…" I stop, struggling with what word I should use.

"Magically complicated?" She snorts softly. "Sorry to make you jump into a master-level relationship situation on your first go. But as much as it isn't in my nature to tell anyone everything about me, I'll do my best to be open with you. And I am always honest. Even when it makes people angry." I hate the pained look on her face. She looks like she's speaking from experience.

"I'd rather be angry about the truth than about discovering a stack of lies." I try to keep a neutral tone. I don't know what's happened in her past, but I don't want to put her in a position where she feels like she has to defend her previous actions. Though, I don't want her to hide her feelings from me either. "Communication's hard sometimes, but I think it'll get better if it's a standard we hold up from the beginning."

She nods and leans her head against my shoulder in a way that makes me think she is as relieved by our conversation as I am. "I want all of our tough conversations to go as well as this one just did."

"You say that like you expect there to be more than just this tough conversation." I'm teasing, but she answers as if I wasn't.

"Of course, there will be. We are both complicated people, and we're attempting something outside of what feels normal and safe for both of us. But it's okay to be unsure or disagree. It's how we handle it that matters." She pats my leg gently, reassuringly, as I consider her words.

"Fair enough. Though I'm surprised that this is new for you. You've done this before, so how is it that you didn't connect with the others like you are with me?"

"I told you." She sits back up, turning to look me in the eyes. "You're different. I sought you out because you would never have even thought to look for someone like me." Something about how she says it bothers me, though I can't put my finger on why. "You deserve attention for what you do, and you deserve to have inspiration beyond the ones who are more than happy to push you into the shadows so that they can shine." She tries to keep her opinion about that off her face but it's a big fail. I still can't figure out why she cares so much about how they treat me, but I have to admit that it's another reason to crush on her.

Momentarily embarrassed by the strong feelings she's causing, I glance down to the laptop and focus on the photo on display. I must have taken it from the couch not too long before I passed out, based on the angle and my sloppiness in framing the shot. It's what appears to be a candid photo of the room, with Peri as a lightly blurred figure almost in the middle of the shot.

There's something off about the shot, and at first, I can't grasp what it is. There's an unfocused quality, but after I stare at the photo for a moment, I decide it's actually coming from me. I blink a couple of times to try to refocus and clear my eyes, and suddenly, everything snaps into crystal clarity—except Peri, who stays stubbornly blurred at the edges.

What draws my eye is the art that Peri has displayed on her wall. No, not the art itself—it's what looks like shimmering energy extending away from the art, stretching out to reach for Peri like mindlessly groping tentacles. I can feel my brow furrowing as I stare intently, trying to make sense out of what I'm seeing. Next to me, I hear Peri's sharp intake of breath.

"So I'm not the only one seeing that, then." My voice is trembling even though I'm trying to play down my nervousness. "You have any idea what that's about, or is it just another mystery I should just accept?"

"I—I know what it's about." She looks away, her eyes darting back and forth between the computer screen and a point somewhere across the room. I feel a twinge of frustration deep inside. Didn't we just discuss being open with each other? But you know, that's not fair of me either. It's obvious that she's really uncomfortable, and I know how that feels.

"Okay." Deep breath, then I continue. "I don't want to force you to talk about something if you're not ready. You've been understanding of my weirdness, so the least I can do is let you have the space to explain it on your own timetable."

She's biting her lip, her eyes locked on the photo, and those tendrils snaking towards her. It occurs to me that seeing them might have shocked her as much as it did me, and the seasick feeling comes back. It doesn't get any better when she stands up abruptly and turns to me, her face pale.

"I hate to do this, but I need to go. Now." She starts stumbling backwards, moving towards the door clumsily in a graceless way I've never seen her move in before. "I'm sorry, I'll explain later; I just need to go—"

And she's out the door and gone. Just like that.

I don't understand what just happened, but that feeling in my gut? It isn't going away.

I could try to chase her. But I don't. What I do instead is go downstairs, through the throng of artists, critics, wannabes, and hangers-on, and I find where the booze table is. Am I being smart? Not a chance. The last thing I need to be doing now is drinking, but I'm not rational at this point. I find a bottle of champagne, not the most expensive one on the table, but it definitely costs more than a week's worth of food. The bottle's still cold, thankfully. When I grab it, I feel a nudge to my left and turn to find Pod at my side. Wordlessly, he inclines his head toward the bottle, and I hand it to him without a protest. He deftly pops the cork so expertly that the sound barely registers in the noisy room and hands the champagne back to me. He raises his eyebrows a little, an unspoken question there that I don't know how to interpret.

"Pod?" He just stares at me intently. "You—you wanna come drink this with me?" I have no idea why I just asked that, but it hits me suddenly that I don't really want to be alone. I don't know. My mind is a huge mess right now. I decide that he'll either follow me or not, and I want to get back upstairs before Joolie spots me and says something, anything, to me.

It's getting dark, and my balcony feels like a hidden refuge. I sit, my back against the wall and my legs stretched out across the balcony floor, and a moment later, Pod comes in and sits next to me. I take a swig from the bottle, enjoying the crisp flavor of the expensive-ass champagne, and then I hand the bottle to Pod. He does the same, then stops to look at the label.

"This is a ridiculous thing to have at a weekday party full of hipsters." He frowns at the bottle, then takes another generous gulp. "Good thing you rescued it. It's going to much better use here." He glances over and makes sure to catch my eye before he winks at me, then drags his fingers through the curly blond hair that's made many a woman lose their mind over him.

I like Pod quite a bit. Out of everyone in the Ants, he's the most real and easiest to relate to, at least in my opinion. He's been through some shit, and it shows for those who know him, but most people see his dark sense of humor and good looks and don't look deeper. I know better, though, and he is often more real with me than anyone else in the house.

"That crowd's more pretentious than the name my parents stuck me with." He says this with a self-deprecating tone softened by a dazzling grin. I mean, he's not wrong, either about the crowd or his given name. Peter Osgood Davies is a perfect name for a CEO or a banking mogul, a rich kid's name. The people who are currently wandering around downstairs definitely have relatives with a name like that. Pod had tried to disconnect himself from that background with some success, so he has a lot of resentment for the rich, artsy people that Joolie goes out of her way to court.

"You know, they're the people who fund our projects and come to our shows, so Joolie's gotta make them feel special."

"Or herself." He takes another slug from the champagne bottle, which is disappearing quickly. "Speaking of, she was talking to anyone who would listen about some new inspiration she found, a creative muse in the making, or some shit. Know anything about that? She looked positively high on the news."

I feel a flush of anger wash over me, and I know I must show it in my face. I grab the bottle from Pod and guzzle some of the champagne in an effort to hide my response, but he's not fooled.

"Whoa, Denny. What happened?" Pod looks genuinely worried, and maybe angry?

"I met someone," I confess, my voice subdued because I want to crawl under my bed and hide rather than discuss this. "She and I—I think we have a connection. But when I got here tonight, Joolie was parading her around the party and talking about having her sit as a model. You know, like how she gets her claws into everything." Unexpectedly, the last part comes out like a hiss. I can feel my resentment roiling under the surface, and I'm embarrassed by how transparent I'm being in my dislike for Joolie's actions, but not for feeling this way.

I can see the same sort of emotions reflected in Pod's face, too, but he looks even more bitter—and on edge.

"Be careful, Denny. When she sets her sights on something or someone—"

"I know, I know."

"You think you know, but it's worse than you imagine." He stops, grabs the bottle from my hand, and then tilts it back in a violent motion. His aggressiveness is so unlike him that I just stare at him, blinking. After wiping his mouth with the back of his hand carelessly, he continues. "She tried to get her fingers on Bethany. And she was the last one of us to see her alive, Denny."

"What?!"

"I shouldn't have said anything." He turns away, staring into the distance, but I can see his jaw clenching in the dim light.

"Pod." Tentatively, I reach out and touch his arm. "What happened?"

For a minute, I think he's going to get up and storm off. But he sighs deeply and folds into himself, drawing his knees to his chest and dropping his head down. After a moment, he turns his head towards me, blond curls spilling everywhere. His eyes are boring into me, his stare is so intense.

"I was gonna ask her to marry me, Denny. I had the ring and everything. And somehow, Joolie found out. She came to me with that fake smile she gets when things aren't going her way, you know the one. But I didn't understand it at the time. I thought she was being genuine, because I am stupid." When he pauses to rake his fingers through his curls, I see his hands shaking. "She told me she was so *glad* that I had found someone who made me happy, and Bethany was so pretty and she wanted to get to know her better. I arranged for them to meet up, and I thought this would be great, that they could be friends and Bethany might even feel comfortable doing things with the Ants. So stupid."

"What happened, Pod?" I'm getting a sinking feeling in my stomach.

"They were supposed to meet for dinner at some fancy place, Joolie's treat. Bethany was excited to finally get to know the person who helped me get my musical career off the ground. I waited up for a while that night, hoping to hear from her how it went, and I finally fell asleep after texting her a bunch of question marks." His jaw clenches again, and it takes a minute before he's able to go on. "I was so freaked out. It wasn't like her."

"No, she would never have just ghosted you. Everyone knew how much she loved you."

"When the cops called me, said they'd found her body in the harbor, I knew right away that someone hurt her. But there was not a mark on her body, so they wanted to rule it suicide? Like that's the only way you can hurt someone." He slammed his fist into his thigh, but his face was eerily blank. "D'you know what Joolie said to me after the funeral? 'You should use your music to get through this. You can lean on us. We're a family; we'll get you through this.' I was drunk, heartbroken, and weak. She stuck to me like a burr for the next couple of weeks, kept me wasted and sedated. Everyone praised her for being so supportive."

"I remember that. Like she was some sort of saint. And she wouldn't let me or Elise near you, either; she told us that you didn't want to see anyone but her or Xan. We didn't know what to do. I was scared that you were going to do something drastic. I guess I thought that Joolie was sticking by you so that you wouldn't."

"She kept me isolated on purpose. And I don't have proof, but I swear she said or did something to Bethany that triggered this. This guy Mickey that I gigged with sometimes told me about six months after that, he saw Bethany that night, coming out of a bar in Fells Point, and she was crying. He thought maybe we'd had a fight, so he didn't think much of it until he heard later how they found her." Again, his hand pushes through his golden curls, which, by this point, are a tangled mess. He won't look at me. He's too upset.

"What do you think she could have done to make Bethany react like that?" At first, I don't think he's heard me, because it takes him a minute to respond.

"Whatever it was, I think it was designed to break us up. Anything that could weaken Joolie's hold on us is dangerous in her eyes, Denny."

He manages to grab the champagne bottle and tilts it to drink the last of it, then puts it down with a thump and lurches to his feet. He wobbles dangerously for a moment, then stumbles towards the door.

"Watch out for her. Don't believe anything she says or does. She'll either do the same to you two or use up that girl right before your eyes if you're not careful."

CHAPTER 6
PUBLIC MEMORY – HEIR

My back hurts so much.

No, wait, my head does.

Why do I feel so hollow inside?

Oh. OH! Last night, the champagne with Pod. The uncomfortable discussion. And Joolie trying to lay a claim on Peri, and the tearful discussion by the fireplace.

The photos.

Sitting up abruptly is a terrible idea, but I do it anyway in my haste to fumble for my laptop. I fell asleep last night on the couch, so it's not that far to reach, but my head hates me anyway.

The images are still there. I had a feeling of immense relief at that, even though I'm not sure why I was afraid they'd disappeared. I realize the photo that rattled Peri so much last night is still on the screen.

"I'm not in the right frame of mind to deal with this," I mutter to myself as I enlarge the section of the image with her in it.

She's still blurry on the edges. And the tendrils of whatever they are, energy or something like that, are also still there, reaching for her like vines stretching towards the light. I stare at the screen blankly for a while, willing myself to understand what I'm seeing. If someone else had handed me this photo, what would I think?

I zoom in more, hoping for answers. The clarity of details is surprising and unnerving. Things should be starting to lose quality at this resolution, but the tendrils only seem to gain more substance and fine detail. I can see crackling energy contained within them, and I feel uneasy the longer I stare at the coiling wisps that stretch eagerly for Peri.

A loud rap on my door makes me suck in a breath in a panic and slam the laptop closed involuntarily.

"Denny? You awake? Someone left a package for you." It's Xan, and he sounds tired, his voice uncharacteristically rough. "I'm sitting it here by the door, okay?"

I hear a soft thump and then silence, and I assume he's gone, so I open the door.

There's a small box, about the size of a book, wrapped in expensive-looking gold and turquoise marbled paper and tied with a wide, textured burgundy silk ribbon. A handwritten label is attached to the top, with my name handwritten out neatly in a Round hand style on cream-colored parchment. Fucking fancy, and I can't think of anyone I know who would send me something like this. Peri? It doesn't seem like her style, but what do I know about that yet?

I bend down to pick it up. When my fingers touch the package, there's a mild shock that jolts up my arms, and I stumble back a bit. What the hell was that?

It's probably a stupid move on my part, but I shake the box a little. A muffled chime comes from it, the faintest soft and sweet note I've ever heard. I have no idea what's happening with this parcel, but I want to see what's inside it more than ever now. I guess I should hurry up and close my door before someone shows up in my hallway and gets nosy, right?

When I untie the burgundy ribbon, the scent of jasmine escapes, underpinned by something sweet yet resinous—frankincense? No, there's a hint of lemon there, making it smell a lot lighter than you'd expect from a resin. I take a deep breath, my eyes closed, and at that moment, I feel calmness and an unexpected happiness wash over me.

"Whoa. That's a rush, right there." My voice echoes a little in the otherwise quiet room, and it knocks me out of my reverie and back into focusing on the package in my hands. The paper falls away to reveal a dark wooden box carved all over with flowering vines. There's no clasp, just small brass hinges almost hidden in the back. For a minute, I inspect the box and contemplate it, trying to figure out what it could possibly hold. Of course, that doesn't tell me anything. Why would it? I'd better just open it up.

With a little effort, the lid swings back to reveal the contents inside: a small beaded leather pouch, a round tin enameled in swirls of blues, and another piece of that fine parchment rolled into a tube and tied with burgundy ribbon. Everything rests on a bed of dried jasmine and is much less messy than you'd think for a package I'd just shaken.

When I take the package over to my sofa and sit down, I hear that soft and sweet chiming sound again. What *is* that? I try the small bag first and smile with satisfaction when it tinkles as I pick it up. I pull open the drawstrings and dump it out on my palm, revealing a dully gleaming silver sphere. It's about the size of one of those rubber balls you play jacks with, no larger. When I shake it in my open hand, it jangles melodically. I am utterly charmed. I don't know what it is or what it's for, but it's delightful.

I slip the sphere back into the pouch, noting how soft the leather is and admiring its beautiful dark blue color. Next, I carefully pick up the enameled tin and examine it. It feels cool and smooth in my hands. It unscrews easily, revealing... lip balm? Cuticle balm? A solid perfume? Whatever it is, it smells strongly herbal and floral, though I don't recognize the scents involved at all. Sniffing it gives me a heady rush, and I feel a bit overwhelmed yet strangely compelled to sniff it again. I resist the compulsion and turn to the parchment scroll, carefully untying the ribbon and dropping it into the lid of the open box.

More of that antiquated script flows across the creamy page. The text takes me a second to read because it's hard not to fixate on how neatly yet free-flowing the letters move across the page. Finally, I make myself focus on the message.

> *Dear Our Photographer,*
>
> *With great esteem, we send you these gifts; were we not enamored with your being, we would not have given you the method to call upon us and see us as we best seem.*
>
> *Bring your device to our home as soon as you see fit, and also the box you now hold. Before you call us forth, touch this unguent to your eyes and all will be revealed. Tell no one whence you go, not even your treasured muse lover. We require this respect and will reward you the same.*
>
> *Until anon.*

I am so confused. At first, I thought this had been something from Peri, because she seems like the type to surprise someone with unexpected and strange gifts. But now I don't know. Peri's a lot of mysterious things, but I can't imagine her using language in this stilted and archaic-sounding way. This whole thing reads like some kind of fairy-tale riddle—wait, *is* it a riddle?

I'd better start off with what I know and work from there.

The letter writers know I am a photographer. They call me "our photographer", so I must have taken their photo at some point. Hmm, I don't like taking many shots of strangers.

They assume I know where they live, as I'm supposed to call them at home. With my camera, too. Do they want more photos of themselves? Maybe?

They know about Peri.

They know about Peri, and I'm not supposed to tell her any of this.

I'm momentarily stopped by a quick flash of pain in my head, a microburst that flees almost as quickly as it came on, but that leaves me with the answer to this riddle, as absurd as it sounds.

Whatever it was I saw through my camera at the park yesterday just invited me to meet them.

I mean, that's the only thing that makes sense, even though it doesn't make sense at all. I'm beginning to think that soon, nothing will shock me or surprise me anymore.

What do I do now? A reasonable person would laugh this all off, I guess. Or think that someone was trying to fuck with them. But I've been forcibly moved out of the reasonable people club, so I decide to follow through with the invitation. I mean, why not? Everything's weird at this point; why not just pile on more weirdness?

There's no expectation of a specific time in the oddly worded letter, but I feel like getting there as soon as possible seems wisest. I don't know why; it's just an overwhelming sense that I've got. I do a slap-dash job of cleaning myself up and getting dressed, then make sure to grab my camera bag and put the box with all of its strange contents safely inside it. I manage to get out of The Compound without running into anyone else, which is no small feat.

The walk to Mount Vernon Place takes less time than usual, maybe because I'm walking so fast that my feet hurt. I go straight down St. Paul Street, so when I get to the park, I'm already at the bottom of the section where I recently took photos. It's uphill from there all the way to the Washington Monument, and if you stand on St. Paul, you can see the entire length of that part of the park.

I don't spy anything out of the ordinary, nothing at all.

Okay. What next? Maybe I should go sit by the wall above the fountain, where I did the last shoot. That seems right, somehow, and when I sit on the ground and lean with my back against the short wall, a sense of calm comes over me. I pull out the box and then take a second to look around me. It's mid-morning, and there's no one to be seen anywhere in the park. I haven't even noticed any cars driving past the park. It feels like I'm the only one around.

The tin opens easily, and I look at it with a frown—I have no idea what this balm is made of or what it'll do—but fuck it, I'm here now, and I might as well follow through. I rub my little finger across the surface of the balm, and the scent gives me that head rush again, making my vision blur for just a moment. I try to calm it down by closing my eyes, and my hand automatically moves to my eyelids and anoints them, one at a time.

I wait for a beat, then remember the chiming sphere. That's the next part of what I'm supposed to do, right? So I take it out of its pouch and roll it around in the palm of my hand so that it jingles.

The vertigo gets stronger, and my hands go to my ears, clasping my head to try and steady myself. The sphere falls back into the box with a muffled jingle, but I barely notice as I try to regain my senses. Before I fall over, totally off-balance, it withdraws, and I open my eyes with a gasp.

Four tall, delicate-looking figures kneel in a half-circle in front of me. One holds a thin finger to its lips, a warning to be quiet. I obey because I'm too busy looking at them to say anything yet.

Their appearance swirls and flows before my eyes. They change from having long to short hair in shades of blue/purple/teal; their faces and shapes move between feminine, masculine, and genderless traits as I watch, fascinated. They're sometimes darker and sometimes paler, but their skin is always a match for their hair, tinted with those same shades like someone had painted over them with watercolors. Their clothes flow and morph along with their appearance too—draped fabric that could be tunics, dresses, or robes at any given moment. They are barefoot, and somehow, I can't imagine them ever wearing shoes of any type. If someone asked me to describe them in one word, I'd choose "fluid".

"You follow directions well."

It's impossible to be sure which one spoke, with the way they seem to shift and change. Their tone is light and airy, but with an undertone that conveys self-assurance and power.

"I—it took me a moment to decipher them. I still don't understand what's happening."

I won't say that I'm freaked out because this whole week has been enough to numb that reaction for me. But I am definitely confused. And there's a part of me, deep in my artist brain, that is dying to capture these mysterious beings on film.

"We hold you in esteem, mortal. You treat our home with respect and reverence, which we have noted over many visits. But you have recently been changed, and we feel moved to protect you." This time, the voice was closer to my right ear, which was a bit disconcerting. "We would not normally act on behalf of a mortal, but we feel a connection with you."

"Your lover moves through the world as she wills, disregarding how she affects the mortals she touches, as all her kind do." This one's tone was a bit deeper, and a touch disapproving. "You may gain much from her, but we caution you to protect yourself."

"She's not my lover. Not yet, anyway." Why did I say that?

"The warning still stands. She will put you in danger, even though it might be unwittingly. In response, we have decided to give you gifts that will show you what is hidden and call to you assistance when truly needed." One of them points to the box, and they all nod, eerily synchronized.

"The unguent allows you to break through our glamour, to see truly. Before, you only saw the afterimages of who we are, but now you gaze upon one of our forms. This will apply to any non-mortal you chance upon, though we caution that sometimes you are better served by keeping the knowledge of what you see to yourself."

The one closest to my right catches my eye and holds it momentarily, and it suddenly hits me: they are serious; all of this is serious. I am at risk in ways that I don't understand in this new world of strange beings and mysterious encounters.

"Let—let me see if I get this right. I can see you because of this ointment I put on my eyes. And I'll be able to see other beings that I couldn't before." I can't help but stammer at the idea that there are more unseen creatures out there.

"Indeed. You will learn to see the true forms of others who hide from mortals the details you would deem uncanny." A soft tinkle of laughter. "As we are sure you find us."

"I find you—I find you beautiful. Impossible not to stare at, honestly, you are so…" I don't have the right words. I'm no poet. Maybe Xan or Pod could do them justice, but I'm not equipped.

They seem delighted by my awkward declaration, though. They shimmy and slide about, their hands moving gracefully through the air as if they were dancing.

"You please us, mortal. This is why we chose to give you a means to call upon us. We are not to be summoned unnecessarily, but if you have need, use the sphere, and we will fly to assist you."

I pick up the silver ball and shake it gently, and I'm rewarded with enthusiastic approval from the beings in front of me. Okay, this is interesting. But what kind of assistance do they mean?

"I don't know what to call you. I mean, how to address you? And I'm not sure what you mean by if I have need." I sound confused and pathetic, but at least I'm being honest, which seems prudent right now.

"Ahhhh. You may address us as Nyxen, for that is what we are. We go where water flows, and our power is that of the great restless bodies as well as the deep, still ponds with secrets at the bottom. We leave it to you to grasp what this means, mortal, and make choices based on your conclusions."

"Nyxen." It feels familiar somehow, like a foreign word that I can almost understand if only I think about it for a while. "And you live here? In this park? Even when they turn off the fountains?"

They look amused at this question. "This space is one of our favorites, and we often rest here. And there is always water here, even if the mortals close off every pipe to these basins."

They lean in close to me, their hair and arms spreading, drifting outwards to shape a circle around me. I can feel a coolness radiating from their bodies and a strange dampness.

"There is always water, Denny Myers. Anywhere there is water, we may be. Remember that."

I make an involuntary movement backwards, freaked out by their closeness and intense declaration, and in the blink of an eye, they seem to disappear. Only some droplets on my jacket and a damp mark on the ground surrounding me hint that they've ever been here.

Holy shit.

Maybe I should run home, lock myself in my room, and reconsider all of my recent choices. But I'll be honest here: as confused and nervous as this all makes me, they've piqued my curiosity. I want to understand what's happening or at least document as much of it as I can. Oh! I never took photos of the Nyxen, and they specifically asked me to bring my camera. I wish I'd been brave enough to think to photograph them when they were in front of me.

Maybe taking some photos of the fountain will do? It's the best solution I have at the moment. Besides, that's a routine that will soothe me and give me time to calm down. There's a certain headspace that taking photos offers, and I need it right now while I process everything that's happened.

I decide on a long exposure photo, pointed in the same direction as the last time I was here—facing the naiad sculpture in the fountain. The last time, it revealed mysteries, so I suppose I'm ready to keep pushing my luck or something. After I attach the shutter release cable, I sit the camera on the marble balustrade, a stable surface if there ever was one. I make sure I have the lens aligned the way that I want, then leave the results to fate as I push down the button and lock it in place.

Nothing changes for me while I leave the shutter open; no great reveals or even a little sparkle. I honestly can't tell if I'm relieved or disappointed in that. Finally, I let the shutter close, put the lens cap back on the camera, and put it back in my bag without looking at the results. I'll do that later.

Later—oh crap. I just realized I have somewhere to be tonight. This is the day I'm supposed to go take photos at The Maithe.

Will I see Peri? Will she want to see me? If I'm being truthful with myself, I should probably question how I'll feel to see her, too. She did run off without an explanation, leaving me confused and hurting. But lately, all I am is confused, so maybe that's my natural state now.

All I know for sure is that I have some time to kill before the party, and that's more time to think about everything that's happened. I'm not sure if that's a good thing or not.

CHAPTER 7
DOUBLE ECHO – THE POSITION

I'm so pissed at myself.

I should never have agreed to shoot this party. I hate parties; I hate being around strangers; I don't even like going to the ones that the Ants throw, and I actually know people at those. This party? I'll know like two people, and right now, I'm not even sure where I stand with one of them. What was I thinking?

I've only done a few sessions of live band photography before. So sure, why not take a gig at my magical maybe-girlfriend's house? No pressure. Not to mention, there's a part of me that fears disappointing Vali for some reason. Her opinion, weirdly enough, matters to me.

Ugh—fine, fine. It can't be much different than shooting Joolie when she's working on some big canvas, right? Or Elise when she's dancing. It's a job. I can focus on that, and maybe I'll stop overthinking everything.

I don't even know what to wear to this party, or show or whatever it is. Vali didn't really say what to expect so I guess I'll just go as the slightly fancier version of Denny that the world usually gets. In this case, that means a pair of loose brown velvety pants, a tucked-in cotton t-shirt that matches, and a mossy green wool sports jacket that I found one day at a high-end thrift store. Paired with my sandy brown hair, I look like something dragged from a clearing in the woods, like a lichen-covered log shaped like a person. I look in the mirror and tousle my hair more—might as well lean into the look, right?

I lace up my beloved, battered boots and check over my camera bag to make sure I have what I need for the night. On a whim, I tuck the same toy camera I took with me on my date with Peri and a couple of rolls of 35mm film in the bag next to the digital camera. Maybe it'll bring me luck.

It's about 6 p.m. and already dark out. Since I'm ready to go and Vali said that I should show up early to take group photos, I head over to The Maithe. It's colder outside than I expected. I consider going back to get a scarf at least, but that risks running into Joolie and then having to explain where I'm going without having her invite herself along, so I'll just suffer. By the time I'm walking up to the huge hulking presence of The Maithe, both my ears and nose are freezing and probably red.

I'm supposed to just walk in, but that feels weird, so I stand in front of the gorgeous glass door for a few moments, contemplating my life choices and feeling stupid. I feel even weirder when the door spontaneously swings open on its own and stays that way, as if it's waiting for me to come in. I look around in confusion before I decide that for my own sanity, I'm just going to believe that it wasn't closed properly, and the wind pushed it open. I walk through cautiously, and before I can close it behind me, the door swings back and latches with an audible click.

Okay then. Okay. It doesn't feel malevolent or anything, but I'd better be ready for more energy tentacles or whatever else this house is ready to offer me. Great.

I attempt to get my shit together by taking a look around. When I was here last, Peri didn't give me much time to assess the rest of the downstairs. But even still, you'd think I wouldn't have missed the huge ballroom to my left, with grandiose crystal chandeliers and a gorgeous wood floor perfect for dancing. There's a stage along the inner wall, opposite the tall windows on the street side of the room, set up for the band that's playing tonight. The Drawback, Vali said, and I recognize that name. They've been playing a lot of shows around town lately, mostly at underground venues or small clubs, but still have managed to raise a big buzz. I think Pod has been trying to get Joolie to book them for one of our parties.

As I come into the room, I see a group of people sitting on the far side of the stage, where they'd been obscured by the drum kit. Vali jumps up from the floor and comes running over to me, a big grin on her face. Something about her seems… different, somehow. I can't put my finger on it.

"Denny! You made it!" She surprises me with an exuberant hug, and I awkwardly return it. She smells like coffee and… spray paint? "Let me introduce you to everyone!"

She gestures toward the group, and I catch a flash of gold paint on her fingertips, the source of the paint smell. It seems overly glittery, catching the light from the chandelier overhead.

"Folks, this is Denny Myers, your photographer for the evening. They/them pronouns, right?" She turns to me to confirm.

"Sure, yes." I feel both awkward and relieved to be that easily accepted. "Nice to meet everyone. If there's anything I need to know or that you specifically want from me tonight, I'll do my best." I'm not looking at anyone directly yet, thanks to my shyness at meeting so many new people, combined with the strange interactions I've had at this house so far.

"Hey, Denny! I'm Sousa. I think I've seen you at the Bean before?" The vaguely familiar guy, a burly punk dude, offers me a thick, muscular hand, and I fully expect to get one of those testosterone-fueled squeezing handshakes. Instead, he grips my hand like we've been friends forever, and I immediately feel at ease. This guy feels inherently trustworthy. I look up as he releases my hand, and it hits me that he's a lot more attractive than I expected. I don't usually find his type of guy to my taste, especially ones that look like they've been wearing the same ripped-up clothes for days, but there's something about him that grabs my attention. I guess that's an important trait to have when you're a musician.

"I spend a lot of time over there, yeah. It's a good place to work, and Vali always makes me feel at home."

"She's good at that." He grins and runs a hand through his short, spiky hair. I realize that there's the same glittery gold in it that's on Vali's fingertips. I feel like there's something else that I should be noticing, but I can't put my finger on it.

"Is that—do you have spray paint in your hair?" I blurt it out, and Vali cracks up.

"He's gonna have a hell of a time getting it out, too!"

"Should I ask why you're using spray paint in your hair?" It's surprising how easy it is to take a teasing tone with him. I'm not usually this outgoing.

"I wouldn't let him use my hair gel!" This comes from the dark-haired guy dressed neatly in all black. He's got an infectious grin and the kind of presence that tells me he probably fronts the band. "I'm Merrick, by the way. Vali told me good things about you." I like the way he carries himself. He seems self-assured but not cocky.

"You're the singer, right? How many people in the band?"

"Drums, bass, guitar." He points in that order to Sousa, himself, and the woman standing toward the back.

"Hey! I'm Lucee, the brains of this unit." She jumps forward, and I can immediately see that while she might be joking about being the brains, she's absolutely the band's heart. It's not just Merrick's snort and Sousa's laugh, but the way they move to give her room. "I hope you get some good shots of us, but more importantly, I hope you have fun! That's what it's all about tonight!"

She's doing this little dance, bouncing from one foot to the other, like it's impossible for her to stay still. Her hair, which consists of many little braids in a variety of shades of green and black, moves in time with her. It reflects and enhances the energy that radiates from her and makes me want to dance around, too. She's got this warm brown skin and eyes that crinkle up when she smiles. Her short black dress is made mostly of tulle with green glitter that matches her hair, and it's paired with fishnets and combat boots. She's just adorable.

The band and Vali are all good-looking people, no doubt, but the last two folks left to introduce themselves are jaw-droppingly stunning. There's no other way to put it. The guy's tall, with the kind of fine facial features and flowing blond hair that makes me think of frock coats and ruffles. He carries himself in a regal fashion, a very different vibe than the one the band puts out. The woman next to him is petite and curvy, with a cloud of dark hair that's mixed with lavender strands. She's almost too pretty to be real. Her features are so symmetrical that I can't help but think what an amazing model she would be. She's wearing a simple black dress, but like the guy beside her, I could see her in something much more period and not bat an eye.

I almost miss it, but there's a subtle exchange of looks between the tall guy and Lucee before she gestures at them and tells me who they are.

"These fine folks here are Cullen and Aisling. They're here for moral support and to up our general attractiveness levels." Lucee winks at me, and I can't help but smile back. She's ridiculously likable.

"I'm told that our title is 'band bitch,' and that it is a term of endearment. I'm not quite sure, myself," Cullen says to me, a twinkle in his eye. His accent is vaguely British, each word carefully pronounced, almost formal sounding. The tone of his voice is warm and humorous, and he suddenly seems much more approachable than I first thought.

"What an outrageous way to present us, you walnut!" The woman—Aisling—playfully swats Cullen on the arm. "So nice to meet you," she directs to me. There's something about her that makes me think that I could confide anything to her and she'd never tell a soul. "If Cullen and I can help you in any way tonight, don't hesitate to ask. We like to be helpful."

I feel surprisingly at ease with these people. I've barely stumbled over my words tonight.

"Okay, that would be great. I don't have much to set up, but having extra hands available is always a good thing." I look around the room, scanning for the best places to do portraits. "I really want to show your personalities. Is there a place you'd like best for me to shoot? Or I can start on the stage and then see where it goes. Your call."

"Why don't we run a sound check, and you can see what we're about and take some pics at the same time?" Lucee asks and hops up on the low stage, gesturing for the others to follow. It's a good suggestion. I nod and turn to make sure that my camera's set up the way I want. There's a tap on my shoulder, and I turn to find Vali standing next to me.

"Here, you'll want these. It can get loud during practices, and these are top-notch." She hands me a small clear container. I can see what I think are earplugs inside, definitely not cheap ones either.

"Oh wow, thank—"

She cuts me off with an abrupt motion. "I don't know what Peri told you, but saying that word is a no-no around here. Just think of it as a cultural difference that will bring a lot of unwelcome responses." She winks at me, a disarming smile on her face. "But I appreciate the thought. We don't want you to leave with hearing damage, you know."

"I—okay. I'll make sure to use them." I don't know what else to say to that, so this will have to do. That wins me another wink before she turns to go sit at the small soundboard stationed across from the band.

Peri did warn me about not saying thank you, as weird as it seems not to thank someone. I just forgot, but that feels like a mistake I shouldn't repeat.

I put the earplugs in, and for a second, everything feels muffled, then that goes away, and it's like I never put them in at all. Whoa. Even when I speak, it's not that weird ears-stopped-up feeling like I've had with other earplugs. The band starts warming up at that point, and I realize that they sound crystal clear, with the right amount of loudness.

I take that as the signal to get to work, and I decide to start out with a couple of wide band shots to warm up. They aren't running any stage lights yet, so the lighting is all from the chandelier overhead. At first, the band members tether in place, adjusting their sound levels. As they start to get comfortable up on the stage, they start jumping around, laughing, and letting their personalities shine, and I start to enjoy this shoot as I watch them goof off. It's hard not to, honestly. I can see why they're getting popular. The band is musically tight in a way that says they've practiced together for a long time, and they're very close with one another. They spend as much time laughing as they do playing, and they make it seem like everyone in the room is in on the jokes. Maybe that'll be different once the room is full of people other than their friends and me, but I don't think so.

They run through a handful of songs, both originals and covers, all with a post-punk feel to them. Once they're finished, it's time for me to do close-up shots. I'm thinking that in front of the elevator might be a great place to start, because of those beautiful brass-inlaid doors. While I'm pondering this, Lucee calls me over to the stage.

"Denny! We've been thinking about where we might sit for the photoshoot. I think we have the perfect place, but we messed around too much, and now we don't have time before the party starts." Lucee's face gets pink at this admission. Even her embarrassment is cute. "It's in a private part of the house, and I think you'll love it. Do you think you would mind waiting until we wrap up our set? I promise we'll pay you well for your time."

Ah, so I *am* getting paid for this gig. That puts me in a good mood, enough of one to stick around longer than I might have otherwise.

"I can stay, no problem. And getting to see more of this incredible building doesn't hurt either." Normally, I'd tack a half-assed smile onto the end of a sentence like this, but the one that follows is genuine. Their banter during the set and the way they go out of their way to make me feel welcome are really warming me up.

"Cool, cool. I might suggest you grab a beer and something to eat before everyone gets here and snatches it all up." Sousa gestures at the far corner of the room. When I turn to check it out, I'm totally taken aback at the spread, laid out on long tables that definitely weren't there when the band started their sound check.

"Our friends know that you're the official photographer and will make sure to keep space for you up in the front, too," Merrick assures me, then shoots a pointed look at Cullen, who is standing off to the side. "Right, Cullen?"

"Of course! If you wish, I can be your personal assistant during the show. Let me be at your service." Cullen punctuates this request with a half-bow, of all things, but somehow, this seems like a natural thing for him to do.

"I don't need much help—"

"Then let me be the ambassador that introduces you to notables and points out those you might want to immortalize on film." His smile seems to convey both reassurance and an apology for cutting me off, or maybe that's me reading too much into things. "Merrick asked me to do this for you, so please forgive me if I don't take no for an answer. Our friends can be a bit overwhelming, and I can help you navigate that."

He beckons to me as he walks over to the tables laden with food and drinks. I meekly follow because what else am I going to do in this situation? Anyway, a drink might help cut the nervousness that's starting to creep in. I'm finally remembering that Peri lives here and chances are good that I'll see her tonight.

"I guess I'll have to accept, then. But just be warned that assistants end up carrying my beverages and catching me before I trip over things." That's a blatant and almost flirtatious lie; what's gotten into me? He's not even my type, and I am anything but a flirt at even the best of times.

"I already spend half my time carrying band equipment, so I may be overqualified for this assignment," he replies with a laugh. Banter is obviously these people's native language. He turns to look at me with an exaggerated critical squint. "You look like a wine person. We do have some wine here, but if you're open to suggestions, I have better options."

"I'm open to suggestions." Why do I feel like I'm flirting? Damn!

"For your consideration." He hands me a clear glass corked bottle, a bit larger than one for beer but shaped more like a wine bottle. "This is mead, made locally by friends who are experts at this type of thing. Give it a try!"

I hold it up to the light and inspect the golden liquid inside. The chandelier's crystals refract through the contents within and make it seem like lights are dancing inside the bottle. I can smell the faint scent of honey, which gets stronger when I uncork it.

Cullen's watching me with interest to see what my reaction is. For some reason I expect the liquid to be thicker, like honey, but it's the same consistency as wine. It's also less sweet than I anticipated, which is a relief. I immediately feel more relaxed, a slow warmth creeping through my body as the drink hits my guts.

"Wow, that's a lot stronger than expected. But good!" I lick my lips, which are a little sticky from the mead. "Definitely made from honey, but not cloying. I like it."

Cullen lights up at my endorsement. "Ah, you have good taste. We also have home-brewed beer, which I do encourage trying if you like beer. Sousa and Sheridan are the ones who make that, and if you enjoy it, they'll certainly soak up some compliments." He waves broadly across the selections piled up on the table, an invitation to partake. "Make sure you eat your fill now; I suspect you will soon be too busy to get back here for a while."

The food is not your typical party food, not by a long shot. There are finger sandwiches, separated into choices for vegans and meat-eaters, indicated by small cards in front of each plate labeled with neat script. I notice that's the case across the table; how thoughtful. Another plate holds small puff pastries filled with herb cheese and fig jam. There's a huge charcuterie board, fancier than some that I've seen at the parties that Joolie's managed to drag me to, and a tiered display filled with small whole fruits—strawberries, plums, figs, apricots, and more. It's not even the right time of year for those. I wonder how much that cost?

"This is quite the spread, Cullen," I stammer, overwhelmed by the bounty.

"We don't do anything halfway, you see," he chuckles, then pops a cheese-stuffed round red pepper into his mouth with a pleased sound. I decide to follow his lead, and grabbing a small plate, I put two of the peppers on it, two puff pastries, and one particularly luscious-looking strawberry.

"We can sit over there if you like. It's a good way to watch people as they arrive." He leads me over to a group of comfortable-looking armchairs then spends the next half hour or so pointing out people he thinks I should focus on as they enter the room, while I mostly nod and enjoy the remarkably delicious food on my plate.

As I drink and eat and Cullen chatters on companionably, I start to notice things that I hadn't at first. There are so many good-looking people in this room! It feels almost unnatural. Thanks to being a part of the Ants, I'm used to rubbing shoulders with rich and talented people, many of whom have taken pains to be the most attractive folks at any event. But this is different, and at first, I can't put my finger on why. It isn't until Cullen kindly bends to pick up my dropped napkin that I see it.

His shining golden hair falls forward as he reaches down, covering his face and revealing his ears, which are as perfectly formed as the rest of him—and pointy.

He has points at the tips of his ears.

There's a moment when he sits back up, and his hair moves back into place, where everything's fine. It's all in my imagination, right?

But then he opens his mouth, ready to say something or another to me. And I see his pointy canine teeth, and there's a weird sort of energy, like a mild electric shock, that moves through my body. Our eyes meet, and that's when I know it's not just me having a moment of confusion or instability. Something isn't as it seems.

"You can see it, can't you? You don't know what you're seeing, but it's not hidden anymore." Cullen's voice is calm, soothing—and a little curious in tone, I notice.

"Something is... what's going on here?" I feel a little dizzy, so I close my eyes and take a deep breath. "I sure am tired of everything being so fucking strange lately."

"Strange in what way?"

"I don't even know where to begin."

"All right, what if instead you open your eyes and tell me what you're seeing now?" It sounds like a reasonable request, so I do as he asks. I crack one eye open and look at him. Still handsome, but looking distinctly... foxy? Like vulpine, I mean. I open the other eye and tilt my head, trying to figure it out. To his credit, he doesn't react beyond sitting there with the ghost of a smile on his lips.

"So you have, um, ears."

"So do you." At this point, either he's fucking with me, or I'm really losing it.

"Mine are your average everyday ears, though."

That does it, he sputters with laughter he can't contain anymore.

"Mine are *also* everyday ears, but I'll let you off the hook. Here," and he pulls his hair back to reveal one perfect, pointed ear. "You aren't imagining it. But I'm at a loss to understand how you saw it."

Surprisingly, I feel relief rush through me. I'm not losing it! I'm still confused, though Cullen's unbothered demeanor is diffusing any fear I might have.

"What if I told you that this isn't the strangest thing I've encountered lately?" I've instantly got his attention laser-focused on me. Saying that reminds me of the Nyxen and their gifts. "Oh shit, I think I understand it now."

"I think you need to explain this to me in detail, Denny. What happened?" He's as serious as can be, no sign of his dazzling smile from just a moment ago.

"I don't know if I'm supposed to say anything, but I guess I'd better tell you what happened. Have you ever heard of, um, Nyxen?"

Cullen's eyebrows shot up, and his eyes widened. "You encountered Nyxen?"

"I was, uh—I was invited to meet them."

"You'd better tell me the whole story. Very few mortals interact with Nyxen and live to tell the tale, Denny."

CHAPTER 8
BOOTBLACKS – TRAVELING LIGHT

I don't tell him everything that's been going on. For now, I keep it to the strange invitation and meeting with the Nyxen and the gifts they gave me. I do confess that other strange things have happened, but it would take more time to explain than we have at the moment.

"That is fair, but I do want to hear the whole tale once The Drawback is finished playing and we're away from the crowd." His frown looks out of place on his handsome face. "And you are correct; their ointment is what is allowing you to see true, though it seems that their recipe is weaker than one we might give you. Do you have it with you, by chance?"

I take the small tin from my jacket pocket, holding it on my outstretched palm for him to see. He plucks it from my hand and inspects it from every angle, stroking a digit over the enameled lid before he opens the tin and lightly sniffs the balm.

"Their blend is most certainly different from our own, but that is not surprising. I sense nothing alarming here, at least. I would recommend re-applying now, Denny, before the band takes the stage. It will give you a chance to adjust."

I want to ask what I'll be adjusting to exactly but decide that's a stupid question that will be better answered by just doing as he says. A swipe across each eyelid gets a nod of approval from him. He crinkles his nose and points to one of his ears, then taps his chest. Okay, that's pretty clear. I follow his instructions and apply the balm to those places as well.

"What will that do?"

"It will assist you in understanding words and subtext that you may not otherwise, and in seeing clearly with your heart as well as your eyes. I think you may find this even more helpful than true sight." His smile seems wistful, and I get the feeling he's thinking of something that has nothing to do with me. "Why don't you look around the room and tell me what you see now?"

For a second, I'm afraid to break his gaze to do as I'm bid. I've already seen some extremely odd and confusing things; I don't know if I'm ready for more. But it's not like I could even leave this place without seeing the other people in the room. I'm pledged to this course, and I'm just going to have to keep an open mind and stay calm.

I turn slowly and the first person I see in the crowd is a thickly built man with rich brown skin that seems to gleam with a faint golden hue. His outfit, a longer-cut black dress jacket over wide-leg pleated pants, is exquisitely tailored and must have cost a fortune. His chest is bare under the jacket. If my chest looked like that, I would probably skip a shirt, too. He has short, spiked hair, which helps me see his pointed ears and delicate-looking horns that sweep away from his forehead and over his hair to curl up at the tips.

Horns. Sure.

The person next to him, however, makes me intake my breath in a quick gasp. They are tall and muscular, as pale as a sheet of paper, with an air about them that immediately assures me that "they" is surely the correct pronoun to use.

I wish I had that effect.

They have what I'd call a strong face, with a pronounced nose and full lips. Their ears are also quite pointed but with more of a slant backward, made obvious by the shaved sides that offset the rest of their long hair. It hangs in braids—wait, did some of them move on their own?

"Cullen, tell me those aren't snakes on that person's head." My voice is calmer sounding than I'm feeling internally.

"I cannot confirm if that is true or not, I'm afraid. Perhaps you'll be the one brave enough to ask them." Cullen casually winks at me, but I can tell that he's carefully watching my reactions. "How are you faring? This can be overwhelming for mortals. Though since you've met Nyxen, you already have some experience in mixing with non-mortals."

I glance over to the stage area and spot Lucee. She looks much the same as she did before, except there's more of a presence about her. I can sense something different, but there's no horns or ears or glow.

"Lucee isn't one of you?"

"Ah, our Lucee and Merrick are special. They are what we call 'mortal-born.' In other words, they started out as mortals, just as you are, but were given magical essence from us. They earned it well, I should add. There are very few mortal-born with us and each one is quite unique. In Lucee's case, she also happens to be our leader. Merrick is our champion."

"How—?" I cut myself off, feeling like maybe I'm overstepping myself, and rethink what I'm going to say. "I'd love to hear that story one day if you feel that you can trust me with it."

"Ah, I'd love to share that at another time." Cullen's approval makes me feel like I scored some points in my favor. I don't know why it matters to me, but it does. "For now, let me introduce you to some of the people I think you should know, especially if you are brave enough to rub elbows with Nyxen."

To my surprise, he gives me a neat courtly-type bow, and that's enough to distract me from questions I have about needing bravery when it comes to the Nyxen. I sputter a little, and he returns to upright with a laugh.

"There, that signals to the room that you're to be respected and serves as a bit of a tension-breaker for you as well, I'd wager." He doesn't give me any time to respond, instead waving over the folks I'd been staring at a moment earlier. "Let me lead the introduction, if you don't mind."

The two strangers approach, and I can tell that they're both curious about me. The stockier one even gives me a subtle up-and-down, and when his eyes meet mine, I realize they're golden-colored.

"Who's this, my friend? A new addition to our gathering, I see." Oh, his voice is deep and resonant, and I could listen to him speak for hours. He's also got a killer smile. Are any of these people just average-looking?

"This is Denny, our photographer for the evening. They were invited by Vali, and they have recently become *aware* of our community, so I thought it wise to introduce them to some of the favored of this house." Cullen's slight stress on "aware" is delivered with an accompanying knowing look.

"I see, I see. Then let me offer my name and assurances," he says to Cullen before focusing again on me. "I am Daro, of Tiennan House. And any friend of Maithe House is a friend to me. If you need assistance, call on me, and I will answer." He bows his head slightly, and I feel myself respond in kind without meaning to.

"I, um, I'm pleased to meet you." I scramble for a way to politely thank him without using that phrase. "Your kindness is, uh—"

He cuts me off with a laugh. "Ah, no need to struggle for the right words, Denny. I see that you respect my offer and our ways as well. I like this one, Cullen. No pretenses here."

"Vali always finds good people."

Huh. What about Peri? Does she find good people, too?

"I am Karsten, also of Tiennan House, though of late, I have been here more often than not." They have a surprisingly soft, kind voice. Karsten steps forward to offer a hand, and I take it nervously. Their grip is firm, and they hold my hand for a few seconds more than I think is necessary before letting it go. Again, I feel like I've been assessed. Hopefully, I passed whatever the test was meant to check.

"Glad to meet you, truly," I manage to get out without stammering this time. I guess I do okay because Karsten rewards me with a pleased expression.

"You'll find I'm a quiet friend to have, Denny, but one willing to answer questions at length. Don't be afraid to ask." They push back a few sinuous strands of hair or whatever it is, and I almost—almost!—blurt out a question about it in my curiosity. If they want to explain it, they will. I settle on a grateful smile instead.

"Who else has our new friend met?" Daro asks.

"You two and our esteemed leaders. Not that they would like being referred to in that way." That's obviously for my benefit, although I'm not sure why. I suppose they don't like getting special treatment. I can get behind that. "Ah, so many people have arrived now. Denny, I don't think we'll have the time to introduce you to anyone else right now. I'm sure the band will be starting soon, and you have work to do. Let me take this plate and bottle for you, and then we shall get you set up as you need."

"If the music begins soon, then you must excuse me while I find Tully. She'll want a dancing partner," Daro says with a grin before striding off into the mass of people. I'm left with Karsten, but before I can attempt asking them anything, there's a tap on my shoulder.

"Denny? Is that you?"

I'm not prepared for who I see standing there. It's Raúl Morro, the painter whose work I'd commented on in Peri's room. He looks much different from when we went to the Institute together, like he's fallen on hard times. He's rumpled, greying, and his once-handsome features are sunken in a way that I associate with the very ill or addicts.

"Raúl? Whoa, it's been ages. What brings you here?" I try to keep the shock out of my voice.

"It *is* you. ¡Menos mal! I was hoping I was right, that I'd find you here." He looks around nervously, and I catch the movement of his hands clenching and unclenching. From the corner of my eye, I see Karsten standing very still. It seems that Raúl doesn't notice them at all. His next words escape from his trembling lips in a desperate flood. "You need to get away from her, Denny. She's no good. She'll ruin you; she ruins everything. She's not what you think, not at all."

"Raúl, what are you talking about?" I don't like where this is going.

"You know, you know who I mean. Peri. Peri Linden." Her name in his mouth sounds like a curse. "She's dangerous, Denny. She'll use you up. You'll think meeting her is the best thing that ever happened to you. She'll make you feel like you're clever and talented, and people will notice your work, and you'll be on top of the world. Until it comes crashing down because she's sucked you dry and left you scrambling while she walks off on the arm of another artist, and you're just washed up."

"I... Raúl, I don't know what to say. I don't have anything like that to lose, anyway. I'm just a photographer." Even as the words are coming out of my mouth, I feel a flicker of doubt. I think how Peri built me up and flattered me at the coffee shop. Joolie and her courting of Peri. The photos I took in Peri's room and the flickering tendrils of energy connecting her to Raúl's painting and the other works on her wall. How I felt when she left my place suddenly. I don't want to believe his unhinged rantings, but...

"I can see it in your eyes, Denny. You're considering what I'm saying. Something's not right, and you know it." He's slightly rocking back and forth, and the look in his eyes is unsettling. How much does Raúl know about what Peri is, or any of the people in this room, whatever they are?

There's a soft noise, and I realize that it's Karsten clearing their throat. "Denny, we should get you set up to work, yes?" It breaks whatever dark spell that Raúl's words have cast over me, at least for now.

"You're right. I need to get in place. Raúl, I'll take your warning into consideration."

"No, you won't. I had to try, though." He looks stricken, and his whole body is tense. I'm a little afraid that he's going to cause a scene, but Karsten takes my elbow and leads me away before Raúl can do or say anything else. I turn to look back at him and see his face shift from haunted to sullen before the crowd swallows him up.

"That one is dangerous," Karsten says in a low voice. "Be careful, Denny." We move to a spot in front of the crowd, and I spy the band getting ready in the darker space behind the stage.

"You said I could ask you anything. Is that still okay?" Karsten answers me with a solemn nod, so I continue. "Do you know Peri? Since she lives here and all, and you said you spend a lot of time here."

"I am aware of her. There are those who live here that don't easily mix with the other residents but are still welcome as part of the House. That mortal seems afraid and angry, but I will tell you something that you might not yet understand. This is a reaction familiar to many of our kind, received when we do not continue to provide them with the wonders they've glimpsed. The world unseen by most mortals is filled with addictive magics, Denny. You should be mindful of this."

"I—I don't know what to say to that, but I appreciate your candor about it." My voice shakes a little, and Karsten touches my shoulder lightly, just long enough to calm me down. I don't know how they know it'll work, but it does.

"You've made friends here already, Denny. I suspect you will continue to do so, as Vali is a good judge of character, and it has been made clear that you are welcome, even if your connection with Peri falters." I don't like thinking about that. I'm sure it shows on my face as Karsten pats my shoulder again and then changes the subject. "Is there anything I might assist with?"

"I don't think so, no. Unless you don't mind watching out for the crowd for me? I tend to get swept up in taking photos, and I might not realize that I'm in the way or in danger of getting jostled around." I don't say it out loud, but it wouldn't be the first time something like that has happened to me.

"I don't think you'll have much to fear in that regard, but I'll be nearby to protect you if needed." Karsten seems pleased that I asked. I suspect that being useful is important to them. I'll try to keep that in mind.

At this point, the band is getting up on the stage and the room lights go down while the stage lights brighten. There's a general movement of the party toward the stage, and I can tell that people are excited for the band to get started. Surprisingly, there's plenty of room in front of the stage despite the crowded floor.

I have my camera out of my bag and ready to go, which is a good thing because the band doesn't take long to start playing. For a moment, I wonder what happened to Cullen, and then Sousa starts banging on his drums to get the room's attention, and I'm just grateful for the earplugs that Vali gave me earlier.

"Hey, HEY! Welcome to The Maithe, old friends and new friends! Hope you're having a good time so far!" Merrick's loud greeting is met by cheers and whistles from the crowd, and he grins at the reaction. "Good, good, and don't forget to try the beer. It's brewed in-house and Sousa and Sheridan will have my hide if I don't mention that!"

Lucee waits for the laughter to die down a little before she steps up to the mic. "Yes, yes, we'll be here all week; try the beer. Anyway, we're The Drawback!" She hits a chord on her guitar, and the sound reverberates through the room, drowning out the cheers from the audience; then the band slams into their first song.

I start snapping shots immediately, but I have to pause about halfway through the first song to just listen. Wow, these folks are *good*. They're talented enough that I can't figure out if their first song is a cover or an original until they mention after they're finished that it's one of theirs. They've got this post-punk, edgy aura, but somehow, they manage to put out upbeat vibes. The entire room's captivated. I try to capture that in some of my shots of the dance floor, filled with bodies just enjoying the tunes without a care in the world.

The energy is sweeping me up, too. I'm so into it that I'm taken by surprise when I feel a tap on my arm in between songs. I turn to find Cullen behind me.

"It's easy to lose yourself in their act, isn't it? But you might want to try and keep focus for the last couple of songs. There's usually a great light show." He winks at me, and I'm not sure what that means. "You'll see," he adds.

He's cut off from saying more by the powerful sound of Lucee's guitar as the band jumps right into the next song. Merrick's voice somehow carries over the pounding bass and drums, and the crowd responds eagerly, dancing wildly and singing along at the top of their lungs. I don't know this tune, but it's obvious that they all do.

I'm busy grabbing a million shots when something weird happens. I know, I know, when *hasn't* something weird happened lately? But this is, for lack of a better word, breathtaking.

Everyone in the audience is fully into what's happening in the room—the music, the dancing, the lights. I can feel the energy building. So it's not really a surprise when the lighting sort of *shifts* and becomes… I don't know how to explain it—more all-encompassing and multi-dimensional? I'm sure I'm not making sense.

Usually, when there are lights at an event, they bathe the room, but you always know that they're coming from fixed points. They're flat, projected onto everything in their way indiscriminately. This was not that, not by a longshot.

The lights seem to move around us in ribbons, weaving in and out of the mass of people in multicolor streams and waves that rise and fall to the music. When a dancer crosses paths with one, it breaks into a million pixelated dots of color, like rainbow fireflies, only to reconnect a few minutes later. As the dancers catch on to this, they go out of their way to break the streams of light with radiant, gleeful looks on their faces. Their joy is impossible to ignore. It's contagious.

I'm moving backwards through the crowd, trying to get behind them to grab shots of the entire room with the band at the front. As I pass through one of the ribbons of light, I sense as it breaks apart and everything feels… effervescent? The only way I can describe it is like I've jumped into a giant vat of champagne.

Just as quickly, the feeling passes, and I find myself at the far end of the room, near the big windows. I climb up on a chair to see over the audience. I don't know what's different about being above everyone in the room, but I find myself removed from what's happening on the dance floor. The curtain is drawn back on what the band is doing—and the big reveal is that it's coming from *them*.

Not from lights or projectors; there's no equipment like that on the stage. Now that I can see it, I don't understand how I didn't before. The sound's different, too. They're still an amazing band, with appealing voices and catchy tunes, but the overwhelming richness of the sound is a bit reduced. The overlays, the extra instrumentation? It's all gone. I think I like them even better without it, but I can see how having the enhancement adds to the whole effect and sweeps the listeners up.

I quickly snap some shots, both of the band and the audience, before I jump down from my roost. When I hit the floor, I expect to be caught back up in the same experience the rest of the room is having, but taking myself out of it momentarily seems to have broken the magic for me. I wonder if that's because of the ointment?

I hear Merrick from the stage announce, "We're The Drawback! Thanks for coming to our party. Now go eat and drink something; I bet you're starving!" There's a collective laugh from the room and lots of cheers, including from me. They've easily won me over. I feel strangely refreshed, not something I usually feel after a concert. I start to head back to the stage, but a commotion in the middle of the dispersing audience catches my attention.

It could be a scene out of a movie, the way it happens. The crowd parts like a human curtain, and Peri and Raúl are revealed to me. He grabs her by the arm and yells something at her, though I can't hear what, thanks to the noise in the room. She recoils and tries to pull out of his grasp, but he's too strong and won't let go. I can tell that he's hurting her, and I feel a flush of anger start at my chest and spread through my body. It doesn't matter what kind of unfinished business he thinks he has with her; I'm not going to let him treat her this way. I don't even think before I start running for them.

The next three things happen in a flash.

Peri sees me first. She starts shaking her head vigorously, fear in her eyes, trying to warn me off. I see why when Raúl turns in my direction, and I spy the small, gleaming knife in his other hand, the one that isn't gripping her wrist tightly.

He looks around, panicked, and for a second, I think he's going to stab her before I can get there. The blade moves faster than I can see, and then I hear her cry. He drops her arm and pushes her away before turning to run, disappearing into the mass of people who haven't seemed to move at all as this unfolds.

Time starts back up again, and the crowd lurches forward as I finally reach Peri. I want to check her over, make sure she's unharmed, but she clings to me like I'm the safest person in the room—and maybe I am, at this point. I realize that no one else seems to have noticed anything happening. It's like we're in this blind spot in the middle of the dance floor.

That is until I look up and meet Joolie's eyes. She's staring at us from across the room, the expression on her face an unsettling mix of greed and fear.

CHAPTER 9
CREUX LIES – MISUNDERSTANDING

My attention is jerked away from Joolie as Karsten spins me around to check for potential damage. I see Cullen doing the same to Peri, a confused look on his face.

"There's blood here, but I see no wound. Are you unharmed?"

"I—I think so?" Peri's eyes are huge, and her voice shakes. She holds her arms out in front of her for us to inspect, and it's true; her left arm is all bloody, but there's no gash. There's not even blood on the floor, just on her arm—no, as I look down, I realize there's some of her blood on me where I held her, a darker spot on the brown of my t-shirt.

"You definitely got hit by that knife. Is there somewhere that we can clean the both of us up?" I'm doing my best not to panic. I don't know if I'm succeeding.

Cullen nods, his face all business as he hurries us to the curved staircase at the far end of the ballroom, then up to the second floor. I don't question him. I'm busy trying not to think too much about what all this means.

He leads us into what looks like a bathroom for residents, with an old-fashioned standalone tub and a surprisingly large sink.

"I'll get you some towels." While he pulls them from a cabinet on the other side of the room, I motion Peri to the sink and wash off the blood. There it is, the faintest pink line of a scar that slants across her forearm, and when I look at her incredulously, she won't meet my eyes.

"I told you." I say it louder than I mean to. "There. He cut you. I'm not even going to ask why it's healed already."

"You know why." She avoids meeting my eyes. "I'm not mortal. I'm like these folks," and she gestures at Cullen and Karsten, "But not. He thought he knew what to do to get a fix from me. I don't know how he got the idea."

"A—a fix? Like an addict? By making you bleed?" I can hear the pitch of my voice increasing, edging into freakout mode. Karsten puts a hand on my shoulder in an attempt to calm me down. "Can you, can anyone explain this to me?"

Peri starts crying, and Cullen, who is obviously uncomfortable, hands Peri a towel while shooting me a concerned look.

"Karsten, can you take Denny to the library? I can finish here, then when we rejoin you, Peri will explain everything." The way he says the last part makes it sound like he won't be giving Peri a choice, and I'm a little surprised by the steel in his otherwise genteel voice.

The library is a wide open space, and I realize that it must be above the ballroom. There are big tables with chairs around them as well as groups of comfortable-looking velvety armchairs scattered about, and that's what Karsten and I settle in. I'm starting to calm down a little, finally. Being in Karsten's soothing presence seems to help.

I look around the room curiously, taking in the shelves filled with books that line the walls and the big windows framed by burgundy curtains. The room smells like old books, well-kept wood, and…coffee?

"Karsten, is that coffee I'm smelling?"

"Oh yes. There is always fresh coffee up here. The house is diligent about things like that." They smiled, and I could swear I hear fondness in their voice. The folks who run the house must be really nice. "Did you want some? Check that table over there."

I wander over to where they indicated, and I find one of those swank silver serving urns, all the fixings for coffee that I could ever want, and a variety of mugs. The mugs aren't fancy at all, but rather the kind of novelty ones that people collect, all different. I pick one up and it has a giant sandworm rearing up in the desert on one side with the inscription "I'd rather be riding the worm" in big orange letters. Another says, "This Could Have Been Beer." I bet that's a popular choice. I put down the sandworm one in favor of a black mug with the picture of a spiral galaxy and an arrow pointing to a tiny spot with a "You are here" message and fill it with black coffee.

I blow on it on the way back to my chair, then risk a sip. It's the perfect temperature, and I gratefully take a bigger swig. I feel like I need it at this point.

Cullen clears his throat quietly as he walks in with Peri trailing behind him. I'm grateful to have the mug in my hands because it gives me something to hold onto and hide behind when I see the look on her face. She looks positively miserable.

"Why don't you sit and explain to our friend Denny what you've told me? Karsten and I will give you space." His voice deepens just enough to enforce the seriousness of his next words. "However, I expect you to leave nothing out." Cullen holds her gaze until she nods, then he turns away and takes a chair across the room, Karsten closely following.

Once they're out of earshot, Peri whimpers, "I didn't mean to scare you. Or leave you in the dark."

"Well," I manage to get out, but it takes a moment for me to come up with the next words. "I feel like I've been stumbling around for a long time, I guess. I don't usually let people in, and this hasn't really made a case for changing that." A cynical laugh escapes before I can stop it, and Peri's shoulders sag. I don't mean to make it harder for her, but you know what? I'm so tired of everything being weird and unexplained.

"It's not fair to you; you're right." She rubs the place where the knife cut, her hand stroking the faint scar. "I got scared when I saw that last photo. I told you that obsession is a risk for the mortals who become *entangled* with me. And he—Raúl—is very much an unwanted entanglement. I was afraid that something like this might happen, and I didn't want you to get caught up in it, too."

"So explain it to me. How is he entangled with you?" I can't keep a hint of contempt out of my voice when I say that word. Or maybe it's jealousy. I don't like what I'm feeling, not at all.

Get it together, Denny. Of course, she had lovers before she met you.

"We met at a party, some grungy art show opening at Mobstadt, right before it got shut down for safety reasons. I had just come to Baltimore and didn't know anyone, not even these folks. I was living at a hotel, and all my belongings were in storage. And I made the same mistake I'd made in the last place I'd lived." She sighs deeply, and I wonder what she's going to tell me about those mistakes.

"I met Raúl while I was looking at his paintings. They were interesting enough back then, textural and complex. Not so different from what they became, really, except for the lack of magical depth. But I'm getting off track. We talked, and he was attractive. I was desperate to connect with someone, anyone."

"So you got involved with him."

"I let things go too far. It was foolish on my part. I wanted a friend and ended up with an obsessive lover who realized much too quickly that being with me changed his work in ways that he craved." She swallows hard before going on. "When I say entangled, I mean that he was addicted to what he could get from me. The energy, the magic, the inspiration. All the things I offered you freely. But I never offered it to him. I can't say that he stole it, that's not fair—but it wasn't his to use in the ways that he wanted. And it changed him.

"I told you that exposure to those like me can create obsession. Involvement with me can change people, especially if they are tapping into my magic, and even more so when there isn't the kind of connection you and I have."

She stops abruptly and hangs her head, staring at the ground. Me, I can't seem to sort out my feelings. I decide to talk through what she's told me and my reactions to that, and maybe it'll all come together.

"So you didn't choose to share that part of you with him. You just wanted companionship, and he—what—realized that something was happening with his art?" She nods, her gaze still downturned. "And eventually, he figured out that it was because of you?"

"No. Not while we were together, if you could call it that. After I stopped seeing him, he must have figured out that it was me, that I was the catalyst, and he came to my hotel room and confronted me. He demanded to know what happened, how I'd bewitched him, as he called it, because now he couldn't paint. He said his talent had dried up. He would start paintings but never finish them because they felt flat and lifeless, and somehow, it was my fault."

"Oh shit. That's why he disappeared from the art world."

"Yes." Her voice is barely audible. "He was devastated, bereft. He said he loved me, needed me, and had to have me back in his life, or he was ruined. He fell to his knees and begged. He wouldn't leave. I finally ran to the lobby, and security threw him out when he yanked me to him and shouted at me."

"What did he shout, Peri?" I'm not sure I want to know, but I have to ask.

"You've destroyed me. How can you be so cold? I'll get you back somehow." Her voice is flat, monotone. I feel a chill go up my spine, both from her tone and the words.

"So, um, cutting you like that. Why would he do that?" Again, I'm not sure I want the answer.

"Some people believe that blood from a magical being confers special powers. Maybe that's what his aim was."

"Really?" I'm aghast and rattled by this idea.

"Or maybe he just wanted to hurt me, and you stopped him. But I think he would have done more if that was the case. He just as easily could have stabbed me, right?"

We both consider this unsettling thought. But something's nagging at me, and finally, it just tumbles out because I need to know.

"You didn't know that we would have the connection that you claim we have, not until you showed it to me. So, knowing what can happen, why did you approach me?"

"I…" When she speaks again, her voice shakes. It occurs to me that neither one of us might like her answer. "I was lonely, and you intrigued me. I find you attractive. And you are incredibly talented but trapped in a parasitic relationship with people who think nothing of using you for their own gain." Again, she pauses, then faintly adds, "I wanted to save you, and I thought you could save me, too."

"I wasn't looking to be saved. I want to be seen and valued for who I am. I want to be important for reasons other than what I can do for someone."

"That's what I want, too. No one sees me; they see what I can do for them." Her voice is full of resentment and pain.

"I never thought about anything other than wanting to get to know you and, if I was somehow lucky enough, getting close to you. I never asked for any of this. I didn't even know to want it."

"That's part of why I was drawn to you, Denny. I wanted you to see how amazing you are. And I wanted others to see your talent." She reaches a hand out to me, but I'm not ready for that, not yet.

"But then you immediately did things that changed me, Peri."

"I didn't do anything! Things just happen when I'm around. I can't direct it, Denny. It chooses the recipient; I'm just the conduit. I swear. I don't control anything."

Suddenly, I'm mad.

I know I'm going to ruin everything with the next words out of my mouth, but I can't stop myself. How dare she play the victim in this?

"No, you're a cypher. You could have warned me, and you could have told me what to expect. But you said nothing. You let yourself be powerless to this energy that flows through you. And you've put people in danger because of that, including yourself."

"That's not fair, Denny! I don't know how to control this. You see what it's done to others. Why would I give it to you, knowing that? I'm telling you, it chose you, not me."

"You chose to bring it to me. You could have let me crush on you harmlessly or changed your routine until I forgot about you or moved on. You were the one to escalate this, to introduce yourself, to bring it into my life. And now I'm changed, and everything around me is changing." I pause, then add in a whisper, "All I ever wanted was to know you."

"And now you do." She takes a deep breath, and this time, when she reaches for my hand, I stupidly don't resist. Despite all this, I don't want to pull away from her. "You know me better than anyone has, which, sadly, isn't saying much. Everyone wants my energy without consequence or commitment. They want this breezy and cheerful girl to light up their lives and give them meaning, to somehow give them direction and make them better. And then when I give them that, things go wrong. They want more; they always want more, and it eventually destroys them.

"Anything we do in this life creates changes, Denny. You couldn't know me or care about me without being changed. But I hoped that with you being you, someone who doesn't want to possess me like the others have, you would transform in ways that made you truly believe in yourself. And then you would be free, and so would I."

"But what if I don't? What if I become like Raúl? What if I don't recognize myself anymore? I don't know how to be the person that you seem to see in me, Peri. You want to save someone who is a stranger to me."

And that's it; I'm well and truly crying now. This time, she's the one holding me, both of us on the floor between the chairs, her arms tight around me. She lets me sob until I can't anymore, then gently kisses the top of my head.

"I don't know all the answers. But I do know that you're not like Raúl and that our connection is very different. I want to be here with you, no matter what, no matter who you are at that time. Maybe we don't need to try to save each other. Maybe that'll happen along the way, if we do this right."

I don't realize how much time has passed until my knees start to hurt, and I still don't know what we're doing or how to resolve this. All I know for sure is Peri, and what she has to offer, scares me. Yet I still want her.

"Peri." She loosens her grip on me enough that we can look into each other's eyes. "I can't stumble around in the dark about this anymore. I was warned that you were dangerous, and I guess that's right. I can live with that; at least, I think I can. But I need to understand more of what's happening before it happens. I need you to be open with me like you promised you would."

"I understand." Her nose crinkles then, and her eyes narrow a little. "Wait, who told you that I'm dangerous?"

Before I can answer, there's a soft noise, a throat clearing, and I look up to find Cullen and Karsten standing over us.

"Perhaps it's time that you tell us why there are Nyxen warning your lover to be wary of you?"

CHAPTER 10
THE FOREIGN RESORT — SHE IS LOST

P eri's eyes dart back and forth from Cullen to me, then back again. "Wh-what's a Nyxen?"

Cullen regards her, his head tilted as if he's considering what she's said. After what feels like a lifetime of us all just staring at each other, he holds out a hand to her. "You truly don't know what I mean. Then let us sit and share all that we know because this is perplexing to me, and I'd like to understand what's happening before we go further."

I don't know how he does it, but that simple request just drains away the tension in the room. Peri takes his hand, and to my surprise, Karsten offers theirs to me, so I allow myself to be helped up off the floor. When Peri stands next to Cullen, it strikes me how alike yet different they are. I haven't paid attention to what the ointment reveals about Peri until now, but I can't not notice it at this point.

It's weird. She's undeniably beautiful. But it's not the same as it was when I was mooning over her daily. I'm not even sure I can explain it, but let me try. Before, she was earthy, yet somehow ethereal in my mind. She's still those things for sure—but I can sense an aura about her that was previously undetectable, and it's unsettling. It's like if you've known someone forever, and then suddenly you find out that they've had a secret life, and now you can't recognize them at all. Which is why this is so strange, because it isn't like I've known her that long and she's always been a mystery, so why does any of this bother me? If you'd asked me before our first date, I would have said that the mystery just made her more alluring.

Shows what the fuck I know about dating, or people—or anything, really.

Don't get me wrong. I still want her, and I still want her to want me. That hasn't changed. But if I compare her to Cullen, another magical being who I barely know, I would say I understand him better than my actual love interest. It's a reality check. This whole day, with zero irony intended, considering everyone involved, has been a reality check.

Magical being.

Who I barely know.

I don't know how to reconcile those words.

"Denny? You with us?"

"Huh?" Oh shit, how long have I been stuck in my own head? Karsten pats my arm comfortingly, which makes me relax a little. I wonder if they know what it's like to mentally wander away during important conversations because everything's overwhelming.

"I'm sorry. Can you repeat that?" I'm grateful for the understanding look that Cullen gives me.

"I can. I was just asking you if you would tell Peri what happened with the Nyxen, as much as you feel comfortable. Don't rush; take your time. It's completely normal to feel overwhelmed in a situation such as this."

"I can do that. Just let me tell it without questioning me until I'm done, okay?" I direct that to Peri, and she nods, her eyes big as she watches me. "I need you to understand that I don't think the Nyxen are going to approve of me telling you, but I'm going to do it anyway. It's important."

Everyone nods, and I start from the beginning when Xan brought me the box with the invitation in it. Karsten looks enraptured by the idea of correspondence and gifts from unknown magical creatures. Peri sits up in alarm when I get to the point where the Nyxen appear, and all three of my small audience seem entranced when I describe what they look like. After I finish, they sit in silence for a few moments, thinking about what I've said.

Finally, Peri tentatively ventures an opinion. "I guess I can't fault their attitude about muses. They aren't wrong. I've definitely made a mess of things."

"Seeing it and owning it are good first steps," Cullen says. "Now, what will you do about it? That's a thing to consider." He turns to me. "You took photos of them? They allowed that?"

"I have to say that I'm not sure. They talked about me doing it, and I took photos of what I think was them from a distance, but I haven't looked at all of the results. Everything's happened so fast, you know." I feel sheepish about it, but it's really been a non-stop roller coaster ride.

"I would dearly like to see those at some point if you feel comfortable sharing them. I've only heard of Nyxen, but I have never seen them. They are legendary elementals," Cullen confides, and I see Karsten nodding in agreement.

"I think that would be okay. They did tell me to bring my camera with me, after all. Though I don't understand why they've taken an interest in me or why they would invite me to call on them if I need them. It's quite the compliment, but I don't get it."

"Respect goes a long way with our kind," Karsten says thoughtfully. "And they seem to respond favorably to your admiration of them. As so few have a chance to see them, I am sure that was refreshing and desirable."

"I'm not sure how I could have reacted any other way. They are unlike anyone else I've ever met, and at this point, that's saying something." I gesture vaguely around me, and Karsten stifles a laugh. Cullen looks amused as well. I feel a little more of the tension slip away. Maybe I'm starting to accept everything that's been happening?

"They don't like me, though," Peri mutters. I have a flare of frustration and impatience at her comment.

"You admitted a minute ago that you understood why. Would you rather just not like them back, or are you going to make the effort to prove them wrong about you?" I do my best to keep my voice calm and non-confrontational.

"Is that how you see me?" She's got her head tilted downwards, her hair spilling forward, so I can't see her face, but the pain in her voice is impossible to ignore. "Dangerous? Capricious? Or just unwilling to change?"

"Peri." I take a deep breath before I answer, considering my words. "I can't sum you up in just one word or even three. And I wouldn't describe you in unpleasant terms like those. Like anyone, you've got positive and negative attributes, and I guess the Nyxen have only seen your bad side. I only saw your good points until just recently. Neither is an accurate depiction of who you are and judging you on either is unfair to you."

She lifts her head a little and asks me, "Do you think less of me?"

"Ah, fuck. Can I just say that you're now more human to me, as ironic as that is? Maybe it's better that I have a realistic image of you now. We're a little closer to equal this way." At this, Cullen makes a sound of discomfort, and I shoot him a curious look.

"This is just familiar to me, that's all," he explains with an embarrassed shrug. "Lucee and I dealt with some power imbalances in our relationship when she first came to the Eleriannan. It took a while to understand each other and find equal footing. You see, she was mortal, and I am Fae, so you can see where the similarities might lie."

I give myself time to absorb this information before I reply. "Eleri-Eleriannan? That's what your, um, people call themselves?"

"Oh, this is going to take a moment to explain." He chuckles softly. "We are complicated, so don't worry if you forget some of this. We, in general," and he waves his arm in a circle to indicate the people in the room, or maybe the building, "are called Fae. We've had other names as well, some more flattering than others. Fair Folk, Faery, Good Neighbors, and so on. We prefer Fae, generally. And definitely not fairy; that is a fighting word."

He pauses to let me take all of that in, and I'll admit that I appreciate it.

"So what's Eleriannan?" I don't stumble over the unfamiliar word as much this time.

"We have what you might call factions in our world. Mortals like to divide us as 'Seelie' and 'Unseelie', but it's much more complicated than that. Lucee has been doing work to soften the divisions we had amongst us, but there are still three worth noting: Eleriannan, Gwyliannan, and Grimshaw. I am Eleriannan. Karsten is Gwyliannan. Beings from all three factions come to Maithe House, though that is a fairly recent happening."

"There are a lot of words I don't know happening here, I have to be honest." This earns me a sympathetic grin from Cullen and a nod from Karsten. "I might have more questions down the road if that's okay."

"You may ask me anytime, Denny. I understand how confusing and overwhelming this can be. But there's more to explain, so bear with me. There are different types of Fae as well, and not all of us are considered pretty. I want to warn you now because, until this point, you've only seen the beautiful or alluring of our cohort. Some you may find downright frightful." He pauses again, watching my face for a reaction. I glance at Peri, and she nods slightly, her brow creased.

"Okay. Will they mean to hurt me? Are they dangerous?"

"Ah, my friend, we are all dangerous in our own ways. But yes, some require caution. I would advise that all of us are to be treated with care and a healthy respect. That will take you far in your dealings with Fae and other non-mortals."

"Non-mortals, like the Nyxen?"

"Nyxen and other elemental beings. Avatars. And yes, muses." He inclines his head toward Peri, who, to my surprise, starts to blush.

"So you are not the same type of… being? Is that the right way to say it?"

"That is fine," Karsten affirms. "We are all beings here. You as a mortal, and we as what you would term magical."

"So if I am a mortal—does that mean you are *not* mortal? Can you even die?" Suddenly, I'm feeling a little freaked out. I know you'd think I would have been freaked out long before now.

"I can die. Muses die. It just takes effort," Peri says. She looks uncomfortable.

"Fae are the same. We won't die of old age, at least as far as I know, but we can be killed. It takes a lot to kill us, and generally one of our own to accomplish it, but even that isn't guaranteed to work. We had a war between factions recently, and that brought us casualties. It made us all the more aware of how precious our lives are." I look at Cullen in shock, and he continues, "I'll tell you the entire tale at some other point if you wish. It would take some time to do that now, and you'll want to connect with the band again this evening in order to finish your task, yes?"

"Oh crap, I've been so distracted with everything that's happened I totally forgot why I'm here! But I certainly want to know more about you and your history when we have the time." I glance over to Peri, then back to Cullen. "But what do we do now about Raúl? Is he still a danger? That's probably the most pressing worry to me, more than anything else."

"Vali can ensure that he does not enter here again, so he will be barred from Maithe House until we and the house allow it. But that won't protect you outside of the property, so I think we should have a chat with the others to see what may be done. Is that amenable, Peri?"

I think that's the first time I've heard Cullen use her name. I wonder if he was mad at her for her lack of action, too?

"I'll gladly ask for help. I was completely taken by surprise to find him here and so unhinged. Though I suppose I shouldn't have been, and for that, I apologize." She's looking at me when she says this, and despite everything that's happened, my heart does a flip-flop at the earnest look on her face. I'm a complete sucker for her.

I consider how I should answer and settle on, "I accept your apology," because even if I could thank her for it, I feel like an apology is the least that should happen. I don't mean that in an accusatory way because what's done is done. But I hope she stops holding things back from me, especially important details that could keep either of us from getting hurt or killed.

I think she gets it because she nods slowly, the smallest hint of relief in her expression. I can work with that.

"We really should get Denny back downstairs and reunited with the band," Karsten says in a mild voice, and Cullen answers with contrite agreement.

"Yes, yes, you are correct, as always, my friend. This needed to be addressed, but any other questions can be answered as we go. Ah, Lucee will have my hide for keeping you."

We go downstairs and see that the crowd has thinned out a bit. I'm unsure what time it is, but I'm not tired, which is good because I still have a job to finish. I suppose I should feel bad because my personal life got in the way, but you know what? Everything's so beyond normal here that I'm just going to believe getting off track in unpredictable directions is the way things go around these folks.

I'm not sure how it happened—just a week or so ago I would have found all this uncertainty frustrating, yet I would never have said a word about it. I'm used to the drama of The Ants, and I navigate it by generally ignoring and avoiding engaging in it, no matter how much it pisses me off and makes life difficult. Not that it's always easy to do.

But as much as I protested to Peri about how I've changed, it's obvious I've become bolder and less tolerant of poor treatment, as demonstrated by my reactions tonight. I'm not mad about it. I'm honestly kind of proud of myself for confronting her, considering how idealistically I regarded her.

And it doesn't escape me that Peri has the tendency to avoid conflict as much as I do. Calling her out on it feels like a wake-up call for me, too.

Maybe I can be capable of having a healthy relationship with someone? It would certainly be a first. I mean, look at my current circle of—well, I wouldn't call them friends. Except for maybe Pod. He's good.

I find Lucee over by the table of refreshments, talking to a group of what I instantly recognize as art school students. Vali is nearby, and she's in a deep conversation with some folks, waving her arms excitedly. One is a woman who I identify as another Fae, with golden hair and a big smile. And the other person is… Xan.

Well, fuck. If Joolie's here, I should have expected Xan as well. He seems to be hanging on every word Vali's saying, and maybe a little besotted with her as well. I don't blame him. She's pretty amazing.

Lucee turns while gesturing toward the stage, no doubt telling the students about something regarding her band, and I see her face light up even more when she spies our group approaching. The next thing I know, she bounds over to Cullen and throws her arms around him in an enthusiastic embrace. They kiss, and it's adorable, but also the kind of romantic that feels more real than anything in a movie or book, and it makes me want that for myself more than I can say. I steal a glance at Peri and see she's staring at the couple with a wistful expression. I imagine I'm not the only one who feels it.

"Ah, we're such a spectacle!" Lucee laughs, pulling back from the embrace. She says in an excited, over-loud voice, "Denny! Are you up for doing those portraits yet? I'm still riding that post-show high, and I think you'll get some amazing shots right now!"

I don't look his way, but I can sense Xan's attention focus on me when Lucee's voice carries over to him. I truly don't want to interact with him, not here.

"Did you decide on where you'd like to take them? The library space might make an interesting background."

"I've got some ideas that I think will be perfect; just need to get the go-ahead from the guys. Come with me; let's ask them now!" She grabs my arm, and I'm basically dragged along in her wake. Cullen follows and shoots me an amused grin at her enthusiasm. I whip my head around to find Peri, then hold my other hand out behind me, gesturing to her to take it. When she does, I feel a little warmth creep into my cheeks.

Beyond her, I see one last glimpse of Xan. He's looking at me with— worry? Ah, he's probably imagining what Joolie will have to say about me going to an event without them. I'm sure it'll be even worse since she's got her sights set on Peri, and she saw us together.

We find Sousa and Merrick lounging in the far corner of the ballroom on some velvet-covered furniture that matches the ones I saw in the library. Aisling's curled up on the sofa seat, leaning against Merrick with his arm around her shoulder comfortably. The guys are having some sort of good-natured disagreement that we interrupt with our arrival.

"Lucee, tell this lunkhead that having one of these every month is too much, would you? There's such a thing as building a demand for us, plus I don't think I want to shoehorn too many events into my schedule."

"Sousa, it's not like you've got a million board meetings or something," Lucee laughs. "But I do agree, exclusivity is a thing. Also, I wanna be able to play other venues sometimes!"

"But the whole point of this was to see if there'd be interest, and I think we can agree that there is." Merrick's argument sounds halfhearted at best. I suspect that, at this point, he agrees with Sousa, but he's too stubborn to just give in. He's more than a little tipsy too, judging by the looks of it.

"What if we consider having one a quarter, like around the big holidays? Or…" Lucee trailed off, thinking.

"Or maybe around the traditional festival days, the eves of February, May, August, and November," Sousa interjects. "Take it real old-school, which could give us some interesting results."

"Hey, I found all of you on Halloween. That's worth celebrating, right there," Merrick says with a big grin. That sounds like an interesting story. Maybe I'll get lucky enough to hear it someday.

"You know, I came over here to pull you all together so Denny can get our portraits instead of waiting around for us to come down from our post-show high."

"Ah, Lucee, why didn't you say so? I'm sorry to waste your time like this, Denny," Merrick apologizes. Like I'd want to leave now?

"Oh—you're fine. I was off discussing some things with Peri," I manage to get out before Merrick waves his hand in dismissal.

"I'm terrible at being responsible after a show. All I want to do is lounge around, eat snacks, and drink a beer." He grins, and next to him, Aisling nods solemnly. Her expression makes me want to laugh.

"I guess if I put on the kind of show you all did, that's all I'd want to do, too." Merrick snorts at that, but then stops and regards me with his head cocked a little like he's trying to figure me out.

After what feels like an awkwardly long time, his eyes flicker past me, and although I can't see it, Cullen must be reacting in a way that confirms whatever Merrick's thinking.

"I think there's more going on here than I realized. Denny, who are you really?"

...What?

CHAPTER 11
HOUSE OF HARM – CONTROL

Merrick looks me over curiously like he's seeing me for the first time. I don't know what he's actually asking me or how to answer him.

"I-I'm just a photographer," I manage to stammer out.

"A photographer who seems to have stumbled into things bigger than they expected, eh?" Merrick doesn't sound skeptical or threatening. He sounds amused.

"I seem to keep stumbling repeatedly, truth be told." That gets an honest-to-god guffaw from him. Behind me, Peri squeezes my hand.

"It's my fault," she offers up, and Merrick raises an eyebrow.

"I think we should do this shoot, and you can tell us all about it while we work. This should be fun!" His idea of fun seems awfully different from mine, but at least I feel less like I'm in the hot seat.

We start with the band modeling together on one of the impressive spiral staircases. I don't usually like talking when I'm doing a shoot, preferring to melt into the background while my subjects do their thing, and I capture it on film. Thankfully, Peri takes over the heavy lifting in the conversation. She explains how we met and what happened after, including the strange energy from the art on her walls that sought her out.

I have to take a pause after she explains this because everyone loses their composure when they hear it—except Aisling, who nods thoughtfully.

"You have forged a connection with the artists through their creations. You can't exchange energy like that and emerge unchanged. Do you still communicate with these artists?"

"I do not. Though the last one, the one before I met Denny? He was here tonight," Peri confesses, her face taut.

"He was not only here, he attacked Peri, I'm afraid to say," Cullen says in a disapproving tone and proceeds to explain what happened with Raúl. Lucee looks scandalized, and Sousa has a mean scowl going on. If I saw that directed at me, I would worry for my safety.

"Inside The Maithe? I hope you let Vali know about that. Though the house won't allow anyone who drew blood on another inside these walls to stick around for long," Sousa says.

"I'm curious how that works," I blurt out before thinking, and I get a sly smile from him.

"Ever go into a house of mirrors? Except in this case, every door leads out. It's a thing I dreamed up and put into motion, but The Maithe does it all on its own now. Seems like having a full house of magic-using people amped up its powers."

I'll pretend like I understand how that works.

"Do we have any other places to use as a backdrop?"

We move to one of the inner rooms on the second floor. Lucee explains that all the rest of this level is occupied, but this one is reserved for guests. Then she throws open the door to reveal a room that would go for a pretty penny in an upscale hotel.

"Tell me, are all the spaces on this floor this lovely?"

"Oh, they're each a little different, depending on who lives in 'em, but the basics are the same," Sousa says, understandably proud. I'm starting to realize his outer scruffy appearance hides a lot about him.

Looking around, I'm in awe. There's a big fireplace, and it occurs to me that it had a fire going when we walked in like someone knew we'd be here. I wonder if the house did that as well. Wouldn't that be scary for a house, to start a fire? Does an anthropomorphic house have worries and fears?

Judging by the furnishings, it or whoever chose them has impeccable taste. There's a big, comfortable-looking bed in the far corner. It's got a velvet coverlet with a richly colored pattern that matches the couch and armchairs that face the fireplace. There's an absolutely gorgeous wardrobe on the opposite wall in the same dark wood as all the other furniture, with gilded, scrolled edges. And the inner wall, the one opposite the door and fireplace, is taken up by windows and French doors.

"Oh! What does that open to?" All of my ideas about how this building is laid out are wrong, it seems.

"Stick around, and you may find out," Sousa says with a mysterious air and, to my surprise, winks at me. Well, okay then. Maybe I will.

We get to the work of taking individual and group shots, and I'm enjoying it immensely. The juxtaposition of the musicians against the opulent background works well, adding an almost dreamy tone to the compositions. Cullen must have left and come back because he's got a guitar case that wasn't with us when we started. He opens it to reveal the guitar that Lucee had on stage and hands it to her with care.

"I can't imagine any official portfolio without your guitar in it."

"You're right, of course. This guitar has been through a lot with me in such a short time." Lucee holds it lovingly, and it's obvious it's important to her. I direct her to sit in one of the armchairs at an angle that includes the fireplace. I'm caught off guard when the light from the fire catches purple and green glitter on the surface of the guitar body and makes them sparkle. Until that point, it had just looked like a simple light wood with a clear coat. I wonder if it does anything magical, too.

As I take photos of her, both close up and full body, I notice the gleam of a silver chain around her neck. It disappears into the bodice of her dress, but the way it hangs gives away that there's something heavy attached to it.

"Do you want to pull your necklace out for some of these pics?"

She makes a quizzical face, like she's forgotten she's wearing it, then nods and hauls it out of her dress. The pendant is a silver book covered in filigree etchings, larger than I expected.

"Oh wow, that's a real statement piece, Lucee. I don't think I've seen a pendant like that in person before."

"You can see why I keep it tucked away, though. It's cracked me in the face before when I was jumping around on the stage, and that absolutely did nothing for either of us." She grins, and I can't help but do the same at the mental image. I snap a few images of her with the stunning piece revealed and some of the trio together, and then I think I'm finished. If it wasn't dark—and if I wasn't starting to feel the weight of the day—I might have asked to get some captures on the balcony with those lovely French doors, but that's going to have to wait for another time.

I sit on the floor and start packing up my equipment. Cullen clears his throat delicately. When I look up and meet his eyes, he raises an eyebrow.

"Aren't you forgetting one of the most interesting parts of your story?"

Fuck. The Nyxen. I'm tired of talking about it at this point, but he's right. I need to tell them and see what they think.

As soon as I finish, Sousa sits down on the couch with a big sigh.

"You're a busy one, Denny. Muses, Fae, Elementals. Awfully popular with the magical world."

"That's an understatement. Couldn't tell you why, though. Until just a little while ago, I was the most unremarkable person in the world. I'd say that hasn't changed, but I've definitely had an upgrade in the company I keep."

Sousa snorts at that. "Hopefully, your usual circle is less dangerous and capricious."

I wince and shake my head doubtfully, which gets me another snort.

"Are they that bad?"

"A mixed bag of chronically self-absorbed, ambitious, cut-throat, and devious, with passive and self-destructive for some extra spice. Two members of my collective were here tonight, by the way. Or are? I don't know if they've left. I was kinda surprised by that, but I guess I shouldn't be."

Merrick leans forward from the chair he's perched on, like he's ready to jump up at any moment. "Why is that?"

"Well." I glance at Peri, who's sitting near me on the floor, playing nervously with the zipper on my camera bag. She's been quiet this whole time. "Joolie's got her eyes on Peri, too. She didn't know we already knew each other when I found that out, but that wouldn't have stopped her anyway."

"I went to Denny's house to look for her and stumbled into a party. Joolie didn't know that I wasn't there for her event. Her energy is, well, it's very—"

"Dominant," I finish for Peri, and she shoots me a grateful look.

"She honed in on me immediately, but I don't know how much of that was sensing my power versus me being a fresh face to impress. However, she was quite reluctant to let me escape. I had to slip away to find Denny."

"Interesting," Sousa mutters. "And she just coincidentally showed up here."

"And when she saw me with Peri after Raúl attacked, she was clearly not pleased. She had the kind of look in her eyes that she always gets when she's determined to get her way, but also…" I fade out as I think about what I saw in Joolie's eyes. "Look, she was scared, too. As much as she pisses me off sometimes for taking the easy way and using people to do it, she's not stupid, and she's pretty observant. Maybe she saw more than she should have."

"You think she knows what I am?" Peri sounds unsure, and I agree.

"No, not exactly. But she might suspect that you're not quite normal either." I hate the way that sounds, and I make a face that conveys it. Peri pats my arm comfortingly.

"I know you don't mean it as an insult. That's how she'll see me. And she's never hesitated in using you for her benefit, so what would stop her from doing the same with me, given the opportunity?"

"Is this Joolie person going to be a problem?" Aisling doesn't like it at all, obviously.

"She can be astonishingly single-minded and driven when she's got a target. I assume she's going to be annoying, and chances are good that she'll keep showing up."

Understatement of the year. Also, I'm going to have to deal with her when I go home, which I am so not looking forward to doing.

"We can keep her out of The Maithe. But once you're out there," Merrick points toward the general direction of the street, "it'll be in your hands to deal with her. And Raúl, too. I don't like it." He starts pacing back and forth, and it hits me that these people I just met tonight give more of a shit about me than anyone in my circle of so-called friends do.

Not that I would call the Ants friends to anyone who really knows me.

Not that a person who knows me well really exists.

Except Pod—I guess, I'd call him my friend. Ironically, he doesn't know me very well either.

I'm suddenly tired to death of being so very alone.

Sousa saying my name, jerks me back to attention.

"Denny, I don't suppose you'd consider staying here for a few days? We have plenty of room, food whenever you want it, and the knowledge that you'll be protected by some powerful-ass Fae." He cocks his head in a boastful pose. It makes me want to laugh, which is probably his goal. Why are they all so nice?

"I—I could do that." Oh, so awkward. I don't know how to handle their kindness. "I need to get some clothes. And my laptop; I need to work."

"I think if you could wait until tomorrow, that might be wise. And one of us can accompany you when you go," Cullen assures me with a warm smile. "I don't recommend going there now when things have already been volatile." I sense that he chose that word carefully. I suppose he doesn't want to downplay the possibility of issues, and he's probably right. It's all too easy to minimize what happened after the fact. But I can't forget the look on Peri's face when Raúl slashed at her.

"We have anything you might need for cleaning up; don't worry about that," Sousa stresses. "I would worry less if you went when it's light out. Too many places for creepers to hide."

"You're right, of course. I can do that. I really appreciate your hospitality." I'm rewarded with a big grin for that, so I must have said it properly. "I'm exhausted after everything that's happened. Not having to go home and deal with all that mess now is a relief."

"You could stay with me," Peri suggests in a quiet, almost desperate voice. She's looking anywhere but at my face. I'm not used to this version of Peri, one that's unsure and timid.

"I don't think that's wise," I begin, and I can see her confidence start to crumble, so I quickly add, "but you can stay with me if you want. I don't think you should be anywhere near that art collection of yours tonight." I pause just a second. "I'd like it if you stayed."

To my surprise, she moves a little closer and leans her head on my shoulder. It feels to me like we've switched positions in this I-guess-it's-a-relationship thing we've got going on. Somehow, I'm now the dominant one? It confuses me.

I'd be lying if I didn't admit that somewhere deep inside me, I'm liking how it feels.

We wrap things up pretty quickly—I think everyone else is as tired as I am. At least I don't have a party to clean up after on top of everything else. I wonder if Vali took care of that so the bandmates could get their photo shoot finished? It seems like they have a good system going with their collective living, something I envy.

Sousa explains where the bathroom is and that everything I might need tonight is ready for me when I want it. I definitely want it now, as I'm ready to crash. He also points out I should check in the wardrobe as he's leaving with the rest of the crew.

I'm curious, so I do just that. When I open the doors, I find two woven willow baskets filled with towels and bathroom necessities. Hanging neatly on two hangers are pyjama sets, one for each of us. I turn to Peri, incredulous at this discovery.

"How in the world did they know we'd both be staying here? It makes no sense!"

"The house knows, Denny. It just does. Stuff like this happens all the time. I don't even question it anymore. I'm just glad it likes to take care of us so well." She reaches out to take the set that's obviously meant for her, cut for a more voluptuous figure than mine in a deep red color, and sighs appreciatively when she touches the fabric. "Oh, this is so soft, like a cloud!"

She's right. This is the softest cottony fabric I've ever touched. I'm not someone who obsesses about clothing, as I'm sure you can tell, but the boxy fit is going to be so comfortable, and I love the mossy green shade of the set.

We take turns going to the bathroom. I let her go first and use the time to wander around the room, looking at all the fancy finishes and details. I add a couple of small logs to the fire, too. It isn't that cold in here, but the fire makes it cozy and helps me feel at home.

Peri returns from the bathroom in an upbeat mood and shows off her PJs with a cute spin.

"I can't wait to see you in yours," she says, her tone flirty. I guess this must be her way of taking back some control of the situation and her feelings. I wonder if she's trying to rekindle the same energy we had when she first started talking to me?

You know what? I want that, too. I'm going to let her have this, at least for the rest of the night. We can deal with this mess tomorrow.

"Then I guess I'd better not keep you waiting." I smile for her even though I'm suddenly feeling shy and unsure again.

I can see the relief on her face before I leave the room.

CHAPTER 12
BODY OF LIGHT – DON'T PRETEND

I don't know where I am. Everything's bright on the other side of my tightly closed eyelids, and that's not helping me figure out what's going on or why I'm so warm—oh wait. That's Peri's arm. She's cuddling me in a way that I could escape from easily if I wanted to, which I appreciate. I'm glad she gets that about me.

I'm not particularly good at this whole "waking up" thing. It takes me a while to become coherent, and waking in a strange place just adds to my confusion. I won't even mention the whole finding myself sleeping next to someone part of it because since that never happens, it makes sense that it would make me feel off-balance.

That's not the only reason I'm hesitant to open my eyes, I'll be honest. It just feels so good to lie here with Peri for a few moments without stressful or weird challenges hanging over our heads. I mean—they *are*, but right now, it's just me and her and this comfortable-ass bed and the sun trying to get through my eyelids. It's peaceful and, well, normal as hell. Or at least normal for someone that isn't me. Right now, I can pretend that she's just my crush, and I've been lucky enough to go home with her, and everything's coming up Denny, for once.

Of course, just as I think that there's a tap on the fucking door.

I wait a minute without responding, and there isn't a follow-up, but it's enough to convince me that I should get up. Best to go get my laptop and a bag of clothes while it's early. There's less chance of running into any of the Ants that way, as they're all late risers, except Elise. She should be in the dance studio by this time, though.

I start to move, and Peri tightens her grip on me a little. "Stay, please stay," she mumbles. Her first-thing-in-the-morning voice is deeper and a little raspy, which I find incredibly sexy.

"I don't want to get up, trust me." I really don't. I'm ready to sleep here with her forever if the world will let me. "I should get to the Compound soon so I can avoid running into anyone there. It's probably too much to hope that'll happen, though."

She answers me with a long, low groan that expresses just how much she hates this idea, and I can't keep from laughing.

"I agree. I don't wanna. But the sooner I go, the sooner I'll be back. You can stay here and sleep."

"Nooooo. I should go with you." I'm not convinced she really means that. I wouldn't either if I had the chance to stay in bed.

"Give me something to look forward to, would you?" I'm rewarded with a muffled laugh. "I can pretend you'll still be here waiting for me to climb back under the sheets when I get back."

I'm surprised but pleased when she reaches out to fumble around for me, grabbing my shirt to pull me down for a kiss. My heart is pounding, and I definitely don't want to leave now. Luckily, she releases me before I decide to give in and stay.

"Go, go, go, before I try harder to change your mind," she says with a soft laugh, her eyes still squinting from the sun in the most adorable way.

I listen to her, even though I hate to leave because she's right.

I don't know if I should ask someone to go with me to the Compound or if it would be wiser to try and sneak in and out quietly and hope for the best. That decision is made for me when I duck into the library on my way out in search of coffee to take with me, and I discover Karsten waiting.

"Uh—good morning?" Yes, I'm still clever and smooth. But Karsten smiles at me in a way that my opener definitely doesn't deserve.

"Good morning, Denny! I hope you'll consider allowing me to accompany you today? I'm sure you're capable of doing it alone, but it would make me feel better to know you are safe." They pause and tilt their head in a pose that I assume means they're considering their next words. A few tendrils of snaky hair trace across Karsten's cheek before they continue. "I must confess that I enjoyed talking with you yesterday and would like your company again, as well. I like your calm energy."

"I-I like your energy, too." Well, that was unexpected. I can feel a slight warmth in my face, and I turn to the coffee bar to hide it. "I just need some of this for the road. Still not quite recovered from last night."

We don't talk much while we're leaving the building, just moving in quiet companionship. After yesterday's events, I find it incredibly soothing. Once we're a block or so away from The Maithe, Karsten breaks the silence.

"Forgive my curiosity. I'm trying to understand you and your situation better, so may I ask you some questions?"

"Um, sure, ask away. I'll tell you whatever." I find myself more than willing to open up to Karsten. There's a vibe about them that puts me at ease.

"How did you fall in with the people you live with now? It doesn't seem like a friendly environment."

"I guess you were filled in about everything that happened yesterday, including Joolie."

"Lucee and Cullen told me everything that I missed. I hope that isn't a problem." Karsten says it in an apologetic manner, so I rush to reassure them.

"No, I'm glad they did. It makes everything a lot easier. No need to catch you up there, and everyone's on the same page." Karsten nods, so I continue. "Joolie's at the heart of our collective—the dark, flawed heart—but it wasn't always so bad. When we started, it was more about pooling our talents and power to help all of us. Joolie's family has money. Their way of showing love seems to be buying things for their daughter, so they gave her the building we call the Compound, and we all moved in. We had big plans to do a series of shows together, with art that intertwined in a way that played up the theme and each of our strengths."

"And what happened with that plan?"

"Truthfully? I'd like to say it was all Joolie's fault, but we let her basically take over the Ants. I mean, she's the one who gathered us together, and she's the one who funds everything. But we used to push back in the beginning; we used to have a shared vision. Along the line, we let her wear us down, and we stopped being assertive. And then Pod's girlfriend died, and in the aftermath of that, she stepped into the void and began to really exert control. It was in the name of helping us stay focused and getting us through the tough times, but it ended up being a bid for power."

We walk for a while, both lost in thought, before Karsten breaks the silence with another question.

"How did the dynamic change?"

"Well, Joolie has always been a control freak. I think she can't feel good about herself unless she's the one in charge, the one making things happen. I was always content to let her do that because it's easier that way, both for her and me. I'm not good at being assertive, especially when it comes to my career, and she gave me a job I could live with, at least most of the time.

"After Bethany died, she started planning to put on a big show with her paintings in the forefront, and all of our various talents were supposed to support that main focus. She wanted Pod to write songs based on Xan's poetry about her art. Elise was to do a dance performance in front of the paintings to Pod's songs. And my photos would be on display, documenting the entire process."

I catch Karsten's sidelong glance directed downwards at my hands and realize my fists are clenched. I don't care. I'm angry now.

"Except she never really asked us, you know? It was never going to be about the collective, but all about Joolie Keyes and her vision. And now she's gotten bold about controlling us, dropping reminders about how much we owe her, how we have a free place to live and that she knows everyone and could easily have us blacklisted..." I trail off, too pissed to keep going, and it takes everything I've got not to kick the trashcan we've just passed by.

I'm caught off-guard by the gentle touch on my arm, and when I whirl to face Karsten, the sympathy in their expression pushes me over from rage to a deep, spiraling sadness. My pain must be obvious because the next thing I know, they pull me into a tight hug right there on the sidewalk in broad daylight. Like this is a totally normal thing that happens to me.

And you know what? I don't care. I start sobbing, and Karsten gently pulls me to the side so we can lean against the building, and I can bawl into their comforting shoulder until I'm cried out. They rub my back with care while I sob in big, shuddering gasps. I don't even care who sees me at this point. There's no stopping it until I can get out everything I've been holding in for years. Thankfully, Karsten seems content to let me cry all over their shirt until I'm finished.

Eventually, I pull back, feeling less embarrassed than I probably should, and fish a tattered tissue out of my jacket pocket so I can blow my nose and dab off my face. I lean against the wall next to Karsten, exhausted by my outburst.

"So yeah, that's the situation," I mutter with a self-deprecating laugh, and Karsten responds with a snort.

"Not at all complicated," and they snort again, and now we're both laughing like it's the funniest thing we've ever heard. Several people walk past us and move to the curb to pass like they're afraid whatever's going on with us is catching, which makes us laugh harder.

"I am reminded of that mortal tale of the frog in a pot," Karsten says after we mostly get our shit together. We're walking again, but we've been randomly cracking up for no reason. We're both punch-drunk at this point. "You were fine at first, but the situation kept getting worse, and you had no way to tell because you were living in the middle of it."

I consider that a minute before I answer.

"Yeah. That's pretty accurate. I just tend to go with the flow, and by the time I looked up to see what was happening…" How long have I just accepted Joolie's toxic behavior? "Maybe I'm just as responsible, in some ways. Because of that, I mean. None of us really pushed back after a while. We let her dictate our lives because it was easier and because we were comfortable."

"I don't think it needs to be a matter of blame. What if you looked at it as it is now and question what, if anything, can be done to salvage the situation?"

I stop abruptly, mid-stride.

"Do you think it's salvageable?" The thought truly hadn't occurred to me before this conversation.

"I believe that if all parties want it to be, yes. I think you should consider what you want and need and if those values can align with the rest of your collective. Or if that's the path you want to keep following." They gesture to me to start walking again, and I do, reluctantly.

"I'm back to dreading going home." I punctuate this with a deep sigh.

"Then it's a good thing to know you'll leave soon after we arrive. Perhaps you can look at your stay at The Maithe like a vacation where you can contemplate your next steps?"

"That's a brilliant plan. Thank—um, you're so kind to listen to all my bullshit." I stop before I say the wrong thing or embarrass myself and realize that, for once, my timing is impeccable. "Oh, we're here."

I'm holding my breath as we go in, but no one seems to be around. The downstairs is a fucking mess, which catches me off guard. Usually, Joolie gets the cleaning service to come in after a party, but it looks like that hasn't happened yet. There's empty and half-full cups of booze on every available surface. People must have been dancing at one point because the expensive rug that Joolie's parents gave her for the living room space is rolled up and pushed to one side. At least it didn't get spilled on again.

One part of the open main room has a raised section surrounded by rails. I think it must have been intended for dining, but Joolie had claimed it as her place to paint when we moved in. The lighting is really good there, and of course, it elevates her over the rest of us when she's working, which makes her the center of attention. When there are parties, it serves as a place to keep her art safely away from the crowd and subtly remind everyone that she's a painter.

The reason I mention this is because the light from the windows along the long, open downstairs space is casting its light perfectly on Joolie's working space and the canvas currently on the easel. The painting would be completely unremarkable to me in any usual circumstance: it's covered with thick paint in reddish and earth-toned hues that dominate everything in such a stylized way that it takes me a moment to see what Joolie was attempting to portray.

Also, there's a huge slash across the canvas.

Karsten makes a disturbed noise from behind me. "Am I seeing that correctly?"

"If you're thinking that's an attempt to do a portrait of Peri, then yes."

"I don't like this at all. Why is it destroyed?"

"She could have been frustrated with the painting. Or angry that her subject wasn't in front of her. Or it's some new statement she's making. It's hard to say." I don't like it either. It feels ominous. "We should get my stuff and get out of here."

"I will honestly feel better once we leave."

We make it to my room without running into anyone. Karsten looks through my stacks of books while I fill a canvas satchel with some clothes and a few other things I think I'll need. I reach under my bed, pull out the package that the Nyxen sent me, and stuff it in the corner of the satchel. I make sure I've got everything I need for my laptop tucked into its bag. As I glance around my space to check I've got everything, it hits me that if I never came back to this room again, there would be little I'd miss. How sad is that?

"Are you okay?" Karsten's voice breaks the silence. My emotions must be on full display. I'm not used to that, or anyone much caring either.

"I guess I am. It's just sinking in that all the ties I thought I had aren't really there. I dunno. Let me think about it a bit, and I'll explain it more later on."

"Of course. Whenever you wish to talk, Denny, I'll be ready to listen." I can't read the expression on their face. Could be pity, could be empathy, could be infinite, undeserved patience with my bullshit. It's hard to say.

I decide the best answer to that is a smile, so that's what I go with before I indicate I'm ready to get the hell out of here.

As we're coming down the stairs, I hear it—the dreaded sound of a door opening. Let it not be Joolie, let it not be Joolie, let it...

It's Elise.

"Denny. You shouldn't be here." Her delivery is emotionless and matter-of-fact. Almost robotic.

"I live here, Elise." I don't know what makes me respond like this, rather than just telling her that I was on my way out. Something about how she's speaking to me puts me on edge.

"Joolie is angry. I think it's because of you and what you've done." She's practically boring a hole into me with her stare. She hasn't even glanced at Karsten, which seems odd to me.

"What I've done? I haven't done anything. What did she tell you?"

She slow blinks in reaction to my question, which reads to me as someone astounded by my apparent denseness.

"You know better than to get in her way, Denny. She wants that girl, and she'll make all our lives miserable until she gets her." For a second, I see a flash of something in Elise's eyes; then the mask slips back. "Know your place. Joolie's done everything for us. Let her have what she wants."

"But has she, though?" I'm fighting down anger now and my face feels like it's on fire. "From what I can see, Joolie's really good at having what she wants all the time, and it's usually at our expense. Or have you been performing somewhere lately I haven't heard about?" Oh shit, I didn't mean to say that last part. Elise's eyes widen in shock and hurt and I instantly regret my big mouth.

"You're going to bring it all down, Denny. It'll be your fault. Remember that," she spits at me, then turns on her heel and stalks off.

I realize that I'm shaking, trembling all over. I feel Karsten's hand land on my shoulder, steadying me.

"Let's get out of here. I'm so done."

We bust ass to get away from the Compound, and it's not until we're a couple of blocks away that Karsten finally speaks.

"Something is very wrong in that place, Denny. And the way that woman casually spoke about Peri, as if she was something to possess…I don't like it." I glance over and see an expression I'd never thought to catch on Karsten's face: disgust.

"I think if we weren't walking right now, I'd be punching things," I admit. "It's obvious that either something has drastically changed for the worse or—and it scares me to consider this—that it's been this awful for a while, and I just wrote it off. I mean, I told you how bad it had become, and somehow it's even more appalling?" I can't control the shudder that comes over me.

"Your housemate looked—"

"Possessed? Brainwashed? Creepy as fuck?" Karsten answers me with a snort, and I laugh a little at myself, too. "Yeah, I'm making a joke out of it because otherwise, I can't deal, but something was even weirder than usual about Elise; you're right."

"Brainwashed means influenced by outside pressures, correct? If so, then I would agree. When you challenged her, she seemed to waver at first."

"She's always been all-in when it comes to the Ants, but this feels different. Like I said, it's creepy, like she's under a spell or something. And another thing: she hinted that Joolie would take it out on the Ants if I got in her way. Joolie's never been that kind of vindictive before. She'd make a big scene if things didn't go how she wanted or if we didn't play along, but I didn't get the impression that's what Elise was talking about. It felt more sinister."

"I felt that as well."

"By the way, was it strange that she didn't seem to notice you at all? She was so focused on me and my transgressions."

"Oh," Karsten laughs lightly, "That was because I did not want her to see me. So she didn't."

"Huh? You disappeared or something? Please tell me you can teach me that trick." That gets a deeper laugh from Karsten.

"Not disappeared, though I did refine this skill with help from one of us who can disappear in plain sight. In this case, it's more like I did not want to be noticed by her, so her eyes just slid over me. If you had looked at me, you would have seen me right there next to you."

"Wow. Do you think I could learn that, or is it not something uh, um—"

"Mortals can do?" I nod stupidly, which gets me another grin from Karsten. "Well, mortals surprise me all the time, so perhaps this will be one of those instances. You are already suitably quiet and good at blending into the background when needed. That might be enough."

Well, if that's not an accurate assessment of me, I don't know what is. Out of the blue, it strikes me that Karsten, who seems so much stronger and put together than I could ever hope to be, might be more like me than I realized.

"You pay attention to everything, don't you?"

They consider my question, shifting the laptop bag they'd kindly taken from me earlier from one shoulder to the other before answering.

"It's a survival skill I picked up long ago when things weren't quite as good. Before I gained the companions I have now, I spent time alone and afraid. The habits I gained then serve me well now." They reach out to touch my arm lightly for a second, then add, "I'm glad to say that I'm neither alone nor afraid these days, but there is always room for another friend."

Again, I feel my cheeks flush, but this time it's welcome.

"I-I'd like to call you friend. I definitely need better ones than the ones I thought I had."

CHAPTER 13
SKELETON HANDS – UNWANTED

Back at The Maithe, I feel a deep sense of relief and safety. Vali and Sousa are waiting for me in the hallway by the room where I slept last night. I figure I've already outstayed my welcome—but no; they had a feeling I might be a longer-term resident and want to give me my own space, a room that isn't for guests.

I just met these people, and they're giving me my own room.

When I try to politely deny that I'd need it, Karsten makes a dismissive noise and shakes their head. "Take the room, Denny. I don't advise going back to that other place."

That gets both Sousa and Vali worried, so we explain what happened at the Compound. Sousa's face goes from puzzled to concerned in seconds.

"I don't like this. How much more do you have there? We can have everything brought to your room, no problem."

"I don't own much. It's one room with some books and furniture, but—"

"Look." He's so serious I have to forgive him for cutting me off. "Do you truthfully see yourself going there again? Does it feel safe? Is there anything you get from that situation that you would truly miss? Consider it a minute."

So I do. I think about the beginning, when we first moved in, fresh out of school, and so excited to be Real Artists in a Real Collective. How the first year or so we really did mesh together, and Joolie was more enthusiastic and slightly overbearing, rather than a success hog with an iron fist.

Then I consider how things have changed over time, and how unhappy and adrift I've felt recently. Most importantly, I have to look at Joolie's sudden obsession with Peri and how quickly it's escalated into something threatening. And there's also how Elise acted like Joolie had brainwashed her or scared her into believing that she needs to back up Joolie unquestioningly.

Nothing about being at the Compound feels safe or welcoming anymore.

"Shit. You're right, of course. I don't want to let that part of my life go, but I'm honestly scared by how Joolie and Elise have acted. I don't know how Xan is handling this or what's going on with Pod, but they're both adults and have eyes. I don't know."

I've been staring a hole in the carpet while I've been puzzling this out in my head, but I happen to look up and catch Vali's expression, which triggers a sinking feeling in my guts. I feel so lost. I think Vali is picking up on that, but the kindness and empathy in her eyes just make me feel the loss even more keenly.

"I can arrange it. They'll never see it happen. Just give me the word." Sousa's got the same look on his face. I feel both cared about and uncomfortably vulnerable. I'm not used to people seeing me at my lowest... or seeing me at all.

"I think, um, just leave the furniture except my bookshelves. Just the important stuff. Clothes and books and the like. And maybe they won't notice right away that I've left." I mumble that last part. Saying it clearly makes it feel too real.

"Not a bad idea," Karsten agrees. "The less they know of your plans and moves, the safer you'll be."

I know they're right. I know it. I keep telling myself that so it won't hurt as much.

It's not working.

I must be broadcasting my feelings because Vali asks me, in the kindest voice possible, "What can we do for you now to help you? Have you eaten yet? Do you need someplace special to work? Or just some space to come to grips with everything?"

So many questions, but they're all good ones.

"I guess I should eat. I'm bad about doing that unless I'm reminded, and being hungry won't help me manage any of this." Vali nods encouragingly, and I add, "I have my studio; you might remember that? Where you and I almost ran into each other."

"Ah, yes," she laughs. "That was lucky for both of us. And it's close enough to here; that's a good thing."

"Lucky for me, for sure. I can't imagine dealing with this on my own." My voice catches at that reminder of what's happening, so I quickly follow up with, "And yeah, I should go there sometime soon to develop the couple of rolls of film I took. Most of the shoot was digital, so I can work on those images anywhere, but I need my darkroom for the film."

"I can accompany you," Karsten offers. "I am happy to serve as a bodyguard, and to be truthful, this process of developing film interests me. If, of course, you would be so kind as to show me how it works?"

"Um, I can do that. Maybe we can do it after lunch? I don't like to wait too long to develop my rolls. It gets easy to forget what you've got if you don't do it right away."

That goes over well with everyone, and Sousa sends us off with the promise that a tasty meal will be waiting for us in the library.

The first thing I notice when we walk into the library space is the smell of coffee and savory food. It smells so delicious that my mouth starts to water, and if you know me, you know how rare that is.

The second thing to grab my attention is Peri, lounging sideways across one of the ubiquitous velvet chairs in the room, still in the pyjamas she slept in. She's bathed in a beam of bright mid-day sunshine, and it lights her hair up from behind, so all the burgundy bits scattered throughout the brown curls gleam. There's a rosy glow on her tan skin, too, especially her cheeks, and she looks so vibrantly alive and beautiful that I lose my words and just stare at her.

Luckily for me, I don't need to say anything because she jumps up with an excited squeak and runs over to throw her arms around me. It knocks the wind out of me a little, but I don't mind, not a bit. I bury my face in her hair, still tousled from last night's sleep, and I let myself be in the moment while I memorize how this feels so I can recall it later when I might need it. You know, when I'm left alone again. Right now, though, this moment is enough.

"I was so worried about you," she says, then loosens her embrace as she realizes we're not alone. "Oh, Karsten! Did you go with Denny? Maybe I shouldn't have worried so much since you were there."

"That is kind of you to say. We made it there and back with no challenges, but there were some things that happened you should know about. Let us get some food, and we can explain."

"Of course," Peri agrees, though she seems reluctant to turn me loose. I don't want her to let go either, but the scent of whatever's under those silver domes is beckoning insistently, and once again, I'm unable to resist the call.

"Did you eat already?" I ask her as we move to the side table where the food and coffee are. She shakes her head, then sighs in approval as Karsten lifts one of the covers to reveal what's underneath.

The first platter is filled with some sort of flaky pastries, triangular in shape, stuffed with whatever is making that incredible savory smell. They're sprinkled on top with dried herbs mixed with large crystals of salt, which catch the sunlight and sparkle as I pick one up.

"I don't know what's in this, but I'm volunteering to find out."

"Let's see what's under here—oh, it's soup! It smells SO good."

I don't get to see it right away. Karsten, moving with extreme efficiency, grabs some plates and moves each mini-tureen of soup to them. They hand me one with a grin.

"Too hot for your hands to handle, but not a bother for me. I hope you don't mind."

I shake my head, noting that the soup is bubbling and the melted cheese on top is steaming. Surely, I'd burn off my fingerprints if I touched it with my bare skin. Karsten continues to be full of surprises.

I add my pastry to the plate and take it over to a big table, then head back for something to drink. When we all get settled, we have clear goblets of water, small dishes of berries, and our plates in front of us.

As we eat, we recount what happened at the Compound. When I describe Joolie's destroyed painting, Peri's eyes get big.

"You're sure she was trying to paint me?"

"Not very well, but yeah. It was obviously an attempt at a portrait of you, I guess from memory. It's not that Joolie can't paint people, but I don't think she's done it since art school, you know?"

"I barely met her, Denny. This level of obsession is scaring me." She takes a sip of water, and I see the goblet shake in her hand. When I reach under the table to touch her knee in reassurance, the shaking subsides a little, but it doesn't go away completely.

"Honestly, though, this is classic Joolie. Obsession should be her middle name. Normally, that wouldn't even faze me because she'd just cast whatever aside when the next obsession came along. But because it's you, Peri..." I don't have to finish. We all know it's complicated by who Peri is.

"We think she's influenced others in the group to bend to her plans, as well," Karsten takes over from where I left off. "I know that is also expected behavior, but there was something strange about our interaction with one of them. It was unsettling."

"Nothing that's been happening lately feels normal," Peri sighs. "My gifts are supposed to be beneficial, but I feel like all I do is cause problems."

"The greed of others is not your fault, Peri." Karsten's voice is warm and reassuring, and I can see the concern on their face. "If you made no promises, then they are acting out on their desires alone. None can blame you for that."

"The Nyxen do, evidently."

"Peri—I keep getting, um—" Oh my god, just spit it out already, Myers. "You sound bitter about what the Nyxen said about you. Did they hit a sore spot?" I cringe and stare at my plate, waiting for her to get defensive or walk out.

"Hey. Denny." Her tone is unexpectedly gentle, and when I look up, her eyes look so sad. "If I've given you cause to fear being straightforward with me, I apologize. I want you to be able to ask me questions like that. You should be able to ask me anything. And I think you're right."

I must look incredulous because she's quick to add, "Look, you're quiet, and you pay attention. That makes you a good person to go to for observations. And I trust you. You're not mean, so you wouldn't say something like that just to hurt me. Your question just points out the thing I haven't wanted to look at, where I guess I'm lacking. Or at least my fear of what I'm lacking, which the Nyxen hit with pinpoint precision."

"You're afraid that they're right. That you've been careless with your influence."

She nods, her cheeks coloring a little.

"I was lonely and nervous about starting a new life here, but that's not a good excuse. Or maybe it doesn't need to be an excuse but rather an admission that I wasn't careful during a low point, and now I've made a mess."

"Let me take a second to think about how I want to put this. Okay?" She nods solemnly, and I glance over to Karsten for moral support or something, I don't know. It's a good move because the look they give me back feels positive and caring, like an unspoken "you can do it" if there ever was one. I suddenly know what I want to say.

"Okay, let's look at it for a minute in a neutral sort of way. No blame." Peri nods again, so I continue. "Say it is a mess, and you could have been more careful. And now you know that. I'm pretty sure you won't make that mistake again. You also know that now it's grown beyond anything you did, which has nothing to do with your actions. So, do you keep blaming yourself for your mistakes, or do you take the lesson and accept that you're flawed, just like the rest of us, so we can address what's happening now? That's the real challenge, right?"

She wants to argue with me, to double down on being a fuck-up. I don't let her.

"Before you answer me, Peri, I want you to know that it's okay. It's okay to be flawed. I don't think I could have done any better than you have. I can barely handle being a mortal with the burden of sloppy emotions and the isolation I bring on myself because—because I'm terrified of the power that people have over me when I let myself care about them."

I didn't mean to say that last part out loud, but I guess it's honesty hour here at The Maithe.

"But Denny, you put yourself in a position where I could have power over you. You barely hesitated. And you didn't—you didn't take what I offered you, either. You've never expressed interest in my gifts at all." Her hands are on the table, and she's leaning towards me with a gleam in her eyes. "You've only cared about me as Peri. Not me as a muse."

"Well, I care about all the different parts of you. But you being a muse? That's not why I'm interested. I like you, not what you can do for me. I mean, I'd be disappointed if you only liked me because I take good photos."

Karsten's snort of laughter surprises me. I honestly forgot that they're still here. "Denny, are you implying it's the fault of these mortals that they're obsessed with Peri's gifts because that's all they see in her?" Their laughter stops abruptly. "You know, I think you may be onto something."

The relief on Peri's face as she looks back and forth between the two of us makes my chest hurt a little. I feel guilty for ever doubting her in any way.

We finish our delicious lunch, and Peri expresses interest in coming with me to see my studio and how I work. It'll be crowded with three people, but I'm so touched she wants to know about the unglamorous parts of my job that I can't turn her down.

Peri gets herself together in a much shorter time than I would have expected, for as fine as she looks when she rejoins us.

I might be a bit biased, of course.

She's wearing a long black skirt with a pattern of red swirls all over it and a plain black sweater over that. It's nothing particularly fancy, but on her, it looks elegant. Next to her, I feel a bit shabby, but she doesn't seem to mind, so I won't.

"Found these clothes in the closet, and someone's got good taste because I certainly would have picked these for me." She twirls around happily, and for a minute, I'm only thinking in the present. I suddenly have a friend and maybe a girlfriend, and they seem to like me for who I am and not what I can do for them. That realization shines through any dread I've got about dealing with Joolie or Raúl or anything else that might be hanging over our heads.

"Is that a smile, Denny?" Karsten teases me. "I was beginning to think you didn't smile."

"Hey, I smile. Occasionally. When the situation calls for it."

That wins me laughter from both of my companions. I could get used to this.

The walk to my studio is uneventful unless you count when we encounter a sidewalk covered with autumn leaves that Peri can't resist shuffling through, kicking them everywhere. It's even funnier when Karsten follows behind her. I watch both of them, then shrug and follow suit, which no one expected, including me. I'm rewarded with more laughter. I'm beginning to like how that feels.

"I think this is the most fun I've had in ages," I confess.

"I'll do my best to make fun a regular thing for you, then." Peri reaches over to twine her fingers in mine and swings my hand as we walk. Me? I'm on cloud nine, don't mind me.

She holds my hand for the rest of the walk.

As predicted, the studio is a tight fit for the three of us, but that's okay. Both Peri and Karsten are fascinated by how developing film works and hang on my every word and action. It's not something that happens often in my world, and to my surprise, I'm kinda into it. It makes a task that I do all the time seem almost magical, seeing it through their eyes. Karsten has lots of thoughtful questions, and it surprises Peri that I have to let the negatives dry before I can do anything else with them.

"I'll have to come back to get them, as it'll take a couple of hours. Usually, I arrange it so I have other things I can do while I wait, but I didn't plan ahead this time. Last time, I killed time by going to the park to take photos, but that's where I met the Nyxen, so—"

"I would rather not do that today, please," Peri quickly asserts, her eyes wide and pleading.

"I think I can just leave these here and come back tomorrow or something. This isn't a priority by any means," I reassure her. "Besides, it gets dark earlier these days, and I'd like to get back before then. Just in case. Though…I wonder if Vali is working at the Frisky Bean?"

"More coffee?" Karsten asks, dubious. I'm sure they want us to get to The Maithe before dark, too.

Really, I just want to return to the Bean with Peri next to me. It'll feel like a triumph for me, the person who never gets noticed and seldom gets a win. Is that ridiculous? Probably.

"I guess I don't need to. I'm sure whoever handles the coffee at The Maithe will be happy to fix me up." I can wait. Karsten's right.

But none of that matters. When I open the door, Joolie's standing on the other side, with Xan behind her, looking like he'd rather be anywhere else. My heart immediately starts pounding like I've been running a marathon, and Peri stumbles into me thanks to my abrupt stop.

"Oh look, Xan, it's both the people I wanted to find. Denny, you need to come back home right away. We need both of you at the Compound. I won't take no for an answer."

She smiles, but there's not an ounce of warmth or sincerity in it.

"You-You're not in a position to tell me what to do anymore, Joolie. Those days are over." My voice shakes and I want to run away or hide behind Karsten and let them defend me, but that's not their job. For once in my life, I need to have a backbone.

Joolie, on the other hand, is living up to her vow to reject my refusal.

"Come now." She's trying her best to sound reasonable. "You've been with us since the beginning, Denny. We can't do anything without you! And Peri, well, she's just what we need in The Ants, you know? Someone to inspire us, to bring us focus so we can truly establish ourselves. Isn't that what you're meant to do?"

She directs that last bit to Peri, and I don't like the way she's speaking to her at all. My hands clench up involuntarily, and for maybe the first time in my life, I want to hit someone.

"You don't understand how any of this works, do you?" I'm caught off guard by the way Peri answers her and the almost pitying tone of her voice. Never would I have expected her to speak to anyone like that. "You can't just compel me to give you that inspiration. Nothing good comes from trying to steal it from me, either. Ask Raúl."

"Ha! Raúl told me lots of things, including how you fueled his art to new heights and then snatched away that gift. He also told me that he knew how to get you back. He was wrong, but I think I've got it worked out now. So don't lie to me. I know what to do, and you won't like it if you push me to do it."

Her voice has been rising gradually, but she breaks off abruptly because Xan puts a hand on her shoulder. I guess he's trying to calm her down, but she's clearly annoyed by it and shrugs off his hand with a sharp gesture. Our eyes meet, and I don't think I've ever seen that whipped, dejected look on his face before. He's always been her trusted confidant. I wonder if that's finally changed?

"We're not going back with you." Peri grabs my hand, and it feels like an act of defiance. I might not be fierce for myself, but I'm realizing that I can be for her. I stand up straighter, shoulder to shoulder with her, a wall of solidarity.

"Look, we've gotten off on the wrong foot." Joolie's tone changes in an instant to contrite, apologetic. "We can do so much for each other, and I hate to see that go to waste. Don't you need to inspire people in order to fulfill your purpose? Isn't that a thing?"

Xan's looking sick at this point, and he finally dares to speak up.

"Joolie, we should go. They don't want to do this."

"Oh my god, Xan, SHUT UP!" She turns and pushes him away from her, and he stumbles and catches the railing to keep himself from falling down the stairs.

"You need to leave. Now." It's the first thing Karsten's said this whole time. The way they cross their arms while saying it makes it clear that they're not fucking around.

Joolie visibly blanches and moves back. I'm guessing she didn't realize she was outnumbered, or maybe Karsten was doing that "being unnoticed" thing again.

"You need to leave us alone, Joolie. Forget that you ever knew us. I'm done with you and the Ants. It's over," I tell her in the firmest voice I can muster. My hands are trembling, but I don't think she can see that, thankfully.

"Fine. We'll leave for now, but we're not finished with each other yet. Peri, just think about this: what can you do for a mere photographer? All Denny does is document other people's work and lives. It's pathetic, really. You're wasting yourself on that, and I think you'll get bored soon enough. You'll see."

She's got a spiteful little smile on her face, but it doesn't reach her eyes. All I can see there is fear and a hunger that I haven't seen in a long time.

CHAPTER 14
SLOWDIVE – ALIFE

Karsten makes us wait for another fifteen minutes or so before we leave. It's torture waiting, and none of us wants to talk much. Not here, anyway. I want to hold Peri's hand, but instead, I futz around with my lab equipment while my mind replays everything that Joolie said. She always knows how to cut right to the quick, and today was no exception. I'd call her a bitch, but is she really wrong about me? What do I have to offer anyone?

Finally, finally, we leave, moving much faster than we did on the way to the studio. I glance toward the Frisky Bean as we pass it on the opposite side of the street. Vali's not working. I don't much want to stop in there now, anyway.

Walking into The Maithe feels like a huge weight lifting off me. Even more so when Vali comes bouncing down the stairs and announces, "Perfect timing!"

"What do you mean?" I hope that whatever it is can be done sitting down. I'm exhausted.

"Your stuff's here, Denny! You're officially moved in!" Wow, she sounds so excited about it. "Hope you don't mind that it's the third floor, but it's nice and quiet up there at least."

"Um, wow. No, that's great. How—?"

"Ha, there are some things we just don't question. How The Maithe does anything is at the top of that list. If there's anything you need, write it down and leave it out somewhere. It'll show up for you." Vali grins at me and winks, like she knows how absurd this sounds, but I should just play along with her. So I do.

"Okay, I'll keep that in mind. Do I need a key or anything?" I try to remember if I'd seen anyone use keys anywhere.

"Do you want one? You'll find that anywhere you're supposed to be will be open for you, but some people feel more included with keys. I get that. C'mon up, and I'll show you where you live now."

She gestures over to the elevator, indicating that we should take it, so we do.

Vali shows up a moment later, huffing from jogging up the stairs.

"I used to be able to sprint up those, but I've been kinda lazy lately. I've been trying to break myself out of that habit, so I try to take the stairs more. Not that anyone's judging, of course," she adds sheepishly. "We put in the elevator so people can do whatever works best for them. And now, with Peri living up at the tippy-top..."

"Yeah, how come you're so far away from everything?" I fill in when Vali trails off, but before Peri can answer me, Vali swings open the door to reveal my new room, and I'm left speechless.

The mysterious movers didn't just bring all of my belongings, they've set up the room for me. And let me tell you, it couldn't be more me if I'd done it myself.

The bed is the one that was already here, but the coverlet on the bed is a mossy-colored quilt that I got in a trade with someone in the fiber arts department at my school. It's a Morse Code quilt—the background is black, and the code is blocks of various greens and browns that spell "I want to go home, but I don't know where home is." When I told her that I wanted it, she'd nodded like it made perfect sense. I guess like knows like.

My bedside table with the lamp made from photo slides is here - the lamp was a gift from Joolie back when we were more like friends. My old Victorian-style couch has replaced the one I know must have been here previously. It goes well with the house-standard velvet armchair that's placed near it.

Some of my photos have been hung on the walls, along with a couple of woven tapestries—again, from my art school days—and a decent poster of Rothko's Ochre on Red On Red in a simple black frame. I remember how much Pod hated it and smile to myself.

Oh, I hope he's okay. He'd better not do anything stupid like confronting Joolie.

I realize that Peri's asking me something and I come back from worrying over things I can't fix.

"I'm sorry, what was that?"

"Oh! I was asking you about this mobile. It's so delicate!"

I turn my attention to where she's pointing, and I see that they've hung it in the window where the French doors open onto a balcony. I have to admit that it looks perfect there.

"Oh yeah. It's from another art student at the Institute. She was obviously influenced by Calder, but I like her color choices and materials a little more for my personal aesthetic." I stop and snort softly. "Wow, I have a lot of things from my art school days."

"I like it," Vali says, and behind her, Karsten nods. "I get to see a little bit more of who you are through them. I hope I get to know more about you as time goes on, too."

I feel my face redden a little, but here's the weird thing: I don't feel like retreating. When I answer her, for once, I don't stumble over my words.

"I'd like that too. I realized recently that no one truly knows me. I don't like it much." I look at the mobile again, and a realization hits me. "It's like my life just sort of stopped growing when I joined the Ants. I had creative friends before that, and we traded our work. I don't have a single thing any of my collective made other than my own photos. I halted everything in service to them. I gave them everything."

You'd think saying this would make me sad, and don't get me wrong, it does. But what I feel the most is anger—and relief.

"You okay, Denny? This has been a lot, all at once. I think we'd all understand it if you were feeling overwhelmed right now," Vali says.

"Surprisingly, I think I'm gonna be okay." I think about it for a minute while three faces watch me with concern in their eyes. "It definitely has been a lot. Maybe I should be a mess or angrier than I am. I mean, I am angry, but not like I thought I'd be. But I'm also free now, and the possibilities are exciting. I, um, I feel welcome here. I think maybe I could start to live again, being here."

I kind of mumble at the end because it's scary to admit that I want something this big. I usually hate exposing my feelings like this, but the people in this house…they're really good at making it feel safe to be vulnerable. All I know is that for the first time in a long time, I feel wanted and valued, and I don't want it to end.

"I really want to hug you. Are you up for hugs?" Leave it to Vali to be considerate enough to ask permission. Also, I should have pegged her as a hugger.

I nod shyly, and she reaches me in two big steps, throwing her arms around me in a warm embrace. Next thing I know, Peri and Karsten join her. I certainly didn't expect that, but I let it happen, closing my eyes so that I can soak it in.

"Ahem! Is this a private group hug, or can I get in on it, too?"

The huddle parts enough for me to see Sousa standing on the threshold of the room with a big grin on his face. Somehow, he's managed to get the spray paint out of his hair, which is quite the feat.

"Since you were the one nice enough to invite me—"

"Pssht," he interrupts, but I can tell he's pleased. "Pretty sure you belong here anyway. The right people always find their way here." He moves into the hug-space, and I catch a tiny glint of gold in his hair. Guess he didn't get all of the paint out after all.

"Yer still a little shiny there, Souz," Vali helpfully points out, and I can't hold back a snort of amusement.

"Is that—did I hear you *laugh*, Denny?" Sousa gives me an outrageously astonished look, and that makes me laugh harder.

"I can testify they have quite a good sense of humor," Karsten volunteers. "We have laughed all day. Well, with a few exceptions."

"Why do I feel like there's a story here that we need to know about?" Sousa's smile vanishes.

"Of course there is. I have a feeling those people aren't going to take no for an answer, Souz," Vali says. "Let me guess, you had unexpected visitors at your studio."

"Joolie and Xan. Though Xan really doesn't seem like he wants to be a part of any of this. I think he's following Joolie around because that's what he's always done. I saw his face; he looked scared and sad. And she almost pushed him down the stairs in her frustration."

"What did she want? Besides Peri, obviously." Sousa looks like he's expecting the answer I give him.

"She tried to convince me to come back to the Compound and bring Peri with me. Like everything would be fine if I just came back with her. Things got ugly real fast when we told her no."

"Denny stood up to her! It was so brave because she was unpredictable and scary." I feel my face heat up at Peri's praise.

"You were brave first. That made it easy. Well, that and she was ordering you around like you were a possession. She—I just realized this. She kept appealing to *me*. Like I was the one who could decide if you went with Joolie or not. Like I owned you or something." I suddenly feel sick. "I think she honestly thinks that."

"Until the very end, right before she left," Karsten adds. "She appealed to Peri at that point."

"Oh yeah. Those digs at my art. Because, of course, she did."

"What did she say, exactly?" I wouldn't want the look on Vali's face directed at me.

"Exactly what I'd expect from someone like her," Peri's voice drips with contempt. "That all Denny does is follow people around documenting them, implying that they are the actual artists and what Denny does is nothing important or artistic, so I'd be wasting my time on them. She's a fool."

I could kiss her.

"It's right in Joolie's wheelhouse to belittle me as a way to try and bring me to heel. She usually does when she's feeling insecure, but this seems like a logical extension of that." I feel drained just talking about it. I'm so tired of Joolie Keyes and her endlessly bruised ego.

Sousa breaks away from us and paces around the room a bit, digesting what we've told him. Finally, he turns back to us.

"So she left after you told her to go?"

"Yeah. She was pissed, and I'm sure Xan will pay for that later, but she left. Oh! I almost forgot she implied that she knew how to make Peri come to her, something that Raúl told her about. But we know that Raúl was wrong about how things with Peri work. Right?"

Please tell me I'm right.

"I don't like it. But it's true, he was wrong about what he attempted at the party." His eyebrows knit together as he ponders it. "Val, what do you think? I mean, they can't hide in here forever."

I'm not following him, but she seems to be. "I don't like it either. That Joolie person sounds like she's fooling around with things she doesn't understand, and that never turns out well. Let me think on it for a bit, I'm sure I can come up with something." My face must betray my confusion because she laughs when she turns my way. "Sorry, Denny, Peri. I know you have no idea what we're talking about. Tell you what—it's going to take a bit to explain it, and I'm gonna have to show you, so why don't we take this downstairs, and I'll show you some wild shit?"

Sure, that sounds about normal for how things go in this house, at least in the time I've been here.

There's beer and snacks waiting for us in the library, but I go for black coffee, and Peri wrinkles her nose at the beer and picks a fancy bottle that turns out to be apple cider. I momentarily regret my choice of coffee when she lets me take a sip from her bottle; it's so flavorful and refreshing.

Vali slams a book down on the table, and then a scruffy bag joins it, with markers spilling out from the unzipped top onto the smooth wood of the table. The book has a well-worn black fabric cover, and when she flips it open, I gasp audibly at the colorful art inside.

"Whoa, I know some of these." I point to the page she's just turned. She goes back, and I study it for a minute, taking in the details. It's a small-scale rendering of a huge abstract graffiti piece that showed up one night on a wall near my studio. It was notable for a couple of reasons. One, it's a striking, unique style done in an unusual color scheme. There's a base of shocking pink that swirls like clouds and strange groupings of earthy greens and golds that could almost be stylized name tags spread across that pink field in random places. The entire design had a vibrant quality to it; like if you looked closely enough, you might see it quiver with energy.

The second thing that made it notable is that the wall where it's painted faces a small parking lot. That space is next to a halfway house and had a couple of bad crimes happen, all to folks who live there. You can imagine how it was handled by the press and some of the neighbors.

"I was really surprised that the building owner was okay with this going up here. I mean, I thought it had to be illegal, but they never covered it up." I can't stop looking at the piece while I'm talking. It's compelling, but there's something else about it that I can't quite put my finger on.

"Yeah, that one was sanctioned by the owners of the halfway house. It took some convincing! I said if it didn't have the desired effect, I'd come and cover it up at my own cost." Vali smirks a little, and it's obvious that she's confident about it, but I still don't know what she means.

"Desired effect? What did you think it would do besides look cool?"

Peri's been intently studying the drawing while we've been talking. She cocks her head and then suddenly gasps.

"Oh! I think I see something here! But I don't get it?" She tilts her head from side to side like a puzzled dog. It's ridiculously cute. Vali must think so too, because she giggles at Peri's confusion.

"I have a thing I can do. Basically, my tags hold intentions that I set up when I design and then paint them. Some are small magics, I guess you'd call them, like being able to lock a door against specific people or help you be warmer or cooler when you're wearing them. That was a fun concept to work out, let me tell you."

"Nearly burned my hand with one of her first tries!" Sousa points to the back of one hand. He looks more proud than annoyed.

"Whoa." Peri and I are both impressed.

"Yeah. I have to take a few risks sometimes when I'm working out the kinks. The big magics take longer and require a lot more thought. That's what that wall's about. I keyed it to protect that area and the people who live in the building by affecting anyone near it. It keeps people calm and discourages bad acts. That's a really abstract idea to infuse into art, so it's definitely harder and needs more area to be enacted. That's why it needed to be a wall piece like that." Vali pats the drawing gently, a fond look on her face. "The design is one of my favorites."

"She says that about all of them." Sousa's tone is teasing, but it's obvious he thinks she's incredible. I have to agree.

"Vali, this is something else. So all of these have been used around the city?" I flip to a page that's covered with what's obviously a series of practice sketches. Each one is in the shape of a stylized anatomical heart, and as I look closely at them, I realize the lines that create the image are actually words.

"Whoa, this is intricate! What was this for? I'd love to see the finished product."

"Ah. That's the most important project I ever undertook, to save someone's soul. If you believe in things like that." Her fingers stroke the drawings on the page reverently. "I don't think you'll ever be able to see the end work, and that's both good and heartbreaking."

"Oh. I'm so sorry." I don't know what the right thing is to say. Knowing this group, the explanation could be metaphorical or as face-value as it gets.

"One day, I'll tell you the whole story, Denny. You should know it if you're going to live here, certainly," Karsten volunteers. "It's an important part of understanding us. For now, I can tell you it was used to contain a dangerous being that wanted to subsume us all into itself. That threat is now imprisoned in one of our own, and they are lost to us."

Um, holy shit. My new friends are kinda scary.

Peri breaks the awkward silence. "How does this relate to what you were thinking about earlier, though?" I'm thankful the conversation's back on track. I don't want to think about anyone becoming a living prison for evil things.

"We-l-l-l-l...maybe I can make a design to protect you from these greedy jerks. I'm not sure how it'll work yet because I only just now came up with the plan." She pushes her short purple hair back from her forehead as she tries to wrap her head around the challenge. It's a gesture I've seen her do behind the counter at the Bean, and oddly enough, it feels comforting. I guess because it makes everything that's happening feel more normal.

"Really? Oh wow. I feel like—I don't want to be a burden. You all have been so kind to me, more than strangers probably should be. I mean, taking me in when I didn't have anywhere to go, just everything—"

"Wait a sec," I interrupt Peri. "You didn't know them when you moved in? How did that work?"

"Would you believe that she was personally invited by The Maithe?"

The smirk on Sousa's face could either mean that he's teasing me or wants me to challenge him so he can tell me more. I decide to go with the latter.

"Okay, I need to hear this story. If it were anyone else, I'd say it was unbelievable, but that option's pretty much out these days." I shrug and match his smirk to the best of my ability.

"I think you're going to fit in here just fine," he chuckles. "Do you wanna tell her, Peri?"

"I don't know if it'll sound any more plausible coming from me! I was wandering around this neighborhood aimlessly, despairing because I knew I had to get away from the hotel where I was staying, thanks to Raúl. But I knew no one I could trust and nowhere that I could go where I would feel safer.

"And then I looked up, and there was a flyer stuck to a pole advertising a room for rent right down the street from where I stood. At this place called The Maithe. I thought it was an apartment building." The look on her face is priceless, a combo of awe and disbelief.

"Imagine my surprise when I hear someone in the foyer calling out hello, completely unexpected, and in my mind, uninvited." Sousa laughs, clearly delighted. "When I come down to see what the hell's going on, she's as confused as me. Hands me the flyer, and it hits me. She's here because the damn house has asked her here, all on its own."

"I, um—I guess that's not normal?" It's a stupid question, but really, I'm asking because I want to see his reaction. He does not disappoint.

"In no fucking way is it normal, even for this place!" He thumps the table with his fist to punctuate the absurdity, then throws his head back and laughs. Once he gets himself together, he adds, "I guess it is now, but that was the first time the house unquestionably asserted itself. And who am I to argue with a huge, seemingly sentient, triangular stack of bricks?"

That makes everyone crack up, but even as I laugh, it strikes me just how much Sousa loves this house and everything about it. There's an unspoken sense of pride buried in how he talks about The Maithe. I bet if there were a way to ask the house about it, as ridiculous as that thought sounds, it would express the same feelings about Sousa.

I guess I've hit the point where I accept sentient houses now. I'd better if I'm going to be living inside one. Yikes.

"I'll give it to Sousa; he was really nice about it once he stopped being confused. I told him I was living in a hotel, but it wasn't safe for me anymore, and he didn't even ask for details. He just said, 'If The Maithe wants you here, I'm not gonna argue,' and told me to get in the elevator and see what happens," Peri says.

"And what happened?" Karsten leans forward, captivated.

"The doors closed behind me, and it started going up without me touching anything! When I got out, I didn't even know what floor I was on. I didn't know what to do, so I started walking down the hallway and stopped when I came to the only open door. That was the tower room. Denny's seen it." Peri winks at me, and of course, I blush.

"And that was that," Sousa says. "I sent her to get her bags, and I guess the house did whatever it does to get her other belongings. Until recently, we'd cross paths from time to time, and I knew Vali saw her often when she'd work at the Bean."

"That's where she and I met." He nods like that's obvious.

"Vali told us—me, Merrick, Lucee—about you and that you seemed likely to move into our circles. That's why we decided to have you come and do the photo shoot. I love it when a plan comes together!"

He looks extraordinarily pleased with himself, leaning back in his chair with his arms behind his head, a big grin on his face. Vali snorts and shakes her head at this.

"Yes, that was totally *your* plan, big guy."

"Hey, I'm the one who found Peri wandering the halls."

"And I'm the one who watched these two hovering around each other like hapless fireflies!" She immediately slaps her hand over her mouth. Peri and I look at each other and burst out laughing.

Vali's expression changes from amused to wide-eyed in an instant. "Y'all, I think I might know what I need to do to protect Peri. But you're going to have to give me a little time to work it out."

She grabs her sketchbook and a black marker and starts furiously drawing lines and curves in what look like meaningless patterns. I know better, though, having seen enough visual artists at work.

"We should let her do her thing." Sousa obviously also knows this routine. "I think this is the perfect time to get some more substantial food and beer going. She'll be hungry when she's finished."

"I'm actually hungry again." I surprise myself by admitting it.

Peri squeezes my hand. "You'll find that meals here are always a joy. Everything's going to be different for you in this house."

CHAPTER 15
WINTER SEVERITY INDEX – A SUDDEN COLD

It takes Vali a long time to finish the drawing, much longer than I expect. Which is presumptuous of me to think because how do I know how long a magical drawing is supposed to take?

In the meantime, there's pizza and beer, which we eat downstairs in the ballroom, so Vali can get her draw on without distractions. That's how Sousa puts it, anyway. The pizza is in delivery boxes, but not ones I recognize, and the slices are huge and full of fancy toppings. The one I'm currently enjoying has sun-dried tomatoes, with the best fresh mozzarella I've ever had, and huge basil leaves. There's a smattering of dried pepper flakes across the surface. Seriously top-notch. The beer is one of the lighter house brews, and it suits the pizza perfectly. I switch to water after the first one, and no one seems to care.

Peri's next to me on a couch in the middle of the room, where just recently there was a crowd. She's turned longways on the cushions so that her back's supported against me, and her legs stretch down the length of the couch. It's more comfortable than I expect and it feels pleasantly intimate in a way I'm not used to but very much like. Me, I'm slouched down enough to be relaxed but ready to sit up at any minute to grab another slice of that pizza. Sousa's commandeered another sofa that faces us and Karsten is in one of the armchairs, leaning back, a piece of pizza in one hand and a beer in the other.

"It just struck me how alike you two are." Sousa makes the comment around a huge bite of his slice.

"I wish," pops out of my mouth before I can stop it, and Karsten snorts at that.

"I like you as you are, but I can see it to some degree as well. What makes you say this, Sousa?"

"Well." He swallows a bite of pizza and chases it, closer than I would have, with a swig of beer. "You have some of the same mannerisms. You're both quiet until you trust the people you're with. You're easy to like, but hard to know." He grimaces after that last point, like he knows it might not go down well.

"Fair enough." Karsten tucks a wiggling tendril behind one ear. "What do you want to know about me?"

This makes Sousa, in the middle of another gulp of beer, sputter and almost spit it out.

"Well, I didn't know that was gonna get turned around on me like that; serves me right. I don't have a question ready!"

"I do, if it's not too rude," Peri ventures shyly. "Your hair—"

"Not snakes." Karsten laughs, utterly delighted. "No one ever asks, but I know they all are curious. They are part of me, I guess you could say. Appendages, though not so useful. More decorative."

They pull off the headband they've been using to keep the "hair" out of their eyes, and it falls forward and curls around, each tendril in its own direction as if it was searching for something unknown.

"You may touch them if you like." Karsten invites us in the shyest tone possible. I reach out a tentative hand, and one stretches forward to meet me, tracing across my palm. There's a vague electrical tingle where it touches.

Peri does the same, leaning across me to reach out. A tiny squeak escapes her when she touches one.

"It's soft! But there was a tiny shock, too. Are we hurting you?"

"No." The way Karsten says it, with a soft sigh, implies just the opposite kind of feeling. "But perhaps I'll pull it back now."

Sousa, who hasn't moved to check it out at all, chuckles softly and leans back to put his booted feet up on the coffee table between the two couches.

"Did you know?" I'm genuinely curious.

"Not in the least." His laugh makes me grin, too. "But when you've been around as long as I have, you get used to not asking about these things unless it's offered. If I'm meant to know, the answers will come up in time. Though, I can't say that I've seen anyone quite like you before, Karsten. It's cool."

"I wish I could say that I have, but only my parents, and that was long ago." There's a wistful, faraway look in their eyes. Before any of us can say anything, they give their head a little shake, and the snake-like appendages float up a little, then settle back down to how they're usually styled. "Anyway, this surely is one place where Denny and I differ!"

We let their change back to an upbeat tone lead us. If Karsten wants to talk more about it, they'll bring it up in their own time, I'm sure.

Thankfully, Vali comes flying down the stairs, and the noise her boots make is enough to distract from the previous conversation.

"I've got something! Maybe!" She bounds into the room, then groans happily. "Oh, pizza!" She immediately grabs a slice covered in roasted broccoli and what looks like sesame chicken, and takes a bite. Not a combo I would have considered, but she seems to enjoy it.

"Take your time, girlie. I know you've been working hard." Sousa looks at her so affectionately that it almost makes me want to glance away. Not that I'm uncomfortable, but it's just so intimate.

"Totally worth it, though," she says between bites. "Not gonna open the book until I'm done, because pizza definitely does not add extra magic to the process."

"We've been down here entertaining ourselves by answering awkward questions while we've been waiting." Sousa winks at me and I almost choke on my drink. Peri stifles a laugh at that by hiding her face against my shoulder, and I guess that's a fair trade-off.

"I'm not even gonna ask." Vali gives me a knowing look and rolls her eyes in Sousa's direction. "Not the weirdest drinking game I've heard of, for sure. But let me show you what I've got sketched out!"

She flips open the book to a page covered with drawings and notes in an unreadable scrawl. Karsten pulls the book closer and tries to puzzle it out.

"I see protection here, a ward? It feels prickly. But not…not prickly? Maybe that is the wrong word." Karsten squints, then backs up as they attempt to decipher it, as if the distance makes a difference somehow.

I can't get anything from it at all, so I wait for Vali to explain. I glance to Sousa, but he doesn't even seem interested in trying to guess. I suppose he's used to whatever this is. Peri's leaning forward too, trying to parse out a meaning where I'd swear there's none to be had. It's not even a good design, but composed of lumpy dark masses filled with cross-hatching…

Wait a minute. Those aren't lines. They're words.

I look up from the drawing to Vali, and she raises an eyebrow back at me.

"I do believe Denny's seeing past the surface." She seems pleased by this and not at all surprised, which makes one of us.

"Can you tell me what it is exactly I'm seeing? Because I see words, but I can't read them, and I don't understand the design at all."

"Maybe this will help?" She flips to the next page and reveals the finished image with a flourish.

"Ohhh." Peri sighs, entranced. "They are thistles? How lovely! But how does this work? What will it do?"

"That's the prickly, I get it now. Prickly for protection? Is there more to it?" I should shut up and let her explain, but I'm sucked into the riddle of it now.

The drawing itself is simple enough in concept: a bristly stem of three thistles with serrated-edged leaves. The stem starts out in black ink but shifts subtly to green for the leaves and a muted purple for the flowery tops. It looks like a fine-line drawing, but when I get close to it, I can see the lines that make up the flowery parts are the words I spied on the previous sketches.

"Holy shit," I mutter under my breath, and I hear Karsten echo similar sentiments, just expressed a little differently.

"Astonishing! Vali, you outdo yourself with every new effort."

"Well, gosh. I just wanted it to be pretty because if Peri's going to be wearing it, it should look lovely on her. That is, if you agree to it, of course."

"Are you going to tattoo it on me? I wear it forever?" Peri's hand finds mine and grips it tightly.

"It's like a tattoo in a way, but I promise you it won't hurt. And I can remove it whenever you want. It should make interacting with you against your will very unpleasant for the interlopers. I liked it as a symbol because it represents bravery, but also warns against getting too close."

"What do the words say, Vali?" I'm so curious. "Or does that need to be a secret?"

"Basically, it's a declaration of protection and a warning against harming her. I'm not going to tell you the exact words, but I fill the drawing with my intentions as I create it, and the words support that. It's a weird mishmosh of magic, I'm told." She's clearly proud of that.

"They just don't understand it; that's the problem. Which is their problem, not yours." Sousa dismisses any doubters with a shrug. "She's got a style she developed all on her own, away from any of the Eleriannan. It's a fucking breath of fresh air in a long-stagnant world." He directs this part to me and Peri, and while she nods as though she gets it, I definitely don't.

"You came up with this on your own? How does that work? I hope that's not rude to ask."

"No, not at all. At least not as far as I'm concerned. Though, just so you know, not all Fae might feel the same about questions like that." I take note of her warning. "As for me, I'm not full Fae. I grew up without any knowledge at all of what I am. Half-blood, they call me now, but I had no clue.

And I spent a lot of time in the foster care system, getting shuffled around, so it wasn't like anyone was going to find me and tell me." She shrugs matter-of-factly, like it's all water under the bridge. I don't think I could be that nonchalant about it.

"Anyway, I started using art to cope. I drew on any surface I could, and eventually decided that I liked street art styles the best. And it turns out I also have an innate talent for not being seen when I don't wanna be. I just didn't know that was magic. I thought I was super lucky."

We all laugh at that, but a second later, I think of something Karsten said previously.

"Vali's who you were talking about earlier, who taught you how not to be seen, right?"

"This one remembers everything," they tell the rest of the group. "Something for us to remember, too."

"Duly noted." Vali gives me a thumbs-up. "It could come in handy."

"I'm detail-oriented. I like to pay attention to the small things."

"It shows in Denny's photos," Peri tells them while I blush. "It's one of the things I liked right away about their art."

"Do tell!" Vali acts like this is the most interesting thing she'll hear all day.

Embarrassed, I pick up Vali's drawing and inspect it closely while Peri tells the group about my show at Under The Earth, which she loved so much. It occurs to me that if I took a photo of her work, a known magical quantity, it might show me something interesting. Or not, but I won't know unless I try it, right?

"Hey, excuse me for a second, there's something I want to try," I say as soon as there's a pause in Peri's story, and before anyone can ask me what the deal is, I jump up and sprint up the stairs.

I'm panting by the time I get to my room and grab my camera bag and laptop, and I'm solidly out of breath when I get back to the ballroom.

"What's going on, Denny? No, wait until you catch your breath; I get it." Vali laughs, then eyes my camera bag and raises an eyebrow.

"Oh wow, maybe I need to use the elevator less," I pant. "I just—I had an idea. I didn't want to forget it." I pull out my digital camera and pocket the lens cap before I flip Vali's book back open to the finished drawing she'd made for Peri.

"Oh! I get it. Do you want me to hold the book open?" Peri moves to assist me, and I shake my head.

"No, I think Vali should do it. No, wait—can I take one with each of you holding it open? I want to see if there's a difference. An experiment." I'm freakin' brilliant, I am.

Vali seems puzzled but she plays along. She holds the book open in front of her chest and shrugs, unsure of what to do. I nod encouragingly, take a couple of shots, and then indicate that Peri should take over.

"Might take a second for this to upload onto the laptop," I tell everyone. "This is one of the cards I used to take band portraits on. I haven't had time to process any of those yet."

Once they're ready, I open the first image of Vali holding the book open. I don't notice anything out of the ordinary right away.

And then I do.

"Can you see that?" I turn the monitor in her direction. In the photo, the edges of the drawing seem to be pulsing. Or maybe sparkling. I'm having a hard time seeing it well enough; it's subtle.

"Can you enlarge that?" Vali asks. "Wait, let me come over there; that'll be easier."

Peri moves down, and I follow, so I'm between the two of them. Sousa and Karsten get up and stand behind us, and honestly, I'm a little surprised. Not at Karsten, who always seems curious about things, but Sousa? I assumed he's not interested or has seen stuff like this before, since he hasn't said much in a while. My fault.

"Let me just…" I concentrate on making the image bigger, and the book fills the screen. A chorus of puzzled sounds from everyone is the reaction that gets. Not because of what I've done, but because blowing it up shows everyone the weirdness I picked up on in detail.

It makes sense that it wasn't obvious before. It isn't a flashy thing, more like a vibration. When you look at the photo, everything is crystal clear, from the edges of the book to Vali's marker-stained hands—except the drawing itself. That? It looks like it's shaking on the page. Not that it's blurred…how do I explain this? There's a clear main image and multiple blurs around it, almost like afterimages. Like how a comic might depict movement, but this is in real life. It's totally weird, and yet, looking at it, it makes sense to me.

"Hey, Denny, is this normal for your photos?" Sousa crouches down a little to peer over my shoulder, his voice soft and uncertain.

"Until I met Peri, I've never had anything like this happen. Suddenly, I've got bizarre artifacts, blurs, and, you know, energy tentacles. Completely normal in someone's world. That someone's now me, right?"

My weak attempt at humor lands with him, shockingly. Maybe I'm getting better at people-ing.

"Yep, you're definitely in with us. Weird is totally normal in this house. I don't think I've ever seen an example of someone successfully photographing our magic, though. Not even when something's happened in front of a crowd."

I let that sink in for a moment. Then it occurs to me: I took all those photos during the party. What else did I catch?

"Hey, I wanna check something." I pop out the storage card, replace it with one from the party, and open the folder with images. I don't know what I'm expecting exactly. Vibrations, like Vali's drawing, maybe. Hopefully, not tentacles.

What I get is everything that I saw happening during the time The Drawback was playing. I start at the beginning; ribbons of light cut through the audience, and dancers break them into pixelated fireflies, filling the floor with light. Lucee's got soft clouds of what looks like sparkles surrounding her, and Merrick looks like he's outlined in neon. Sousa's harder to see in the back, but sparks fly where he hits the cymbals, and I can see literal waves of sound coming from the bass drum to encompass the audience.

"It looks like someone tried to illustrate what a rock show would look like if ears could see." Peri's hand flies up to muffle her laugh at Vali's observation. That makes me start laughing, and the next thing I know, we've all lost it.

"Can we see the rest of these?" Karsten requests once we've regathered our composure.

I oblige by slowly scrolling through the rest of the shots, but I stop when I get to the ones I took by climbing above the crowd.

"Huh. That's wild. When I got up here, it's like I was above the illusion, so to speak. I could see everything without the magical enhancements, though I don't know why. And these pics are like—well, you can see."

"It looks like photos of any other band's gig." Sousa sounds disappointed, and I turn and glance back at him in surprise. "Guess I got a little too used to looking cool and out of the ordinary."

"I don't think there's any chance of you not looking that way, Sousa. I liked you all, even without the magical enhancements. I was really impressed, and I don't impress easily."

"It seems strange that being above the floor would change anything," Karsten muses. "But this is magic, so we should expect the unexpected. I imagine that the camera captures what you see because you are the one holding it, so it becomes a tool for the magic to express itself."

"Well..." I start to answer, but trail off as I think about the photos at the park. They don't fit in this narrative at all. "When I photographed what I assume was the Nyxen, I couldn't see anything out of the ordinary. And they didn't show up on film at all like how they appeared when we spoke. I just pointed the camera and hoped for the best."

"You can't expect Elementals to operate under the same set of rules," Sousa explains. "Though I'd like to see what those photos looked like, too. I've never met a Nyxen."

"Few have." Karsten looks like they don't want to meet a Nyxen, either. That's a little surprising to me from what I know of Karsten. "The fact that we have three people in our circle who have met Elementals is quite remarkable."

I turn and give them a quizzical look. "Who else? And I guess there's a question that goes with that. What other kinds of Elementals are there?"

"Cullen and Lucee met several not so long ago. They are unpredictable, ancient beings and dealings with them must be undertaken carefully. There are many kinds of Elementals, though they usually fall into specific groupings connected to earth, water, air, and fire. As you might expect from the name." That last sentence would have sounded snarky from most anyone else, but Karsten manages to make it sound like, of course, I guessed that, and aren't I clever? That's assuming a lot about me, but I appreciate the unspoken vote of confidence.

"Oh, I get it," Peri says. "So there are different kinds of water Elementals besides the Nyxen?"

"All are what have classically been called Ondines, though there are many types. Potamides, who stay with the fresh waters of streams, for example. Or Nereides, who belong with the salty waves of the sea. Nyxen favor unseen sources of water, usually in the darkness. It used to be underground springs that were their home, but mortals have tapped so many of those. Perhaps Nyxen have spread their realm to anywhere that water might flow through a pipe, or even passing between stones." It's obvious how much respect and wariness Karsten has for these creatures.

"Anywhere there is water, we may be." I quote one of the last things the Nyxen said to me. "They seemed quite sincere when they explained how powerful they are, though I didn't understand it then, not really. I think I'm getting it a little bit now. Though I never felt like I was in danger from them. They seem to like me for whatever reason. They said I was respectful?"

"I think that's an accurate assessment of your character, Denny." Vali's declaration makes me blush. Of course. "You don't push. You seem to accept everything that's happened with a grace plenty of mortals lack. You're thoughtful in your interactions and you move through the world quietly. Honestly, I think you're due to make a little more noise."

Okay, this is too much attention on me. My face is hot, so I find a distraction to get everyone refocused.

"I, um, we could look at the photos I took at the park and see if anything showed up? Because I couldn't see anything obvious at the time." I take the initiative, scroll back to the beginning of that folder, and open the first image I see.

Green grass, autumnal trees losing their leaves, the pool with the statue, and…something. I squint at it, unsure, but I know I'm not imagining it when Peri shifts around uncomfortably. Wordlessly, she points right to where I'm looking.

I enlarge the photo, centering in on the spot at the far end of the pool.

"Well, fuck me. I've seen that before and I had no idea what I was looking at." Sousa leans over my shoulder so far that I'm afraid he's going to tumble into my lap, so I hold up the laptop for him.

"Is that a Nyxen?" Peri's hand is gripping my knee a little tighter than I like, but I let her. I get it.

"They didn't look like that when I talked to them. They were more bodied."

The being, if that's what it was, that I'd captured in the photo was more like the suggestion of a body. Instead of a solid form, it was a cloud? A mist? Fog? Definitely something watery, with the reflections you'd expect coming from something made up of many droplets.

"If I was a water, um, being? I'd probably shape myself like this to travel places. If that was possible." I don't feel like I sound convincing, but Karsten, who's leaning down over the back of the couch between Peri and me at this point, nods as if I'm making perfect sense.

"You caught them in transition. And they allowed it. How remarkable."

"So you think I'm right?" I try to tone down the disbelief in my voice, but probably not enough, as I get a reassuring pat on my shoulder from Karsten.

"Trust yourself, friend. You have seen enough unexpected things recently to have a good working knowledge of how magic can present itself. And you have a special connection with these Elementals. You are well beyond any in this room in that regard."

Karsten's kind words fluster me—in a good way—and when I go to close the folder we're currently looking at, my hand shakes a little. I somehow double-click on the folder next to it, and the photo shoot with Peri pops up.

"Oh, wow, these look cool—these are the ones you took on your first date, right?" The corner of Vali's mouth twitches in a barely suppressed smile.

She's teasing me. I'm still not used to people doing this in a way that isn't intended to cut me down.

Before I can answer, I see her smile disappear, and her eyebrows crease as she examines the large thumbnails that I prefer to use in my photo folders.

"Denny, what the hell is that?"

She's pointing at the thumbnail for the image that shows Peri in front of her art collection.

"Are those—are they tentacles?"

CHAPTER 16
BOX AND THE TWINS – THIS PLACE CALLED NOWHERE

Sousa is furious.

"What the fuck is going on with this? Are they a danger to you? I can't have that going on in my house; it's unacceptable!"

I haven't known him for long, but so far, he's been kind and supportive of me and pretty laid back. This is a different Sousa. He's pacing around behind the sofa and Vali jumps up to try and calm him down.

"Souz, nothing's happened so far, so let's not freak out, okay?"

"Fine, fine, nothing's happened yet." He stops his angry circling and looks Peri over carefully. "You *are* okay, right? As stupid as it sounds, I'll go fight a bunch of paintings if they've hurt you."

I try hard not to laugh at that mental image and mostly succeed.

"I think I'm fine—I mean, I didn't even know this was happening until I saw Denny's photos. I've owned these pieces for a while. The big one," and she stops for a second for emphasis, "was by Raúl. The guy who attacked me at the party."

"Oooooooh. Oh shit," Vali murmurs. "Surely he doesn't know how to do this purposefully?"

Peri shakes her head, dismissing the notion outright.

"He didn't even know he was tapping into energy from me until after I left. Whatever happened is something spontaneous, something neither of us saw or understood. He doesn't have the knowledge to create whatever this is." Her expression shifts, reflecting her fear of the unknown potential those paintings hold.

"I could destroy them." Sousa's face is neutral, but he's so full of barely contained energy that he's practically vibrating. I get it. He seems like a take-action kind of guy, and this must be making him antsy as hell.

Peri, however... As soon as he offers to destroy the paintings, she stiffens with a sharp intake of breath. I don't understand the reaction—no, wait. Maybe I do. She didn't make the paintings, but she contributed to them in a way.

I feel shy about it, but I slide my hand over hers, clenched together in her lap, and I give them a gentle squeeze.

"There's some of you in those, right? Will this hurt you?"

"You understand it so well." Ah, the grateful expression on her face makes me want to cry. She turns to Sousa and explains, "I'm tied to that work. I don't know if it'll hurt me if we kill them or if the energy will just dissipate. I've never been in this situation, not that I'm aware of. And it's not like I can go ask another muse."

I can feel her trembling. She's got every right to be scared.

"Maybe we can lock them away somewhere, far away from you," I suggest. "Whatever you want, I support you. I don't know what the effect of them is on you. Maybe the energy is just trying to rejoin you. I don't know."

"That's a reasonable possibility, too." Sousa frowns as he puzzles it over. "We just don't know enough about what this all means. Maybe I'm overreacting. It's just damn weird, and that was my first reaction. Sorry, Peri."

"No, don't apologize. It freaked me out when I saw Denny's photos, too. I've lived here all this time with those pieces on my wall, and I never knew..." Her voice strains and cracks at the end, and then she squeezes herself tightly like she's forcing herself to hold in her emotions at any cost.

I don't know what to do. Do I hug her? Tell her everything will be okay?

Before I can make a move one way or the other, she shakes her head like she's shaking sense back into herself. When she looks up at Sousa, her eyes are wide and wild-looking, but she's playing it brave for him. For all of us, I guess.

"We can go up there and see if anything happens now. Maybe that'll tell us what the next steps are." She lifts her chin a little, doing her best to act undaunted in the face of the possibilities.

"You don't have to do it now," Vali reassures her, but Peri's not having it.

"If I don't do it now, or think about it too much, I might not follow through. Denny, you'll help, won't you?" Like I could ever say no to her.

"I should be more scared than I am, but the paintings and their energy could've done something to me that night, and they didn't. I'll come with you."

It's true. I'm not scared. Maybe that's stupidity or naiveté, who the fuck knows? But whatever this manifestation is, it could have hurt me at any time during our date. Nothing happened, so I'm choosing to believe it's not interested in me. A weird time to get fearless, but I'm not going to argue with myself over it.

"That is a valid point." Karsten's the voice of reason and I'm glad for it. "And extrapolating from that, whatever this energy is, could have easily hurt Peri at any time if that was its intention. Perhaps this is a normal state for works of art created under the influence of a muse?"

"You know what? No matter what the situation, I really want to see them up close," Vali declares. "As someone who makes magical things happen with art, maybe I'll pick up something."

And that's it; we've decided to go to Peri's room and evaluate the situation, like a weird contingent of Fae and mortal paranormal investigators.

Every time I think my life can't get any stranger—you know, I should probably stop here so I don't unwittingly challenge something else to show up.

The elevator's almost not big enough to comfortably hold all of us, but we make it work. I've brought along my digital camera because there's no guarantee that we'll be able to see anything out of the ordinary, such as that is in this house, without it. I feel better with it in my hands, like it's a protective screen between me and the rest of the world.

Peri glances every which way, avoiding anyone's direct gaze. Vali stares down at the floor, seemingly deep in thought, and Sousa's unreadable, a far-away look in his eyes. I assume he's thinking about what might happen when we confront the energies in Peri's room, but it's just a guess. And when I glance at Karsten, who's standing at my side opposite Peri, their eyes are closed and their face, peaceful. It's odd to me that my mood is closest to theirs, but like I said earlier, I just don't feel intimidated by whatever it is that we're going to see. Wish that applied to more of my life, honestly.

The walk to Peri's room is an eerily quiet one, just like the elevator ride. Peri opens the door to her room cautiously, cringing like she anticipates something lunging at us. I can't help but compare it to entering a fairground haunted house, breathlessly expecting that first jump scare.

Absolutely nothing happens.

The first thing I notice is the ambient street light spilling through her window.

It barely illuminates the room. The filmy curtains are pulled back so there's a clear view of the nighttime city skyline. The memory of our first kiss while sitting on the windowsill rushes back to me, and suddenly that's all I can think about.

Focus, Denny. You need to focus.

She fumbles inside the room for the switch, and with a click, the room fills with light. We all stand on the threshold nervously until I can't stand it anymore. Someone's gotta go in first, so I push forward, and everyone else trails behind me. Which, let me tell you, is not usually how these things work. But you know what? I'm not letting Peri do it. I can be brave for her.

I can.

"Those are the paintings?" Sousa looks dubious. "They don't look so scary right now."

"How about we all keep away from them until I look things over with my camera, since that seems to be the key to seeing this energy stuff?" I direct them to join me across the room from the wall of art.

I turn on the camera and mentally curse that I didn't think to bring a tripod. It would have been useful, but I guess we're just going to have to deal with me holding the camera. It hits me then—I've only seen the strange phenomena happening in photos I've already taken. I wonder...

"I wanna try something. Bear with me?" I get murmured assents, which is good because I have no idea what I'm doing, but at least these people trust me to try.

I hold the camera in both hands, turned on, but otherwise just resting there. I close my eyes and think about what I've seen, how the camera has been my eyes to the unseen magic around me. I really, really want the camera to show those things to my friends without having to go through taking the photos. I'm trying to will it into action, I guess.

Nothing feels different.

I check the camera, aiming it at the wall again. Nothing changes. The screen on the back just shows the wall filled with art. Fuck. Like, I could manage to direct magic like that, right? Denny, you're an idiot.

Wait. I have another idea.

I dig into my camera bag and feel a little jolt of excitement when I find the tin of ointment that the Nyxen gave me. I pull it out and get rewarded with curious looks from the others, but I'm too focused to care right now or explain what I'm doing.

I open the tin and rub my finger across the surface, then carefully apply it around the edge of the metal part of the camera lens, making sure not to get any near the lens itself. I turn the camera over, and in an overabundance of caution, I also rub some gently around the edge of the viewscreen. Again, I avoid touching the glass.

"Oh! Do you think?" Vali's excited enough to not even finish the thought. At least someone gets where I'm headed with this.

I hold the camera in front of my face, nervous to even try looking—ah, fuck it. Let's see what we've got.

"Hey, um, so can you all see this, too?"

Tentacles of energized light stretch away from the canvases, reaching straight ahead, presumably towards Peri. They move and sway gently, curling up at the ends and then unfurling again as they try to reach her.

There's a chorus of gasps or loud exhalations, and everyone crowds around me to see what's on the screen. Guess that means I'm not the only one seeing it, then.

"They're reaching for Peri? Are we sure?" Karsten always asks the practical questions.

"We can test it. Peri, do you mind walking back and forth a little? Let's see what they do," Vali says.

Peri moves from one end of the room to the other, making sure to stay far away. I swivel my head back and forth, trying to watch her and observe what's happening on the camera's screen at the same time.

The energy tendrils do indeed follow her movements. At first, it seems creepy, but unexpectedly, the feeling of a deep longing washes over me. It's so out of the blue that I find myself glancing around at everyone else, hoping that I'm not imagining it.

"Do you feel that?"

"Oh wow," Vali breathes, and beyond her, Sousa looks extremely uncomfortable.

"That's from paintings?" His voice is pained. "It's really intense."

I turn to check on Peri and see she's got tears streaming down her face. I don't even think; I just hand the camera to Karsten—who takes it awkwardly—and rush over to pull Peri into a tight hug.

"Are you okay?" I whisper into her ear, and she sighs, then nods unconvincingly.

"I didn't realize that being away from them would affect me, too," she admits. "I must be used to spending time with them and their energy."

"This is strange." There's a slight frown on Karsten's face, and I can't tell if that means, oh shit, or just another odd thing to add to the list.

"What is it now? I'm about at my quota for strange today," Sousa declares.

Me too, Sousa.

"The energy? It changed when Denny embraced Peri." They hand the camera over to Sousa, who looks at the screen curiously, then to us, and then back to the screen.

"I don't feel that sadness anymore. Maybe whatever this is approves of you two together? As bizarre as that sounds." He wrinkles his nose, I guess out of confusion over the whole thing.

"I think we should get closer, Peri." I wait for everyone else to protest, but I'm met with silence. Have they decided that I'm qualified to make a decision like this? I don't think they'd let me be foolhardy, though, and that gives me confidence. They won't let me do anything too stupid.

"Okay. I'm scared, but I believe what you said—if it wanted to hurt us, it had plenty of opportunity before. I'm going to trust in that and you."

Oh, my heart. I sure hope I'm right.

We move cautiously toward the display of art, with Karsten and the others watching nervously through the camera's screen. At first, I don't notice anything at all out of the ordinary, and I'm beginning to feel foolish, like we've been making all this fuss over nothing.

And then there's something to make a fuss about.

We're standing about a foot away from the wall, and Peri decides to put her arms around my neck like she's going to kiss me. I, as usual, fluster a little because that's what I do when we're close to each other. And of course, we're in front of my new friends, with a camera on us. I can feel myself flush, the heat spreading across my cheeks and the bridge of my nose.

But then there's a shift, a change in the atmosphere around us. It's not sudden. It moves across us much like my blushing does on my face—I feel it first in my hands and feet, and then it flows over the rest of my body in a slow wave. Peri's face shows that she's feeling it, too, and she's not at all scared. Rather, she looks elated, abuzz with the tingly and scintillant energy we're being bathed in.

I don't want it to end, especially when she leans forward to kiss me, and the vibes just amp up all around us. I'm intoxicated, and I don't want it to stop.

I don't know how long we're embraced like this, but I slowly become aware of someone shouting my name. And Peri's name. Repeatedly.

They won't stop, so I reluctantly pull back from Peri enough to look around in a daze. That's enough to break whatever's happening between the two of us. Reality comes rushing in like a rough ocean wave, and I stagger and almost fall over when it hits me. Peri catches and keeps me upright, but she's not all that stable, either.

My head's spinning, and I'm relieved when I feel someone's hands grab my shoulders and steer me over to the couch. Through blurry eyes, I see Karsten doing the same for Peri. It takes me longer to realize that it's Sousa helping me. He frowns as he inspects my face intently.

"I'm...I'm okay," I manage to get out. "I don't understand what happened, though."

"You don't? Then I'm not sure any of us are going to be of help." He laughs, but there's a nervous edge to it. Whatever happened freaked him out. I'm not sure I like that idea.

I haven't looked back over to Peri yet, but I boldly stretch out my hand and wiggle my fingers until I find hers. She locks her fingers with mine immediately, and I can't tell you how relieved that makes me feel.

"We couldn't see you." I hate how worried Karsten looks. "You were wrapped up completely in the energy coming from the art. We all saw it, even without the camera. It happened much too quickly for us to stop it, even if we knew how."

"We're unharmed, I swear," I reassure them. "I think whatever it is, liked us being that close, if I can attribute feelings to a phenomenon like this."

"It was mind-blowing." Peri barely manages to say it—she looks completely wasted, like she's been on an all-night bender.

Do I look like that? I don't feel like she looks, that's for sure. I'm invigorated after the experience. I could run laps around the building if I was inclined to run for any reason that wasn't about trying to escape from something.

"Are you sure that you're okay?" Vali hovers over Peri, pressing her wrist to Peri's forehead like my mom used to do when I was a kid to check if I had a fever.

"I just—I need a minute; I'll be fine." She squeezes my hand and then lets go to push herself up from the couch. She staggers a bit, which concerns me, but she manages to get it together and smile weakly. I'm pretty sure that's for the benefit of the rest of the room.

"I dunno, Peri. I don't like it." Sousa rubs his neck, frowning. "I don't understand what's happening, and it feels like you're seriously affected by it. Who's to say it's not dangerous just because you came out of it okay this time?"

"You can't do anything to them!" Her response is loud and vehement and totally unlike anything I've seen from her in the time I've known her. She's tightly clenched her fists like she's ready to throw punches if we argue.

"Whoa, whoa. No one said anything about that," Sousa tries to soothe her, putting his hands up in an appeasing gesture.

"The Maithe wouldn't let anything inside that was dangerous, would it?" I'm hoping my question will diffuse the situation, but the answer I get doesn't help at all.

"Yes and no. The Maithe is still learning about how to identify bad actors," Sousa admits, a sheepish look on his face. "You have to understand that until recently, no one was allowed in the main part of this place but me. The house has gained awareness and grown in power since I reopened the doors, but it's like anyone—it needs experience to learn. I wouldn't have noticed any malice in a wall full of artwork, so how can I expect it to have grasped the possibility of that?"

"It didn't feel malicious to me."

Sousa doesn't look convinced.

"You can't let him hurt the art," Peri begs Vali, her voice wavering.

"Is there a safe place where we could store them instead?" Karsten's sedate demeanor cuts through the tension in the room. "I agree with Peri; destroying them right now seems unwise. We have no idea what that will do to her."

Sousa thinks it over, his brow heavily creased as he debates the possibilities, his mouth in a straight line.

"Souz." Vali walks over to him and puts a hand on his arm. Her voice is calm and soothing, something this party definitely needs right now. "I think you're underestimating The Maithe."

He looks skeptical, but he doesn't argue. "I'm listening."

"It sent Peri up here to live. Away from everyone else, right? Maybe it knew exactly what it was doing. Maybe it wants that power contained here, and this is the safest solution. I mean, it even went out of the way to invite Peri here without involving us at all. That seems significant if you ask me." She looks so reasonable that I can't imagine Sousa arguing against her.

At first it looks like he wants to. It's become quite clear to me how seriously he takes his role as a host, so it makes sense that he's worried about our safety. He doesn't respond right away, taking his time to consider Vali's suggestion. And it's obvious when he concludes that she's got a point because his face clearly communicates how much he dislikes the idea.

"Fine. You're right; you always are." He smiles at her to soften his words and runs a hand through his hair. "Didn't sign up for hosting a room full of succubus paintings or whatever they are, but guess that's not my call."

Vali snorts at that.

"Lots of things you haven't signed up for have ended up working out okay. And I'd rather have the art with us than any alternative."

There's an unexpected touch on my shoulder that startles me, and I twitch in response and let out a gasp before I turn to find Karsten there.

"I'm worried about your friend." They indicate behind us with a subtle head tilt.

I move so I can see what they're talking about and spy Peri sitting sideways in the window seat, her knees tucked up under her chin. She looks like she's trying not to cry.

"You should go talk to her."

I don't have to be told twice.

"Hey, can I sit here?" I pat the seat near where her feet are. She responds by scooting closer to the window, and I take that as an invitation to sit next to her instead.

When I do, she straightens up so that she can stare dejectedly at the ceiling.

"I should be grateful. Everyone wants to solve this problem. But I feel powerless, and I don't know what the problem is exactly. All of this is a part of me. And I wonder how many other pieces of art like this are out there, all attached to me somehow." She closes her eyes and sighs deeply. "Maybe that should be a scary thought. But I don't feel scared by it. I'm just tired. I'm exhausted."

She does look tired. There are dark circles under her eyes that would be more at home under mine. Me, though, I feel refreshed, like I slept for eight blissfully uninterrupted hours.

"Peri?" I guess my tone must be serious because she stops staring at the ceiling and looks me in the eyes, her brows lightly furrowed. "Did you feel like that before we, um, were embraced by the paintings?"

She shakes her head slightly. No. Of course not.

"Because I feel amazing. Never better."

I expect a different reaction than the one I get. Instead of surprise or questions, she just smiles at me so sweetly that it makes my heart flip-flop a little, then her head slides down, and she slumps against my shoulder. Before I can even move to accommodate her better, she starts softly snoring in my ear.

This would be adorable in any other circumstance, but right now, all I can think about is why is she so drained, when I'm ready to take on the world?

I glance over at the paintings covering the far wall, a sinking feeling in my stomach. I swear I can see the barest glimmer of pulsing movement.

CHAPTER 17
TEMPERS – STRANGE HARVEST

In the end, we don't make any decisions at all. Karsten is kind enough to point out to Sousa and Vali that Peri's exhausted, and nothing with the paintings is likely to change suddenly if it hadn't before our visit. Why not regroup and think a bit before we make any bold moves?

I'm paraphrasing, of course. Karsten speaks much more elegantly than that.

Everyone reluctantly agrees, and Karsten helps me get Peri to bed in my room. She's wiped out, but I'm no such thing, so I trail Karsten down to the library, where we discover Merrick on one of the couches next to Sousa, a mug of coffee in his hands. The mug's another one from the mismatched collection that lives next to the coffee maker, and it's emblazoned with "GO JUICE" in blurred, jittery red letters on a white background. Other than that, it looks like it could have come from some run-down diner.

"I was just filling Merrick in on everything that's gone down tonight," Sousa tells me, and Merrick raises his mug in my direction in lieu of a hello.

"Let me get some of that before we go any further." I wander over to the coffee station and pick the first mug I put my hands on. It's incredibly plain except for this thin filigree design that runs along the bottom edge of the mug. Upon closer inspection, I realize that the design is a repeating motif of extremely stylized hands all flipping the bird.

Okay then, House. Your sense of humor is something else.

"Oh, you got the one Aisling calls 'elegantly aggressive.' That's her favorite," Merrick says with a laugh.

"The mug selection here is hilariously random." As I take possession of the armchair across from them, I note that Karsten's joined Vali on the other side of the room, deep in an animated conversation that I can't hear from where I'm sitting. "What's going on with them?"

"Vali wanted to toss some ideas at Karsten without us annoying them." Sousa rolls his eyes, and Merrick makes a derpy face. "Evidently, we're bad at not interrupting." I can't help but laugh.

"Doesn't matter anyway; I came over to talk to you." Merrick grins, but I'm immediately on guard. What did I do now?

"Uh, what about?"

"Nothing bad!" He looks genuinely surprised that I'm worried. "Sousa thought that you might relate to someone else who got sucked into this whole world of Fae-ness unawares. I know that for me it was really confusing."

"He had a tough time assimilating at first. In his case, because he was being hardheaded about the whole thing." Sousa rolls his eyes again.

"Yeah, yeah. Despite getting a gorgeous and incredibly kind girlfriend in the process and having a bunch of magic powers piled on me, I had some trouble accepting my fate." He says the first part in a mocking tone, but he's earnest when he continues. "I think I know how you're feeling, at least to some extent. You can ask me anything. Whatever I can do to help you feel like you belong here; because you do."

"Why—why are you all so *nice?*" I don't mean for my voice to break, but it does anyway. "You don't even know me and you've still been nice to me, like you've known me for years."

"If you were asking Vali, she'd say something like there are more nice people than mean ones. Before I met her, I would have argued with that. And until I met Merrick and Lucee, I spent most of my time rattling around this big-ass place all alone." Sousa pauses to rumple his hair with one hand, then adds, "Meeting them changed me for the better. And as I learned to let more people in, I realized just how isolated I'd been. We're building a family, a community, made up of people who share the same needs and values."

"Most of us have some kind of fucked-up background," Merrick shrugs like, of course, we all do. "Lucee's dad tried to force her to be something she isn't. Vali was abandoned by her parents and was unhoused before she came here. Aisling was rejected by, well, everyone."

"What about you?" I don't know what gives me the confidence to be that direct. Maybe it's because they're both being so honest.

"My parents are fine." He shrugs again, but I get the feeling he's underselling the reality. "But I didn't have any drive or vision at all before I stumbled into the Eleriannan. I was basically just drifting aimlessly through my life, offering a whole lot of nothing. I still don't know what they saw in me."

"Don't be a dumbass," Sousa teases him. "They saw the potential in the lump of clay that you cluelessly offered to them."

"Like you did," Merrick grins back affably. Their friendship is so effortless that it's hard not to be a little envious. "Anyway, this is kind of our thing, you see? And you are definitely one of us. If you want to be, that is."

"I…I think I do."

Admitting this aloud releases an unexpected flood of emotions in me. I know it must be noticeable, but they don't push me or even try to fill up the space after my tepid statement. They wait, letting me work it out for myself.

"I'm a lot like you were, Merrick. At least in some ways," I finally say.

"Like what?" He leans forward a little, subtly encouraging me. And even though I know what he's doing, I respond to it, my words pouring out of me in a rush.

"I have a career, but I let other people tell me what to do with it. I always settle for what's easiest instead of speaking up for what I need or want. I stayed with people who were happy to use my talents but stopped giving back anything to me long ago. And now I'm faced with all of you, and you're offering me what feels like the world. I don't know how to deal with it, how to accept it. Except in my case, it's because I don't see how I'm worthy of this."

"Hey," Merrick says in the gentlest voice possible. "You are worthy of it. You know, that was part of my problem, too? I didn't think I was special in any way, and it made me skeptical. I was also scared, because everything happened so fast, and there were a lot of expectations about who I am and would become. For a guy who was used to just skating by in everything, that was a lot to accept! I went from being the front guy in a nobody band to the champion of a house full of immortal, powerful beings. I struggled a lot with why they'd want me."

I'm clearly having a difficult time resolving that version of Merrick with the confident, relaxed guy on the couch opposite me.

"Don't let him fool you. He still second-guesses himself and makes horrible mistakes." Sousa looks entirely too pleased with his playful dig.

"Look, I *told* you that I'm sorry about taking that gig at Thirteen! I thought with the name, it was gonna be a fun spot, okay?" His protests are met with yet another eye roll from Sousa.

"This is why Lucee usually books our shows," Sousa tells me this like he's sharing a secret. "She's another good one to talk to about feeling inadequate or out of place. Seriously, you aren't alone here. And that's kinda the point we're trying to make. You need to get comfortable with the fact that you wouldn't have a room here if you didn't belong. And that's that." He crosses his arms over his chest triumphantly, and despite myself, I crack up.

"Whatever's going on here must be good; you've got Denny laughing," Vali says as she and Karsten finally join us.

She collapses onto the floor in front of Sousa and leans back against his legs in a way that's comfortably familiar, and again, I've got that little pang of envy. I don't know why, except maybe it's hard for me to be that relaxed with someone. Yes, it occurs to me that it's not like I've had a chance to develop a closeness like that before, and it takes time. Seeing it continually makes me ache for it for myself. That's all.

I should cut myself some slack, eh? So much has changed already.

Maybe the talk with Merrick and Sousa did me some good. Wow!

We spend some time talking about how Sousa and Merrick met, and the early days of the band, and how they used to practice in the shabby basement rooms under The Maithe before Merrick ever knew that his drummer was Eleriannan. I love hearing these stories, and how different their bond is from the one I have—had—with the Ants. There's some regret, too, because it could have gone so differently with the collective, and I can clearly see my part of the blame along with everyone else's. I should have been more assertive and outspoken before we ever got to this point.

It's a lesson I'm trying to absorb now, because I don't want to make the same mistakes again. Not when I'm finally starting to feel like I have a home.

"I don't know about the rest of you, but I'm exhausted from all the excitement." Vali stands up and yawns dramatically. "And I let them put me on the schedule at the Bean tomorrow, so I'll need to get up early. Y'all carry on without me, okay?"

She leans over to kiss Sousa before she leaves. When he rumples her purple hair affectionately, I have to hide a smile. They're so good together. I hope one day I'm that comfortable with Peri.

"I think I'm gonna go bang on the drums for a while, get out some of this energy. Merrick, you wanna join? Anyone's welcome to hang out with us unless you want some quiet because we definitely won't be." Sousa stands up, then cracks his knuckles like he's getting ready for a fight.

I consider it while I watch Merrick bound up from the couch and follow Sousa downstairs, their laughter echoing up the staircase as they go. Do I want quiet alone time? I don't think I'm ready to go to bed yet, and I don't want to disturb Peri by working in the room while she sleeps.

"What are you going to do, Karsten?"

"I was going to ask you the same. I'm not ready to retire, but I'd hate to intrude on you if you need time alone." They push back some swaying tendril-like strands that have escaped from their headband again.

"I was thinking of editing all these photos I've taken recently. I can do that anywhere, and company would be nice. Do you think if we sat on the far side of the ballroom, it would be too loud to talk?"

"I think we should give it a try. A little noise might do us wonders." Karsten's wink makes me smile to myself. They're the kind of friend I can imagine having adventures with or just as easily sitting around in a quiet room while we share snacks and read in comfortable chairs. I don't know what to do with that, but for what feels like the first time in my life, I'm ready to learn.

We go downstairs, and as Sousa predicted, they're jamming loudly—but when Merrick sees us, he takes his bass volume down a notch and Sousa gives us a thumbs up. Karsten and I grab seats on the sofa farthest away from the stage. There's a coffee table in front of it covered with containers of salty and sweet snacks. There's even drinks waiting for us: some sort of chilled tea for Karsten, and water for me in a big goblet, very fancy.

Karsten wants to see how I do my work, so I sit next to them. I get their undivided attention as they watch my process, and occasional comments on some of the photos as I scroll through. I'm only editing the ones I feel immediately are keepers, and that astounds Karsten.

"All that work and you're discarding these?"

"You do realize that because they're digital, I'm not really losing anything when I delete them, right? Though I won't actually delete them. I'll zip up the leftovers in a marked file and store them on a huge backup drive. Sometimes I go through my archives and find photos I rejected in case I see something in them that I missed previously."

"Why do you take so many if you're not going to use most of them?"

"That's a good question. It's because when I'm using a digital camera, I tend to take snaps of everything. I'm not precious about it, because there's enough space on my memory cards to take many more photos than I can when I'm using film. But that also means most of them end up being thrown away. For live events like the party, that works in my favor because I never know what I'll catch in all those shots. I'll probably save more of the portrait photos because I took more time to stage them and control lighting and the scene."

"And when you use film, you're even more careful?"

"Usually, but not when I'm using my toy cameras. They're cheap plastic and have light leaks and other imperfections, so serendipity can give you cool results. I don't overthink it. I just try to pick interesting subjects and let the magic happen. It's a fun way to approach photography."

I open the folder from my shoot with Peri and pull up the one of her twirling in the middle of her room. Karsten makes a little noise, and when I glance over at them, there's a smile on their face.

"She's delightful, Denny. You've captured her spirit so well here. I hope I'm not out of line to say I'm glad you found each other."

"I, uh. I'm glad too," I only stumble over my words for a second, thankfully. "And finding her led me here, to all of you. I've been really lucky."

"Perhaps. Or maybe you're finally finding people who appreciate you for who you are and not what you can do."

"That's similar to things that Peri's said to me." I switch over to a folder with all the staged shots of the band in it. "I guess I should start listening to all of you. Why is it so easy to go along with the people who don't have my best interest at heart but incredibly difficult to accept the kindness of those who do?"

"You have to let yourself believe that you deserve kindness, Denny." Karsten pats my arm amicably. "Give yourself time. We will do the same."

I don't usually feel like crying, but Karsten's sweet encouragement comes very close to triggering tears. To keep that from happening, I redirect our focus to the photo on display, a shot of Lucee in the doorway of the guest room.

"Are those glints of purple and green, or are my eyes just tired of all these magic shenanigans?"

"Ah! They make me think of her guitar!" Karsten reaches for the laptop to look more closely, but I stop them and demonstrate that I can enlarge the photo so we can see better. "They look like sparkling rays of color surrounding her. And you didn't edit this?"

"Nooo-ooo. I didn't do anything out of the ordinary at all. And I haven't even looked at these shots before now."

We scroll through some of the others, and to our surprise, all three of the bandmates have similar effects in their photos, each in colors unique to them. Merrick's are blue and gold. Sousa's are coppery, glittering.

"I wonder why these weren't obvious in the shots from the ballroom. Maybe there was too much going on."

"That's as logical an explanation as any." Karsten smiles shyly. "Would you consider doing this for more of the Fae? It could be an experiment to see if the rest of us have these sorts of aura around us."

"Huh. That could be interesting. I wonder if they would mind if I showed them to anyone else, though."

The idea of a gallery show filled with portraits of my new Fae friends has me inspired. I haven't been pumped about the concept of an exhibit in so long that I'm actually a little giddy thinking about it.

"I can't speak for the others, but I think that if those at Maithe House were to endorse the idea, others would follow. That's how it usually goes."

"Is there a, um, a hierarchy here?" I scour my memory for what everyone's told me about the Fae so far. "Lucee's the leader, I remember that. So why wouldn't they follow her directions about it? Not that I want her to order everyone to get a portrait session. I can't imagine that happening."

"She rarely orders anyone to do anything. I would define her leadership as contagious enthusiasm."

This seems so in line with what I've seen about Lucee so far I can't help but giggle at it. Karsten seems pretty amused at their phrasing, too.

"How is it that people follow what folks at The Maithe do, then? Is it just because they're effortlessly cool?" It's my turn to make Karsten giggle.

"Never let Sousa overhear you say that; he will never let anyone live it down!"

"Live down what?"

Like we've summoned him, Sousa appears in front of us, arms crossed on his chest, a knowing look on his face.

"Look at these!" Karsten deflects him with a laugh, turning the laptop in his direction.

Merrick ambles over, water bottle in hand, and grins when he sees the scroll of photos go by. "We look like a proper band in these!"

"What's this?" Sousa asks, pointing at the subtle sparkling surrounding him in his photo.

We end up spending quite some time rehashing what Karsten and I noticed and our idea for more portraits. The guys decide to join us while I go through the rest of the shots, and they excitedly critique each one.

They're more enthusiastic than anyone besides Peri has been in so long. I feel bubbly and light inside, watching them bicker over which portrait is the best—in the end, they chose one of Lucee with her book necklace—and time just seems to fly by.

Is this what it's actually supposed to be like to have friends?

It's late by the time we get through all the shots I took because after we look at the individual pics, we go into the folder of photos from the show, too. I have to playfully argue with them a couple of times over which ones weren't worth using. They think almost every photo is amazing, which is flattering to me, but as I tell them, we can afford to be discerning.

"I can barely see straight," Sousa grumbles and rubs his eyes blearily.

"Could be all the beer you drank." Merrick doesn't look all that more awake if you ask me.

"You staying here tonight, man?"

I think that's a good suggestion. Merrick definitely doesn't look up for a drive, though I don't know how far he has to travel.

"Mmmph. Yeah. I'll be lucky if I can walk all the way to my room, much less home," he mumbles. "I'm sure Aisling'll forgive me." He struggles a little getting up and waves goodnight as he ambles towards the stairs.

"That's it, let's call it a night," Sousa announces. Before we part ways, he calls my name. "Yo, Denny! You did a great job. Let's talk to everyone soon about your idea, 'kay?"

My face flushes at the praise. I know nothing coherent is going to come out, so I nod like an idiot and hustle out, waving goodnight to him and Karsten.

For some reason, I decide taking the stairs is the way to go, like I'm not already tired enough. It takes what feels like forever to get to my room, and I can't hold in the sigh of relief when I open the door and slip inside, trying my best to be quiet so I don't wake up Peri.

I'm tired enough to just pass out in my clothes. I should change, in deference to my girlfriend—I'm still only referring to her like that privately, in my own head—but seriously, I'm exhausted, and I know she'll forgive me.

I carefully put down my laptop on the table and tiptoe across the dark room to the bed. I'm not sure if I can manage to get into the bed without waking her, but I'm going to do my best.

It's not until I fumble around in an attempt to pull the blanket and sheets back that I realize that the bed is still neatly made up, the coverlet tightly tucked under the mattress edges.

Peri's not here.

CHAPTER 18
HANTE. – LIES//LIGHT

I check the bed three times in my panic, then fumble with the lamp and flood the room with light while I hope that I'm just mistaken. Maybe she fell asleep on the couch or, I don't know, on the balcony, anywhere in the room.

I'm the only one here.

Fuck fuck fuck FUCK, don't panic, Denny, she could have just gone for a walk around the building. Maybe she's taking a bath? Or probably she woke up and realized that this is never gonna work and and and...

Okay, you need to stop this right now; you're spiraling and that isn't helping at all.

I do my best to get my shit together and think logically. It's totally plausible that she got hungry or wanted a shower. So I check the bathroom first—nothing—and then I go back to the library, thinking maybe we passed by each other somehow. It's empty, lights turned down low.

I'm about ready to cry at this point. She...she wouldn't have gone up to the tower room, would she?

"You know, this would be the perfect time to be able to talk with you, House," I say out loud. I feel ridiculous, but also I mean every word. "I could just ask you where Peri is, and maybe ask how you felt about those paintings. Are you afraid of them? Are they yet another mundane magical object to you? I'd really like to know."

Of course, there's no response. It's a house. It's not like it has a mouth—

There's an audible ding from the hallway that echoes in the quiet library, and I hear the elevator doors open.

"Is that your way of telling me what to do?" I get silence as an answer. "I guess I'll go check it out."

When I get in the elevator, the doors slide closed behind me soundlessly, and I feel the motion of the car going up. I have a bad feeling about this, and it's not coming from the elevator ride. I know where I'm going.

The doors open on the sixth floor. I sigh deeply, trying to get my feelings under control. I don't know what I'm going to find, but getting freaked out ahead of time isn't going to help anything. I've got to keep my shit together, for Peri's sake.

The elevator dings again. This time it feels more like encouragement than a summons, though realistically both of those interpretations are just me engaging in a flight of fancy.

Whatever, I'm going to indulge in it.

"You're right. I've got this. Don't go anywhere, okay?" I'm begging an elevator not to abandon me. I don't even care how it sounds.

I want to run to Peri's door, but I make myself take my time. I'm treating this as if she sleepwalked up here or just made a totally normal visit to her room to grab supplies or something. Anything to keep my panic levels down.

When I get to her room, I take another deep breath, then put my hand on the doorknob, turn, and push.

Nothing at all happens.

Shit, is it locked? No, the knob turned. But the keys for these rooms are antique metal keys, the kind that you'd expect for a house this old. Maybe the knobs turn on those kinds of doors, no matter if they're locked or not?

"Um, House? What do I do now? I'm locked out. I don't have a key!" My voice tightens and gets a little shrill there at the end because I'm definitely starting to freak out a little.

What can I possibly do at this point?

I can yell.

"Peri? Are you in there?" I knock at first, then I pound on the door, my knuckles complaining about the force I'm using. "Peri!"

I'm crying now, big fat hot tears that drench my face. I don't bother to wipe them away. Maybe she isn't in there. I have no way of knowing for sure until I can get access to her room and see for myself. And I'm not going away until I do.

I reach out and press my palms to the door, leaning so that my forehead rests against the wood right above the brass plaque that has Peri's name beautifully engraved on it. I yearn, with all my heart, to be able to open that door and find her unharmed, on the other side.

"Please. Please let me in. She needs me. I'm begging you," I repeat the words over and over under my breath. I've never wanted anything more in my life.

There's a small click. The balance of the door changes subtly.

I'm unsure if I understand what's happening, but I slowly slide my right hand down to the doorknob, turn, and push against the door carefully.

I'm in.

I'm here, and the paintings are where they've been on the walls, same as usual, and everything else is exactly as we left it when we were here last.

Only Peri? She's not here. I'm the only one in this room.

"Now what?" My voice is a whisper that feels like it's out of place in this room, breaking a silence that I wasn't invited to partake in. I can feel all my panic-fueled energy drain away, and suddenly, I'm so exhausted that I can't even cry anymore. I'm out of ideas and full of despair.

I look to the paintings on the wall, which are as lifeless-looking as they should be in normal circumstances. Of course, they are; it's not like I can see their energy without a camera, and I didn't think to bring one with me. Why would I?

I'm trying not to panic—I really am. I can feel the pressure rising up in me, dizziness, and a pounding heartbeat that thuds dully in my chest and ears. What do I do? What can I do?

I need to sit down, or I might pass out, so I stumble to the couch and flop down like a sack of something useless, which right now I definitely am. I need to get myself together and think, dammit. Why would the house bring me here when Peri's not here? What's the purpose of that?

"I really could use some answers, you know?" I say out loud. "Why did you bring me here? Do you know where she is?"

Weirdly, I anticipate that something's going to happen before it does. There's a feeling in the air, but I don't know how to describe it. Like the feeling before lightning strikes, but much milder—an impending movement of energy. I feel myself tense in anticipation.

There's a strange noise over in the corner by the door, and then there's a hole in the wall.

I sit on the couch, blinking furiously and with my mouth hanging open because, for the life of me, I can't figure out what just happened. There's a hole. In the wall. I can't make sense of it. My heart, which had finally started to calm down a little, winds back up into pounding-in-the-chest mode.

After a minute of sitting there stunned, I realize that it's not a hole. It's a doorway. In my startled and extremely tired mind, all I could see was the blackness of a space that wasn't there a minute ago. It occurs to me that since nothing's come out of it, I'm probably supposed to go into it. Great, just great.

Reluctantly, I get up and walk over to it. The first thing I notice is that it isn't a doorway as much as a hidden alcove, and it holds a ladder that's attached to the wall and goes up into darkness. Obviously, I'm meant to go up there.

The second thing I spot is the place where the panel that had covered the entrance has gone. It's like a pocket door, but it's made to look like the wall, so it blends in perfectly. Wow, that's clever. Wish I'd known about that before the house freaked me out by moving it.

I don't want to climb up there. It's dark and I don't know what I'll find, but if there's any chance that Peri's there, I know I need to do it.

The ladder is made from the same beautiful wood as the house's staircases, and it's set far enough away from the wall to keep my toes from banging into it as I climb each wide rung. If I wasn't freaking out right now, I'd be enchanted, but at this moment, I can't stop to think about it.

I call out Peri's name as I get near the top, with no response. After what feels like a million years, but I'm sure is really only a few seconds, I emerge into a shadowy space. I lean over the ladder to touch the floor while I wait for my eyes to adjust and realize that this must be the actual tower on the corner of the house. There's two towers on The Maithe, on the right and left front corners of the building. I hadn't really thought about how that worked, but this makes sense. There's some ambient light coming in from a window across the room from me, and between that and my vision finally adapting, I'm able to see what the room holds.

It's a circular space with a high ceiling and white walls that follow the shape of the pointed roof as they go up. It feels a lot like being in a tent, one with a window. There's a garment rack to my right, filled with all of Peri's clothes. They're much duller in the twilight of this room. I see a table with some bottles and things I can't identify, and a tall oval standing mirror.

In the middle of the room is a futon, and there's a pile of something in the middle of that. Peri? Surely, she didn't sleep through my noisy climb up that ladder.

Even though I know deep in the depths of my heart that it's not her, I force myself to pull myself up and gracelessly crawl into the tower space and across the floor to the bed.

They're bedclothes, wadded up like she'd gotten up in a hurry. That's all.

It's finally too much for me. I'm exhausted and scared and the blankets smell like whatever perfume Peri wears, like apples and cloves and amber. I can't hold back the tears that come, hot and intense, and I'm sobbing into her pillow, and I can't stop.

"Denny? Oh, Denny! Please wake up. I'm so sorry."

I hear the voice first, calling me from the darkness of the deepest sleep I've had in ages. I feel like I'm being pulled up from the depths, and I don't want to open my eyes. The bright sun shining on my face has other ideas, though, and so does the owner of the hands shaking my shoulder.

"Mmmmpf, let me sleep," I groan. "Turn off the sun, would you?"

"Tell me you're okay, and I'll let you sleep as long as you want."

"...Peri?" It's an effort to force my eyelids open, but when I do, there's Peri kneeling beside me, her lovely face scrunched up like she's about to cry. "Holy shit, you're here. Where were you?"

Despite being incredibly groggy and sluggish, I want to sit up and hug her, yell at her, shake her, and make her promise she won't disappear like that again. Maybe all of those things at once.

But before I can do any of that, she's flung herself across me, hugging me tight. It's involuntary; my arms go around her, and I'm hugging her back, and then she's sobbing into my shoulder, and somehow I'm comforting her.

"It's okay. We're okay. I was just so worried about you, I couldn't find you anywhere." Instead of the anger or fear or desperation that dominated last night, all I can feel now is relief. She's safe. She's with me. I bury my face in her hair and breathe in her familiar scent. She's warm and soft, and I just want to hold her forever.

She finally calms down a little and moves into a position that's less her hugging me tight and more gently embracing me. Her head is nestled into my chest and that triggers a variety of feelings, none of which I have much experience with. Her hand is idly playing with the hem of my shirt, and the soft movement of her fingers have my heart suddenly leaping around in my chest. Surely she can hear it.

I should be asking her where she disappeared to, but I don't want this moment to stop.

"Denny?"

"Hmmm?"

"I didn't mean to scare you." She grazes her lips across my collarbone. For the first time in my life, I'm sorry that I'm wearing so many clothes because all I want is for her to kiss me there.

"I didn't think you did."

"I woke up from a deep sleep, and all I could think about was the paintings and what everything that happened yesterday could mean."

That sobers me out of enjoying her pleasant affection.

"Damn. It was too much to ask to have one day where we just get to have a regular relationship."

I can't keep the whine out of my voice and I cringe a little at it. Peri, however, gives me a tight squeeze.

"I know. I'm sorry for that, too. I should come with a warning label." The amount of regret in her voice makes me feel bad for complaining. But I'm not wrong to want something less weird and stressful, am I? Or is that just how it is to be involved with Peri?

"That's the thought that made me decide what to do last night." She's clutching my shirt nervously now. I can't see her face well enough at this angle, but I can imagine the nervous look.

"What was it you decided, Peri?" I keep my voice even, free of emotion. It takes a lot of effort.

"I thought about the hold the paintings have over me and how drained I was after what happened yesterday. It felt amazing while it was happening. I've never felt more alive. And you, you were the focus of everything, and that was the feeling I've wanted all along." She sits up abruptly, turning so she can look me in the eyes. "Tell me you weren't re-energized, revitalized by that."

"No, I totally was. It was like I had the best sleep of my life. But was it at your expense?"

"If it had been just you and me exchanging like that, no. That's the proper way it works—I give you creative energy and inspiration, and your creations give me back that energy. It's a two-way street.

"But those paintings didn't come from a proper muse/creative exchange. When Sousa called them succubi, he wasn't completely off. They're still taking their life, so to speak, from me. I don't get anything from them." She wrinkles her nose like she's still confused by the concept. "But because part of me is in there, I don't want to destroy them, either. As long as they're here, I'm going to be affected by them."

Phew. That's a lot to process.

"So your choices are to hold on to them and have them leech off of you or destroy them without knowing what the outcome will be. There aren't any other options? That just doesn't seem right to me."

"I honestly don't know, but I feel the same way. I just couldn't think of any other answers. And obviously no one else here had different ideas. So I took things into my own hands." I can see her fidgeting with the edge of the blanket, and I immediately know I'm not going to like the rest of this story.

"And what does that mean?"

"First, I came up here and sat in front of the artwork while I thought about what to do. Then I, um…I went to see if the Nyxen would talk to me."

I don't say anything because I can't make sense out of what she's just told me.

"Oh, I hate that look on your face! Denny, I'm okay. Nothing happened. They didn't show up for me. I guess they didn't have any answers, or they didn't want to talk to me. But I talked to them, or at them, I suppose. I just thought that as Elementals, maybe they'd know something we don't."

She's practically got the blanket knotted up in her hands at this point, and I reach over and take it out of her grasp. She grabs my hands instead, and I let her squeeze them tight instead of strangling the bed linens.

"So you what? Went to the park to see if you could find them in the middle of the night?" She nods, a sheepish look on her face. "And you sat in that dark park all night long, all by yourself?" She's braver than I would have been.

"No one else ever came into the park, so I sat on a bench by the fountain and I talked. I told them everything that's happened, that they were right about me and that this is all my fault. And that I want to try to fix it and do better." She pauses and waits for me to meet her gaze before she continues. "I want to change for you, but also for me. I need to communicate openly with you so we don't leave each other guessing. I know last night isn't my best example of doing that. And I need to clean up my messes."

"Like this unfinished business with Raúl?"

"And anyone else that I might still have connections with. He's not the only one I have work from. He's not my only dalliance, I guess you could say." She pulls away and stands up, then paces nervously towards the window. She looks ashamed, and I hate it.

"Hey. You shouldn't feel bad because you had relationships, or flings, or whatever, and they left connections. But you're right; if they're still affecting both you and the people in your past, something should be done."

The grateful look on her face makes my heart ache.

"That's what I think, too. So when I went to talk to the Nyxen, I asked them for advice. I told them that their words to you were really wise, especially concerning me, and that I thought they might be able to suggest what I should do next. Even though no one ever appeared, I said I knew they were listening, and if they would consider advising me, I would be grateful." She shrugs, with a look on her face that's only slightly disappointed. "Now it's up to them, I guess."

I fall backward onto the futon with a sigh and a thud. She's right; nothing's changed, so there's nothing to it but to wait. I'm still exhausted from last night, and the adrenaline I had from Peri waking me up has worn off. I just want to go back to sleep and deal with this after I wake up.

"Look, I was up half the night freaking out. You can't just disappear on me like that, okay? Promise me you won't do it again."

I let my eyes close—they're so heavy, I could fall asleep in an instant. A moment later, Peri slides under the blanket and I feel her arm wrap around my middle. I don't have a chance of staying awake now; I'm so warm and comfortable.

Before I slip into unconsciousness, I hear Peri's voice, soft in my ear.

"I'll be here as long as you want me."

All I know when I wake up is it's much later in the day, based on the angle of the light coming in through the single window. A lot of time's passed since we fell asleep.

Obviously, we both really needed it.

I start to move around, and Peri rouses enough to mumble an adorably sleepy complaint. I hate to get up, but nature is calling fiercely, and my bladder isn't going to take no for an answer. My stomach joins in with a complaint about being ignored, which surprises me.

"You're getting awfully used to regular meals, aren't you?" It answers with another growl.

"Mmmpfh. Okay, okay." Peri looks impossibly soft and cuddle-able right now, curled up on her side with her arm still loosely across my waist. She's making it really difficult to go do what I need to do.

"Peri? I need to get up. You should sleep, though."

"Unnnng. You should stay."

"Can't. Have to do important mortal business." This is a joke I would never have made a few weeks ago. Living here is starting to rub off on me. "Come find me in the library when you're awake?"

She makes a sound that I interpret as a positive because I can't wait much longer to visit the bathroom. I kiss her shyly on the cheek and drag myself away from the futon before I change my mind. There's a part of me that worries about leaving Peri alone with all the art, but again, she's lived all that time with it, and nothing extreme happened. Not until I showed up, I guess. So I'm just going to trust that it'll be fine because nature's calling, and I'm at its mercy.

I realize when I'm halfway down the ladder that I don't know why the house wanted me to come to her room when she wasn't even in the building. Maybe it was trying to keep me distracted while Peri begged for advice from the Elementals. I don't think I would have been able to sleep in my bed without knowing where she was. Being surrounded by everything of hers was a comfort, at least. It makes as much sense as anything. It's not like I understand how a house thinks.

I find the bathroom nearest Peri's room and do all the needed bathroom things. I'm glad there's one close by, no matter where you are in the house. I really want a shower, but I need to get clean clothes, so I'll have to head back to my space for that.

I'm washing my hands when I hear it. Drip, drip, drip.

It's not coming from the faucet, and the toilet's silent—the tub? The Maithe's not the kind of place to have plumbing issues. This feels out of place.

There's a tap on my shoulder, and I look up from my hands and the faucet with a jerk. My eyes meet the watery blue ones of a Nyxen, reflected in the mirror from where they're standing behind me.

A scream escapes me and echoes off the bathroom walls. The Nyxen's eyes widen, and they step back from me as I turn and throw my still-wet hands up in front of my chest.

"Shit! How the fuck?—no, that's a stupid question; I know how you got in here." I'm so flustered that I'm babbling. "But why?"

"That is a much more useful question," the Nyxen agrees in a calm, almost lulling tone. Good try, but it's a little late to soothe me at this point.

I slide away from the sink and put my back against the wall next to it. I just need something solid behind me, you know? The Nyxen watches me, and I have no idea what it could be thinking. Or why it's here.

"Is it a question that's going to get answered?" I ask, more sharply than I intend, but I'm still a little freaked out. The Nyxen seems to take it in stride.

"Your lover, the muse. She came to petition us last night." The Nyxen looks faintly amused at this for reasons I don't understand. It shifts in my vision, hair growing longer and body thickening until I realize it's taking on Peri's shape. "She told us of her plight and took ownership of what part she played in creating it. And most importantly, she said that we were right to warn you and that she learned to accept our judgment."

The Nyxen, now wearing Peri's face, looks quite smug. It's an expression I've never seen from Peri.

"You didn't answer her, though. She thinks her efforts were in vain, though she stands by what she said. She told me so," I add before the Nyxen can call me out for speaking for her.

"We needed time to make a decision. And we were unsure of her intentions at first. She has grown since you came into her life." It stares at me for a minute, which I find extremely disconcerting. "So have you."

"A lot has happened." I shrug, like this is all something that happens on a normal day.

"You moved from fear to acceptance quite rapidly. Not any mortal can do that."

"Like I said, I've been getting a lot of practice." If only I was as truly nonchalant about everything as I'm projecting right now.

"Or you've acquired some bravado." The Nyxen laughs, a light tinkling sound like rain on a windowpane. "I like it on you, Denny Myers. May it serve you well."

I don't know what to say to that, so I just duck my head like a bow. When I look back up, there's still a smile on the Nyxen-as-Peri's face. It's both comforting and freaky all at once.

"Discuss what I have said with the muse and call us here when you are ready. We will come and offer our advice to those who care to listen."

"Does that mean—are you talking about other people who live here?"

"I certainly expect that the caretakers of this house will want to greet us. Include them."

And before I can say anything else, the Nyxen's form seems to dissolve from the top down. A damp mist lingers on my skin, and then it, too, disappears.

Holy shit.

CHAPTER 19
WINGTIPS – THE EYE THAT FOLLOWS SUIT

Before I talk to anyone about what's happened, I need to get myself together.

I really want a shower, but I can't stop worrying that a Nyxen's going to randomly show up in the tub with me. It's ridiculous, but I already feel extra vulnerable when I'm wet and naked. Now, I get to worry about something else while I'm in the bathroom.

Imagine explaining this to a therapist.

Instead, I go to my room to find an outfit I haven't slept in. I pull on some clothes I find in the wardrobe, a plain brown tee and these pants that I'm frankly in love with. They're denim but baggy cut, and the color's a mossy green from one direction and a brown that matches the tee shirt when you catch the material from the other way. They look great with my boots. At least no matter what happens, I'll be dressed in clothes I like, right? I add an unzipped black hoodie for comfort and head off in search of food.

I find Karsten already in the library, stretched out on one of the velvet couches, long legs crossed at the ankles, and face buried in a book. Either I'm quiet, or they're really lost in what they're reading because they don't react right away, and when they do, it's in the form of a few strands of snake-hair floating up past the edge of the book's cover.

"Don't let me disturb you," I say in a low voice as I wander over to the coffee bar. Today's mug choice is a black mug with the silver outline of the microscopic creature known as a tardigrade on it. There's text that reads "virtually indestructible" on the other side.

"I could learn a lot from you, water bear," I tell it as I fill the mug with hot coffee from the urn. There's a couple of dome-covered plates nearby, and my stomach growls enthusiastically at the sight.

"Yes, yes, let's see what our options are," I mutter to my midsection.

One plate's got an assortment of cut fruit laid out beautifully. I hate to disturb the display, but I do it anyway, taking some sliced strawberries, orange sections, and raspberries that look like gleaming little jewels. When I lift the next dome, I have to suppress a squeak of delight. Popovers! How are they so fresh and warm? I can't stop myself, and I take two. I can never find popovers these days, but when I was little, it was something Mom used to bake for us as a treat. The smell of them gives me a rush of nostalgia.

I don't want to bother Karsten, but when I sit down at the long table with my breakfast, they close their book and come over to join me, a mug of tea in their hand.

"There's a story to be told, isn't there?"

"You say it like this happens all the time." My mouth is full of delicious popover, so it comes out muffled.

"Does it not? There truly are few dull days here at Maithe House." I look up from my plate and catch Karsten's unexpected wink.

"I want to clue Sousa and Vali in so I don't step on any toes and also because I think they should know. But basically? The Nyxen want to help."

Karsten sputters into their tea.

"Water elementals are usually the least likely to offer assistance. We were lucky once to have their help. At least, we assume that's what happened because they never showed themselves or took credit for it. We were grateful but shocked."

"Yeah, I can totally see that," I answer. "They don't seem the type to be easily moved, which is why it felt weird they told me to call if I needed them when we first met."

"The oldest of our kind, the magical beings, respond positively to those who are well-mannered and respectful. You must have impressed them greatly." Karsten nods thoughtfully. "I can see it, knowing you. And now they make good on their offer?"

"But not for me. Peri won them over to her side." I pause to let that sink in. "She went to appeal to them last night. In the dark of night, in a park in the center of Baltimore City. Alone." I try to keep my voice neutral about it, but I'm sure I'm failing.

"That was ill-advised, but I can understand her desperation." They take a deep breath and let it out in a long sigh. "She came home unharmed, though."

"Yes. The Nyxen never appeared. She wandered around talking to them, hoping they were listening to her. Eventually, she came back and told me what she did. Then, one came to visit me. In the bathroom. I was not expecting that at all." I deadpan that last bit and get the anticipated big-eyed reaction of disbelief from Karsten.

"Oh, shit."

Okay, that caught me off-guard. Have I ever heard Karsten curse before?

"That's almost exactly what I said!"

"Here? A Nyxen appeared here?" I nod solemnly, and they frown. "You are right; you need to tell this to Sousa and Vali. He'll have opinions about a being that powerful materializing unexpectedly inside Maithe House."

"No doubt. But also? The Nyxen asked to meet them and wants them included, which I'm assuming means that they know Sousa will insist on being involved. I have a feeling that we don't have many secrets from them unless they want us to have them."

Yeah, that creeps me out.

"You said that where water is, they are. This makes sense." Despite their calm words, I suspect Karsten's creeped out too.

"If they've been paying attention, they probably know us pretty well. Super. At least one of us knows the other side." I shove some fruit in my mouth before I say something stupid and potentially Nyxen-insulting.

Karsten lets me finish the rest of the food on my plate before they ask more questions.

"When do they want to meet?"

"It's our call. I told them I needed to talk to Sousa and Vali first. And, of course, you, too. I want you there if you want to be. I trust you and your judgment." I look at the table and feel myself blush a little admitting this, but it's true, and I want them to know it.

"Denny."

Karsten moves one of their big hands to cover mine, giving it a light squeeze.

"I am honored to be included and to be trusted by you. I don't take that lightly."

I get brave and look up. They have such a kind, caring expression on their face.

"I'm having a hard time adjusting to the idea that I have actual, genuine friends now. I'm sorry that I get so weird. I don't know how soon I'll get used to it, but I'll try to be less—whatever this reaction is, I guess."

Karsten squeezes my hand again.

"You have actual, genuine friends, Denny Myers. We're powerful companions to have, and I feel confident in saying that we all truly care about you. I'll keep telling you that until you believe it." The smile they give me is dazzling, and once again, I'm reminded that my new friends are something special and magical.

I know you'd think that with everything going on—so many strange, otherworldly beings and events—it would never leave my mind that I'm surrounded by Fae. But they are warm, comforting, and just so *normal*, even when we're discussing magical graffiti or energy tentacles. My hopeful-girlfriend, the muse, feels more real, grounded, and on my side than anyone in the Ants has ever been. Even Pod, the one I'd consider myself closest to in the Ants, hasn't been so reliable or concerned about me.

"I guess I'd better learn to believe it. Because I'd hate for you to have to keep repeating yourself." I turn it into a joke to make it feel less awkward for me, and thankfully, Karsten rolls with it, rewarding me with a laugh.

"What's so funny?"

Peri stumbles into the library, somehow still looking sleepy despite having obviously taken a shower before she came down to find me. Her hair is curlier than usual and hanging past her shoulders in its still-damp state. She's wearing an oversized, open-knit tunic sweater in a soft mauve over black leggings, and how she manages to look so pulled together no matter what's happening is something I find extremely attractive. I'm not complaining about the lacy sweater, either.

She waves at us but doesn't join us right away because the pull of caffeine at the coffee bar has her attention. I can't blame her. When she sits down next to me, she's also got a plate filled with two flaky-looking biscuits smeared with butter and honey and three pieces of bacon. I don't remember seeing any of those choices when I put my breakfast together.

"Couldn't sleep anymore, so I gave up and decided that at least I could have a nice, long bath. It's easily been the best thing so far about my day, though these biscuits are a close second," she says before she takes a big bite. If I was the one eating those, I wouldn't have been able to do it half as gracefully.

The sound of the front door to The Maithe as it opens carries up the staircase to us, and I recognize Vali's laugh immediately.

"Excuse me, I'll be back in a moment," Karsten says and gets up from the table. I hear their footsteps echo down the stairs, so I guess they're going to let Vali know that I need to talk to her and Sousa.

"I like that you two are becoming close," Peri tells me. "I don't know Karsten all that well, but they seem kind and loyal. You need that. You deserve better friends."

"I used to think I was lucky to have the community that I did. But now,

I see how messed up that situation was, and how much better off I am now, even with all the strangeness that's been happening. Which is kind of what Karsten and I were talking about when you came in."

"What do you mean?" She's got honey on the back of her hand, and I point it out before I answer.

"Well, in general, I mean all of this." I gesture around me to include The Maithe and all its inhabitants. "I stumbled into a magical world, thanks to you. I know it's not all a bed of roses. I'm sure there's plenty of Fae baddies out there too. But it's been a hell of a lot more welcoming than my previous situation was."

"I think a 'bed of roses' is a pretty apt description. Gorgeous, luxurious, hidden thorns. I like it." She snorts at her joke, and I consider it before I answer.

"I keep being warned about the thorns. But so far, it's been the mortals I already knew that I've been worried about."

I drain the last of the coffee in the tardigrade mug and stand to go get a refill. Before I can get very far, I hear the thump of heavy boots on the stairs. Time to stop pretending that it's a normal, pleasant morning and get ready to talk about Nyxen.

"Denny, what's this I hear about visitors to The Maithe?" Sousa asks as he comes in, then drops a big Army-style rucksack on the long wooden table. It looks old, possibly vintage military surplus, and very well-used. I hear a cacophony of clangs and rattles, and it dawns on me that the bag's full of spray paint cans.

Vali sits opposite him, pushes the bag farther down, and then jumps back up to join me at the coffee bar. She seems nervous, edgy.

"I think you've got the right idea." She grabs a mug and fills it, takes a big swig, and then refills.

"There's not enough coffee in the world today, let me tell you."

I go back to my seat at the table, and Karsten gives me an encouraging look before I begin explaining what's happened.

Everyone's kind enough to keep from interrupting me until I finish, though when I describe the Nyxen's sudden appearance in the bathroom, Peri gasps and grabs my arm a little more tightly than I'd like. By the time I'm done, everyone's looking thoughtful.

Sousa finally breaks the silence. "Makes me wonder how often they've been here before now."

"I should probably mention to them that randomly showing up in the bathroom isn't great for my anxiety." That gets me a laugh from the entire table. "Anyway, the important part of all of this is that Peri made a good impression, and they want to help. We're supposed to summon them when we're ready to talk."

"I wish you'd waited until I put on that tattoo to protect you, Peri." Vali frowns. "But I gotta say that you're brave to go out in the middle of the night to talk to them."

"I was afraid that if I had it, they might not want to talk to me, since they don't like me much already."

"I get it. But we should consider applying the tattoo to you soon if you still want it."

"I-I do."

"You're not stuck with it forever, remember? If you decide you don't need it or want to change up what it does, I can remove it or replace it. But I'm the only one who can do it, so keep that in mind."

Vali reaches behind her, grabs a beat-up black canvas messenger bag hanging off the back of the chair, and pulls out her black book from it.

"Here we be." She opens the book to the page with the finished version of the beautiful thistle design. "You won't be able to see it, but I thought it would look amazing if we placed it between your shoulder blades. It'll work no matter where I put it, though."

"No, I like that a lot." Peri surprises me by immediately pulling her sweater over her head and then moving her hair to the side. "Will I feel it?"

"You might feel something, but it won't be painful. Denny, can you pull down her tank top a little so I have enough room to place this?" Vali's gone all business now, focused on the task at hand.

I do as I'm asked, even though the brush of my fingers against Peri's soft skin makes me flush. I forget about that right away, though, because as I watch, Vali reaches out to the page and just scoops the drawing up into her hand. Where the image was on the page is now blank.

I'm never going to get used to this magic stuff.

She moves next to me and carefully grasps the tattoo between her finger and thumb, and with one swift motion, she neatly transfers it to Peri's exposed skin. She gives it a gentle pat, and it seems to settle in.

Vali indicates that I should let go of Peri's top, and it moves back into place, covering part of the thistle design. All I can see is part of the flowers peeking out from the tank and blossoming at the nape of her neck.

It's beautiful and looks perfect on her. There's no way to tell that it's not actually a tattoo. The design is even raised slightly, like it's been inked into her skin.

"How does it look? Do you like it?" Peri twists this way and that, trying to spy a glimpse of the art that's now a part of her back.

"Why don't you go to the bathroom and check it out?"

She looks at me like I'm a genius, which is ridiculous but I'll take it, and sprints off to the bathroom down the hall.

"If I ever decide to get ink, I know who I'm going to." Vali grins at my declaration.

"Tattooist to the Fae and Fae-adjacent, just one of the many services that I offer."

"Where you might not get the tattoo you want, but the one you need," Sousa quips, which makes Vali hold back her laugh with a snort.

"Too true, Souz, too true. I do try to take into account personal taste and appropriate designs whenever possible. What a drag it would be to have to wear something on your skin that you hate!"

Peri loves the tattoo. She comes back practically bouncing, and I suspect some of that bounce has to do with the confidence of feeling like she's got protection. It's got to be a relief for her because it sure is for me. I've had this underlying feeling of anxiety for days now, and even though my tearful breakdown in Peri's bedroom eased it somewhat, it's still lurking below the surface.

"Look, it's not going to keep you from getting hit by a bus or even stop everyone from fucking with you, okay? But it will make anyone who tries to hurt you regret it. Like messing with a porcupine. It's doable—but is it worth the effort?" Vali cocks her head and winks at Peri. "Still, don't put yourself into unnecessary situations. It's a backup plan."

This doesn't take the wind out of Peri's sails at all, though I think maybe it should, at least a little. But let her feel invincible for a bit, I guess. I get it. I feel small and vulnerable all the time.

"When will we speak to the Nyxen?" Karsten asks. "If they have suggestions, sooner is better than later."

"Are you ready for that?" Sousa directs the question to me and Peri.

"I don't think I'll ever be ready to talk to the Nyxen. But I guess now is as good a time as any." I look to Peri, and she shrugs, trying to look nonchalant about it.

"What Denny said."

"Can you call them, Denny?"

"You want me to call them here to the library, Sousa? Or is there somewhere better?" There's a part of me that doesn't like the idea of them coming into this space. Maybe it's because the library has felt safe and welcoming to me since I've been here. As much as the Nyxen claim to like me, they don't really exude "safe and welcome" vibes.

"Sure, you're probably right. This is more of a private space for people who live here, not ones who come in through the drain or whatever. Let's take this to the ballroom." It's pretty funny, but I can't help but wonder how wise it is to joke about how the Nyxen get around.

"Let me stop by my room and get what I need to call them. I'll meet you down there."

I don't know why I'm thrown off when Peri follows me to the room. We don't say anything on the way up because stairs don't go well with small talk, especially not when you take them at the speed that I do. I go right for the box that the Nyxen gave me once we're in the room and tuck the bag with the jingling sphere into my pocket. Before I close the box back up, I spy the small tin of ointment, and a thought occurs to me. I grab the ointment and put it in my pocket.

"Hey, Peri, this might be a weird question."

"Hmm?" She's staring intently at the Rothko print on my wall like all the answers to our problems are hidden somewhere in its blocks of color.

"So... when you look at the other people here, you *see* them, right? I mean, you see them. All of them."

She looks at me like I'm speaking a different language at first, which I don't blame her, because I probably don't make any sense at all. Then her forehead creases under those heavy bangs of hers, and her eyebrows knit together.

"What do *you* see?"

"I, um, I see things like pointy ears. And horns, and..." It's obvious that I'm making a fool out of myself.

"I see those things, too. I wasn't sure at first that you actually saw the same, but playing with Karsten's, um, hair? That convinced me that you were fully clued in. But why did you think to ask me about it?"

"It's stupid, but I thought that maybe since you didn't see the Nyxen, maybe there were other details—I dunno. Like I understand anything that has to do with magical beings." I look up at the mobile hanging in front of the big windows. Anything to not look her in the eyes.

"It's not stupid!" The vehemence in her voice forces me to turn back to her. She points at me, thrusting her finger in my direction to punctuate her words. "You need to stop doing that. Cutting yourself down. It was a good question. You don't know what I know! How could you? Asking questions helps you to figure that out."

I consider that a minute. I guess I don't actually understand what she knows, do I? Or anyone in this house. Assuming that we're all on the same page isn't very logical.

I don't want to think about the other part of what she said, but I make myself.

"Do I cut myself down that much?" That's a bullshit question, and she says as much.

"You know very well that you do, Denny, and if I can say it honestly, it sucks. I like you so much, and it hurts to watch you undermine yourself like you do. I understand that you've been taught to think about yourself like this by the people around you and how they've treated you. But everyone here likes you, Denny! We think you're smart and funny and much braver than you give yourself credit for, and I think it's fair to say that you wouldn't even be here now if it wasn't for all those things about you."

She stops talking long enough to draw close to me and puts a hand on either side of my face, cupping it gently. When she does, tears well up in my eyes, and I want to be embarrassed, but honestly, it just feels so good to have someone fight for me like this. Even if it's actually me they have to fight against.

"You are strong and kind, and I'm crazy about you. Now, could you stop being so mean to yourself? Please?"

She softens the request with a kiss, brushing her lips softly against mine.

"If I promise to do my best, do I get another one of those? As a treat?" My voice breaks a little at the end, and I'm rewarded with her delighted giggle and then another, longer kiss.

The Nyxen are going to have to wait a few more minutes.

CHAPTER 20
FEARING – PICTURED PERFECT

To my surprise, no one seems to care that Peri and I took our time getting to the ballroom. I'm sure I'm still flushed from kissing Peri, so maybe that keeps them from asking. I'm floating just enough to not care too much. I mean, I care a little. It's me, so of course I do. But I wouldn't trade those last minutes for anything.

Some of the chairs and sofas have been moved around to make a kind of living room-type setup, with the furniture making an open U shape. It makes for a nice presentation area in the middle. As usual here at The Maithe, there's also a low table that has several food and drink selections arranged on it. When we find seats on the couch, I take a handful of caramel popcorn. It's salty and a little spicy, and I realize it's got crab seasoning on it. Unconventional but delicious.

Karsten sits on the other side of me, and Vali's slung sideways across one of the armchairs, one leg hanging over the armrest comfortably. Sousa, in what I'm realizing is a normal thing for him, is pacing around the area like a nervous cat.

"I do wish you'd sit," Vali grumbles. "You're making me edgy."

"You know I can't." He sighs, and she exhales audibly and nods. "Anyway, let's do this. Before I wear a rut in the floorboards or something."

"I don't know how long it'll take for them to answer. I've only ever done this once," I tell them as I take out the little bag. I open the drawstrings and let its contents fall into my cupped hand.

Karsten leans over to look at the sphere with interest. I let them see the silver ball by opening my hand somewhat, then I close my fingers around it loosely and shake my hand.

The tinkling sound is sweet, both quieter than I expected and yet reverberating. It sounds like many chimes playing all at once. The sound builds in intensity and lingers after I stop the motion of my hand. It echoes in my ears much longer than should be possible.

It's funny. If this was a group of anyone else I know, I'd expect a "Is that it?" comment by this point. But these people, these magical beings, they know that a small gesture can have big effects. And yet we're still all caught off-guard when the Nyxen appear in the midst of us.

It's not a flashy effect. It's more like a coalescence of mist or steam that gathers itself up from the air around us and turns into a swirling mass, growing in power and speed until it forms into two bodies that seem made of water and air.

They've chosen to appear as a male and female, at least for now. I'm not sure, but I think the female-appearing one is the same one that came to me in the bathroom. I don't have any solid evidence for it; it's just a strong feeling of familiarity.

"Ah, Denny Myers, you listen well. You have brought the leaders of this house and the little muse—but who is this?"

The female-appearing one bends to examine Karsten closely, obviously interested. It reaches out to brush one of their hair-tendrils curiously. I don't know how to react to that. It's so bold!

I feel relief wash over me when Karsten chuckles lightly and tilts their head forward to allow the Nyxen to run its fingers through their snaky-hair. And when I say fingers, I mean that in the loosest sense because the Nyxen's hand seems to turn to a thick fog as it trails through Karsten's tresses. It must feel nice, judging by Karsten's reaction.

"We've not seen one like you before," the Nyxen tells them. "You are new to us, and we see very few new things these days. What a delight."

It's obvious that they are delighted by the look on their faces, like kids at Christmas with an unexpected present. I glance over at Sousa and see him visibly relax. The Nyxen acting like this over Karsten is really disarming.

"I'm honored to be the source of a new experience." Karsten grins and sits up. "I am Karsten, and I don't think you'll find many Fae of my kind."

"Karsten." The Nyxen says their name carefully, as if it tastes wonderful in their mouth and must be slowly savored. "How did you come to be invited to this gathering?"

"They are my friend, caring and true. I trust them and thought that it was important that they were part of this meeting." I don't mean to speak up. It just comes out of my mouth unbidden. Maybe my subconscious thinks it's important to say it.

Karsten colors slightly at my words, and the Nyxen both react with soft laughter.

"Finally, you have friends worth defending! This pleases us. And this one has come far as well." The male-shaped one points at Peri.

Peri, on the other hand, looks strangely confused. I squint and raise my shoulders in a "what's wrong?" motion, and her confusion only seems to deepen.

"I—I can't see anything," she mutters. "You are all talking to nothing."

Why did I expect this, somehow? My head snaps around to stare at the Nyxen accusingly.

"Why can't she see you? Is this why she spent all that time talking to you, sight unseen? That doesn't seem very kind."

I'm answered by the tinkling laughter of the two Nyxen, and my fists ball up at my sides. It feels like they're bullying Peri, and I don't like it at all.

"Who said that we were kind, Denny Myers? Not we, surely. But this is none of our doing. The muse cannot see us for the same reason that you could not see us without the ointment; she is not of the same make as your Fae friends. Her magic differs enough to keep us out of view. She is more like you than she is them."

It looks smug and not at all ashamed to have withheld this bit of information at a time when it could be a handicap for Peri.

Wordlessly, I dig into my pocket, pull out the ointment, and then hand it to Peri. She looks at it, then around the room nervously before she cautiously opens it and slides her finger across the surface, then over her eyelids.

When she reopens her eyes, her mouth makes a big O.

"Oh my. You are so beautiful..." She fades out, dazed by what she can finally see.

The Nyxen laugh again, but this time, I'm not quite so charmed by it.

"Please don't treat her with contempt again," I tell them, my voice more steely than I thought I had in me. "She apologized in depth and thought highly enough of you to come to you for advice. And she is one of us. And im-important to me."

I stumble over the last words, but I make up for it by standing up to stress how much I mean what I'm saying. I fully expect the Nyxen to get angry, but they surprise me.

"Today, our Photographer learns to take a stand. We are glad to see it."

I feel a gentle mist caress my cheek, and I manage not to flinch or react too much.

"I would fight for any of the people in this room, but especially Peri," I tell them with as much defiance as I can muster. "They've all had my back in ways that no one else has ever bothered to do before now."

"Then let us join that list and discuss what we can do to help you." The way it's said implies that I'm the one being unreasonable and dragging things out.

It's obvious that I'm never going to get apologies for the way they've treated Peri. This is the closest they're going to come, by offering assistance to us. I guess when you're an Elemental you never have to say you're sorry.

"No need to give me your names, brave ones," the other Nyxen addresses Sousa and Vali. "We know who you are and what you've done for the City."

There's a stress on the word *city*, a very Proper Noun sort of distinction, much the way Sousa speaks about The Maithe. Please don't let the city of Baltimore also start speaking to me through things like elevators and flyers. That might be my line in the sand.

"What are your thoughts on the paintings?" Sousa ignores the compliment the Nyxen has given him and Vali. He seems uncomfortable with it, which scans.

The more masculine Nyxen smiles widely, as if it expected that response. It drifts over to where Peri sits next to me and crouches down to inspect her face. To her credit, she stares back boldly at it. If she's afraid, she's hiding it well.

"Tell me, museling, have you considered what you would have us do? We could destroy the paintings easily, but you professed fears about what might happen. We agree; it may not end pleasantly for you." It watches her face for a reaction, and when it doesn't get one, it stands back to its full height. "We have a proposal."

The Nyxen come to stand together, then begin to subtly blur at the edges, bodies indistinct from each other where they touch.

"Let us take the paintings. We will store them someplace secret and safe, and over time, our element will wear away the paint and the magic along with it. That energy stolen from you will slowly return. It should not harm you that way."

"I...are you sure? I mean, not to question your wisdom; that's not my intention." Peri is quick to reassure them. "I am—I'm just scared. I've never had to deal with this." She twists her hands in her lap as she speaks, and I reach over wordlessly to put a hand over hers.

To my surprise, the Nyxen seem to soften a little. The more female-presenting one sinks down to our level in a gracefully fluid motion and moves towards me and Peri. I'm left wordless when it reaches out and trails one damp finger gently across our hands, entwined in Peri's lap. Peri sits frozen in place like she can't believe what just happened, and she doesn't want to break the spell. I don't blame her.

"I have changed my mind about you. You have power but are a young, hapless being. But, tiny muse, you are making efforts to gain sovereignty and repair the mistakes that were made. You are correct to want to break these bonds that were created without understanding what they mean and the repercussions they hold. We will assist you if you allow it. You will owe us nothing in return."

There's a collective reaction of surprise from the rest of the room at the Nyxen's words.

"You will make this bargain for all of us?" The other Nyxen sputters, and as I watch, their colors shift to a stormy mix of green, grey, and the darkest blue. It would be beautiful to watch if it wasn't happening during such a tense moment.

"We value our Photographer, yes? Then we will do it for them." It stands and faces off against the other watery being, arms crossed and face set in determination.

I don't like this at all. I don't want us to be at the center of some power struggle between immensely powerful and capricious beings. Before I can talk myself out of it, I stand up.

"I, um, I have a question."

I have the undivided attention of two pissed-off elementals. Good going, Denny.

"I don't understand something. Why do you hold me in such esteem? What makes me worth fighting over?"

"We are not fighting over you." This is from the masculine one, in a tone like I'm being dense. "We are in opposition over helping the muse without recompense."

"But if I asked, would you require me to return a favor?"

"No!" It sounds genuinely offended, and I don't understand why. So I ask, because at this point I'm really confused.

"But why am I exempt and Peri isn't? What makes me so special to you? I asked you before, but I still don't understand why such impressive beings would involve themselves in my life and problems."

The Nyxen blinks at my questions, genuinely surprised.

"You are quiet and mindful. You have always shown respect and appreciation for the small, otherwise unnoticed delights around you and honor them by taking images to share with other mortals. That is a form of service in our eyes, to bring awareness to those who overlook what is meaningful in this world."

"We find you unpretentious and refreshing and have taken an interest in you," the other Nyxen adds. "Our time is long here, and small distractions are of value. You, Denny Myers, have become valuable to us. You give us something positive to anticipate, and that is rare. Put simply, we like you."

Well, shit. My stomach does a little flip-flop of emotion. I wasn't expecting them to lay it out quite like that.

Fuck it, I know what I have to do.

"I don't want you to argue over helping Peri. I'll repay the favor instead. It's the least I can do."

"Denny!" Vali's panicked voice blends with Sousa's loud, "No, Denny!" I can see Peri quivering nervously out of the corner of my eye.

"Is this your freely given choice?" The Nyxen are both watching me carefully. The kinder one keeps quiet, but there's a sadness in its face that wasn't there before. The other one looks almost impressed.

"You didn't have to consider Peri's request, but you did. You didn't have to befriend me or come to tell me what was happening. It's only right that I return the favor from one friend to another. It's not like I have many friends, right? I need to treat the ones I do have well."

I seem to have rendered everyone speechless.

I can feel the tension in the room when the Nyxen that challenged me finally speaks up.

"It has been a long, long while since any called us that. Too many have forgotten or ignore us." It pauses again, considering. "We chose well to reveal ourselves to you. We will do this for you, our friend."

There's a collective exhalation of breath, but more than that, I feel some sort of energy wash over me. I look down at my hands and realize that there's a fine, damp vapor covering them, enveloping me. It feels refreshing, energizing, like walking under one of those misting tunnels that they put up at summer festivals. I don't know what it means, but I'm not going to forget it anytime soon.

"You are too kind," I murmur, because I don't know what to say that isn't me thanking them profusely.

"What do you need us to do?" Peri asks them. I glance over at her; her face is paler than usual, and there are tears in her eyes. I can only imagine what she's feeling right now. I'm not even sure what I'm feeling.

"Do nothing. Stay away from the room where the objects live until sunrise tomorrow. We will remove them and hide them in a place known only to us. You will be aware of their slow erasure, but that should not be troublesome. We will inform you when they are fully destroyed." I notice that the words the Nyxen uses to speak to Peri are still formal in tone, but its voice has softened, and it doesn't seem as annoyed by her mere presence.

I don't know if that's because she's changed their impression of her or if it's due to our newly declared friendship, but I'll take it. Peri seems to visibly relax at its words, so that's good too.

"Sousa. Vali. We will not overstep or stray from our mission here. Although we can enter this place any time we wish, you have been kind enough to welcome us. We respect that."

The Nyxen drift, flowing together and then apart again as they move to where Sousa stands. The effect reminds me of small waves dancing across the surface of the ocean, fluid and almost playful. His eyes dart back and forth between the two of them and Vali as they circle around him, inspecting him curiously.

"Was there something you, ah, wanted to ask me?" He's definitely nonplussed but trying to hide it.

"You were born here," one says, and the other continues, "You are of this land."

"As much as one of my kind can be, I guess. I love this place with all my heart. I would defend it with my life."

"You have no need to convince us. We know you have put your life on the line to protect it. You convinced others of your kind to wake from their apathy and do the same."

"Not just me. There were others who helped. Once-mortals, other Fae. We rallied together. I just helped as much as I could." Sousa looks uncomfortable with the attention they're giving him.

"You are modest, but we were there." The more masculine Nyxen points languidly at Vali. "You were also a leader then, as now. You, who have also befriended greater powers like us."

My attention snaps to Vali. She did what now?

"I do what needs to be done. I'm lucky enough to be connected to powerful beings who are sometimes kind enough to help." She shrugs and adds, "I'm nobody, really. I'm just someone trying her best to leave the world in a better state than I found it."

"A nobody does not befriend numina, Vali Dawe. We respect your choice to put your work before your ego, though." Tinkling laughter escapes from the Nyxen. "We know better. Your stature looms large."

I wish I understood everything that's being said here.

"We are glad that our Photographer lives here now, in this seat of power. Keep them under your wing, and we will not hesitate the next time we are called upon."

With that cryptic exchange, the Nyxen swirl together in a coalescing cloud of fog and droplets, which abruptly explodes outwards and evaporates in an instant. The five of us are left staring at each other in confusion.

"So," I finally break the silence, "that went to interesting places."

"I can't think of a better time for a beer." Sousa seems to be in a daze. "Your friends are a bit much, Denny."

I turn in surprise to stare at Vali when she bursts out laughing.

"Hi pot, meet kettle," she manages to wheeze out, doubled over.

"I have no idea what you're laughing about; my friends are all quite normal supernatural beings." Sousa's retort triggers a giggle fit from Karsten. Peri and I look at each other, bewildered. It's not that funny. Is it?

"I'm sorry, I'm sorry." Vali struggles to contain her giggles and mostly succeeds. "Get me a beer too, Souz? I think I need one before we make any other plans."

"You know what? Me too, if that's all right." I guess I've earned one tonight.

"I'm not your dad; you can have a beer if you want!" Sousa calls over his shoulder as he heads to the hallway on the far side of the ballroom.

Vali makes a rude raspberry noise. "It's always all right, Denny. You live here now! You're one of us; you don't have to ask." She grins at me then, softening her words. "I get it. You're just being polite, and that's always a good plan around folks like all of us. I just want you to feel at home. There's a kitchen full of food, plenty of coffee and beer, and whatever else you might want, and it's all yours. And once you've been here for a while, I'm sure the house will reveal even more of its secrets to you. I think it likes you, too."

"That's good because I absolutely like the house. And I promise I'll get used to all of it eventually, but it's definitely in my nature to be cautious about expressing my wants."

I sink back down onto the couch, and Peri slips an arm around me and gives me a half-hug.

"You were amazing, Denny. I can't believe how brave you were!" She pulls back a little from me and studies my face, concern in her eyes. "Hey, you're shaking. Are you okay?"

"Me? I'm fine—"

Much to my embarrassment, my voice breaks off in a squeak, and I realize that I'm hot all over, and everything feels like it's closing in on me. I haven't had a panic attack like this in a really long time, and I'm not ready for it at all.

"Whoa, whoa. You're okay. I'm right here; we're all here." I hear Peri talking to me from what feels like a mile away. I feel cool hands push my head forward so that I'm leaning with it between my knees. I always thought that was for people who were in danger of passing out, but it seems to help, so I'm not complaining.

Peri's rubbing my back gently, and Karsten's there with a hand on my arm, which also strangely seems to help. And Vali's in front of me—my head's down, so I can't really see her, but she's talking me through the panic attack in a soft, soothing voice.

"Concentrate on the floor, Denny. What do you see? It's so smooth and shiny. And my voice, you can hold onto that as an anchor. I hear Sousa coming from the kitchen, too. He's got beer for us, and that will calm us down. I bet Peri's hand feels nice right now, stroking away all that tension, right? You've got all of us here with you. We're here, at The Maithe, and we're all safe."

She's good. Really good. I can feel myself calming down, my back relaxing and the shivering easing up. By the time Sousa gets to us with the beer, my breathing has calmed down a lot, and I don't feel the ringing in my ears as much.

"Hey, I heard you could use this," Sousa says in the kindest voice I've heard from him. He hands me one of the beers. "Don't drink it too fast. Give yourself time to settle, okay?"

He sits in one of the armchairs, I assume to give me some room. It's thoughtful because I don't think I could handle one more person hovering over me now. Not to knock the support I'm getting at all, I'm just at my limit.

I look at the bottle in my hands for a minute before I take a drink. It's an old-fashioned brown glass bottle, the kind with a long neck, wide shoulders and a ceramic flip-top. It could be a reproduction, but it feels genuinely old, like Sousa found it somewhere down in the basement. Knowing him, it's totally possible.

I pop the lid with my thumb and take a sip. It's cool but not overly chilled, which makes the flavor even more prominent. It tastes like a beer that should be in one of those bottles, if you know what I mean. Much too complex and authentic to come from some big brewery.

I guess that's a metaphor for my current situation, in a way. You can't take on a life like this, one so different from anything you've experienced as "normal" beforehand, and expect it to feel like an everyday existence. Complex but authentic. That's my life now.

I take another swig of the beer and feel myself slowly relax. Maybe I'm not always going to be safe, but I feel like I can count on these people to have my back when I need them.

"I can't guarantee that I won't have a panic attack again, but I think it's finally settled for me that, as scary as it is sometimes, this is the life that I want. With all of you in this beautiful and strange house, because even when I'm scared by the magic and all the unknowns, I've never felt more like this is where I'm supposed to be."

"That's what we've been telling you!" Peri kisses my cheek with an audible smack, and I can't help but crack up. When everyone else joins in, it's the best sound I've ever heard.

CHAPTER 21
LUSH – SECOND SIGHT

When I tell you that everything settled down for a while, this is what I mean:

The paintings quietly disappeared. We never saw the Nyxen take them, but when we checked—after waiting the amount of time that the Nyxen told us to wait—there were blank places on the wall where the greedy art, as I've privately been calling it, used to hang.

I still didn't like the idea of Peri sleeping there. Okay, I know that's not the whole truth—I prefer it when she stays with me. But I also get nervous thinking about her there on her own, and I don't particularly want to sleep there right now, either. So she's been staying in my room for now. I still wake up some mornings and can't believe my luck.

Peri told me that she feels useless because everyone here has some sort of interest, hobby or job, and all she's good for is inspiring other people to be creative. I think she's got a point: she needs something that makes her feel fulfilled beyond being a muse. I know I personally wouldn't be satisfied with that. So I encourage her to try exploring things on her own, because I'll support whatever she tries. I'm repaid by seeing her do the cutest happy dance ever.

It's so amazing to be able to inspire that in someone with the most minimal effort.

She's been dabbling in all kinds of crafts in her search for a hobby, including jewelry making and painting. She even borrowed one of my cameras for a while but was disappointed when she couldn't get results like I do. I had to remind her that I went to art school and it took a long time to refine my skills. She got it, but the next week, I found her trying out polymer clay, and I haven't seen her with a camera since. That's okay. She'll figure it out. It's fun to watch her experiment in the meantime.

I have endless amounts of work to do here, and I'm enjoying it. I edited all the photos from the night of the party and the band loved them. Vali asked one of her connections to frame some of the best of the bunch, and she and Lucee came up with plans to do a show in the spring featuring them. Lucee was worried that she might be stepping on my toes, but I'm terrible at contacting galleries and setting up shows, so I'd much rather she did it, you know? I told her that anytime she wanted to play manager for my career, she's more than welcome. She laughed, but I think maybe, just maybe, it tempted her a little.

Peri and I have also been following Vali around the city as I take photos of her various projects. She regularly volunteers at a local community garden, organizes waterway and trail cleanups along the Jones Falls, and takes food and other useful goods to some of the camps of unhoused folks around the area. One day, she marched us to the underside of a couple of train bridges where encampments had been hassled, and I did a series of shots while she threw up graffiti pieces that she'd designed to protect those living in that dangerous environment.

Those shots are special. I managed to capture the mood perfectly as Vali used her art and magic to create shadowy spaces that conceal those seeking refuge. Raggedy tents and carefully arranged belongings were surrounded by a glittering curtain of containment, protecting but always holding the encampment separate from the rest of us. It's a visual record of her work, but it looks like social commentary via art. There's an honesty in the photos and a warning, too: this is not enough. This is a stopgap. Hiding those in need away from their oppressors won't fix the problem.

I'm proud of this work. I'm furious that this story needs to be told. Vali says that's how she feels all the time and that she'll make an activist out of me yet.

It makes everything I did with the Ants feel so small, so worthless.

I don't know how I lived like that for so long. My days are now filled with activities I feel good about and I think are making me a better artist and person. My nights are sometimes cozy, spent snacking and reading or working in the library, and occasionally energetic if there's a band practice or visits from some of the other Eleriannan.

I don't think about Joolie or the other Ants for a while, not one bit.

That's a mistake.

Nothing about today seems different from any of the last couple of weeks. Peri and I roll out of bed when the sun wakes us up, too bright to ignore. I rouse first because I'm a much lighter sleeper than Peri is. The sunlight feels like it's blazing through my eyelids, but once I open my eyes, I can't complain. The way it highlights Peri's olive skin where the sheet's slipped down and exposed her bare shoulder is just exquisite. I have to pause a moment to admire it, to take in the reddish glints glowing in her curls that spill across the pillow and how the light causes shadows in the folds of the sheet that hugs all her curves.

She's just breathtaking to me. I hope I never take this for granted, because never in my life did I think it was possible to have someone so lovely not only want to be in my bed, but with me every day. When I think about how I mooned over her every day at the Frisky Bean, without any expectation that she could actually want someone like me…

Impulsively, I lean over and kiss her sun-warmed skin, her shoulder smooth under my lips. I get a pleased little squeak from her as a reward, and then she reaches back, trying to snag me and pull me back into cuddling with her. It's so tempting, I have to admit, but we have time-sensitive plans for today, and I don't want to mess that up.

"You're really hard to resist, but don't you want to go to the farmer's market today? Cullen's supposed to show you how he makes his apple pie, and they always have the best apples—" I'm interrupted when she turns in my arms and presses her lips against mine. Again, I'm not complaining.

"You know that's just an excuse to get him to bake for us, right? I'll never make a pie as good as his." Her smile's almost as brilliant as the morning sun. "But you're right. If I want pie, we should go. And they have those little donuts in a bag you can't seem to resist, too. Any chance to entice you to eat more." She pats my bony hip affectionately.

There was a time when that would have made me blush, but amazingly, I seem to have gotten a little more comfortable with flirting. I guess constant exposure to it helps. However, when she slides the sheets back and gets out of bed, I still get flushed. It's hard not to stare at her.

Of course, we've been quite intimate at this point. And every single time, I still turn pink over it, which Peri adores. She says it's the most honest compliment she could get, which I suppose is true, as I sure can't control it.

"It makes every touch or kiss we share that much more intense," she told me once after some particularly impassioned sex. "Loving you makes me feel everything in such a different way like I never have before."

Saying it like that, using the word "love"—made my head spin. I didn't answer back; I just hid my face in her hair and held her close. But maybe I should have. I honestly don't know what love feels like. I could just be obsessed with her, for good reason, too. But it doesn't feel like it used to in the days when I would sit daily at the coffee shop and wait for just a glimpse of her.

Like I said, I still feel a flash of happiness every time I wake up and find her sleeping next to me. I hope that never fades.

Because we've dragged ass getting out of bed, we rush through getting dressed and doing all the usual morning things, like play-fighting each other at the sink while we brush our teeth. After I run a damp hand through my short hair, she comes over, carefully adjusts a few pieces of it, and smiles.

"I hope you don't mind. It's just so cute when you have these little pointy bits."

"I trust that you're working to improve my ever-scruffy appearance. You know I don't have an eye for that kind of thing."

"I think you have a very suitable style, and you always look fashionable in your own way. Not scruffy at all."

"I'd question your taste, but as that might cause you to reassess our relationship, of course, you're right. I am the height of fashion."

I think hanging around with the band may be improving my ability to banter. I get a laugh out of it from Peri, at least.

"Let's ask Karsten. They'll give you an honest answer."

"Does Karsten care about fashion? They wear pretty much the same thing every time we see them."

"We can ask them that, too. I bet it makes them laugh."

We find Karsten waiting for us by the front door. They do indeed laugh, and assure me that I am "tidy and dapper," which is an interesting description for sure. Quite unique.

We're amused again when we see Karsten's reaction to the free shuttle that will take us near the farmers market. Today's shuttle is one of those vehicles they call a "trolley" with cute red paneled sides and wooden benches and panels on the inside. Karsten is completely charmed by it.

"I have been traveling by foot or motorcycle for too long; look what I've been missing," they gushed. "This is delightf—"

The loud noise everything on the trolley makes as we drive over a series of bumps in the road cuts them off mid-sentence. Laughing, we hold off on conversations until we get to our stop.

"I didn't think they were running those for anything but tours these days," I comment after we exit. "I haven't seen one in ages."

"Maybe they knew we were in need of one." Karsten has a look in their eyes that implies they know more than they're letting on. Or maybe that's just how I'm choosing to interpret it because I've been spoiled by living in a magical house that often anticipates my needs.

"I appreciate the ride, but I think it's going to take a few minutes to get over all of my bones being rattled." Peri grabs my hand and swings it like we're little kids. I can't stop grinning.

"This day just started, and it already feels like the best day ever."

It doesn't take long to get to the sprawling farmers market, which is bustling with shoppers and vendors of every type and description—a perfect representation of Baltimore. The city has several weekly markets at different sites spread around the city, but this one under the Jones Falls Expressway is the largest and always has a wide variety of food, crafts, and performers to enjoy.

We immediately find the apples and spend what's probably too much time sampling different varietals and cultivars until we find just the right choices. We make sure to take some for snacking as well as pie apples because they're just too good not to have on hand.

Licking sweet apple juice from our hands, we wander around the vendor spaces. We occasionally have to shout at each other over the noise from the crowd, musicians, and the sounds from cars as they pass overhead on the expressway. We don't mind. It's all part of the experience. We even have a good time as we wait in the very long line for fresh mini-donuts.

While I munch on still-warm cinnamon donuts and drift along with the shoppers, I stop to watch a quartet of musicians perform a unique blend of what I can only call Celtic-style hip-hop. There's a fiddler who looks exactly like what I'd expect, with long, curly red hair and pale skin spattered with freckles, dressed in a long green gown. She looks like she was ripped from a book of Celtic mythology. There's a thick, bearded guy in the background with an acoustic guitar that he occasionally switches for a pennywhistle. Both of them sing, too. And there's a DJ laying down beats, a curvy woman with her braids piled high on her head. She's covered with eye-catching geometric tattoos that stand out against her tawny brown skin. She's hyping up the crowd, and they're eating it up.

The show-stopper, though, is the frontman. He's young, but his confidence grabs my attention. He's got thick locs that hang past his shoulders and commanding eyes that I can't help but focus on. He effortlessly switches from rapping to singing in a style that both blends perfectly with the music and yet stands out as the obvious jewel of the band.

He's absolutely mesmerizing in a way that reminds me so much of my Fae friends. I turn to Peri to see what she thinks because surely she sees it too—

Except she's not there next to me. In fact, I'm all alone.

Huh. I guess they didn't notice that I'd stopped to watch the band and kept walking. I know Karsten wanted to get tea, so I hustle over to the tea vendor's booth. Karsten is indeed there, doing a taste test while animatedly chatting with the owner, who looks like he's completely awed—and maybe a little smitten—by Karsten's appearance.

"Thought I'd find you here," I say as I sidle up to Karsten. The vendor looks a little disappointed until Karsten introduces me as "my friend Denny," and then he brightens right back up. It's cute to see his obvious interest in my oblivious-seeming friend.

"Did you find a tea you liked?" I glance around us, but I don't find what I'm looking for. "Where did Peri go?"

"She's not with you?" Karsten asks distractedly as they sniff one of the tea samples. "You know, I think I'll take both of these. They're too good to choose between."

The tea vendor beams like he's just sold Karsten a car or house. I bet he puts extra samples in the bag. And his phone number.

"I thought she was with you, actually. I stopped to watch these amazing performers, and I guess you both didn't notice. Hmm, she's probably up ahead of us."

We start walking again, and I scan the crowd, looking for Peri's curly hair. It's so crowded in the aisle it's difficult to see anyone in particular, and Karsten and I struggle to stick together.

"Perhaps we should look for a place to sit and wait for her to find us? We aren't going to be able to do much otherwise until this throng disperses." Karsten seems uncomfortable in the crush of people, and I'm not loving it either.

"I can't fault that logic. The market should be closing in about twenty minutes, so that'll make it a lot easier for us to reunite. Right now, everyone's trying to get their last-minute shopping in before the end."

We manage to spot a free table near the exit and lay claim to it. The table's one of those ones that you stand at, because I guess chairs in this environment would be no good. It's fine, I can see better this way. I share the rest of my donuts and a bottle of water with Karsten, and I tell them about the musicians I'd found so enchanting while we wait for the crowd to thin.

Still no Peri.

"You don't think she went home without us, do you? I suppose I can call her, but she's not always good about bringing her phone with her when we go out."

"Do that." Karsten frowns. "This feels wrong to me."

I pull out my phone and first text her a string of question marks because maybe I'm overreacting, you know? It's a big crowd. It's possible she couldn't find us and gave up, though I don't truly believe that.

I wait about five minutes, then with a sigh, I hit "call" and listen to what feels like endless rings before it goes to voicemail.

"Periiiiiiii. We're worried. Call me back." My heart's sinking even as I leave the message. "She could have left it at home." I'm not convincing anyone, least of all myself.

"They're rounding up the last shoppers to leave. I think we have to assume for now that she's gone back to Maithe House." Karsten doesn't look confident about that at all.

We wait outside of the exit until it's obvious that no more shoppers are emerging. I'm doing my best at this point not to panic, but I've also sent approximately 41047 messages to Peri's phone. Karsten watches me text her for the millionth time, then puts their hand over the screen.

"She would have answered you by now, Denny. Let's go home. Hopefully, we'll discover that she is there, safe and sound."

"I'd be happy just to have her fuss at me for blowing up her phone with texts."

Karsten tilts their head in a way that tells me that they have no idea what I mean, so I explain the slang while we walk to the bus stop. I wish it distracted me as much as I need to be distracted right now.

The ride home takes forever, or at least that's how it feels. I stare out the window, watching the sidewalks for any glimpse of Peri. Karsten doesn't say much, but I know they're doing the same, watching the other side of the street. It feels useless, but that's all we can do right now.

When we finally make it back to The Maithe, I start calling for Peri as soon as I burst through the door. It doesn't magically summon her from wherever she is, but it does conjure up a confused Vali, who answers back by yelling down the staircase.

"She's not up here! I thought she was with you?"

I walk over to the stairs and look up. Vali's hanging over the curved rail, hair in her eyes, a confused look on her face.

"We got separated. We couldn't find her anywhere at the market, so we thought maybe she came home." I can't keep the worry out of my voice, and the way Vali's face changes, she feels the same.

"This isn't good. Not at all." Next thing I know, she's down the stairs and pulling me towards the steps that head into the basement level. "Sousa's down here checking on the beer he's got brewing. Let's see what he thinks."

I'm expecting a dark and musty space, but the area that's been set aside in the cavernous basement is well-lit, with shining steel equipment and long work tables. Sousa's washing dark bottles in the large steel sink when we show up, but he immediately gives us his full attention.

"Hey, didn't expect to see any of you down here. What do you need?" His genial smile fades as he looks from me to Karsten to Vali and then back to me. "Okay, this looks bad."

"Maybe I'm overreacting, but I don't think so." I launch into a summary of what happened at the market. "I don't think she'd leave me behind," I finish, and he nods solemnly in agreement.

"No, she wouldn't. But we should search the house to be sure, then we can decide what to do next."

"What if..."

"What if what? Don't hesitate if you've got ideas, Denny."

"Well, what if I asked the house if she's here? I know it can't speak, but it helped me the last time she disappeared. It can't hurt, right?"

"It did—what did it do, exactly?"

"Told me to go look in her room for her, basically directed me. I know, it sounds weird."

"Noooooo, actually I can very much picture how that went down. Though as far as I know, I'm the only one who's experienced that kind of communication with The Maithe before."

I kind of expect him to look annoyed about this because it's obvious that he has a special bond with this place. But no, he seems intrigued.

"So how do you do that, Denny?" Vali's also obviously curious about this new revelation.

"Last time, I begged it to help me find Peri." I look up towards the direction of the ceiling and address the house because I don't know any other way to do it. "House? I don't mean to only talk to you when there's a problem, I'm sorry. But I need your help again if you would be so kind. I'm scared, House. Peri's missing, and I don't think she came home, but you're so big, she could be anywhere. Can you tell me if she's here?"

We're all quiet and motionless as we wait to see if The Maithe is interested in helping me or even listening. I'm holding my breath, scared that it won't help, but also afraid that I won't like whatever answer it might have for me if it does.

Nothing.

"I guess it was too much to ask; I'm sorry." I try as hard as I can to hide the disappointment I'm feeling. I can't blame it; I don't know how it would answer this question, either.

"We can split up—" A loud ringing noise cuts Vali off mid-sentence. "The doorbell? Who could be here?"

We troop up the stairs, Vali in the lead and me right behind her. My heart's pounding in my chest, but that's not from the sprint up the steps. The bell rings again as we reach the ground floor. As we round the corner to the vestibule, the door opens on its own, light flooding the dark entrance.

But there's no Peri there. In fact, there's no one at all. Fuck.

I don't mean to be rude, but in my desperation, I push past Vali to stand in the doorway, my hand shading my eyes from the bright afternoon light as they search the street for any possible sign of my missing girlfriend. As I look to the right, I spy the back of a curly head of hair that I instantly recognize.

"Pod?"

I don't think my voice is loud enough at first, but he slowly turns, trying to puzzle out who's calling his name. I step out onto the sidewalk so he can see me and wave, one arm high in the air.

It occurs to me after I've already committed that Joolie could have gotten to him like she did to Elise, but no, this is Pod we're talking about. I remember how he looked when he talked about Bethany. There's no way he's going to fall under Joolie's spell.

"What the hell, Denny? I've been so worried about you! You disappeared from the Compound without a trace, not even a crumb left in your room!" He runs up to me and sweeps me up in a hug, which is a generally very Pod move, but not at all something he would normally do to the reserved and shy Denny he's known.

I surprise even myself by hugging him back tightly, and I blink back hot tears.

"I didn't mean to scare you; I'm so sorry. It all happened so fast."

"It's her fault, isn't it? Joolie, I mean. Denny, she's been so unhinged lately. I'm glad you're out of there." He steps back and holds me at arm's length. "You look good! Healthy!"

"Pod, I... Shit, there's so much I want to tell you about. But my girlfriend's missing—"

"Missing?" Instantly, he's on alert. "Wait, girlfriend? Is that the girl you were so upset about the last time we talked?"

"Oh, so much has happened, and I don't wanna tell you about it out here." I frown, unsure of what to do, but suddenly Vali's right there to support me.

"Hey! I should introduce myself; I'm Vali." She sticks her hand out cheerily, and he shakes it, immediately swept up in her warm personality. "I'm one of Denny's housemates. Denny, did you want to bring him inside to catch up? We can check the rest of the house and see if she's around."

The way she says it downplays our worry about Peri, and I guess that's smart. The look on her face is reassuring, but there's an undertone to her words that makes me think she doesn't trust him. After everything that's happened with Joolie, that makes sense.

"Is the ballroom good?" I ask her, and she nods.

"Perfect. We'll get to work. Nice to meet you, man."

"Pod. Should be easy to remember, right? Nice to meet you."

He gives Vali one of his warmest smiles, the kind that makes all his groupies swoon, which, under normal circumstances, would amuse me to no end. I mean, he has no idea yet how good-looking my new friends all are. Pod on his handsomest days doesn't compare. But right now, I'm too worried about Peri to pay it that much attention.

And now I need to catch Pod up on what's been happening without giving him too many details. This should be fun.

CHAPTER 22
TWIN TRIBES – SHADOWS

I'm debating internally what parts of the story I feel comfortable telling to Pod. I manage to distract him by pointing him to a huge table of snacks and beverages that—of course—The Maithe or someone in it had left out for us. He has a hard time believing that it's just for us, which is understandable given the sheer amount of things we have to choose from. Even I'm not used to the idea of little sandwiches and random finger foods appearing any time I want them.

"So you manage to eat regularly these days, is what you're telling me," he says in between bites of a tiny quiche. "Tasting this, I can see why!"

"It's always like this here; it's great. And there's no one to force me into taking vanity photos of them."

"Denny, what's going on? Did your leaving have something to do with Joolie? Because she's been incredibly unpleasant to live with since you moved out, even more than usual."

He looks at me with those big, clear blue eyes of his, and all I can see is concern for me. That seals it. Maybe he won't believe me, but I'm going to trust him.

"Come sit down over here, and I'll tell you what's happened. You have every right to be skeptical, but I'm gonna ask that you suspend disbelief for a bit because you know me."

I lead him over to a semicircle of chairs and couches and sit facing him so I can watch his reactions. If he looks too disbelieving, I guess I can edit myself, but I don't plan to. I need for him to understand what's happening.

I start from the beginning when I went from stalker-lite to discovering that Peri had also been watching me and why. When I get to the part where she tells me she's a muse, I wait for him to express skepticism or look at me like I'm ridiculous, but he keeps his face impressively neutral.

I gloss over the details about how Raúl's paintings react to her to some degree, and I leave out the Nyxen entirely, as well as the fae-ness of my new friends. But I don't minimize how Raúl went after Peri or how Joolie behaved when she and Xan came to confront us at my studio. When I tell him how Elise acted after I came back to the Compound, he waves at me to stop talking, a frown deeply creasing his forehead.

"Ah fuck, Denny. This all makes sense to me. I'm glad you got yourself away from them because they've been getting more erratic and unpredictable every day. I mean, I don't get all this about muses, but Joolie obviously believes it because she's been muttering about them for weeks. And that Raúl guy? He's been staying at the Compound until recently. Joolie was doing some sort of huge project with him. Something with a big-ass canvas." He ran a hand through his blond curls nervously, his mouth in a thin line.

"Ugh, Raúl was there? But you said was—he's gone now?"

"Yeah, they got into a terrible fight. I was upstairs and I could hear it; that's how loud it was. Lots of yelling, screaming, and then I heard some stuff get broken. That's when I ran downstairs to see what was going on. Made it just in time to see her pushing him out the door and Elisa helping her. Elise had a big scratch on her face, and Joolie looked like a hot mess. But that Raúl guy had a mark on his face like someone punched him, plus a lot of scratches. Stuff was knocked around all over Joolie's painting loft. I guess they got into a fistfight? It didn't look good."

"Wow, shit. That's wild. What did she tell you about it?"

"To mind my own business, she was fine! I offered to help clean up, which was a mistake because she practically took my head off. Then Elise suggested I go somewhere else and get laid since that's what I'm good at these days. That's when I decided that I'm sick of the lot of them. I was in your neighborhood looking at places to rent when you spotted me.

"I'm so done with the Ants, Denny. I don't know what's happening in that house, but it ain't good. Xan pulled me aside later and tried to apologize for Joolie, saying she's been under a lot of stress and she's obsessed with her latest project. But I knew something wasn't right, and now I know why." He takes a long drink from the beer in his hand and then gives me a concerned look. "I shouldn't believe anything you told me. But I do."

"That's a relief, at least. I wasn't sure if you would. But now you see why I'm worried about Peri. She wouldn't have just wandered off."

"You think Joolie dragged her off?"

I don't want to even think about that possibility.

"Peri would fight her off. I mean... I hope she would." I remember how Raúl jerked her around at the party and how passive she was. "Shit. I don't know. You think she kidnapped her in the middle of a crowded farmers market? That seems extreme, even for Joolie."

Pod doesn't look convinced that they wouldn't try it, and in my heart of hearts, neither am I. But still, something doesn't feel quite right.

We're interrupted from pondering it further by the sound of boots coming down the stairs, and Sousa, Vali, and Karsten appear a second later in the ballroom. Sousa's frown turns into a curious look when he spies Pod next to me.

"Hey, don't I know you? You're a musician, right?"

Before Pod can answer, Sousa diverts over to the table and grabs two beers with one hand and one of the small sandwiches with the other. When he joins us, he hands one of the beers to Pod.

"Perfect timing. I just finished this one, thanks." I see Sousa cringe at that, like it physically hurt him, but Pod's oblivious to it. "I'm Pod. I do gigs with me and an acoustic, so if that's your scene, you might have caught me."

"Don't let him fool you; he's really good. He plays folk with a modern edge, and he'll make you fall in love one minute, then want to go fight someone with your bare fists a couple of minutes after that. And he's the only one of the Ants I'd voluntarily invite inside The Maithe if that tells you anything."

That makes Sousa nod appreciatively and stick out a hand to welcome him.

"I'm Sousa. That's a pretty powerful recommendation to come from Denny, so I'd say you're welcome here."

Pod looks embarrassed, which, unsurprisingly, is a charming look on him. But I think I caught him off-guard with the praise, which he confirms.

"I'm not used to Denny being this talkative. Or outgoing. It's a nice change." He smiles at me, and now it's my turn to be embarrassed.

"So, uh, I was filling in Pod on the truth about Peri and our story. How she's, um, a muse and how Raúl attacked her and all. And he believes me, so there's that. He thinks maybe Joolie has something to do with it."

Well, that was a rambling mess. And I don't know how to signal to them that I didn't disclose who and what they all are when I enlightened Pod about Peri's status. All I can hope is they read between the lines and pick up what I didn't say.

"Given the recent interactions you've had with her, that wouldn't shock me. But how would she have managed to drag Peri off? There's too many unknowns here." Sousa scowls and takes a swig from his beer while he thinks about it like somehow it holds the answer. Don't I wish it was that easy?

"She was there, and then she was not," Karsten murmurs, then straightens up suddenly. "Ah, I am lacking in manners. I am Karsten, and I was at the market with Denny and Peri."

"Karsten is a good friend to me." Pod glances between the two of us and nods.

"I'm so glad you've found better people to surround yourself with, Denny. It's about time. Because fuck the Ants."

I can't help it; a snort escapes me, and Pod raises an eyebrow at my little outburst.

"I don't disagree, but you've been saying that for a while now, yet you didn't leave, either. Why have they been so hard to walk away from?" I honestly want to understand this. Why didn't we leave before now?

"I don't know if this is true for both of you, but when you don't have a family, and then you find a group that takes that place, it can become really easy to ignore or deny their toxic behavior." Vali's got a look that says that she knows all too well what that's like.

"We've all got experience with that firsthand," Sousa adds, gesturing to Vali and Karsten.

"Especially if it happens slowly. It's an insidious poison that slowly rots from the inside out."

I can see the echoes of pain in Vali's eyes. Whatever they're talking about must have really divided their friend group.

"So, how did you all deal with it?" I'm genuinely curious. I can't imagine anything like that happening here, between the people I've met.

"Withdrew. Buried our heads in the sand until everything got to the point where it couldn't be ignored anymore." Sousa looks disgusted when he says this. It must have been truly bad. "And when it finally came to a head, it changed all of us. In the long run it's been for the best, but we lost so much. Inaction almost cost us everything."

"I had no idea." It's such an inadequate response, but I don't know what else to say.

"We are stronger now," Karsten tells us. "We're still rebuilding our community, and I'm sure we will always be working on strengthening it and our connections to each other. Our friendships were hard-won."

"I don't think that will happen with the Ants. Or maybe one day it will, but I won't be there to see it." Pod doesn't look too sad about that prospect.

"No. I don't think either of us will. But I don't want to lose touch with you. Have you moved your stuff out of the Compound already?"

"Not really. I've been drifting between places with my guitar and a bag of clothes. No, not people that I'm sleeping with. I promise you, that's over. I want real connections now."

"I didn't say anything!"

"You didn't have to. It's okay; you'd be right to call me on it. I don't wanna be that guy anymore."

He looks contrite, which makes me both uncomfortable—because I wasn't aware it was so obvious that I didn't like what he'd been up to—and relieved. It's not that I'm against him having sex with whoever he wants. I've just worried about how extreme he's been about it. He was never like that before he lost Bethany. I know it was how he coped with grief, but I don't think it was healthy for him.

The rest of the room is steadfastly trying to ignore our little veer off-topic, so I save them by bringing us back to the original subject.

"So, do you think you'd be able to go spy and see if Peri's there?"

Pod thinks about it, his brow furrowing as he considers his options.

"Honestly? I don't think they're even aware that I've started the moving-out process. Joolie's been avoiding me since the night she fought with Raúl, and of course, where she goes, Xan goes."

"What about Elise?"

"Haven't seen her, either. In fact, the house has been remarkably quiet since that blow-up. When I left today, I don't even know if anyone was there. Which I guess makes sense if they were out trying to kidnap your girl." I watch him fidget with the beer bottle, and the nagging sense that he's leaving something out overwhelms me.

I start to ask him what's going on, but Vali beats me to it.

"There's something you're not telling us."

"Uh, why would I do that?" He doesn't look up from the bottle, and I get this cold feeling inside.

"You tell me," Vali says. Again, I start to open my mouth, but she shoots me a look with a little shake of her head. Okay. I don't know what's going on here, but I trust her.

Pod shuffles his feet nervously and looks like he'd rather be anywhere but here right now. What the fuck is going on?

"Look, I don't know you. But Denny says you're their friend, and that's enough for me to believe you're not in on whatever bad things may have gone down. You've gotta clue us in on what's happening, though. This is bigger than you. We've got the power to fight for Peri, but if you know something that could help us..." She breaks off when panic flashes across Pod's face. He manages to pull himself together quickly, but it's enough to confirm the anxious feelings in my gut.

"Shit. I didn't want to bring it up until I could go there and look for her myself."

"What are you not telling us, Pod?" My voice is high and strained, completely different than my usual calm, low tones. I don't even recognize it.

"Look, she's—I saw some of Joolie's recent paintings when she wasn't around, and they've been disturbing. The last one, the one she was working on when she got into the argument with that Raúl guy? It was dark, man. I honestly didn't think Joolie had this kind of style in her. A woman, a naked woman was the main subject; she took up almost the entire canvas. And Jools had her painted like she was lying on a table, like the canvas was the table, you get me? But she was tied to the surface in so many places, like she was strapped down and then mounted to the wall. Am I making sense?" He looks sick.

I feel sick.

"And it's all in reds and silver and black and white, the starkest thing I've ever seen her paint. And Denny? It feels fucking powerful in a way that Joolie fucking Keyes has never been able to manage. It's easily the best thing she's ever painted, and it's terrifying."

I look over to Vali, then to Sousa and Karsten. They look as shocked as I feel. I watch as Vali schools her face, shoving away the unease—I guess so at least one of us can figure out what to do next. In that minute, my gratitude knows no bounds. My head is spinning, and I can't think straight. Having Vali take over is a relief.

"Okay. I get why you didn't want to tell Denny." Her voice is soothing, like this is all no big deal.

"You do?"

"Look, when regular people are confronted by stuff that's wildly out of the norm, it's natural to deny what they're seeing, even to normalize it. And you probably didn't want to scare Denny more than they already are. I get it. But this is important info."

She jumps up and starts pacing around, and it hits me how hard she's working to be the calmest person in the room. I think maybe she's reached her limit.

It's okay, I have an idea. I'll push down my feelings and take back over for a bit. I think I can do that.

"If I showed you a photo of Peri, do you think you could tell me if she was the one in the painting?"

Pod nods, his lips a tight line.

I pull out my phone to show him a recent selfie that Peri had sent me. It's one of the few photos I have of her that I didn't take with a camera. In it, she's lying back in bed, curly hair spread out on the pillow, a flirty look on her face. She'd sent it to me the other night when I'd spent too long in the library working on editing photos on my laptop, and she'd grown tired of waiting for me to come to bed. I hadn't intended to ever share it with anyone, but now wasn't a time to selfishly keep it to myself.

My heart starts pounding in my chest when he exhales hard. "I was hoping I'd be able to say that it wasn't her."

Now I take a turn at pacing around. I don't know what to do.

"I-I want to go with you. If they did something to her—"

"No." The way he cuts me off is absolute. It doesn't stop me from arguing. "You think I want to go back there? But it's Peri! She would do it for me!" My voice is shaking, but I've never felt more determined in my life.

"I couldn't live with myself if something happened to you too, Denny!"

The look on his face and the tears in his eyes—it stops me in my tracks.

"I'm not Bethany," I say in the gentlest voice I can manage. "I know what Joolie's capable of, when she didn't. And I won't be alone."

He turns from me, pain written across his face. I hate being the one causing it.

"Hey, I don't mean to insert myself here, but I might be able to help." Vali steps between us, looking about as unsure as I've ever seen her. "I have a few tricks up my sleeves, too."

Pod's unconvinced, and truthfully, I'm not sure what Vali means either, but I indicate that she should go on.

"Denny explained to you about Peri's, um, unusual talents. But I've got some, too. And if you let me go with you, I can do my best to protect Denny, at least." She moves next to me and puts a hand on my arm. "Is it okay if I show him what I can do? Will you do this with me?"

I think I know what she wants to do.

"You can do that to me? Will I feel it?"

Pod's looking at us like we've both lost it. "Do what?"

"Watch us and you'll see."

I glance over to Sousa. His mouth is a thin line, lips pressed together tightly. I can't tell if he's worried about us doing this, or Pod's possible reaction, or some unknown third option. On the other hand, Karsten is standing next to him with an encouraging expression. I decide to focus on them. I need the positive vibes right about now.

I realize that Vali's muttering quietly to herself, though I can't quite make out what she's saying. It sounds like a chant, calming and repetitive.

The next thing I hear is Pod's gasp.

"What the fuck! What is this magic trick bullshit?"

Before anyone can stop him, he lunges forward and right into us. Vali and I both stagger back, and she loses her grip on me. I fall to my knees in front of Pod, who gapes at me like I grew two heads.

"Where the hell did you go, Denny? You disappeared, and now you're back!" He grabs my shoulders and shakes me a little, like that might make me vanish again, then hauls me to my feet.

"Ugh! You knocked me down hard!" I glance over to Vali, but she's not there.

No, wait. There's something there where I know she should be. A shimmer, almost imperceptible, in the spot where I last saw Vali as I went sprawling. I reach out a hand and connect with something warm.

"That's my chest." I hear her voice, amused, come out of seemingly nowhere.

Sousa snorts with barely contained laughter. I jerk my hand back like it touched something hot. Vali reappears a second later, a big grin on her face.

"Not the first time that's happened," she confesses, then looks up at Pod from her seat on the floor near me. "You okay?"

"I am extremely confused." He sinks down on the couch and takes a couple of deep breaths, his face pale.

"It's a talent I discovered last year that I have, along with a few other interesting things I never knew I could do." Vali shrugs like this is just another day in her life. "I used to use it when I did graffiti so I could throw pieces out in public without getting caught. Only I didn't know that's what I was doing. I just thought I was extremely lucky."

"We've all got different talents like that here," Sousa says, and Karsten nods in agreement. "Look, we don't share this with just anyone, so I hope we can trust you to keep it to yourself."

He sits across from Pod and reclines back, his arms crossed on his chest. To me, it looks like he's waiting for the other shoe to drop, for Pod to reject what he's been shown and storm out or argue or something else equally drastic.

"Shiiiiiit." Pod breathes out the word in one long string. He looks at me, then at Vali, then back to me again. "If it wasn't you, Myers. If it wasn't you bringing all this to me, I wouldn't have believed a word of it. Still don't know if I fully do, but I'm trying to get my mind around it. I mean, you tell me your girlfriend's a muse, and I can rationalize that to some degree. We're creative people; we're always looking for muses. Joolie going off the deep end to steal yours? It sounds totally reasonable because that's what Joolie does.

"But disappearing right in front of me? And I can touch you, but you're fucking invisible? Naw, that's harder to explain, to understand." He gulps the rest of his beer, gripping the beer bottle so hard I'm afraid it'll shatter.

"I know. It all feels unreal. I wouldn't blame you if you didn't believe any of this and left in a huff, never to speak to me again, but I hope you won't." I sit down next to him and take the beer bottle from his hands. "There's so many amazing things I've learned about since I fell in with these remarkable people and sometimes it's overwhelming, but I've never been happier here. And I think that Joolie is a threat to the one who makes me the happiest. If you can't help me look for her, I understand. But I really could use your help."

I've got tears in my eyes, again. Loving people hurts more than being alone. There are so many more opportunities to lose what you love.

We sit there, wordless, while we let him think. Karsten comes to sit next to me, a comforting presence in this uncertainty.

Finally, Pod speaks up.

"If I say yes, will you—Vali? Will you show me how you did that?"

"If you help us, I'll even do it to you!" She grins at his astonished reaction. "You wanna know how it works, right? Or at least see it from the inside because even I don't quite understand how it works."

CHAPTER 23
HEMLOCKE SPRINGS - SEVER THE BLIGHT

It takes us a while to figure out the plan. First, Vali spends a little time demonstrating to Pod the ins and outs of making people invisible. Watching his face light up after she makes him disappear and reappear is the only thing good about this day.

Well, that's not fair. The market was amazing until Peri vanished. But it's all sucked since.

He gets a little less enchanted when he realizes that Vali can only make people invisible if she's touching them.

"I'm still learning, you see. When I started doing this, I couldn't extend it to anyone. I didn't even know that I could move around and maintain this magic at first. I've been practicing, but it takes a lot of effort. I'm sorry that I can't do more yet."

"You've got nothing to apologize for," Karsten tells her. "You've worked hard on this skill, one that none of the rest of us have to this degree. We are lucky to have this option at all!"

Vali's smile expresses all the thanks for their support that she can't say aloud.

"It must be something to live with these kinds of abilities." Pod sounds a little envious about it. There's a wistfulness in the way he's watching Vali while she demonstrates how she can make objects she's holding blink out of sight.

Vali must sense it too because she asks me, "Hey Denny, do you have that tin of ointment on you? I think it's time we give Pod a gift."

It's starting to get dark by the time we decide we're ready to attempt our sneaky entry into the Compound. Sousa volunteers to drive us over in his van, pointing out that if by some miracle we do find Peri, we can get her out of there fast. Karsten comes along for extra support, too.

The plan is for Pod to go inside the Compound like nothing's happening, as casually as possible. Vali will keep in contact with me as we follow him in. We'll play it by ear from there, depending on if Joolie and the rest of the remaining Ants are around, but we're going to do our best to see if we can find Peri or any potential clues pointing to Joolie's involvement in her disappearance.

There's a moment during the short drive over to the Compound when I doubt myself and question this course of action. Maybe we're overreacting? What if Peri just ran off, and we're assuming that Joolie's to blame? Why aren't we calling, I dunno, the police or something instead of sneaking into my former residence?

I must be showing my inner thoughts on my face because Karsten gently shakes me out of it by putting one thick hand on my shoulder.

"Trust yourself and your feelings, Denny. Don't talk yourself into uncertainty. We know something is wrong with the people in that house, and the chances are very strong that Peri is there, possibly against her will. We'll know more soon."

"You can't get cold feet now, Myers. You've already blown up everything I know as true with the stuff you've told me and what your friend here can do." Pod gestures to Vali in the front seat next to Sousa. "If I can buy into all of this, you'd better be able to stick with us."

I can't help but laugh at the way he says it, despite my nerves tying my guts up in knots. "Okay, you're right. Both of you are. I guess my brain just decided to rebel. And I'll just say it: I'm scared. But I'm good at people not paying attention to me, so I'll try and pretend that it's a normal thing we're doing here." I rumple my short hair nervously, and Karsten gives me a reassuring pat.

"You can do this." In an interesting twist for me, I believe them.

"Let's go before any of us get cold feet." Vali gestures to me and Pod, and we follow her out of the van.

She stretches out her hand to me, and I take it and hope my palms aren't too sweaty. She closes her eyes and does the mumbling thing for a minute, and I find myself standing there wondering when it's going to happen. Then I see Pod's face and I know that it worked.

"Freaky deaky, I swear. Hope I won't trip over you two," he says, shaking his head.

"I'll try to be careful," I say, and his eyes widen and eyebrows shoot up.

"*Wow,* that's weird. Your voice is coming out of nowhere." He shakes his head again. I can totally sympathize. Encountering this kind of magic really throws you for a loop.

There's a lot of traffic on the streets, but the sidewalks are empty. We look up at the side of the house from where the van's parked, checking for lights in the upstairs levels or signs of the occupants.

"I don't see anything that would tell me that someone's home." Pod explains for Vali's benefit, "Don't be surprised that the downstairs lights are on. They always are. Doesn't mean anyone's here."

But when Pod opens the door, the lights are not on, and that immediately puts me on my guard. He walks in and fumbles for the switch that turns on the overheads, and Vali and I try to stick close but not too close to him.

I have to stop myself from gasping when the lights reveal the state of the room. Saying that it looks like a brawl happened here is seriously downplaying the destruction and mess all around us. There's broken furniture, smashed dishes, and torn-up papers everywhere. A series of trashed canvases are scattered around the back of the room, near the elevated part where Joolie paints. Wine is spilled over everything, and splattered up the walls.

Vali squeezes my hand, and I'm immensely grateful for that reminder that I'm not alone in this.

"It wasn't this bad last I saw it," Pod mutters, then adds for our benefit, "The canvases, that's been building up. And some things got smashed when the fight with Raúl happened."

"Maybe you should look around upstairs?" I try to speak as quietly as possible. "Vali and I can look around here for clues about what's been happening."

"No, I don't wanna leave you two here alone. Let's check this out, then we can go upstairs together."

He takes matters into his own hands by crossing the room to the raised workspace, kicking aside debris as he goes. I want to caution him about the noise he's making, but I'm afraid to speak loudly, just in case we're not alone.

"Fuck," I hear Vali mutter behind me, and I silently agree.

"See anything that stands out?"

"No, this just looks like a rumble went down in here. Maybe we should look at the canvases."

We weave our way carefully over to where the biggest pile of smashed-up wood and canvas is and start to examine the ones that aren't completely destroyed.

"I'm getting weird feelings from these," Vali says, then she shudders. "Ugh, that's a creepy sensation!" She points to a piece of fabric that's been ripped away from the wood supports and is curled up against the wall. "Wanna flip that over and see what's on the other side?"

She's got my right hand in her left, so we have to work together to turn and smooth out the canvas. I glance over at her and notice that her nose and forehead are wrinkled up like it's painful, or at least unpleasant, for her to touch the painting. I don't feel anything—no, wait. There's the barest tingle when I touch the fabric, like my fingertips are starting to fall asleep. Once I notice it, I can't ignore it.

It doesn't matter once I see what's painted on the other side, though. Because I want to throw up when I see it.

Part of Peri's face is cut off where the canvas was ripped away from the rest of the painting. Her head is thrown back in an expression that someone who didn't know her might have mistaken for ecstasy, but I immediately see the pain in the set of her jaw and the lines on her face. My heart starts pounding at that, but I feel like it's going to burst out of my chest when I see that she's barely clothed in the image, thick ropes cruelly binding her across her body.

It's freshly painted, barely dry. The feeling of wrongness from it is overwhelming.

Next to me, I hear Vali's sound of revulsion, and her hand tightens on mine. "We need to find her. Now."

I glance over to Pod, who's on the far side of the dais, pawing through the debris. His expression darkens, and when he stands up, there's a crumpled grey towel in his hand, stained dark in places. He gestures in our general direction for us to come over.

"What is it, Pod?" I ask once we're close enough.

"Is this—tell me this is paint, Denny."

He holds out the cloth in front of him, and I reluctantly take it to inspect it. I drop it in a panic when I realize it's still damp.

"Oh shit, that's blood." Vali's voice comes from far away, even though she's right next to me. I feel everything closing in on me, and a buzzing starts in my ears. "Denny? Denny, stay with us! We'll find her, Denny."

I do my best not to pull away from Vali, clinging to her hand as I lurch forward and find a place to lean against the railing enclosing the platform. Vali's stroking my back with her free hand and telling me to take deep breaths. I can't see Pod from this angle, but I hear him ask what's happening, and Vali answers that I'm having a panic attack.

Slowly, I come back out of the well I've fallen into. It feels like hours, but it probably has only been a few minutes. There's another part of me that's worried that Joolie will show up while I'm uselessly panicking, and that almost sets me off again, but I manage to push it into a dark corner. One emergency at a time, right?

"We're gonna save her, Myers. Couldn't do it with Bethany, but—"

He shuts up abruptly when we hear the keys rattle at the front door.

"Quick, go upstairs! I'll distract her," he hisses at us, and I don't even think. I hold onto Vali's hand and pull her towards the staircase at a sprint. Thankfully, she's right behind me.

I hesitate once we're upstairs. We should go all the way up and hide in my old room, but I desperately want to hear the interaction between Pod and Joolie. Vali doesn't object, so she must be thinking the same.

Or she thinks I know what I'm doing, which would be a terrible mistake. I hear Pod open the refrigerator and rummage around as Joolie enters.

"What are you doing here?" The voice is sharp and demanding, and not Joolie's. Elise.

"Uh, I live here? Or did you forget?" Pod does a good job of sounding mildly annoyed.

"Hardly." Her voice drips with disdain, which isn't something I associate with Elise at all. It's bizarre.

"Funny. Anyway, what the hell happened down here? Go away for a day or two, and everything goes to shit, I swear."

The fridge door thumps shut, and I hear wine bottles rattle when it does. I wonder if everyone here's just living off of alcohol at this point.

"Joolie's too busy with her new work to worry about things like cleaning up. It's beneath her, anyway. She's inspired right now."

Wow, Elise really became a fawning acolyte, didn't she? I don't understand how that happened. Does Peri's energy affect her, too?

"Surprised she doesn't have Xan doing it," Pod says this in an offhand way. I hear a cabinet open, so he must still be playing the ruse of looking for a snack.

"There's nothing in there. And Xan's busy taking her to get more paint. She used up so much this week. She's been busy." The admiring tone in her voice makes me sick.

"Good for her." There's an awkward pause. "Hey, if you see Xan before I do, will you tell him I need to talk to him? I've got a question about something we're, um, working on."

"Fiiiine." I can practically hear her roll her eyes. "But he's busy with Joolie's project, you know. Anyway, I need to check on something."

I hear the crunch of her shoes on the debris covering the floor as she turns and walks away from Pod toward the stairs.

"Oh shit," Vali whispers. I try not to freak out as I pull her away to the back of the hallway, by the door to Joolie and Xan's space. I don't know why, but I flatten out against the wall like I'm not already invisible.

Elise is light on her feet and makes almost no noise coming up the stairs, which is unfortunate because I feel like I need something to drown out the pounding of my heart. Surely, she'll hear it.

I think at first she's going to her room, but no, she's headed right for us—right to Joolie's door. I didn't think she'd ever go in there on her own. Joolie's not the type to allow anyone in her room without her. In all the time I've lived here, I've only been inside a few times.

When Elise passes by us, I'm sure there's no way she won't catch us. I try to breathe as shallowly and quietly as possible, frozen in place. Vali is completely motionless, but I can feel her hand shaking in mine. I'm not the only one who's afraid.

Elise puts a hand on the doorknob, then hesitates for a second, turning to look around the hallway behind her curiously.

"Thought for sure he'd follow me up here," she mutters and then turns the knob and opens the door.

She moves fast, but before the door closes behind her, I get a glimpse of something that set my heart off again: the golden olive skin of a bare, curvy leg, escaping from the black bedclothes to hang over the edge of Joolie and Xan's bed.

I can't stop the squeak that escapes from my lips. My hand flies up to cover my mouth too late. Vali turns to me with panic in her eyes, and she squeezes my right hand tightly. We stand there, frozen, waiting for Elise to come back and search for whatever made the sound, but she must have been too focused to hear it, thankfully.

Before I can figure out what to do next, I hear Peri's sleepy voice through the door.

"I need to go to the bathroom. Where were you?"

"Hush. I can't watch you all the time; that's why you're chained to the bed. Can't trust you to just stay here where you belong."

We hear the rattle of metal, which I guess is the chain that Elise referenced. I want to cry.

"Get up. Go take care of yourself. Oh my god, just stand up, will you?" There's a fumbling noise, a thump, and then sounds I can't identify. "I'm not going to help you. Joolie told me not to touch you again."

"Don't you want to? I know you do." Peri's words are slurred, but the seductive tone is impossible to miss. "I could—it could be you instead of her. Everyone would come to see you dance."

For a minute there are no sounds at all from behind the door.

"You need to shut up." I can hear it in Elise's voice; she's either crying or close to. "I'm not important. Not like Joolie. You're supposed to be for her."

"You're important too. I can show you. I can show the world." A pause. "But I can't from here."

"Ahhh!" Elise's shout is full of anguish. "Go! Go do what you need to do, leave me alone! Hurry up before I change my mind and leave you to piss the bed!"

There's a slamming noise, and I have no idea what's happening. I'm ready to bust through the door and get her when the sound of pounding footsteps on the stair treads echoes through the hallway.

It's Joolie and Xan.

They breeze by us without even suspecting we're hiding right next to them. At this point, I'm about ready to have a coronary. I don't know how much more I can take.

Joolie throws open the door, and Xan trails behind, his arms full of bags from the art supply store. It's open a bit longer this time, but I can't see Peri.

"What's this?" Joolie's so shrill that it echoes in the hallway. "Why is my treasured muse on the *floor,* Elise?" She disappears from view, presumably to help Peri up.

I hear Elise start to stammer out an answer. There's a slapping sound, then another, then silence.

Xan comes to close the door, and the last thing I see is the look on his face.

Haunted. Trapped. Scared.

Vali looks over to me and mouths, "We need to go." Her eyes are huge. I shake my head, but I slowly start backing up anyway. I'm not taking my eyes off of that door until we're at the stairs—both because I don't want to leave Peri, and to make sure that we're not discovered.

Somehow, we manage to get back downstairs without making a sound. Getting out is going to be a little trickier.

Pod's still in the kitchen space, hunched over with his elbows on the counter and his head in his hands. I can't see his face, but the posture is one of someone who is utterly exhausted, which I feel in my bones.

We make our way over to him, carefully picking our path through the scattered debris. When we're close, Vali clears her throat just enough to let him know we're near.

"Pod, we need to go," she says and reaches out to grab his jacket. To my surprise, he jerks his shoulder, pulling away from her.

"I need to stay," he says in a flat tone. "They need me here."

"What's this bullshit?" I say, possibly louder than I need to. "Pod, what the hell is going on with you?"

"I have an idea," Vali says, her voice grim. "You won't like it."

"I don't think we have time to discuss it. Pod, you can come back, but right now, you need to go with us." I grab at him with my left hand, and that's when I realize my mistake.

He turns and pushes me away, and that throws me off-balance. I start to flail around to try and stop my momentum, but it's too late. As I stagger, then fall to the ground, my hand slips free from Vali's.

Several things happen at once.

There's a loud thump when I hit the floor and the clatter of garbage scattering.

Vali, still invisible, gasps.

As I scramble to get up, I hear movement coming from upstairs.

We need to get the hell out of here.

"You're coming with us, damn it," I hear Vali exclaim, and then I see the ludicrous spectacle of Pod being dragged across the room by invisible forces. She's strong but not fast enough, so I join in, pushing him toward the front door. Strangely, he's not fighting back. He's more dead weight than anything.

I hear feet coming down the stairs, but we make it out of the Compound before I ever see who it is. Suddenly, Vali appears, her hands locked around one of Pod's arms.

"Get him to the van, hurry!"

But as soon as the brisk autumn air hits us, Pod seems to snap out of it. Next thing I know, he's the one dragging us over to the van and pushing us inside. As the door slides shut, Sousa starts up the van and takes off.

Before he can pull away, I look up and see Joolie standing on the deck connected to her space. She's watching us with an intense stare, and although it should be impossible from where I am in the middle of the van, I feel like she's looking directly at me.

CHAPTER 24
ECHOBERYL – SWAMP KING

"Oh man, my head hurts bad." Pod groans as he bends to cradle it in his hands.

"What happened in there? We were starting to get worried." Sousa's got a nervous edge to his voice, though he manages to keep his face neutral. I can't tell if that's because he's busy driving or if he's trying to downplay his emotions. I suspect it's the latter, because Vali seems like the type who doesn't want anyone thinking she can't handle herself.

"Oh, nothing, just some of the creepiest shit I've ever seen going down and the people perpetrating it showing up halfway through our search." Vali looks like she wants to jump out of the van and run back to confront them all.

I haven't said anything since we took off. I don't know what to say. I can barely get my mind around what we saw and heard. I don't even realize I'm shaking until I feel Karsten pull me close to comfort me.

In another time, that small act of kindness would have broken the dam and I would have been sobbing into their shirt. But now? I can't feel anything, and my eyes stay dry. I can't even stay focused on the conversation happening around me or Vali telling Sousa what went down. I just stare at the back of Sousa's head numbly.

I'm so out of it that I don't even notice when we get back to The Maithe or when Sousa and Karsten herd the three of us up to the library. I finally start to come back to reality when Karsten presses a mug of coffee into my hands, and I absentmindedly drink half of it in one gulp.

"Is that helping?" They hover over me protectively while I silently slide down onto the couch. "I'm worried about you, Denny."

"Give them time," Vali says from somewhere behind me. "It was awful. Horrible."

"We need to rescue her." I hear my voice like it's coming from outside of my body, flat and emotionless.

"We do." Vali doesn't sound confident.

"I-I don't understand what happened," Pod says shakily. I turn to look at him; the first time I've really focused on anything since we left the Compound. He's wide-eyed, sweaty, and fidgety.

"She got to you, somehow." Again, my voice sounds lifeless, alien.

"I'm afraid it wasn't Joolie," Vali says. She comes around the couch and takes a seat on the floor in front of me and Pod. "I think it's worse than that."

"What could be worse?" I'm not sure I want the answer.

"You aren't going to like it, but hear us out." Sousa sighs deeply, like he's considering his next words carefully. "I'm not an expert in how her kind works, you understand, but after listening to Vali's explanation of what happened, I think that it's actually Peri who caused it." He comes over and crouches in front of me, his face full of concern. "Not on purpose, you understand? But I suspect that what's happened to her has sort of short-circuited her, for lack of a better description."

"It's like she's broadcasting on high volume," Vali adds with a frown. "I think what Joolie's done to her is making it so that instead of connecting with one person, like you, Peri's abilities are just casting out to anyone in the vicinity. Which is why when your unpleasant housemate that showed up first—"

"Elise."

"Yeah, Elise. That's why she's being extra hostile and protective, and why Pod was basically mesmerized. I think it's filtering through Joolie's control of Peri. And after looking over the rejected painting from that maniac, I'm pretty sure I know how she's holding her beyond the chains."

I watch as Vali's jaw clenches, and she looks away from me, her mouth set in a hard line.

"It's the blood. Isn't it? She was painting with Peri's blood mixed in."

Again, my voice sounds like it's coming from far away, outside of me.

Now I think I know why. There's a part of me that understood this from the moment I saw that stained and stiff towel, but the other part— the part that's sitting here interacting with everyone—didn't want to admit it. Because recognizing that Joolie could do something like that changes everything.

I've been trying to shelter myself from the sickening reality that the

Joolie I thought I knew is now something much more monstrous than I ever suspected.

I suddenly become aware that everyone is staring at me, in various stages of shocked understanding. Except Vali, who's nodding grimly because she's figured it out, too.

"It's all starting to make sense. That's why Raúl cut her." Karsten, normally one of the gentlest people here, looks like they want to hit something. "He was planning this all along, or at least something along these lines."

"Maybe. Or maybe he stumbled into the discovery. He looked just as shocked as any of us after he sliced her arm. I don't want to give him the benefit of the doubt, but it didn't feel purposeful to me." Do I truly believe this? Or is it that I want it to be true?

"You are right, we shouldn't assume anything." Karsten comes to sit next to me on the couch and pats my knee comfortingly.

I've never been one to lean on anyone for support, but the way Karsten's been by my side through this has been such a relief. I glance over at them, and when our eyes meet, I feel a sense of calm wash over me.

"So we can't just rush in to save her, as much as we want to." Sousa is adamant. "We need to have a plan because there are too many unknowns here."

"I didn't feel affected, if that means anything." Vali pulls her knees up to her chest and rests her chin on them, a thoughtful look on her face.

"Me either, though I guess my connection with Peri might change how it works on me?"

"Are you sure? Because you've seemed really off since we split from that place. I know it's been traumatic, so maybe that's what I'm seeing."

I consider her question and think about how distant I've been feeling.

"You know, maybe you're right. I thought that maybe I was just dissociating. I've felt almost like I'm outside of my body since we ran out of there. But it could be something different, caused by being in that house."

"… and close to Peri." Vali cocks her head when she adds that, like she's expecting me to argue about it.

"Sure, I guess so. I hate that idea, but you're probably right. What do I know about magic, and what happens when the people who are full of it are captured and tortured?" Just saying it aloud makes my skin crawl.

"Tortured?" I suddenly have Sousa's full attention.

"If you had seen the painting that Joolie destroyed, you would understand. She had Peri bound in that image, and she looked like she was in so much pain—"

I can't finish the sentence. All the emotions that have been holding back until now break free, flooding my senses with grief and anger. I jump up from the couch, tears blinding my eyes, and whirl on the rest of the group, who are watching me with their mouths open.

"We can't let her stay there and suffer! How can we just sit here and discuss this like she's not hurting even now? They're holding her captive! They're abusing her just so they can feel like they're fucking special!"

The volume of my voice rises with every word until, at last, I'm screaming, my hands in fists at my side. My face is burning and tight from the suppressed anger and fear finally exploding from me. My head and heart are pounding in time, inescapably loud.

I want to smash things. No, I want to smash Joolie's smug, shitty face.

I scream again, a wordless sound that echoes through the library, wrung from my bent-over body in anguish. No one comes near me. They let me rage unchecked, averting their gazes so that I can have this moment to deal with emotions I've never expressed before. Maybe they know that's what I need.

I finally crumple to the floor on my knees, tears blurring my vision. I feel a warm hand on my shoulder. Of course, it's Karsten. I let them comfort me like that for a minute, connected yet with enough distance that I don't feel too awkward because Karsten gets that about me.

But I can't stay still. I'm angry and scared, and I don't have an outlet for it. I don't know how to rescue Peri on my own, and I don't understand why the rest of them aren't rallying to get her.

"Why aren't you talking about what we can do? Why aren't we marching over there and busting her out?" My voice is raspy from all the screaming. Small and powerless, like me.

"Denny," Karsten begins, then pauses with the faintest exhalation of breath.

"Please don't tell me that you can't. Not you especially, Karsten."

"We want to do it safely, Denny." Sousa looks like he wants to cry. Another time, I might find that touching, but right now, I need anger. "We don't want them to hurt Peri in our attempt to free her. They're unpredictable—this whole situation is unpredictable. We have to be careful and not make it worse. You understand?"

"I could go back in and spy some more," Pod offers. Pretty brave of him, and more than anyone else has volunteered.

"I think that's a bad idea, you know? Considering we weren't in there that long, and we ended up having to drag you out because you were affected," Vali reminds him. His face goes from hopeful to crestfallen in an instant.

"I've gotta be of help somehow. I can't watch Joolie destroy another person on my watch."

I forgot about Bethany in my anger and fear for Peri. This wasn't the first horrible thing Joolie has done; how could I let that slip?

I need out of here. I need to get out of this house, away from all of the uncertainty for a little while, and get my head together. Right now.

"I—I have to take a walk. Clear my head." I'm met by confused and concerned stares. "I know what you're thinking. I promise I won't do anything rash. I just want some fresh air, and a break from all this heaviness so I can stop reacting and start coming up with solutions. I'm too emotional. Walking will help."

"I can come with you." Karsten starts to rise with me as I stand, but I wave them down.

"I'll be okay. I think I need to be alone for a bit. I'm not thinking clearly."

Surprisingly, no one seems to object, though it's easy to see that both Pod and Karsten don't like the idea that I'm going off on my own at night. Sousa seems to be deep in thought. Vali looks angry, but not at me. At least, I don't think it's directed at me.

"Watch your back, okay?" she says to me as I start to leave, and I nod my head with as much reassurance as I can muster, considering.

I don't know where to go. I stop at the foyer to grab my heavy, oversized black hoodie, which mysteriously is thrown across a bench rather than in my closet. I put it on, then pat the door jamb appreciatively as I open the front door. I'm glad the house is looking out for me. I'd probably catch my death of cold otherwise.

I don't get more than ten steps away from The Maithe before I realize it's raining. Fuck. I put my hood up and zip the hoodie up all the way. That seals out most of the damp chill, at least for now.

The weather matches my mood. I keep my head bent as I start walking, not really thinking about where I'm going. I'm just trying to release some of this pent-up energy and emotions. Unfortunately, walking like this gives my brain time to analyze everything.

We have to find a way to get Peri back without hurting her. The Ants, I don't care about so much.

Can't call the cops, even if I would, which I wouldn't. Joolie's rich, white, and persuasive. I have absolutely nothing to show as evidence. There's no reason law enforcement would listen to me or go check it out.

Can't break in by myself and try to set her free—I'd be outnumbered and there's no telling what might happen. Sickeningly, I can't put it past

Joolie to decide that if she can't have Peri, then no one can. I don't want to back her into that corner. She could decide to take me out and get rid of a nuisance, too, and that would be one less person to fight for Peri.

It's possible that the Fae could call in reinforcements. Don't know if that would help or hurt. There'd still be a chance that Joolie would take out Peri in her selfish desire to own her and enslave her for her powers. I mean, she's already bled her in order to imprison her.

I have to stop and let the nausea that thought induces in me pass before I can start walking again.

Holy crap, I'm almost to the waterfront already. I've walked almost a mile without even noticing, lost in my thoughts. I find myself turning left from Charles Street onto Baltimore Street, walking past restaurants and then a cluster of high rises of concrete and glass. I see my reflection, and I look disreputable at best. The buildings get shabbier once I cross Calvert Street, and there's a lot of construction happening, so I have to watch where I'm walking.

When I reach what's called "The Block," the infamous area for strip clubs and other unsavory businesses, I start to consider turning back. I don't even know why I've gone this far. There's nothing out this way for me, and my jacket is starting to get soaked through.

Instead of turning back or heading north, I make a right and wander closer to the harbor. This is probably a stupid decision. It's not the safest neighborhood, and because of the rain, there's hardly anyone on the streets. The people I've passed so far haven't given me much of a look, thankfully. It's probably because I look like I belong here, soaked through and shambling.

I pass some more boarded-up buildings, a mission, and a parking garage. It's right about then that I start to feel it: a pull, a whisper in the back of my head that tells me to go to the water.

I turn left on Water Street. It seems obvious, you know? And I follow that to the end, picking up speed as I get closer to what's calling me like I'm being towed in. A detour around a parking garage, and there's my finish line: a wide brick and concrete sidewalk, which borders a short wall made of dark grey-greenish stones. Beyond that? The Jones Falls, emerging from its underground passage to ultimately spill into the Inner Harbor. It's the waterway the city was built around, once powerful but now more subdued. And that's where I'm supposed to be.

It's not a pretty stretch of water. It starts out that way, far outside the city, where it flows past fields and rich people's houses before it enters Lake Roland, a human-made body of water surrounded by a lovely natural area popular with hikers. It passes over a dam before continuing on through the city, snaking along the Jones Falls Expressway and then next to Falls Road before it disappears into pipes that run under the city. It empties out into the harbor after it passes where I'm standing now, at the mouth of the culvert that ushers the stream back from its chthonic journey. It brings with it all the trash that's made its way into the water, which gets collected by an adorably anthropomorphic trash wheel before it can reach the harbor.

All that doesn't explain why I felt compelled to come here.

"You look lost, yet I know you are not." The voice is soft and deep, with a spoken rhythm reminiscent of waves lapping against the shore.

Aw, seriously?

I turn to my left and seated on the stone wall under a scraggly-looking tree is a Nyxen. It strikes me immediately that this is not one of my Nyxen, as much as any Elemental could be called mine. I'm not even sure how I know it because they are such amorphous beings, and even this one can't seem to settle on an appearance. It keeps shifting between long and short hair or whatever the watery substance is on its head. Otherwise, it's surprisingly stout in build, quite different from the Nyxen I know, and almost squat. It still has that blue-green-purplish hue to it, though, as much as I can through the meager shadow the tree provides.

"I don't believe we've met before?" I keep my voice light and noncommittal.

"We have not. But you have the blessings of my cousins on you, mortal, and that is rare indeed. And you look troubled." It chuckles in a low voice. "More than looking troubled, you are broadcasting it loudly. And luck is on your side, as I believe I may have insight for you."

"It's true that I don't know what to do. But I can't afford to be in the debt of someone as powerful as an Elemental, especially not now." Oh, I can't afford to disrespect it either, crap. "Your offer is much appreciated, though." Fuck it, I add a little bow at the end. Can't hurt.

The bow earns me delighted laughter from the strange Nyxen.

"Ah, you've been well tutored! Not that one such as myself stands much on ceremony. As you can see, I'm hardly fastidious." It gestures to the dark, polluted water below us. "No worries, mortal. Your bond with my cousins speaks well of you. No need to return favors for me."

It gestures me closer, then seems just as quickly to change its mind.

"I am used to staying in the shadows, but let me step to you. The reputation of my kind is not a good one, and deservedly so. But I will not harm you. I will come away from the water to prove that."

As it emerges from under the shelter of the tree's branches and few remaining leaves, the streetlight's yellow-toned glow illuminates the Nyxen's stout body, revealing all the details that were hidden before.

It's not a Nyxen at all.

It looks similar in face and colors, and how it shifts, but the resemblance ends there. Its sturdy frame is not as streamlined as the Nyxen I know, but rather bumpy and textured. It takes me a minute to realize that the bumps are actually barnacles. They cover its ankles and wrists heavily and less so across the rest of its body. Its hair is mixed with long strands of seaweed, and there are clumps of it wrapped around the creature's body as well. I catch the dark shine of a mussel shell in its hair as the not-Nyxen throws its head back and laughs heartily.

"Ah, I see that I have surprised you! You thought I was the same as my cousins, yes?"

I nod, speechless.

"That tells me that you have not had much experience with Elementals. Yet you are properly cautious and respectful. I like that. I see why my cousins have marked you."

"I—I am marked? What does that mean, exactly?"

Again, it laughs. "Not like a sign or a marking you would recognize. But there is an essence around you that signals to any of my kind that you have been favored by one of us. And being unaware of it means you do not take advantage of that favor. Though I would suggest to you that occasionally, you should." It leans closer to me and winks. I can smell the familiar tang of brackish water and a hint of something fishy. It's not unpleasant, surprisingly, because normally I would find it so.

"So, um—if you aren't a Nyxen, then what should I call you? If that's okay to ask?"

"At least one culture calls us Nereides, and that is as good a name as any. Once, we were known as beautiful, but as you can see, I reflect my home." It indicates the dirty canal behind us with a wink. "Unlike my cousins, I live here in your harbor's waters with others of my kind, and we are not as bound to each other as the Nyxen. Their bonds are by necessity, you see."

I didn't, but that was something to puzzle out later.

"So, is there a name I can call *you*? Or would you prefer I didn't? I would give you my name in exchange…" Maybe that's not the wisest offer, but I've made it this far through being polite, and I don't see any reason to change that.

It looks me up and down as if judging my worthiness, which is fair enough. For my part, I stand there trying to muster all the confidence I can, which, as we know, isn't much. After a moment, it nods thoughtfully.

"You're a trusting child, aren't you? Luckily for you, it's a charming attribute. You may call me Dorcha, which is a name I have never offered to any but my own kind before today. Perhaps that makes me a trusting child as well, now." When it smiles, its whole face creases up with the expression. It's surprisingly endearing. I probably shouldn't let down my guard, but it's making that difficult.

"I'm Denny. I'm also known as the Photographer, at least by the Nyxen I know." This gets me another full-faced smile. "I'm still new to this whole interacting with beings that are much more powerful than I am, so I hope you'll forgive me if I make mistakes."

"Points for your honesty, Denny the photographer. You are respectful and thoughtful and that counts for a lot, especially when dealing with water in any of its forms. But perhaps I should tell you what you need to know." Again, it winks at me, and all I can think of is sunlight flashing on ocean waves.

I'm not sure how to answer, so I nod encouragingly like the fool I am.

"You can see that everything that you mortals discard eventually finds its way to me and my kin. It travels through the waters of the city to come to rest in the harbor. They've put a device now at the end of this channel to collect debris, but the emotions, secrets, and everyday concerns that travel with the trash escape those sorts of traps. And my kind? We hold it all. Those are our treasures."

It moves a little closer to me and holds my gaze with an unnerving stare that makes the hair on my arms and the back of my neck raise.

"Water never forgets, Denny. And we Elementals know all the secrets the world wants to wash away."

"There's always water," I mutter, remembering the Nyxen's words, and Dorcha's face lights up.

"Yes! You understand! We are everywhere. We see it all. And there is a thing I have seen that I know will matter to you. Let me show you."

Before I can react, Dorcha reaches out a cold, damp hand and grabs my wrist. A squeal escapes my lips as it pulls me close, pressing its clammy body against mine. Darkness rushes up to surround me, and the scent of brackish water and sea-foam fills my senses.

CHAPTER 25
SWORD TONGUE – DROWNING

The water is dark and cold, and I swim freely through it, nimbly avoiding the trash that appears in my path along with random crabs and jellyfish. As I rise upwards, I see glassy halos of yellow lights grow from diffused pinpoints to soft orbs. Then my head breaks the surface, and I realize I'm seeing street lights that illuminate the piers in front of me.

Beyond the structures that jut into the harbor and define the water's edge here, there's a street and old buildings—wait, I know where I am, though I've never seen this part of town from this vantage point. When I hear a car pass by, making the distinctive rattling sound of driving over cobblestones, I know it for sure. This is Fells Point, and in front of me is the Broadway Pier, with the long, dark bulk of the City Pier building to my right.

The Broadway Pier is a wide open space with benches and lights that encourage the public to walk or sit and watch the boats or the occasional crab pass by. There are thick metal bollards along the concrete edges of the pier that one can tie a boat to, although I don't remember ever seeing one docked there besides the water taxi.

I can hear the occasional strain of music echo over the water, so the bars that make up a large portion of the businesses down here must still be open, but since there's no one using the pier space, it's probably late. Close to closing time, I'd guess.

There's a small part of me, in the back of my mind, that thinks I should be panicking. I don't swim all that well, and I don't even know how I got out here. And it's harbor water—cleaner than it used to be, but still not something I feel comfortable being exposed to full-body like this. I'm probably insulting Dorcha by thinking like this about where it lives...

Oh.

OH!

This is a memory of Dorcha's.

How? But that doesn't matter, does it? What matters is why. Why am I here?

I get my answer almost immediately. I hear a commotion headed towards the water, arguing and someone crying, loud footsteps echoing off the old brick buildings. When the first person lurches into view, stumbling from either drunkenness or poor footing on the cobblestones, I realize that I recognize her. It's Bethany, Pod's girlfriend, who died.

Immediately, a chill runs up my back that has nothing to do with how long I've been in the water. Oh shit, this can't be that night.

But of course, there's Joolie following her, chasing her down while saying something that makes Bethany stop in her tracks and whirl around to face her angrily.

I move silently through the water, getting closer so I can hear what they're saying. I can see their faces clearly now: Bethany's, tear-stained and red; Joolie's, calm and almost emotionless. I know that's a ruse, though. I see that one of her hands is clenched into a fist.

From this distance and with the refraction from the water assisting, I can hear their voices clearly. I wish I couldn't.

"He doesn't love you, you know. Not like he loves us. He won't let you come between us. The Ants have so much to accomplish, Bethany. He'll come to hate you if you hold him back. And I know how much that'll hurt." Joolie delivers this statement as if it's the most compelling argument in the world. Like she's telling Bethany this to save her or something.

"We're gonna be engaged, you idiot. He bought me a ring. Doesn't know that I know, but I saw it. Why'd he plan to marry me if he thinks I'll hold him back?" She slurs her words a little, and I cringe at that. Just like Joolie to get her wasted and vulnerable, then try to convince her that she isn't wanted.

"You keep saying that, but why do you think that he sent you off to have dinner with me?" Joolie's smile is poisonous. She pauses for effect before adding, "Of course, he doesn't want to hurt your feelings."

"You-you're telling me he asked you to tell me that he's d-dumping me? He'd never do that. He wouldn't." I can see her bottom lip quivering as she tries to deny the bullshit that Joolie is feeding her, but it's obvious that drunken Bethany is buying it.

I want to jump out of the water, force myself between them, and tell her that Joolie is lying and that she should go get Pod and run far away. But it's a memory. I can't do anything but helplessly watch this unfold.

"It's not like I want to be the bearer of bad news, you understand? I like you, Bethany. You seem like a sweet girl." Oh, the condescending undertone makes me want to break things. "I want you to be happy. That's never going to happen with him. He's too dedicated to us."

"No. You're wrong. You HAVE to be wrong! He was so excited for me to get to know you; he said this was an important dinner..." She trails off at the knowing look Joolie get at her words. Finally, she whispers in a small, broken voice, "I don't believe you."

"I understand," Joolie says. "It's a pity that it has to be this way. You deserve better."

She looks around the deserted area like she's just realized that they're all alone out there.

"Hey, let's get you home, and you can figure out everything there. Pull out your phone so we can get you a rideshare."

This is the most reasonable and kind thing that Joolie's said tonight. But drunk, hurting Bethany isn't having it. I don't blame her. I would probably feel the same in her shoes.

Joolie grabs Bethany's purse, trying to help her get her phone out, and Bethany jerks it away violently. Joolie stumbles into her, and Bethany reacts by pushing her away.

I know without having to see it what's going to happen next, but I'm unable to do anything but witness it.

Joolie loses her temper and pushes Bethany back. It's honestly not that hard of a shove, but Bethany is uncoordinated in her inebriation, and she stumbles back, then slips on the damp bricks of the pier. I watch in horror as she flails in a desperate attempt to stop her backward momentum.

When her head connects with the bollard, there's a dull thump, loud enough to echo back off the City Pier building. Her body slips down the side of the protrusion, and I guess she's unbalanced and enough drunken dead weight to just slip over the edge of the pier. She disappears over the side, hitting the water with an unexpectedly small splash.

Oh shit. Oh fuck.

I'm suddenly swimming over to where Bethany disappeared—well, Dorcha is. I'm along for the ride, which is fortunate because I'm reeling from what I've seen. We're there even before Joolie comes to the edge and looks over.

I've never seen that look on her face before. She looks sick. And...

ashamed? She's crying, ruining her perfect dark liner as tears stream down her face. For a minute, I think she considers jumping in after her, but no, she just leans over the edge, looking like she's going to throw up.

She's like that for probably five minutes, just hanging there, watching the water for any signs of Bethany's body. She doesn't move until the voices of some other drunken bar patrons echo across the water and startle her into standing up. She quickly wipes off her face with a tissue she pulls from her purse, and just like that, it's like nothing ever happened. She takes a couple of deep breaths, then turns and briskly walks away. The last thing I hear is the clacking sound of her boots on the cobblestones as she crosses the street in front of the pier.

The next thing I know, there's a tilting feeling of vertigo, and I slip under the surface, disoriented. I feel my body struggling, thrashing about wildly to try and get control, and then I'm falling backwards.

I hit the bricks hard with an audible gasp. Dorcha towers over me, and for a second, I want to scrabble away from it, my heart pounding in my chest.

"Nothing has changed, child. I'm not going to hurt you," it tells me, a half-smile on its dark-water-colored face. It extends a seaweed-wrapped hand, and for a minute, I consider rejecting the help up. It snorts at my hesitation and tolerantly waits for me to finally take the assistance offered.

"You could have—you should have helped her," I finally manage to get out. I'm shaking, overwhelmed by everything I've just witnessed. I wrap my arms around myself and squeeze tightly, trying to ease my nerves and calm myself.

"It was too late, Denny," the Nereid says, shaking its head in emphasis. "The mortal would not have survived. And as much as you will not like to hear it, it is not in my nature to help. Or hinder, for that matter. I do not generally get involved in mortal matters. Others of my kind are more likely to meddle, but I have little patience for most mortal foolishness."

"But you're helping me."

"You have less foolishness than most. Or perhaps I've grown soft." It throws its head back and cackles at that. It reminds me of a seagull's raucous call. "This solves nothing for you, but I have given you information that, if you spend time to understand, may give you a breakthrough. Or not."

Dorcha shrugs, and I get the impression that if I don't figure out how this piece of the puzzle helps me, it will consider me less clever than it thinks I should be. Right now, that doesn't matter. I need to take some time to think about what I've seen and process it. And I'm exhausted. I don't think I can walk back home, not after everything that's happened.

"I have nothing more to tell you, Denny the photographer. You may find my cousins to be more helpful. After all, you are bonded with them." The Nereid looks me up and down, frowning. "You mortals are so delicate. Too far from the water taxi, too fatigued to return home by foot. You could sleep here." It gestures toward the scraggly tree and the wall it grows beside. It seems like the number one way to get killed, bitten by rats, or robbed.

"Uh, probably not the safest option."

"I could watch over you."

Yeah, like you watched Bethany drown.

"I have people who will be concerned about me. Maybe one of them will come get me." I pull out my phone and realize I don't have anyone's number but Pod's.

"Denny! We've been losing it over here; where are you?" His voice is so loud that I have to hold the phone away from my ear.

"Uh, it's a long story, and I can explain later. But can someone come get me? Please?" My voice cracks at the end. Great.

There's a rustling noise on the other end, and then Sousa's voice, thick with worry, comes through.

"Tell me where you are. I'll be right there."

I struggle to explain, but when I blurt out "canal", even though that's not the right word, he insists he knows where to go and that he'll be right there and don't move. And then I'm standing there with the phone in my hand and my head spinning.

The last thing I remember is the ground rushing up to meet me and cold hands.

"Do you think they'll wake up soon?"

"The best we can do is be patient. Denny's been through a lot. Give them time."

"There was something there, Vali. Something was standing over Denny, but it backed off and disappeared when Karsten and I got out of the van." That's Sousa, his voice rougher than usual.

I think I'm starting to snap out of it. I can feel the world coming into focus, my internal lens gradually finding the right setting until I feel comfortable enough to open my eyes.

"Mmm, my head feels funny." It takes a minute for my vision to clear. Everything seems far away, including my body. I'm stretched out on one of the library couches, like I'd just decided to take a nap here.

"Are you okay? Did you get hurt?" I look for, then find Vali. She's not crowding me, which I appreciate, but she looks like she really wants to check me over for damage. I hate that I've worried her. She's already got enough to worry about.

"I-I'm okay. I think." I slowly sit up, and a groan escapes me despite my best effort to keep it to myself. "I feel like I've been beaten up, but I promise no one hurt me."

Ugh, everything aches.

"What can we do?" Sousa looks like he'd go out and take on an entire gang of people if I told him that they were to blame. It's fierce but also strangely endearing.

"Um…something warm to drink?"

In less than two seconds, there's a piping hot mug of something in my hands, thanks to Karsten. I glance at the mug, helpfully emblazoned with "NOW WHAT?" in big white letters on black.

"That's a good question, mug." I take a swig of the beverage, which, to my surprise, turns out to be a rich broth. I let it warm me up, and I can slowly feel myself start to come back to reality.

Thankfully, no one presses me to explain anything until I've emptied my mug and Vali's refilled it. Pod kinda looks like he wants to cry, but he's being so patient with me.

I am not looking forward to sharing my story with him. Not at all.

"So…there was another Elemental."

When I tell them this, I expect the loud, incredulous, questioning reactions of the Fae in the room. I didn't count on Pod's reaction, which is flat and emotionless. But of course he has no idea about Elementals. I'm afraid that this is going to challenge his willingness to believe, though he's been remarkably accepting so far.

"Is that what I saw with you, Denny?" Sousa asks.

"It said it would watch over me until you arrived, so probably so. I mean, I was unconscious. I just passed out; no one's fault. I was so tired after what it showed me."

"Denny." Karsten leans forward, pats my arm. "Why don't you tell us what happened from the beginning?"

It's a reasonable request and what I need to get me back on track. So I explain how I managed to get to where Sousa retrieved me, through a combo of angry-walking and feeling drawn to the spot. When I describe meeting Dorcha and what it looks like, I see Pod shiver, his mouth open.

I try to recall everything it said to me, and then I recount where Dorcha pulled me close and shared the memory of what happened at the Broadway Pier. I'm trying not to focus on Pod's reactions too much, just so I can get the tale out without breaking down, but I can see him out of the corner of my eye. It's not pretty.

The part of the story where Joolie and Bethany fight is one of the most difficult things I've ever had to share with someone. But it's like I can't stop myself. It's just spilling out, every uncensored and unpleasant detail. When I describe how Bethany flew back, striking her head, there's a throaty, heart-wrenching gasp from Pod that makes me halt.

"Don't you dare stop," he demands. "I need to know how it ends." He fiercely wipes tears from his face with the back of one fist.

I want to reach out and somehow comfort him, but I have to be the one to tell him this heartbreaking tale. I hate that it has to be me.

When I describe Joolie's reaction when she realizes what she's done and how she leaves the scene, the room's absolutely quiet.

Finally, Pod breaks the silence.

"No one helped."

"I asked Dorcha why it didn't help Bethany. It told me that it was too late. Nothing would have saved her." I don't include the part where it added that it's generally not inclined to help. I don't think that will do any good in this situation.

"If an Elemental says that she couldn't be saved, I'd believe them," Karsten tries to reassure him. "Everything that could have gone wrong in that situation did. There was nothing to be done."

"She didn't even report it. She just walked away and went on with her life!" Pod's voice increases in volume, and his hands clench at his sides. He stands up, propelled by his anger and hurt, and I don't know what he's going to do next. He looks like he's ready to march over to the Compound and beat Joolie to a pulp.

Just as quickly, he slumps to the ground, burying his face in his hands as he sobs. I do the only thing I can think to do: I slide off the couch and crawl over to him, and pull him over so that his head is in my lap. I let him cry with great shuddering sobs, stroking through his golden curls until he's finally exhausted himself.

We're all left staring at each other awkwardly while Pod lets his grief out. Once he's calmed down some, Vali takes a napkin from one of the tables where food is usually served and wets it down with water from a crystal pitcher.

She hands it to me, and I pat Pod's shoulder gently and give it to him once he sits up and registers what I'm offering. After he's pressed it to his face a few times and seems to have finally calmed down for the moment, he looks at each of us with big, sad eyes.

"So, what do we do now?"

My brave friend.

I would never say that to him because it would make him mad. Because what choice does he have, right? Except that the love of his life died, and he's this strong, and me? Mine is being held captive, and my response is to run away and walk in the rain.

I need to be at least as resolute as Pod.

"Dorcha said something right before I passed out. 'You may find my cousins to be more helpful. After all, you are bonded with them.' I was too exhausted to pay it much mind, but maybe it had a point."

"Cousins? Bonded?" Pod's rightfully confused.

"It's a long story that I'll make sure to tell you in full later, but this wasn't my first time meeting an Elemental. I've recently connected with some that live in Mount Vernon Park. They're water Elementals, but different from Dorcha, hence the 'cousins' label. They call themselves Nyxen." I remember our last meeting with them and what they told us, and suddenly, I feel a glimmer of hope.

"When they took away Raúl's paintings of Peri, they said that they would help us. Well, they specifically said they wouldn't hesitate the next time they were called, so that's not quite the same. But I think they'd help if I asked."

"I worry about you putting yourself into their debt, Denny," Sousa says, frowning. "You saw how they reacted when you offered to do that before. Making that kind of bargain with any of us is tricky at best, and with beings that powerful? It could be disastrous. They might not even mean for it to be, but rarely do those kinds of oaths go well."

His warning deflates me a little because I know he's right. I'm messing with powerful beings that I don't understand. But I don't think we have much of a choice.

"Dorcha specifically used the word 'bonded', and that caught my attention. They've shown up for me unbidden and even invited me to meet them. I've tried not to ask for much and made it clear that I'd rather not go that route. All I can do is put it at their feet and see if they'll pick it up."

The frown hasn't left Sousa's face. If anything, he's even more concerned.

"Bonded is definitely a curious choice of words. You didn't promise anything to the Nyxen?"

I think back through my encounters with them.

"No, not that I can remember. I've tried to be honest and transparent when I've spoken with them. From the first, though, they've said they feel a connection with me. And that I should call them if I need assistance." I don't know what else to add. How do I justify being found worthy by some water Elementals, even though they've insisted that I am from the beginning?

"Sometimes, these powerful beings just see to the heart of who we are, Denny," Vali tells me. "But here's something else: you named them as your friends. That's a pledge that they'll take seriously. Friends help each other."

"Dorcha told me that I don't take advantage of the Nyxen's favor enough." I remember back to the conversation with the Nereid and all the stress it put on bonds. "It seemed to imply that connections like that are important to the Nyxen, though not as much to the Nereid. Nereids?"

"Nereides might be the proper plural? I admit that I know little of water Elementals, but from what you've described, this differentiation makes sense." Karsten sweeps back some of their snake-like hair before continuing. "You told us that the Nyxen seemed to flow together, joining, then reforming into individuals. Perhaps that is the bond that Dorcha referred to?"

"Hopefully, they understand I don't want to be absorbed." I'm joking. A little. "But that makes sense, Karsten. Dorcha was very clear that Nereides don't function like that. They are individuals and operate in that way. More like us, I guess. I dunno." I'm starting to feel overwhelmed by everything that's happened today.

"You look done." Sousa's never been more right. "We've all had a really long and stressful day. Nothing is going to be solved now, at this late hour. You must be exhausted. You too, Pod."

Pod nods, subdued. I can't begin to imagine how he's feeling. I know how scared and angry I am about Peri's situation. But as unhinged as it all is and how traumatic it must be for Peri, at least I'm not worried about Joolie killing her. She's not worth anything to Joolie if she's broken or dead.

At least that's what I'm telling myself so that I can keep calm while we figure out what to do to get her back.

"You should stay here," Sousa tells Pod. I'm grateful that he's offering it. I don't think The Maithe would let Pod run off half-cocked or hurt himself. I'm not sure how exactly it would stop him, but that's none of my business.

"I appreciate that, man. I don't know where I'd go otherwise." His eyes look haunted.

"I'll get you set up." Vali gestures for him to follow her. I hear her explaining to him to meet back here in the morning as they leave, her voice echoing in the stairwell as they walk to the next floor up.

"You need to eat, Denny."

I wave away Karsten's concerns with one hand. "I'm too upset and tired to eat. I'll make up for it tomorrow, I promise."

"You know how I said that promises to the Fae are a big deal, right?" Sousa winks at me, and at that moment, I'm more grateful than he'll ever know for his weak attempt to lift the mood.

CHAPTER 26
ZANIAS – UNSAID

It isn't difficult to live up to my promise to Karsten. I wake up absolutely famished, my stomach growling at me angrily. I guess that's because I'm getting used to regular mealtimes. The food here does make eating much more enticing.

I feel like something that got scraped off the sidewalk on Baltimore Street and brought home to stand in for the regularly scheduled Denny. I should have taken a shower before I fell asleep last night, but the need to sleep was too overpowering. At least I took off the clothes I'd been wearing.

I pick up the hoodie I tossed on the floor last night and cringe. It's stiff and crispy on the front, and it smells weird. I guess it's seawater? And seaweed, because there's a piece of it wrapped around one sleeve. Gross. It must have happened when Dorcha pulled me close and dragged me into that memory.

Thinking back on that, I shudder a little. It's a little easier to stomach in the bright light of daytime, but so much could have gone wrong. And what it showed me...

Okay. I need to focus on practical things for a bit. That way, I'll be ready for the unpredictably magical parts of my day.

My new life among the uncanny residents of The Maithe hasn't stopped being strange to me yet. I wonder when I'll just take it all for granted?

I'm half on edge the whole time I shower, waiting for the Nyxen to show up. I have a feeling I'll be like that for a while, looking over my shoulder every time I'm in the bathroom. I get through the whole morning routine without a visit, thankfully.

I dress for comfort today—baggy brown corduroy pants that roll at the ankles, a black tee under a darker brown loose cardigan. Everything's oversized, which makes me feel safer. Black socks and my short scuffed combat boots complete the look, such as it is. I rumple my hair and decide that's good enough for how I feel.

The library's deserted. There's almost always someone else here, so I'm a little surprised. But there are silver domes set out on the usual table, so the house is aware that I'm awake, at least. I grin and give a thumbs-up to the otherwise empty room.

"You know how to make me feel cared for," I say out loud. I have no idea if The Maithe is paying attention, but considering how involved it's been with other things, I'll have to assume it's always tuned in. That should feel creepy, but honestly, it's sort of comforting.

I lift one of the domes and find tiny puff pastries filled with a mix of grilled vegetables and what turns out to be seitan bacon. Under another one is a platter filled with all kinds of cut fruit. I can't suppress the sigh of happiness at this spread.

I let myself fully enjoy my meal without any distractions from my phone or books. Before I'm finished, Pod quietly wanders in, looking half-awake. I wave and point him toward the table of food.

When he joins me, he's got a plate with items that must have been under the third dome because I hadn't seen the little quiches or sausage links that he's chosen. I like that there's options for different eating preferences. The house, like its occupants, is considerate.

"Hey, Denny." He's got dark circles under his eyes. I wonder how much he actually slept.

"Hey, yourself. You were comfortable last night?"

"Mmmph." He nods, his mouth full of quiche. It's the most normal thing, and for a minute, I almost forget about what's happening. Once he swallows, he adds, "Too many dreams, though. My mind kept playing over everything you told us about. Denny—"

He pauses long enough that I need to prompt him to continue.

"What is it?"

"How do you do this?" He looks like he wants to run his hand through his hair, but instead, he picks at one of the quiches on his plate nervously.

"I, um. I don't know, really. I just watch all the magic unfold all around me, and there's this part of me on the inside that marvels and maybe screams, depending, but on the outside? It's still in observer mode, I guess. Like always."

He takes a long sip of coffee and gets a faraway look. Then he puts his mug down and focuses on me with a more intense stare than I'm used to from him.

"You aren't really like that anymore, though. The Denny I've known would never have done any of the things that happened yesterday. You take action these days. You aren't waiting for other people to make decisions for you anymore.

"I think I like this version of Denny. You're afraid sometimes, but you're fighting for what you love. You're so much stronger now."

I feel myself turn pink, but he's not wrong. I like this version of myself better, too.

"I didn't think I had any of this in me. But maybe I just needed the right people around who believe in me."

"You definitely weren't gonna get that before. I mean, I've always believed in you, but I let…"

I wait for him to finish, and when he doesn't, I do it for him.

"We all let Joolie call the shots. And now we know what that cost us. She was being malicious, yes, but it even got away from her in the end. And now look at her." I take a swig of my coffee while I think about what I've seen and how to talk about what feelings I have about it. "Pod, I don't think she means to be this destructive. She's like this chaotic and needy force that destroys things without understanding what she's leaving in her wake. And that's not excusing any of this. But she's messed with forces beyond her understanding now, and that's amplifying the effects of her greed and manipulations."

I hear a soft sound, the clearing of a throat, and then Vali and Karsten walk in, both much too awake for this time of day.

"Hey, didn't want to startle you," Vali tells us. "I only caught the last of what you just said, but it echoes some of the things I've been thinking about. Have you ever read Plato?"

I shake my head no, then crinkle my nose as I remember Philosophy 101 class.

"Some, in high school. Long ago. I remember more about Aristotle, truthfully."

"I spent a lot of time in the library when I was in my teens because the library was infinitely better than being at my foster family's house. I would read anything. One of the things I read was a collection of Plato's writings, and the other night I remembered something interesting. He talks about muses and madness in the text of Phaedrus."

She sits at the table with us, and Karsten trails behind, clearly interested.

"What does he say? You've got my attention," I tell her.

"Keep in mind that this is a mortal talking about magical things through his lens of understanding, so he's not going to have the whole story. But he goes on about what he calls divine madness being a gift and a noble thing. He specifically talks about the kind that brings prophecy and divine inspiration that enhances the various arts, as well as the madness of love or attraction. It's very much of its time and culture, if you know what I mean, both in language and some, um, moral choices." She grimaces uncomfortably at the thought. "But what pertains to this discussion is that he gives four examples. From Apollo comes prophetic madness, like the Oracle at Delphi. Dionysus brings ritual madness, and Aphrodite, erotic madness.

"He calls possession by the Muses the third kind of madness. He refers to 'poetic madness', but I would argue it encompasses the arts in general." She pauses and looks at me meaningfully.

"Following so far, I guess. But how does this apply? I don't feel mentally unbalanced, if that's what you're implying."

She squints at that.

"Are you *sure* you haven't felt like that at least some of the time? Denny, a lot has happened. You don't have to be in the middle of an unhinged rager like the followers of Dionysus threw to get there, you know. You've genuinely been touched by a muse, and gifts were given. That's enough to disturb things outside of the norm. I really don't like this term 'madness,' either. But that's what he used, so, you know." She's obviously uncomfortable with pushing me to examine this, but she's not willing to let the topic go.

"I'd be lying if I said it hasn't been disturbing sometimes. I've been dissociating lately when things have gotten bad, like what happened last night. But that's not directly because of Peri, it's because of everything happening around her. And she didn't have anything to do with a lot of it." I can hear the defensive tone in my voice, and I cringe a little. But I'm not sure that I like what Vali is implying.

"You don't like this train of thought. But let's ride it to the station at least, okay?"

She smiles at me reassuringly, so I sigh and nod. Sure. Let's do that.

"Let's just say that having her in your life has upended it, even though that wasn't her intention, and she didn't specifically set those actions in motion. Even the Nyxen said that she's been less careful than she could have been about her engagement with others. Right?" Again, I nod, so she continues. "It happened even though she specifically sought you out and chose to give you her magical gifts. So, what do you think happens when people try to steal that from a muse? When they try to take through strength or guile, what wasn't offered?"

"You're saying what, exactly?"

"Plato says that the one untouched by divine madness won't be admitted to the temple. They can't compete with the divinely inspired and they won't get the results they crave. But what if it's worse than that? What if that person is actively punished for their hubris or suffers deeply because they aren't equipped to handle the powers they tried to steal? Attempting to use those powers without the authority to do so could damage anyone who tries, and cause hurt to those who get caught up in the muse's misdirected energy."

The four of us sit there, looking back and forth at each other, stunned.

"Well, fuck," Pod says.

"So basically, having Peri there is amplifying everything that's already wrong with Joolie." I consider what I'd been saying when Vali and Karsten had walked in. "Do you think that because they've both stirred up chaos, even if it was unwittingly, that might also play into how bad the energy is at the Compound right now?"

"If that is the case, then they are chaotic on opposite ends of the spectrum, Denny. Peri has always seemed to desire lifting others up, especially you. Whereas Joolie looked to enrich only herself." Karsten leans on their elbows thoughtfully, watching for my reaction.

"Fair enough. Joolie really did care about others a little more when we all came together, though. I feel like I should make sure to remember that. She's not always been a monster."

I hear Pod's grumble before he responds. I'm expecting him to rage, but he surprises me.

"She paid for my first gig, did you know that? It was at this space that was really hot at the time in Hampden, but they had a pay-to-play policy. I was poor enough that I didn't want to do it, even though I knew playing there would be a huge boost to my career. I could have gone to my parents, but you know how that would have gone, fucking poorly." He shrugs and runs his hand through his hair. "I didn't even ask her. She did it without telling me beforehand and even drove me to the gig. Not Xan, her."

"She never drives." I'm a little shocked at this revelation.

"Nope. And she shouldn't; she's a terrible driver! But she did that, and I'm not even sure anyone but me knew about it."

"She's the one who introduced me to the landlord for my studio space, because I complained about wanting something private and quiet. She used her parents' connections to get a good deal on the rent and paid a few months off ahead of time for me. She's always been good at using her fortunes that way, at least. But you know that we paid for it later, Pod."

He sighed deeply.

"Yeah. But like you said, later. It wasn't always like it is now. Her ambitions changed her for the worse, Denny. I don't know why. I guess she got tired of watching others succeed while she struggled to get her work noticed. Wasn't until she started roping all of us into doing shows as a collective that she got any real notoriety. Except that it wasn't great publicity."

"Her paintings were always noted as the weakest part of our exhibits," I explain to the others. "The reviews weren't flattering for her at all. Our contributions didn't suffer the same fate, which made it worse."

"I don't understand why she tried to come between you and Bethany," Vali says to Pod. "Was she that insecure?"

"She knew that I was moving away from The Ants. She was beginning to lose control of us, and she thought if I left, the others would certainly have drifted off eventually." He's looking down at the table like all the answers are hiding in the beautiful wood grain. I can only imagine how this is weighing on him.

"She became desperate." I can see how much this story is affecting Karsten. Their eyes reflect a kaleidoscope of emotions. "And she made poor choices thanks to that, and those choices have shaped who she has become."

"I wish I could reset everything. Find a way to talk to her, you know? Maybe if she'd opened up about how much she was struggling—"

"You know she would never have admitted it," Pod interrupts me.

"You're probably right. But seeing it like this, from the other side, it feels a lot more clear. I wish I knew how to fix it."

The entirety of the situation feels soul-crushing. Joolie's descent into the horrible person she's become is so evident in retrospect, but not only do I not know how I would have stopped it, it's too late to dwell on that now anyway. Joolie's an adult, and she's made her choices. Maybe she'll find a way to come back from this when all is said and done, though I don't know how she could possibly atone for what happened when she tried to break up Pod and Bethany.

Right now, I need to come up with a way to get my girlfriend out of her clutches before more harm is done to everyone left at the Compound.

I stand up from the table, determined.

"I think it's time I talk to the Nyxen."

No sooner do I say it than there's a shift of pressure in the room, a movement that coalesces from seemingly nowhere to gather as mist before me and shape into one of the Nyxen.

Just one, this time. I don't know what to make of that. And I didn't have to use the sphere to summon it, either.

"You seem surprised, friend photographer. Did you not think we would come when called? We are as good as our word." It winks at me, and I realize it must be the same one that was so supportive the last time we met.

"I'm only surprised you came so quickly, not that you're here. I believed you when you said you'd come when we need you. You've always kept your word to me."

It laughs at this, delighted.

"You grow bolder every day! Being here is good for you, Denny Myers. You will need to be bold in order to steal back your lover."

"Should I assume you've been here listening the whole time?" It laughs again, crystalline and clear, this time at me. Sure, I deserved that. "Stupid question, okay. So you know that Peri's being held captive. And that's made everyone in that house affected by her magic in really unfortunate ways."

"If you had called us when you crept unseen in those hallways, all would be over and done." Is it scolding me? I definitely feel chastised.

"I didn't know that was an option, and to be honest, I wasn't at my most clear-headed. I'll try to keep that in mind in the future."

I try to sound grateful for the suggestion, though it would have been nice if the Nyxen had just shown up rather than waiting for an invite. It must work because the Nyxen seems mollified.

"The mood in that place was not going to yield clever solutions. Yet you managed to escape before you were caught up in it, and that itself can be considered a success. Next time, you will not forget your friends the Nyxen," it tells me in a conciliatory tone.

"I rarely forget you, it's true." I'm just being honest, but that swings the Elemental back over to amusement. Thankfully.

"You encountered a cousin. And they showed you what has passed and what it witnessed." The Nyxen abruptly turns to Pod, like it's suddenly realized that we're not alone in the room. "The loss that keenly hurt this mortal, the one you have not introduced. But no matter, we know who you are."

The wide-eyed look on Pod's face plainly says that he'd rather not be perceived by this strange, flowing creature.

"Pod was one of my housemates at The Compound. And here, too, at least for now. He's the only one from that place that I trust."

The Nyxen seems to consider that, then leans forward to inspect Pod closely, its eyes darting back and forth to get every detail. I watch as Pod swallows nervously and puts his hands flat on the table like he's bracing himself against something unexpected. I'll give it to him; he's being much calmer about it than I would have expected. Things have been weird lately, sure, but not Nyxen-in-your-face weird. That's a different level of weird entirely.

"You were brave to go into that corrupted house with our photographer. You were almost swept up in the ill-cast net of muse-magic, and yet you've stayed steadfast. Nothing around you is once as it seemed, eh, mortal?" It winks at Pod saucily, and I suspect it's enjoying his discomfort a little too much. Maybe I've become too blasé about random appearances from the Nyxen, and it misses getting those reactions from me. Who knows?

"I-I can't let Joolie hurt someone else. I'm not brave. I'm determined." Pod manages to stutter out this declaration, though he's close to the edge of panic. In a weird turn of events, I suddenly see how I must look to the people currently around me. It's a relief—I'm used to being the one person in the room who isn't used to magical beings. Now, I'm not so alone.

The Nyxen's expression softens at Pod's confession, and it nods in agreement.

"That little nuisance of a mortal has caused enough hurt and trouble, both for herself and those around her. You understand that beings of my stature do not generally stoop to meddle in mortal affairs, yes? But stealing a muse and attempting to subvert her powers for personal gain, those things are unbalancing acts. They cause ripples that are far-reaching." The Nyxen pauses, then glances my way, and its mouth forms a hard line. "And she has caused pain to my friend, and that will not do."

Something about the way it's acting sets off warning bells in my head. I don't know what it is, exactly, but there's a possessive sort of change in the Nyxen's tone that gives me an uncomfortable feeling. I want to catch Karsten's eye and see if they're picking up anything concerning, but they're tightly focused on the Nyxen. I'll have to ask later.

"What should we do? I'm willing to go back and fight for Peri, but I'm afraid they'll hurt her more than they already are. Everything there was so volatile. Me marching in to claim her back could set Joolie off, and who knows what she'll do then." I try to keep the fear out of my voice and mostly succeed.

"The answer is quite simple, Denny Myers. Here is how you will fight for your muse: you will surrender."

"What?!" Pod and I say at the same time. Loudly.

The Nyxen throws its head back and laughs, its whole body shaking and shimmering in amusement at our reaction. For once, I don't find it charming. I just want this over with.

"I'm not just going to give up on Peri." I can feel myself getting angry. My jaw's clenched so tight that it hurts.

"Keep that anger about you, as long as it keeps your head clear. You must act a part for this plan to work, and the emotions needed are anger and heartbreak. I expect you will play your scenes perfectly and leave the rest to me and my kind. Do you understand?" The intensity of the Nyxen's stare is boring into me as it waits for my answer.

"I'm supposed to pretend to surrender my connection to Peri. How does that even work?"

"Does it matter if you can actually cede the connection? That mortal won't know what's possible; she'll believe it if you tell her you can do it." Karsten says this like it's obvious.

"Yes! That is exactly right, clever one. The usurper must be made to think she needs the other paintings and images made from the muse's influence and that you have them in your possession. She must believe that only when she holds these will your connection with the muse be broken." The Nyxen still has me fixed in its gaze. "You will need to convince her that she cannot do it through her willpower alone."

"I'm not a good liar. I fluster too easily, and I stumble over my words." How can I pull this off? I feel sick inside, but I know I can't back down. "It's for Peri, so I'm going to try my best and hope that's enough."

When it hears my reluctant agreement, the Nyxen finally breaks the eye contact with me and nods firmly, as if it's got everything sorted out. I feel a rush of relief like my head was just released from a vise that was squeezing tightly, and I slump back down into my chair, exhaling loudly.

That gets me concerned looks from the others at the table, but I wave their concerns off with the weak sweep of one hand.

"I'm fine, I'm fine. So, Nyxen friend, I invite Joolie to come and take some art off my hands. Then what?"

It does this little dancing move, giggling as it sways around in front of us, arms outstretched and flowing mist-hair following behind it. It looks all too pleased with itself.

"Set the meeting at our park late at night. We will ensure that no others see. Let us do the rest. We will take care of the details for you, Denny friend."

Something about the way it says that...

"Should it be a specific day?" Vali sensibly asks. I get the feeling she's not picking up any unnerving subtext. But that's reasonable; the Nyxen are consistently unnerving.

"When Denny comes, we will be there and ready. No more needs to be said."

The Nyxen leans forward then, close to me. Uncomfortably close, enough to get my heart suddenly pounding in my chest. I can feel a dampness in the air coming from its rippling body, and purple-toned blues and greens are shimmering and reflecting in my vision. It reaches out one finger and caresses my face gently, leaving a moist trail like a tear's path on my skin.

"Friendship is a kind of ownership, Denny Myers. I hope you understand that. We have a connection now for which we are both responsible and must tend carefully. We Nyxen rarely befriend any, especially beings as delicate and fragile as mortals. We will care for you. But of course, you must do the same for us.

"You may find your role in this friendship more challenging than you expected. I am sorry for that."

With those words, the Nyxen evaporates in much the same way that it had previously, leaving me confused and not at all relieved about what I've agreed to.

CHAPTER 27
SELOFAN – GIVE ME A REASON

The consensus is that I have really put my foot in it by declaring the Nyxen my friends.

Once it does its vaporizing trick, Vali stands up so violently that her chair turns over, clattering on the floor, and declares she's going to go get Sousa so we can get his insight. Once she leaves, both Karsten and Pod turn to me and start talking excitedly at the same time until I have to hold up my hands to make them stop.

"Please take mercy on my fucked up head and go one at a time? I'm at my wit's end here." My voice is sharp to cut through their chatter.

A faint blush spreads across Karsten's nose and cheeks.

"I am sorry. My manners have taken a back seat to my concern. Please, Pod, do go first." They look uncomfortably chastened. Now, I feel bad about the tone I took a moment ago.

"I'm sorry, too. I just—Denny, what did that, um, Nyxen—is that it? What did it mean? I don't like how it approached you like that. I mean, far be it for me to dictate or even understand your relationship with anyone in your new circle, but..." He sighs, clearly disturbed but not sure how to communicate it. He's probably afraid he's going to inadvertently insult someone under this roof, and I can't argue with that instinct. I'm not sure how I haven't accidentally pissed someone off yet.

"I called them friends, and I meant it, but I guess I need to learn what their ideas about friendship entail. It's not the first time I've run headlong into a commitment without fully understanding what I was agreeing to. Not that it's the same, but that's how I ended up in the Ants." I can't help the derisive tone at my own expense. Whatever happens between me and the Nyxen is my own damn fault.

"You called them friends in good faith, Denny. There is no reason to assume they did not do the same." I agree, but the problem is that Karsten doesn't sound like they fully believe what they're saying.

"They're going to help me get Peri back. That's generous, especially as it's out of character for them to act like this, as they've made clear. I'll take that as all the good faith I need."

The reality that I don't have much of a choice hangs unspoken between the three of us.

"What did it mean about ownership, though?" Pod won't leave it alone. I need him to let it go.

"The Nyxen's statement that you must care for them is open to interpretation, but in context and at face value, they want you to help them like they are helping you. While that's fair, there's no way to know what reciprocity looks like in their mind." Karsten tucks a few hair-tendrils back behind their ear. I'm starting to recognize their nervous tics at this point.

"For mortals, that usually means things like moving each other's sofas and sharing a pizza. Not some open-ended obligation in exchange for rescuing one's muse girlfriend from obsessed ex-roommates. I've got to assume that the requirement will be proportional, whatever that means."

I'm interrupted by Vali pulling Sousa into the library, his boots clomping noisily as he moves from the carpet runner of the corridor to the smooth wood floor in the study space. He frowns at the sound.

"Maybe I do need to start implementing a no-shoes policy here, damn. So what's this about a plan?"

As we relate our interaction with the Nyxen to the best of our memory, Sousa's face gets more serious. When we're finished, he lets out a long exhale.

"I warned you about making bargains with our kind, Denny. And this is even more fucked, because Elementals are well beyond my understanding. Who knows what they consider a fair trade?" He flops onto the couch with a sigh. "I'm in to help however I can. But I can't shield you from the pledges you've made. I'm sorry."

"It's okay. I'm not expecting you to."

I get up and go over to refill my coffee. I have a feeling I'm going to need it. When I come back, I sink down to sit cross-legged on the floor across from him and Vali. We sit there in silence for a bit, everyone kind of in their own semi-miserable thoughts. At first, I'm unhappy about everything too. I've made a big mess, even if it's in the name of saving Peri.

But the more I think about it, the less it bothers me. Maybe that's stupid—no, I've made mistakes and assumptions, but I've taken every step with the best of intentions. Isn't that all anyone could do?

"Hey. I need everyone to listen to me for a minute." I gesture for Pod and Karsten to come nearer. Pod takes one of the velvet armchairs, but Karsten joins me on the floor. Irrationally, this makes me feel warm and fuzzy inside and emboldens me to continue.

"Everything that's happened to me lately is because I've been open to it. Maybe that's a fault and not a positive trait, but for the longest time, I was closed off and alone, and all the magic in my life had disappeared. Then I saw Peri, and I dared to have a dream of my own again. I never thought it was attainable, but that didn't stop me from thinking about it every single day."

I pause when her face appears in my mind, her sparkling eyes and big smile making my heart ache. She's always believed in me and wanted better things for me, even when I didn't think I deserved it. I owe so much to her.

"I let myself have that dream, and the day she finally spoke to me, she confessed that she'd been pursuing me, too. She told me the thing that most people would have found ridiculous, that she was an actual, real-deal muse, risking that I'd laugh it off and leave. I was skeptical and confused, but I took a chance. And then as time went on, I took another and another, even though sometimes I was scared. I took the gig you offered, Vali. I let myself be friendly with everyone here at The Maithe. And I found myself face to face with water Elementals who flattered me and involved themselves in my, until recently, very normal and dull mortal life.

"I never rejected any of it. In fact, I've been actively accepting, more so than anyone who knew me previously might believe." I nod at Pod, who thoughtfully nods along with me.

"You're right. You're a million miles away from the Denny of just a few months ago. I like how open you are now," he confirms.

"And what I've gained is that I like the version of me that I'm becoming. Having you all in my life has changed it for the better. So what I need everyone to understand is this: I'm agreeing to whatever obligations that these new connections and friendships require. I walked into this with my eyes as open as a clueless mortal like me could manage, but I don't think even if I knew more, I'd do anything differently. It's all been worth it." I take a long sip of coffee to hide my emotions from the rest of them. Yes, I know I'm probably as transparent as a windowpane, but let me pretend, okay?

"Can't argue with that." I'm surprised by the respect in Sousa's voice. When our eyes meet, I see sadness there, though I don't fully understand why. "You're one of us now, Denny, for as long as you want to be. Whatever you decide, I'll support you."

"I can't help but think that Peri wouldn't be in this situation if it wasn't for me, so I'll do whatever it takes to get her freedom back." I lean back, throwing my head back to study the ceiling as if it's the most interesting feature in the room. "I'd march over there right now and demand her back if I didn't know that Joolie would be relentless in trying to break the connection Peri and I have. I'm convinced that at this point, she'll stop at nothing to make it happen so that she can have complete control over Peri's powers."

"It is not your fault." Karsten punctuates their denial with a fist thumping the floor. It makes a resounding thud. "Peri purposefully chose you. Neither of you could predict what would happen after. You certainly are not responsible for Joolie's terrible choices."

"What Karsten said," Vali echoes. "You are right not to go there to try and pry Joolie's hands off of her, though. What I saw at your old place chilled me to the bone. Let's do it the Nyxen's way."

"Especially as you've agreed to it. You've pledged yourself to who only knows what; don't piss them off on top of it." Sousa winks at me in an attempt to lighten the mood, but the warning's still a good one to heed.

"I hear that." I keep my voice light and add a raised eyebrow, hoping it conveys that I appreciate both his teasing and his advice. "I guess the next move is to get Joolie to Mount Vernon Park tonight. Do I—should I call her? I have no idea how this should work."

We all look back and forth between each other, unsure how to proceed. Finally, I mutter, "fuck it," and dig my phone out of my pants pocket.

My hands shake when I pull up her contact info and hover over the call button. I briefly consider texting, which I vastly prefer, but getting an answer might never happen if I go that route. With a sigh, I commit to the call and put the phone on speaker so everyone can hear.

Ring. Ring. Ring.

Voicemail.

Joolie's overly-cheery-with-an-edgy-undercurrent voice comes over the speaker, directing me not to even consider hanging up without leaving a message. I roll my eyes but nervously wait for the tone and stumble through what I need to say.

"It's Denny. I have, um, a... Fuck it, this is about Peri." Pause; take a deep breath. My voice is shaking. "Look, you win. I can't be the reason she gets hurt, you understand? I can't live with that. I don't want to walk away and let you have her, but for her sake only, I will."

More deep breaths.

"But you can't break the connection between the two of us without the art I made with her. And I have some of Raúl's, too. You need all of that. Call me back, and I'll explain."

I hit the end call button and let the hand holding my phone fall limply into my lap. I just want to collapse on the floor and sleep for a million years or until all this is over, whichever comes first.

I feel Karsten's hand rest on my shoulder, and I've never felt more glad to be surrounded by actual, dependable friends who have never flinched at supporting me.

Pod stands up abruptly, startling me out of my thoughts.

"I should go over there and tell her in person. You know she'll probably never listen to that message, or she'll put it off as bullshit. Let me tell her." He looks ready to run out the door at any minute.

"No, man, that's a really bad idea," Sousa says, and stands up too. I wonder if he's thinking he'll need to physically block him from going. Pod's got the look of a man on a mission.

"Remember how messed up you were when we snuck in?" I ask him. "You were totally under whatever spell was being caused by Peri. I can't imagine it's any better now. And what if the Nyxen's plan doesn't work for some reason? We can't lose you too." My voice breaks a little at the end as panic grips me at the thought of Joolie ensnaring my only ally from the Ants.

"I'll do it."

Everyone's attention shifts to Karsten, and they shrug as if it should be obvious.

"I've been there already. I have seen the players involved. I won't be affected by Peri's uncontrolled energy. And I can certainly handle any of Joolie's ill-advised shenanigans."

"I hate that this idea makes sense."

Karsten smiles reassuringly at me. "I certainly do not want to add to your worries. But Denny, you may rest assured that I will be able to carry out this mission and return unscathed."

"I don't doubt you in the slightest. I just don't want to put you in harm's way just to—"

"To help my friends? This is what we do here, you know. That's what friendship with the Fae means."

That gets a half-smile from me, but it fades as I take what they've said and apply it elsewhere.

"And what about Elementals? Is it the same? Is that why you've been trying to warn me, Sousa?"

He folds his arms across his chest with a big sigh.

"I truly don't know for sure, Denny. They are much more powerful than any of us and, quite honestly, terrifyingly unknowable. They *seem* reasonable when you interact with them, but I have no way to judge if what you think they're saying and what they actually mean are the same. And beings that command that kind of strength are often painfully unaware of the delicate nature of mortals." He paused and sighed again, closing his eyes with the exhale and then reopening them with a frown. "I'm not at all saying that I don't trust them. I appreciate that they seem to care for you and want to help. I just know that next to the Nyxen, we're all puny and fragile. Hopefully, they'll remember that, too."

"I'll make sure to remind them regularly." He snorts in appreciation, if not full approval, of my vow.

After Karsten leaves, I'm full of nervous energy. Pod's not much better; he's been pacing around the library so much that by now, he must know every inch of it. Finally, Sousa gets to the point where he can't take it anymore, and he groans loudly and jumps up from the couch.

"Look, man, you've gotta calm down some. Why don't I take you over to where you're stashing your stuff so we can set you up here? At least it'll pass the time, and you won't be wearing out your shoes and my floors."

"You don't want him to get started on that, man," Vali adds, laughing. "It's one of his greatest fears."

Pod looks back and forth between the both of them, then to me, as if he needs my permission or something. It's sweet, truthfully.

"You should go." I wave like I'm sweeping him out the door. "I'll be fine—well, I'll be a nervous wreck, but that means I've got that task covered, and you should take whatever distractions you can get. Besides, I'll be glad when you're officially moved in."

"Another musician is a great addition to the crew here, too," Sousa says. "Though you don't have to join in on anything you don't want to. If you decide you'd rather spend every day locked in your room, no one will argue."

That gets a grin from Pod.

"I did enough of that at the Compound. It'll be cool to live somewhere people actually like and support each other. I miss that."

"I'll keep Denny company. We'll see you when Pod's settled." Vali shoos them out, then grabs my coffee mug and gets us both a refill.

"I'm glad he's going to be with us." The realization of what I've just said hits me suddenly. "Us. Wow."

"Now that's something I'm glad to hear come out of your mouth. It's finally sinking in." She sits on the couch and gestures with my coffee that I should come join her, so I do.

"Can I ask you something? It's been in the back of my mind for a bit."

"Sure, shoot."

"Why didn't the tattoo you gave Peri work?"

Vali's in the middle of taking a long sip of coffee when I ask this, and the question causes her to sputter a little in surprise.

"That's a good question. But the answer's simple enough: I think it did work, just not in a way we might have expected. I couldn't protect her from Joolie getting her hands on her, but at the same time, we both saw that Peri's not fully under her command. She's able to fight back in some way. Otherwise, Joolie wouldn't have to chain her up, right?"

Wait a minute. The way Vali described how the design should work comes back to me, and I can't stop thinking about it.

"You said that the design would make it very unpleasant for people to interact with her against her will. Do you think that explains some of what we saw at the Compound? Like… maybe that's adding to the effect that the attempt to steal Peri's magic is already causing?"

"It could be." She drinks more coffee, obviously contemplating what I've suggested. "It's like this. I'm usually pretty detailed when it comes to setting the objective of my designs because most magic needs that specificity in order to work as intended. But every once in a while, you need to leave space for the magic to take the lead; you know what I mean? Especially when you're working with another Fae or related being because their personal magic can sometimes interfere with mine and even neutralize it if I try to be too specific."

"I'm obviously not the one to understand this, not yet anyway. But maybe it's like when I work with my toy cameras? If I attempt to control the end result too much, it never comes out as well as when I just let fate and the inherent quirks of the camera do what they will."

I catch myself running my hand through my hair, tousling it nervously. I should probably stop drinking so much coffee. I'm already full of pent-up, restless energy, and it's got nowhere to go.

"That's a pretty good analogy, actually. Sometimes you've just gotta give the magic room to do what it will." Her face changes, suddenly full of concern. "You doin' okay, Denny? Your hands are shaking."

Oh, so they are.

"I think… I think it's all finally, truly catching up to me, Vali." I stop, take a deep breath, and fidget with the buttons on my cardigan. "I'm afraid if I stop or talk about my feelings too much, the wall I've built in order to hold all this back while we do what we have to do is going to bust wide open. Then I won't be of use to anyone. After we get Peri back, then I can freak out. But the strain is getting to me." My voice cracks a little on the last couple of words, and I have to fight down the internal panic and nerves. I'm not going to give in to it until it's safe. Until Peri's safe.

"I get it." Her voice is soft and reassuring. "But I like how you said, 'When we get Peri back.' You're scared, but you're thinking positively. Look, once we take care of this, I think you should get out of the city for a week or two. Go someplace totally free of pressure or stress. I bet Lucee would loan you and Peri a room at House Mirabilis for as long as you want to get away. That's where the rest of the band stays when they're not here, and it's a charming place. There are a lot of our folks who live there that you haven't met yet. If that sounds like something you'd enjoy, I can make it happen. You deserve it."

"That sounds amazing. And strangely normal, except for all the new Fae we'd be meeting." That gets a chuckle from Vali, which somehow manages to calm me down. Laughing feels like the right antidote to all this built-up energy.

Vali spends some time telling me more about what it's like at House Mirabilis. I'm fully distracted by her description of the house and grounds when we hear the sound of the front door as it opens, echoing up the stairwell. I see Karsten's face appear in the library doorway, and my anxiety ramps right up again.

Karsten, however, understands that we're both a bundle of nerves and immediately says, "It is arranged. It was quite simple, if unpleasant."

I feel a sigh of relief escape me involuntarily. Could it really have been that easy?

"She opened the door for you? What happened?"

"The scared man—Xan, I believe? He was the one who answered my knock and was at first relieved to see me. I suppose he thought I'd come to put an end to what's happening at the Compound. When Joolie came at his summons, and I laid out our offer before her, the fear in his eyes was evident.

"Despite being swept up by the madness enveloping that house, he wants out, Denny. That is plain to see, although Joolie seems blind to it."

Karsten eases into the velvet armchair and covers their eyes with one hand. They look as exhausted as I feel. I get up and pour a glass of water from a crystal pitcher on the far table and bring it over for them. Karsten takes it with a grateful smile and drinks it in several gulps.

"Ah, that's a help. My apologies—I am resistant to the energies around that group, but even still, being near it is taxing. And Joolie is, to put it plainly, toxic to be around for long. Her greed to possess Peri's gifts is poisonous."

"What did she say when she saw you?" Vali asks.

"She was at first taken aback, and I think she feared I'd come to fight her for Peri. I could see her change from guarded to calculating as I explained why I was there. Denny, you will have to be the meekest version of yourself when you meet her tonight. She believes she has broken you, and I even implied that she might lure you back once the art of yours and Raúl's are in her hands. She thinks she has won, and all that's left is to fully claim Peri as the spoils." Their face plainly says what they think of that idea.

"I can do it. I have to." I try to sound more confident than I am. I'm not sure how successful that is.

Karsten confirms that Joolie understands to be there around midnight. They also assured Joolie I would meet her alone but to expect backup to be nearby for both safety's sake and to ensure the trade would be completely unnoticed by others.

"You can do that? I know when I met the Nyxen there, it felt like we were outside of time or something…"

Karsten is amused by my question.

"I did not reveal to Joolie how we would keep the meeting private, of course, because she should be shielded from the existence of other magical beings, if at all possible. We have many ways to keep ourselves a secret from the greater world. If the Nyxen do not arrange it, then I will do it."

"And what about Peri? How do we get her back? I know the Nyxen said to leave it to them, but I'd feel better if we had a backup plan." I try to push down the voice in the back of my head that's telling me it's all going to go wrong and that maybe we should just rush over there and bust into the Compound to steal Peri away; damn the consequences.

"If she's not returned to you—to us—tonight, Sousa and I will drive over there and beat down the door to the Compound and take her back." I've never heard this steely voice from Vali before, nor have I seen that kind of determined look. "I trust the Nyxen will do what they said they will, but if things go south, then all bets are off. Okay?"

"…Okay." I've never wanted to thank someone so much in my life. But I can tell by the way Vali's looking at me I don't need to say it.

All that's left to do before then is gather my part of the trade, and somehow find a way to pass the time until our scheduled meeting.

I copy my photos from the very first date night, which seems like a million years ago at this point, onto a new memory card. I'll have to trust that Joolie will believe these are the only copies because I'll be damned if I'm deleting the originals. I decide to print out the portrait of Peri in front of Raúl's paintings with the tentacles reaching for her. I feel like it's both a way to show what's on the memory card and also a warning, not that I think she'll be clever enough to get that.

Though I've underestimated her already, so maybe I'm wrong about this, too.

CHAPTER 28
DRAB MAJESTY – A DIALOGUE

In the nighttime city, darkness is usually something to be avoided. Nothing good happens in the dark corners or alleys of Baltimore. If there isn't something already going down, chances are there will be at some point. At least, that's how I've always understood it to be here because I have a propensity for cluelessly wandering around with my camera and not paying attention to my surroundings beyond finding subjects to shoot. So I needed to be warned, "for my own good."

The warning stuck.

Mostly.

But tonight, darkness will hopefully be on our side. There are plenty of shadowy areas in the small green spaces of Mount Vernon Park, and I plan to meet Joolie under the trees near the naiad statue's pool, the same place where the Nyxen introduced themselves to me what feels like a million years ago. Although there are antique-style iron street lamps placed along the park's perimeter, I've never felt them to be particularly illuminating. Keeping my fingers crossed that holds true this evening.

Vali suggests I dress for courage, and I'm not sure how to interpret that. I know what she means; I'm just not certain that any of the clothes in my wardrobe impart a particularly courageous feeling. It's all earth-toned and loose-fitting in the closet of Denny Myers, clothes designed to blend in rather than stand out.

Maybe that's a strength, though.

Maybe my game plan should include looking like the mild and anxiety-ridden version of myself that Joolie's expecting.

I decide to go with that, and in the end, I keep on the baggy brown corduroys and the black tee I'm already wearing. I switch the cardigan for my favorite raggedy plaid shirt, which sticks to the color palette I've got going but adds subtle blues that are hidden in the weave. I'd like to think that's my quiet nod to the Nyxen. Maybe they'll notice.

I need a bag, but the usual camera bag feels like too much—no, fuck it. You know what? If there's one thing I know for sure, Joolie would expect me to have it with me, so I'll stick to that script. I put the memory card in a small zip-up pocket on the side and the print of Peri down inside the bag next to my camera. It's going to get a little bent up, but that's the least of my problems tonight.

I lace my boots extra tightly, nervous overcompensation in hopes it'll ward off stupid mishaps. All I want is to get this over with and somehow come home with Peri by my side. Or come home and find her waiting for me in the library, eating some tasty food that The Maithe cooked up and drinking coffee from a ridiculous slogan mug.

That's not too much to ask. Is it?

I look at my reflection in the oval mirror next to the wardrobe. I don't do that often because I generally dislike what I see there, but today...well, today, I need to check and make sure I'll pass Joolie's inspection if she chooses to be suspicious.

Plain. Scruffy. Freckled. That's all normal. But do I look meek enough? Am I the same Denny she expects, or close enough to fool her? Because there's no denying—as much as I'm loath to admit it—I'm not the same person that I was before the day Peri spoke to me and changed my whole world. But is it obvious?

I guess it doesn't really matter. I'll go do this and do the best I can, and hope the Nyxen can do what they said they will. And...

And if it doesn't work, I don't know what I'll do. Jumping on Joolie and punching her until she lets Peri go is definitely not off the table. Doesn't matter that I've never hit another being in my life, nor do I want to start.

I'm not giving up until I know Peri's free.

I'm ready early, which, thanks to anxiety, is usually the case for me. But in this case, getting to the park ahead of time isn't a bad idea, so I head downstairs to see if I'm the only one.

I peek in the library on the way down and find Karsten staring out one of the windows. The way their hands are clasped behind their back gives me the impression that they're on edge, too. When I step into the room, they turn and give me a weak smile, and it hits me that they're worried about *me*.

"I'll be fine." It just pops out. I didn't mean to say it aloud.

"You will. But permit me to feel uneasy on your account, my friend. I don't like all the unknowns we are working with tonight." They sweep back a few errant strands of snake-hair restlessly.

I'm not used to seeing normally calm Karsten unsettled like this.

"I guess if you do it, that frees me up to concentrate on other things." It's a weak attempt at humor that somehow manages to land, judging by the twitch of their lips.

"That's it, Denny. Keep focused on what matters. I'll do all the worrying." Their laugh is self-deprecating, but at this point, I'll take it. "I know we are waiting for Vali, and I suppose Sousa as well. But what about Pod? Tell me you aren't bringing him with us."

"No, that would be a terrible idea. He's been incredibly quick at adapting to this new life and all the magical people in it, I'll admit. But although I think he's gotten to a calmer place when it comes to what happened between Joolie and Bethany, I don't think I'd trust him not to go at Joolie if he saw her. Especially since we have no way to predict how she's going to behave tonight." I swallow hard, thinking about the possibilities. "I need her to trust that I'm still the weak Denny she knows and expects to collapse like a house of cards if threatened. Pod can't be relied on to stick to that script, not that I blame him."

Boots on the stairs announce Sousa and Vali before they come into the library. Sousa's got a frown on his face. Vali just looks focused and determined.

"I like your friend, Denny, but I'm a little worried he won't stay put tonight. So I left him in the capable hands of Merrick and Lucee under the pretense of showing him where he can set up practice space and maybe jam together." Sousa runs a hand through his short hair, which is more tousled than spiky tonight, for a change.

"I'm glad you're both here early. I was thinking we should leave as soon as possible. Set the tone for the evening, you know?" Vali grins, standing tall in the face of the unknown.

Of course, it's easier for her to be brave. It's not her girlfriend who's being held captive and probably in danger.

Okay, okay, that was an uncharitable thought that Vali doesn't deserve. It's my nerves talking, but that doesn't excuse it. And I need to get that out of my system now because it's a weakness I wouldn't put past Joolie to use to her advantage if she gets even a whiff of it.

"You ready for this, Denny? Are you going to be okay?" Vali knocks me out of my reverie, and I immediately feel even more rueful because it's obvious she's really worried about me.

"I'll be good. I'm sorry; my brain's just been busy lecturing me about having the right mindset for this. I don't want to screw everything up." I wince at how pathetic that sounds. "Well, no doubts that I'll be able to play up weak-ass Denny of old because it's obvious they still live here in the same brain."

"Dude." The non-nonsense way Sousa says it almost gets a laugh out of me despite myself. "Look, you're always going to have access to the Denny you used to be. Key words to keep in mind here are *used to* because you've grown way past that person. I know it doesn't come easily to you to trust yourself, but we trust you. You can count on that if nothing else." He crosses his thick arms across his chest like he's defying me to contradict him.

Deep in the back of my mind, I realize he's wearing a shirt with the sleeves cut off. Have I ever seen him with a sleeved shirt?

I don't know what to say, so I nod and manage not to stare at the floor too much as I do it. From behind me, Karsten's comforting hand lands on my shoulder and gently squeezes it.

No matter what happens tonight, no matter if I succeed or fail, I have this. I've got these people who believe in me and want to help me for no other reason than they like me.

But I'll be damned if I'm going to lose against Joolie Keyes. Not when it comes to Peri.

It doesn't take long to walk to the park. Sousa follows with the van, even though we're literally just a few blocks from The Maithe. He reasons that if anything bad happens we might need transportation at hand, and he and Vali can stay in it, hidden, unless I need them. I can't argue with that.

"The park's as dark as I hoped." I keep my voice low as we carefully maneuver the few stone steps into the park, trying not to stumble in the shadows.

"Why don't we pause a moment and let your eyes adjust?" Karsten asks, just as quietly.

I do as they suggest, and after a minute or so, I adjust to the low light.

We walk the path that runs between the iron fences of the park's boundaries and the center section, and pass the big statue of George Peabody that presides over the grass and trees like a benevolent ruler.

The sidewalk slopes downward gently, and we follow it to where there's a bench and a couple of metal café tables and chairs. They're tucked into a shadowy space under the trees that run along the line of the iron fence. The pool with the naiad statue is right across from us. The fountain's been turned off for the season, but there's still water in the basin—murky and greenish, from what I can see. I wonder how the Nyxen feel about that and if the water quality affects their mood any.

"I'll be close by, but not so near that I might alarm Joolie," Karsten assures me, pointing toward another dark clump of trees further down the path. "I'll listen for any sign that you might need my help. Do not call my name, understand? If there's reason for me to interfere, I'll want the element of surprise on my side."

To my surprise, they pull me into a tight hug.

"You can do this," they whisper in my ear before letting go. I don't have time to respond, either to agree or deny it, because as soon as they move away, they disappear into the gloom.

Before I can even catch my breath, there's a weird shift in the atmosphere, something I'm learning to associate with the Nyxens' presence. I feel off-balance, so I close my eyes, trying to steady myself. When I open them, there's a large parcel wrapped in plain brown paper leaning against the bench.

Raúl's paintings.

I step to them, ignoring the hair rising on the back of my neck, and look the package over just so I can reasonably claim that I know what's up with them if Joolie questions me. Running my hands along the edges confirms that each painting must be individually wrapped inside the larger package, which is reinforced by twine tied around the whole thing. I'm not sure how the Nyxen make these things happen, but this works for me. Thinking about them sitting around a table, carefully wrapping each painting, and trying hard not to soak the paper through with their damp fingers is a good distraction from my nerves while I wait in this dark-ass park.

I don't get to be amused for long.

The sound of bickering voices floats up from the direction of Calvert Street, at the bottom of the hill that the park spans. It takes me only a moment to pick out Joolie's sharp tone and a little longer to discern Xan's quieter, deeper voice. Fuck, was that Elise, too? Did she bring the whole damn collective with her?

I try to fight the sinking feeling in my guts while I listen to their steps echo on the pavement. There's some more grumbling and a shuffling sound, and then I see their forms start to take shape as they come up the path. By the time they make it to the seven granite stairs that ascend to the fountain area, I can see them much more clearly.

Joolie's in front, as I expected. It's disturbing how glowing and robust she looks. Batshit, but physically hearty. Xan trails right behind her, looking like he'd rather be anywhere else. It's obvious they've been quarreling, though over what, I'm not sure. Compared to Joolie, he looks like a ghost of himself, thin and wan.

Elise is behind them, and she doesn't look happy either. Her hair, normally a silky curtain, hangs around her shoulders lankly, ragged. That shocks me because her hair is a source of great pride for her. But I forget all that when I spy the fourth person in the little group, the one being pulled along by her arm by Elise, feet shuffling zombie-like on the pavement.

Peri.

My stomach does a panic flip-flop, and for a minute, I'm afraid the sound of my heartbeat, pounding so loudly that it's echoing in my ears, is going to overwhelm me. So I give myself a fucking pep talk, of all things, because that's what's always worked during panic attacks.

Breathe, Denny.

(I take in a deep breath.)

You've got to calm down.

(I exhale in a slow, controlled stream.)

She needs you to keep it together for her now.

(Another deep breath. Another exhale. I feel my heartbeat slow.)

I swallow hard, choking down the fear clenching at my throat, and step out of the shadows under the sparse cover of almost-bare autumn trees so I can face Joolie and the rest of my former collective.

When Joolie sees me, I don't get the expected reaction right away. She skids to a halt mid-stride, her face changing from bitchy to alarmed in an instant. I mean, she's here to meet me; what is she expecting to find? I wasn't just going to leave the paintings on a bench and run away, but maybe she hoped it would be that easy.

It's okay, though. I'm going to give her some classic Joolie-ego-boosting moments in just a second. That should hold her for a while.

"Denny. We weren't sure you'd actually show." Her voice is light, artificially so. The grin she puts on is as well, though as I keep my posture slumped and I add a defeated look to my face, she seems to gain confidence.

"I said I'd be here. I'm no liar."

"No, you've never been good at that." She laughs breezily, and I can see her relaxing, taking up her familiar role with me. I try not to let it go to my head.

"Can we just get on with this?" Elise's normally smooth voice crackles in irritation.

I've been trying to avoid looking at the rest of them, just staying focused on Joolie. Unfortunately, the outburst from Elise makes me glance her way, and it takes just a flicker of attention to look away from her and over to Peri.

I shouldn't have looked.

She seems miserable, but she's making no move to break away from them. Elise isn't even clenching her arm anymore. She's drifted apart from Peri and is standing with her arms folded disapprovingly.

Despite the fact there's no moon out tonight and barely any light coming from the park's lamps, Peri looks illuminated in the gloom, a shining jewel that stands out from the rest of us. She's utterly beautiful in a way that's different from how I've always seen her. Before, she was soft and luscious, like velvet or rose petals—but vibrant, too, in a way that made me buzz excitedly when I was near her.

Now, she's got a tangibly sharp and glittering energy that surrounds her. It simultaneously calls and repels me and leaves me breathless. It's still exciting, but in an unhealthy way instead of the nourishing feeling I've come to associate with her.

And all that softness I love about her has been overshadowed by a wide-eyed, unfocused gaze and an unnerving blank expression.

It's like they only brought the shell of her along with them. This Peri is a dazzling, empty husk standing in the place where my vibrantly alive girlfriend should be.

My attention, thankfully, is torn away from her by Joolie's smug voice addressing me.

"—you brought the goods?"

"What?" I sound sullen, but really, I'm just covering up my shock at seeing Peri like this.

"I was asking if you brought what you promised." She's speaking to me slowly, enunciating each word like I'm too stupid to understand otherwise. Normally, this would enrage me. Today, it's a good thing. Go on, underestimate me.

"I said I would." I sigh deeply, letting my shoulders slump even more. "There's paintings here that Raúl made under Peri's influence. And my photographs from our time together are here." I point to my camera bag, then unzip the pocket and pull out the memory card.

"I have a print as well, so you can see what's on this."

It takes me a second longer to get the photo of Peri out of the main compartment of my bag, mostly because I know I'm going to feel sick when I see the image of her before everything happened. And I'm right; even though it isn't so easy to see in the darkness, her glow comes through in the photo and tugs at my heart in a way that makes me want to lose it right there.

Handing this over to Joolie feels like a desecration, even though I know rationally it's just a print. I feel a little relief when she prods Xan to come take it from me while she goes to check out the paper-wrapped paintings.

Close up, I realize how awful he looks, too. I've never seen Xan Pang, a guy who wouldn't dare step out to the corner store while less than impeccably groomed, in such a sorry state. I'm not sure when he's last showered, and I think he's got at least a five-day bed head going on. Damn.

It's obviously a reluctant gesture when he puts his hand out for me to give him my files, and before I can surrender them, he fixes me with a wide-eyed stare.

"I don't want to do this," hisses out of him between narrowed lips, like steam escaping a valve. His eyes dart back and forth after his confession. Checking to see if he's been noticed, I suppose.

I don't know what to say to him, so I nod as discreetly as possible and pass him the items, but not before he grabs my wrist with his other hand and steps closer than I'd like.

"Don't let her win, Denny."

Joolie's barking reaction breaks up our little tableaux before he can say anything more.

"Leave them alone, Xan! The only reason I even have you here with me is to carry these, so why don't you do your job?"

Wow. I'm used to her careless cruelty with Xan—the kind that comes from knowing that no matter what you do, that person will be by your side—but this is so much worse than usual. He slumps at her words and slowly walks over to her, defeated.

"Show me what she gave you."

She practically snatches the photo print from his hands, stepping toward the weak light from the park lamp in an attempt to try and make out the details.

"It's the first portrait that I took of Peri." Unbidden, my voice shakes when I say it. The gravity of what's happening is starting to get to me.

That must work in my favor because the photo immediately becomes precious to her. She smiles in delight as she greedily studies it.

"Oh, this must hurt to give up," I hear her mutter. It's not an observation born from compassion.

I turn my focus over to where Peri's standing, nearby but not next to Elise, who is obviously playing the part of lookout in this weird scene. Her head is swiveling back and forth, trying to keep watch over the park for unwanted interruptions.

Peri, on the other hand, is still in that zombie-state, her attention unfocused and her stance loose and ungainly, so very unlike her usual graceful self. It takes me a minute to realize she's wearing the outfit she put on for our trip to the farmers market—have they not even allowed her a change of clothes?

Or maybe she's too traumatized to care.

I don't like this train of thought.

Lucky me, I don't get more time to worry about that, because suddenly Joolie's up in my face.

"So now what? I have Raúl's paintings, and I've got your photos. But I don't feel like anything's changed. She's not acting any differently." She gestures impatiently at Peri, and her face frowns up like she's ready to throw a tantrum about it.

I don't have an answer for her. Now would be a great time for the Nyxen to show up, just saying.

CHAPTER 29
LYCIA – A FAILURE

"I, um—I was told that you needed all the art that was made under the influence of a muse to claim a connection not, um, freely given."

I'm stumbling over my words in my desperate attempt to convince Joolie, but I needn't have bothered. She accepts it easily, and I realize she thinks she's got me thoroughly broken at this point.

If I was the old Denny, that would be 100% indisputably true. I would have buckled well before now. Even now, I'm struggling internally to keep going with this ruse—but not because I'm weak and spineless, not anymore. It's because I'm afraid of what this loose cannon might be capable of, and I don't want her to hurt Peri any more than she has. I don't even care about what happens to me.

No, that's not true either. I do care. I want to win so I can finally have a happy life with someone who loves me and encourages me to love myself. I want something enough to fight for it because I'm worth fighting for, too.

"I bet this is killing you, isn't it?" She's too close to me, and when I try to back up, her hand shoots out and grabs me, a fistful of plaid shirt clutched by one bony fist. She pulls me near, then quickly switches to grip my scrawny arm tightly, yanking me back as I start to stumble. "But I bet if I told you that you could come back to us, you'd do it to be near her. Even though she won't want you anymore."

"I—I don't understand what happened." It comes out of my mouth unprompted, and as I say it, something *does* break in me. All the frustration and fear turn into hot tears that well up unbidden, and I don't even feel disgusted with myself like I usually would. I just want to hear it from her. I want to hear her say it out loud.

"Oh, look at you, I've made you cry. I know how much you hate that," Joolie coos, a half-smile on her lips. "You're such a disappointment to me, Denny. I did so much for you, made it so you had a home, a family, a career. Like you could have done that on your own! You've always been so wishy-washy, and you would have ended up a nobody doing kid's portraits or, at best, insipid photos for local media. A waste of all this talent."

She jerks my arm downwards, and suddenly, I'm on my knees, connecting painfully with the pavement. I can't help it—I gasp when my kneecaps hit, and that seems to fuel her cruel tirade.

"You haven't been a real part of this group for a while now, but I let it slide. Until I found out you'd found a muse, a real muse, not just some romantic bullshit relationship that artists like to slap that label onto. That idiot Raúl isn't good for much, but I have to thank him for that tidbit, I suppose. He's the one who told me who the mysterious guest at my party was. And then he told me how to keep her."

My mind flashes back to the party at The Maithe, and the flash of his knife as he attacked Peri.

"That didn't work for him. He never was able to make their connection anything like what he desired because she didn't want him." I glance over to Peri. She's still vacant, swaying back and forth slightly. "I don't know what you did to her to make her like this. But you've only captured her body. She isn't working with you, and she isn't giving you all of her. That's why you came tonight. You still don't have what she and I have."

As I'm talking, I can see Joolie get angrier, her whole body tensing up and her brows coming together. Really, any time the Nyxen would like to show up…

"You!" she explodes, leaning down to yell into my face. "I am so fucking sick of you! I've been working my whole life to be someone, to have someone notice my work, to find my way for my art and drag all you ungrateful coattail riders along with me!" She gestures widely at Xan and Elise, both of whom look like she's slapped them. "I work twice as hard as any of you, with half the results, and somehow, you are the one who ends up with an actual muse. You, a useless, spineless fool who thought it was beneath you to just shut up and do what I say for your own good!"

She's screaming at this point, her whole body shaking, and when Elise breaks away from Peri's side to come put a hand on her shoulder—I guess to try and calm her—Joolie whirls around and shoves her away. Elise stumbles back and hits the ground with an audible sound, but I don't think it's because she's been knocked on her ass.

Elise mumbles, "I was just trying to help," but Joolie's not even paying attention.

"Bring me those," she snaps in Xan's direction, and he hustles to deliver the paintings to her, shooting me an apologetic look when he hands them off.

In return, I try my best to signal with my expression that he should do something, anything. I'm sure I just look desperate.

Joolie violently rips the rest of the paper off of the paintings and throws them on the sidewalk, with no regard at all to their value, then stands menacingly over me. I can see her hands tremble, even though her fists are clenched.

"What do I do with these? Raúl didn't tell me anything about this!" I can see the desperation in her eyes. It's got her so close to the edge that any small challenge could send her spiraling over. "I painted her portrait the way he told me to do. And she came to me, she walked right in my door! I've got her, but she won't connect with me. You're the one who called me here. Obviously, you know how to fix this—tell me how to make her mine!"

"That's the problem, Joolie. You've only ever wanted to possess her. But she's not a thing to own. She's a person! You can't get from her what she's always given to me freely because you don't understand what it is to love someone without taking from them. You only want her for what she can do for you."

She steps between the paintings on the ground to grab my shoulders and shake me hard, so hard that my teeth rattle in my head, and I cry out in pain before I can stop myself. But I keep talking, the words jerked out of my mouth as she shakes me.

"Everyone in the Ants loved you at one point, and look what you did to all of us! You stopped looking at us like friends or family and instead thought about what we could do for you. And look what it got you!"

She stops me from talking by slapping me across my mouth, and the pain makes stars dance in front of my eyes. When I try to back away from her, she slaps me again, and I can feel the intensity building between us. The look in her eyes makes me honestly fear for my life.

"Release her to me."

"I can't. I don't have a hold on her, Joolie. She chose me, not the other way around."

"Bullshit! Give her to me, and maybe I won't destroy your career in this town, too."

I am suddenly so, so tired. All of Joolie's scrabbling greed to be important, to have power instead of just living to create the art that brought us all together—it's exhausting, and I don't know how she's lived with it for so long. I honestly feel sort of sorry for her, to be trapped in such a small and unimaginative world while being surrounded by people with the drive and vision to do and make what their hearts desire.

"I don't care about that, Joolie. If you truly knew me, you'd understand that. I'm sorry that I can't help you be who you want to be. But I'd never help you by using the powers of someone else. I won't help you suck her dry so you can pretend to be a success."

For a minute, I think I've actually reached her.

All the anger drains from her face, and her eyes narrow with pain. She stares intensely at me, like she's absorbing everything I've said. Then she turns to look at Peri, still standing in her zombie-like stupor. A branch moves in the light breeze that's picked up while we've been talking, and it makes the weak light from the street lamp glint in Peri's hair like tiny stars. Even in her dazed state, she's incredibly beautiful.

A small noise comes from Joolie; I can't tell if it's a sigh or a gasp, it's so quiet. She turns back my way and cocks her head as if she's assessing me.

And then she lunges at me, pushing me back so that my shoulders smash back into the pavement. I only avoid my head doing the same because of quick reflexes.

Next thing I know, she's on top of me, her hands in a tight grip on my shoulders, bashing them into the pavement repeatedly.

I sputter and flail around helplessly, trying to push her off. Her knee is on my right arm, and my left isn't as strong, but I do my best to batter at her with it while my legs kick around uselessly. I'm not a fighter, and it shows. I catch a glimpse of Xan, still standing where he'd handed her the paintings that are now strewn across the ground. He looks like he wants to be sick, but that's not helping me at all.

"Xan—" I try to call out to him, but Joolie hisses and slams me down again, and this time I'm not so quick at keeping my head from missing the concrete. All I can see are stars.

I'm in serious trouble, and my once-friends are going to stand here and watch me die.

"Joolie, this is too much!" I hear Xan's yell, but it sounds like it's far away because my ears are ringing.

I want to fight back. But everything is spinning, and I close my eyes the next time she slams me down because the pain is taking over my consciousness...

"Enough."

The words reverberate throughout the park, loud enough to make me force my eyes open to see who spoke them. Joolie's not on top of me anymore, but I still can't move.

"Get up, Denny."

Was that inside my head, or did everyone hear it? I can't make sense of anything at this point. I'm staring up at the sky, but I can't see stars. Everything's covered in clouds—wait, when did it get so foggy?

"I can't get up. I'm hurt." My voice feels weak, as if it can't penetrate the air around me.

I hear a sound, an exhalation, like someone is exasperated or barely containing their contempt. Maybe that's a bad interpretation; I have no way to know. But a moment later, I hear boots on the sidewalk rushing toward where I'm lying on the ground, and then I see Karsten's worried face appear over me.

"Let me see," they fuss and carefully cradle my head with one hand so they can check my skull with gentle fingers. "No breaks," they sigh with relief, but I see blood when they pull away their hand.

"That—that's inconvenient," I manage to get out, and Karsten sputters a little at my stupid joke while they wipe the blood on their pants.

"Let me find something to clean this off." To my surprise, Pod appears in my line of sight, hands them a bandanna, and then pulls the beanie off his head and gives them that as well.

"Why? How?" I mutter, and Pod shakes his head, his eyes wary.

"Tell you later." He indicates that I should sit up.

I don't want to move. And then when Karsten tries to help me sit up, the whole world does a tilting thing and I'm sure I'm going to throw up everywhere. It feels like it takes forever to finally get into a sitting position, but in reality, it's no time at all.

The entire park is enshrouded in thick fog, much denser than should be possible for the amount of time that's passed. I can't see beyond the trees or past the edge of the terrace where the fountain is. The sky is oppressively heavy with clouds, and everything is damp and clammy like it might rain at any moment.

Xan is kneeling not too far away from us, his arms wrapped tightly around himself. If I had to guess, I'd say he's in shock, which I guess is reasonable enough considering everything that's happened. I can't tell for sure, but I think he must have been coming to help me. I don't know what stopped him.

Peri's moving listlessly behind him. She's still wearing that heartbreakingly glazed expression. Elise isn't paying any attention to her captive. Instead, her gaze is fixed on something on the other side of me, a look of horror on her face, her body stiff and unmoving.

I slowly turn, reluctantly following her stare. What's got her so scared?

Two Nyxen have a furious and terrified Joolie encompassed in their grasp, watery arms forming rope-like appendages that hold her tightly. She's strangely quiet even as she rages against their restraint. A third Nyxen has its back to me but turns when I'm as upright as I'm going to get, like it knows I'm watching.

"Ah, our brave photographer has rejoined us at last. And look what we have caught for you!" Its face shifts from masculine to feminine, then back again, but the entirely too proud look stays regardless. Today, I'm not as enchanted by its charms.

"You pulled her from me."

It pauses, and its expression changes from pleased to confused as quickly as a shift in the weather from sunny to storm.

"You wished her to keep pummeling you? But no, we did nothing but appear, and she jumped back in horror at our arrival." It seems amused while recounting this part of the story. "Easy enough to scoop her up and hold her until you roused. We allowed your friends to come help with that."

I don't know why that makes me want to get up and challenge it, but justified or not, I can feel the ire building inside me. I feel Karsten's hands steadying me as I make an abortive attempt to stand, then sigh, defeated by my body. My frustration bursts out of me as I address the Nyxen.

"And now what? You didn't show until Joolie beat me almost senseless. Peri's still…whatever is going on with her. She's a fucking zombie, and I don't know how to undo it. My head's all busted up, so help me out here: what do we do now?" I'm almost shouting by the end, and when I stop, my head rewards me with a small explosion of pain across the back of my brain. I can't help it; I shut my eyes tight and whimper until it lessens.

When I open them back up, the Nyxen is crouching down and peering at me intently.

"You are more injured than we realized." It reaches out and strokes damp fingers across my forehead, and mercifully, the pain fully recedes. "We are not beings that heal, but that should help for now."

I carefully nod, not wanting to test the results too much.

"But what happens now? I did as you told me to do."

"Ah, Denny. You won't like what we are going to tell you." It glances over to Pod, who is still standing behind me protectively. "But that one might."

"Huh?" Pod is obviously caught off-guard by being included. "What do you mean?"

The Nyxen eases itself into I guess what would be considered a sitting position for one of their kind. Its body flows across the pavement in little streams that dissipate into the ground where they end. One slowly seeps into the sidewalk under my leg, and I can feel the moisture through my pants. I try not to let it distract me.

"I told you before that the mortal we now hold has caused power shifts and created problems that we find quite alarming. And she has hurt you, caused you physical damage. These things, we will not allow to pass unpunished." It shifts slightly toward me, and I'm again struck by the possessive nature of how it's acting. "We are not vindictive beings. But certain actions must be met with the proper responses. In this case, as you mortal beings might say, restorative justice is in order."

It looks pleased with itself, but I still don't understand.

"Please, can you explain this to me in simple terms? I'm just a mortal, currently with a broken head. Why won't I like it?"

I'm getting a bad feeling about this.

"Leave the details to us. But when we are finished, she will be ready to atone for her actions."

"You're saying that I'm not going to approve of your methods."

"As much as we treasure you, you must understand this: in this matter, your opinions carry little weight. We will follow our own path."

In my mind, I imagine a dam breaking and the water flooding everything in its path. The Nyxen's words have that same kind of energy. I'm not going to win this fight. I'm not even sure I want to, if I'm being honest. I want her to have consequences for her actions. But...

"Just don't hurt her, okay? Please? I'm not going to argue with what you decide. I mean, how can I? You're more powerful than I'll ever be. You are doing me a favor by even entertaining my opinions. But I don't think I could live with myself if I knew you were going to hurt her."

The Nyxen starts laughing at this, the kind of laugh that adults have at the expense of children who say incredibly naive but adorable things. And then it reaches out and gently pats me on the head, and then I'm sure it's patronizing me at best.

"Oh, sweet, lovely Denny. We will tell you nothing of our methods, and that way, you may sleep at night with a clear conscience. Anything that happens to that one," and it gestures dismissively at the still-struggling Joolie, "will be brought about solely by her own actions."

Obviously, the discussion about this is over because the Nyxen swells up to a standing position, gathering its watery body up into itself like a waterfall in reverse. It stands over me, staring at me in a manner that leaves me feeling uncomfortably judged.

Then, unexpectedly, it extends a hand to me. Or what I guess I'd call a hand.

I take it cautiously and I find myself being enveloped by waters from the body of the Nyxen, surrounding me and carefully raising me to my feet. It all happens too quickly for me to react, but when the Nyxen withdraws, I'm left with my mouth agape and my palms moist, and not from sweat.

"You are favored by us, Denny Myers. And it is time for you to give something in return."

Oh, here we go. Fuck. Behind me, I hear Karsten's sharp intake of breath.

"You must decide who it is that you serve." It stares at me, swirly blue-green eyes locked on mine in a challenging gaze. "You gave your talent and time to those who did not see you as anything but a commodity to be used for their own gain. Then you looked to tie your fortunes to a being that cares for you but planned to shape your destiny to their own vision. Now, you can choose for yourself. Will you yoke your talents to another force or invest in yourself?

"I hope you will repay us by choosing your freedom."

It doesn't wait for my reply. The Nyxen turns away abruptly from me, ethereal mists swirling about it like skirts in a breeze. It moves swiftly to join the other Nyxen, who have just stood there silently all this time while they held Joolie in their fluid grasp.

And before any of us even have time to react, they seem to melt into the fog surrounding us—all of them, even Joolie.

They're gone, just like that.

CHAPTER 30
CRANES – INESCAPABLE

We all stand there in stunned silence for what feels like an eternity, staring at the space where Joolie and the Nyxen had just disappeared until the unnatural quiet over the park is broken by a strangled cry.

I whirl on my heels in shock towards the source of the wail, and I'm rewarded with a microburst of pain and stars clouding my vision. It clears in time for me to see Peri sink to her knees, her head in her hands. Unexpectedly, I see Elise go to the ground next to her and put an arm around her shoulder, which Peri half-heartedly tries to shake off. I'm stumbling over myself to get to her when she lifts her head and puts out a hand to warn me off.

"Don't come near me yet! I'm broken, I'm contaminated, I can't—I can't break free of what she did to me." She's got tears rolling down her face, and all I want to do is go wipe them away and hold her, but everything about her is telling me to keep my distance, so I do.

"She's gone, Peri. What else do we need to do?" I use the gentlest voice I can muster, keeping my own worry out of it. She doesn't need that right now.

She shakes her head, obviously in distress, and this time, she does shoulder off Elise from touching her. At least she's in a mental place where she understands who not to trust. I don't even know how much she remembers from the past couple of days.

I'm trying to figure out what to do next when the last person I expect to hear from drops a question I hadn't even considered.

"You said that Raúl's paintings are important. What about the ones Joolie did?"

I turn to stare at Xan, mouth ajar.

"I didn't see any intact paintings when I was there. Did Joolie hide them? You should know if anyone does." I try to keep my contempt for him out of my tone, and I totally fail. Honestly, I don't care much.

"I don't blame you for hating me—"

"No, we're not doing this now. Where did she put the paintings? If you want my feelings about you to improve, you can start by helping us. I mean, it's the least you could fucking do."

At first, he jerks his head back like I've sucker punched him, but then he straightens up a little and nods resolutely.

"Right. You're right. I guess they're in—she started using your old room as her studio. Like, she got secretive about it after she started using the, um, the blood..." he trails off, hunching in on himself as soon as he admits aloud the fucking atrocities that Joolie did and that he witnessed.

I can't get angry right now. I can't get angry right now. I can't.

I've got to keep my shit together. For Peri.

I can get pissed later.

"I remember that," Peri says, though she sounds uncertain. "I was angry that she took me to your space. Just another way to try and claim me from you." Her face reflects what I'm sure are a thousand horrors, and again, I have to push down my fury. I look away so that she can't see my feelings, which I'm sure are written all over my face as much as hers are.

"We can go there," I tell her, my voice rough. "Let me grab Raúl's canvases, and we can get Sousa and Vali to take us. They're parked nearby, so you won't even have to walk far."

"Those paintings aren't important anymore," she says flatly, and to my surprise, kicks one of them toward Xan. "Whatever the Nyxen did to them worked. I don't feel connected to them at all."

I cautiously approach the painting, which is lying face down on the pavement, and flip it over with two fingers. The wooden frame that the canvas is stretched on hits the cement with a damp, hollow thud, and then I'm looking at something much different from what I saw displayed on Peri's wall.

All the bright colors that were once there are now faded, lifeless. I don't need to look at it through my camera to see that whatever magic was embedded into the design has fled.

"We should bring them anyway. We can't leave them here." I signal to Xan that he should pick them up, and he does, eager to ingratiate himself with me. I'm not buying it but I can use the help.

"What—what are you going to do to us?"

I turn on my heel to glare at Elise, ready to bark out something cold and disdainful. But when I see her standing there with her head bowed, meek and submissive, all my anger drains away. I'm left feeling empty and exceptionally tired of cleaning up Joolie's messes.

"It's not my place to do anything to you, and what would I do, exactly? You and Xan have a lot to atone for, but that's between you and Peri. Me, I'm done with both of you."

"I couldn't fight her. You understand? She's always had me trapped; I didn't know how to break away. But you did! You're so strong, and I didn't see it. I should have followed you."

She's wheedling, trying to flatter me in order to forgive her, and at another time, it would have worked. But not now, not after she conspired with Joolie to keep control of Peri.

"When are you going to stand up for yourself? You need to stop looking to people to follow and learn to make your own choices." I shake my head, disgusted. "That's been the problem we've all had. And Peri's the one who's paid the price. I'm done talking about this for now. Peri, let's get you to the Compound."

"I'm ready to finish this." Her face is pale and tense with pain, and my heart wants to break seeing it.

Getting to Sousa's van while she's in this broken state is a struggle. She won't let anyone touch her, not even me. I try not to let it hurt me, but it's just another kick when I'm already down. I think I understand why she doesn't want anyone close to her, but I can't help how it makes me feel.

She's moving slowly, swallowed up in her emotions, taking stiff and painful-looking small steps. We're forced to go at her pace.

When we get to the van, Vali looks at me questioningly, and whatever expression's on my face gets her to open the door silently. I let Peri climb her way to the window seat in the middle aisle before I stop everyone else.

"I'm not letting you ride with us," I say to Xan and Elise. I expect them to argue, but the objection I get comes from an unexpected place.

"Just let them in," Peri says in a dead, emotionless manner. At that moment, I hate the Ants and what they've done to her with every ounce of my being.

I move out of the way and point to the far back of the van like it's a punishment. I want them as far away from us as possible.

Pod and Karsten get in next, and before I follow, Vali grabs my arm to stop me and scans my face with concern.

"It's almost done," I tell her. "At least, I hope it is. We need to go to the Compound so we can undo what Joolie did."

She doesn't say anything, just nods like this all makes sense, and maybe to her it does. She understands painting and intentions, after all.

I expect Sousa to object to Xan and Elise's presence, but he's grimly silent for the short drive it takes to get to The Compound. I sit next to the door, Karsten between Peri and me, and I've never felt so much distance between the two of us. Peri doesn't look at anyone; instead, staring out the window in a way that obscures her face from me.

I feel like I've lost her forever.

Maybe that's for the best. I don't know anymore.

The tension in our group doesn't improve when we arrive at our destination, not that I expected it would. We all get out of the back, but Peri stops Karsten before they get any further.

"You should stay. Explain everything to them." She tilts her head in the direction of Vali and Sousa, still in the front seats of the van.

"Whatever you want, of course." Karsten frowns, and I know they'd rather come with us. "But if you need me, call out my name, and I'll be there."

"We won't be stupid. I promise." I'm lying, of course. I have no idea what's going to happen, but I might as well reassure my friend.

Even walking to the front door, Peri keeps her distance from me. I can feel the energy between us tugging at me, or at least I imagine that I can.

The house is a disaster, and our footsteps echo as we pick our way across the trashed main room. I didn't think it could feel worse than the last time I was here, but there's unspoken pain and desperate wishes crushing down on me, and I can barely stand it. How the rest of them could come back to this is beyond me. Especially Peri, who was the focus of all these desires.

She leads us up the stairs at a surprisingly breakneck pace to my old room, passing by the level where Joolie and Xan's space is with her head down, focusing on the steps. By the time we get to the bedroom door, we're all panting, out of breath—except Peri.

She pushes against the bedroom door, and it swings back violently, crashing into the wall with a loud bang. She either doesn't care or isn't hindered by the darkness of the room, because it's Xan, next in line after Peri to enter the room, who flips a light switch.

I wish he hadn't.

The room is flooded with unforgiving bright light from the overhead fixture, and it illuminates the paint-covered shambles of the room. Against the walls are stacks of canvases in various stages of being worked on, and there's an easel set up near the door to the balcony. Paint is spilled all over the once-beautiful hardwood floor, now scuffed and pigment-smeared, and there are brushes and empty, crushed tubes and cans everywhere. There's an off-putting sticky-sweet smell under the odor of solvents, paint, and spilled alcohol.

"These are so different from how she used to paint," I say to myself as I flip through some of the stacked canvases. She'd moved to a more figurative style, all centered on Peri as a central focus. We had seen this in the destroyed paintings downstairs, but in these, she'd found more success. They were some of the best things I'd seen Joolie do, with an honest quality that she'd never been able to achieve previously—mostly because she'd only approached her art with a mercenary mindset.

There was still something off about these works, though. An uneasy energy, an angle that didn't quite align, a disturbed quality that was repellent. In someone else's hands, it might have been intriguing, but the vibes in all of these paintings feel nauseating, at least to me.

"Go get everything from downstairs, every scrap of painted canvas you can find," I order Elise, and to my surprise, she turns to do so without a whisper of objection. I hear the flurry of footsteps going down the stairs, then the faint echo of her digging through the garbage covering the floor as she searches.

"There should be a key painting here, one that is the most important—"

"This one." Xan cuts me off, but I don't care because he's holding the door to my old closet open, and inside, I see the image of Peri, larger than life.

She'd put it in the back of the closet and shoved some boxes and old suitcases in front of it in a weak attempt to hide it. Why she'd need to do that in a house full of willing acolytes is beyond me, but considering how unbalanced everyone in the house had been during our last visit... Ugh. I just need this to be over.

I glance over to Peri, and she's stopped still in her tracks, a look of revulsion and panic on her face.

"I-I can't get near it. It won't let me!" She tries to move forward, and it's like she's pressed against an immovable wall. As hard as she strains, even pushing against nothing with both hands out, her feet just slip and scramble uselessly in place.

She turns to appeal to me, her eyes wide. "Denny, I can't do this alone."

"I'll do it."

When I say that, she sinks to the floor, seemingly defeated.

"I wanted to do it. I want to—I need to break this hold she's got over me. But here I am again, helpless to take back control. If I ever had control."

If it was me, I'd probably be curled into a little ball, broken and useless. And she's slumping, her face wet with tears, sure. But she's not giving up. She asked for help. She's not collapsed or withdrawn anymore. I need her to see that she's stronger than she thinks.

"We can do this together, Peri. You and me. You showed me how to believe in myself and you made me stronger. Let me be here for you now. You wanted us to save each other, so here's our chance."

I don't wait to see her reaction. For once in my life, I'm just going to do what needs to be done, even if it risks everything for me. Things between us are already different and weird because of course they are after all that Peri's been through. I don't know what will happen when we destroy this painting. It could change everything.

Xan helps me move the boxes blocking the painting without me even having to ask. I don't say anything, but I notice. He also gives me a hand at pulling it out of the closet, leaning with me to slide it bottom first because it's too tall to get past the clothing rod otherwise.

It's awkward, and we pull it into the room loudly, displacing the debris scattered everywhere, then finally letting it fall to the floor with a loud thud.

It's similar to the image Pod had described to me, what feels like ages ago—the painting at the start of everything. But Joolie must have painted over parts of it later on, changing it to be more like the version on the destroyed canvas downstairs, reinforcing her assertion of control over the muse.

Honestly, I can't look at it too closely; it's too disturbing. I can sense the despair and fear Peri must have felt radiating off of the canvas, and it's like standing too close to a toxic dump while poison seeps into my skin.

"What do I do now?"

No one in the room answers me. I don't have the Nyxen to ask. They've already done enough and I think they've made it plain that they want me to figure out the next steps on my own.

"I can't use water. But…what about fire?"

I glance at the fireplace, once one of the rare comforts of this place for me. If I cut the canvases away from their frames, I could fit them in the fireplace. I know that the big painting, the vile one, is the most important to get rid of first.

"What do you think, Peri? Can we burn them without hurting you?"

She blinks slowly. The harsh overhead light doesn't do the circles under her eyes any favors as she stares at me. I can see how this ordeal has worn away at her, and it breaks my heart. But her voice is filled with defiance.

"Burn them. At least I'll be free."

"I don't want to hurt you."

"You won't be the one doing it. You never have."

I don't know how to argue with this. I wouldn't want to be trapped like she is, either. Even though I allowed myself to be trapped in a different way.

"Please, Denny. I can't do it myself. It has to be you."

She doesn't ask the other two people in the room, but I understand why. It's beyond not trusting them, or them being her captors.

I'm the one that's connected to Peri. She's right. It has to be me.

I set the fire, pulling just enough wood to burn up two canvases. Peri says those are the only ones Joolie painted with blood, so I send Xan to put the rest of them in the shower and turn the water on them. Nyxen-style elimination, but faster. It doesn't seem to make Peri feel any worse, at least not from what I can tell. Elise finally returns with an armful of canvas pieces wadded up in her arms, looking like she must have dug through every inch of the downstairs on her hands and knees. Her hair is tangled, and there's stains on her pants and hands. I can't help but feel a little satisfaction at seeing her in this state after what she's done.

In the meantime, I get to slicing the big painting from the support frame, using an old paint-splattered box cutter that Xan finds for me.

"You can drop it over there." I point to an area near the fireplace. "Come help me with this."

Surprisingly, Elise does exactly that, with no complaints or questioning. In fact, both she and Xan have done everything I've told them to do since we got here. It's how they used to jump when Joolie ordered them around. It makes me uncomfortable, but I can see how addictive this kind of control must have been for someone like Joolie.

We struggle with the task because the box cutter isn't particularly sharp, but I manage to free the fabric from the wood and tightly roll it up into a tube shape. I then go to the other scraps of canvas, do the same with them to the best of my ability, and stuff the lot of it into the fireplace on top of some firewood. I add some paint-daubed newspaper that I scraped off of the floor. It's not elegant, but fuck that, I just want this to burn fully.

Peri watches from an enforced distance. She tried to come closer when I was fighting the big painting, but it repelled her right back with some cartoonish physics that, at a different time, might have made me laugh. Not right now, though.

"I want you to be a part of this. So here." I walk over with the box of fireplace matches and hand it to her. "Light one, and I'll do the rest."

Her hands shake as she gets one of the long matches out and strikes it across the bottom. It flares to life, and she quickly hands it to me like she's scared of it.

"No matter what, I'm here with you." I walk the flame over to the pile of wood and fabric, carefully shielding it with my hand.

Then I touch it to the papers I've stuffed under the logs and watch as they catch fire.

I don't expect much to happen right away. Fires take a little time to get going, and I've never burned fabric before, much less a painting. That's why when it bursts into a small fireball, I jerk back from a crouching position to hit the floor hard.

"Denny!" I hear Peri cry out while I scramble backward through the debris on the floor, away from the flames, as quickly as I can.

"I-I'm okay." That's not quite a lie. I'm not sure, but I think I'm unhurt. My heart's pounding in my chest harder than it ever has in my life, and I have to struggle to catch my breath.

And then the paintings start to burn.

The flames grow tall, almost too big for the fireplace, and I scramble to get the fire extinguisher in case it gets out of control. The heat is intense, much more than any fire I've ever set before, and I can feel sweat trickle down my forehead and run down the side of my face. Xan darts across the room and swings open the glass doors to the balcony, and I'm grateful for the cold rush of air.

"What the hell is that?" Elise's scream is shrill and panicked, and my first instinct is to cover my ears, but instead, I look away from the open door and instantly regret that I let my attention slip. Not that I would know how to stop what's happening.

The paintings are reaching out to Peri, wicked barbed tentacles of energy stretching toward her in an attempt to wrap her up.

I don't want to take my eyes off the fire, but I've got to get to Peri to help her somehow. I back up blindly, leaving the extinguisher where it is until I've almost reached her.

"Don't get too close, Denny!" Elise shrieks. I wave both her and Xan back because the last thing I need is for them to get hurt, too. Someone's got to get us out of here in the end, no matter how this goes.

Peri's hands are raised in front of her in a protective stance. Her eyes are wide and full of fear, but she's clenching her jaw. I can tell that she's not going to go down without a fight.

I'm not going to let her go down alone.

The grasping, seeking tentacles aggressively surge forward, searching for her. I don't even think—I can't; if I stop to think this is all over—I just throw myself between her and the ethereal strands with all my might.

There's a deafening shrieking sound as the tentacles jerk back away from me like I'm made of acid or poison, and then a burst of light blinds me as I hit the floor with a hard thud. I know I should be hurting, but the surge of adrenaline coursing through me tells me to keep moving, so I scramble up as fast as I can.

The light is coming from Peri. No, from behind her?

As soon as I see it, time feels like it slows down to a crawl. I'm doing my best to slog my way over to her through air as thick as molasses. Despite the open door, the room fills with a layer of smoke, and the light coming from behind Peri shines through it like the sun trying to shine through clouds. It gives her an almost angelic appearance.

It finally dawns on me that it's coming from the tattoo that Vali gave her. The thistle design is glowing like it's on fire.

The tentacles seem to have regrouped, and as I watch in dread, they lunge out toward her once again. Whatever she's trying to do to fight them off, even with the protective sigil at her back to aid her, isn't enough to stop them.

Fuck this. I don't know what comes over me, but I'm just so goddamn tired of the greed and insecurity of all these artists that tried to make Peri their salvation, their ticket to greatness. She offered it to me, thinking that was what she was supposed to do. She's never had a choice to be her own person.

I want that for her now that I've tasted it for myself. Even if that means I have to give it up.

I take a deep breath, step in front of her, and grab the energy tentacles with both hands.

And then I hold on for dear life while I yank them toward me as hard as I possibly can.

"No, Denny! What are you doing?"

I hear her screams from far away, another world from where I am now. It's just me and this parasitic energy, this need.

I let it pour into me, fill me up with pulsing electricity, vitality. I feel myself buzzing with it, alive in a way that I've never felt, vital and vibrating and desperate to touch the one who made it. Desperate to touch Peri, to embrace her, to reunite with her—

I've made a mistake.

I'm too far gone now, though. The energy from the paintings has control and I'm trapped here in the body that's now housing this uncontrolled power. I watch in horror as Peri runs to me. I'm helpless to stop whatever's going to happen, a voiceless witness.

My body lurches forward, and my hands of their own volition reach out to grab her arms and pull her close. There's a surge that moves through me, the energy gathering itself up into a tight ball in my middle before it flows out of me through my arms and hands to rush into her.

She takes in that energy willingly, wrapping her arms around me and pulling me closer until I feel like she's going to absorb all of me along with the forces that were trapped in the paintings. Our lips meet and she's kissing me, energy flowing between us there too, blinding in its brightness until that's all I can see, all I can feel.

"Denny? Denny!"

Shit, did I black out again?

It takes me a minute to come back to myself, and I'm definitely not ready to open my eyes. I'm sitting mostly upright, if you can count being on the floor with my upper body slumped over my knees upright. I shift a little, and I feel debris move under my rear. Okay, I'm still in my old bedroom. It's cold; why is it so cold? Didn't we have a fire going—

Oh shit. Peri.

My eyes snap open, and I try to sit up straight. I instantly regret it because everything tilts, and I feel like the floor's falling away from me. I close my eyes again and try to breathe through it, and slowly, everything stabilizes again.

"Is Peri...is everyone okay?" Ugh, I sound pathetic and small.

No, let's be real. I sound utterly exhausted.

There's a shifting sound, and then a soft, warm hand touches mine, almost like they're afraid to do so.

"Do you think you can open your eyes now? I'm right here." I can hear the worry in Peri's voice, so I do my best to do as she's asked, cautiously.

At first, I can't focus on anything. The world's a soft blur, and I can't help but think that's for my protection. Am I ready to see what's happened?

"I feel weird," I mumble. "And my eyes don't want to focus."

"I think you might have a concussion." I feel her hand run through my hair, gently touching my scalp as she checks for wounds. "There's some blood back here. You're really lucky it's not busted wide open."

"Mmm. Again, huh? Maybe this time, it knocked some sense into me. That would be a first."

After some effort on my part, I'm able to get my eyes to cooperate. I turn my head slowly and finally look at Peri.

Oh fuck, she's so beautiful. But it's different now, somehow. She's not the same person I mooned over every afternoon at The Bean, a beguiling ray of sunshine that I couldn't help but stare at. There's something darker and unfamiliar there now, and yet I feel like I'm connected to her in a deeper way than ever before.

She smiles at me, self-conscious and blushing, and laughs a little.

"I'm still myself, Denny. But now you see all the parts of me you couldn't before because you idealized me. And I guess...well, I buried them away, so I forgot about that part of me, too." She swallows nervously before she continues. "When I said that the Nyxen were right about me, I had no idea how true that was. I pushed all my power down inside me and let myself believe that I had no control over my fate or who I let myself influence. And you had to pay the price for that along with me. I wanted us to be free, but now we're tied together even more tightly."

"We are? But I don't feel different. I feel like myself, just a really beat-up version." She frowns, and I shake my head, careful not to start the world spinning again. "No, listen. I don't know what it means. But I feel in my guts that we are free. I wanted to be with you from the beginning. I've never fallen in love with anyone before, but you gave me all the reasons that I could. I mean, I almost feel stupid saying it because it's so obvious we've been connected since the beginning. Whatever's happened today just enhances that. It's not a trap, it's a bond—and one that I don't want to lose."

She's still blushing, but now her eyes are filled with tears, too. I carefully reach over and wipe one away that's trickling down her cheek, and she stifles a sob.

"I-I never thought you'd say it."

"Say what?"

"That you love me. That's why I didn't say it because I didn't want to pressure you."

"But you do?" My heart does a little flip-flop.

"I've loved you since that first date, Denny. Even though you were scared and skeptical, your eyes lit up when I showed you who I am, or I guess what I was pretending was all of me. I knew then. And those photos you took confirmed that I was right to love you. Though I'm sorry, it's been awful since then."

"The only thing that was awful was everyone else that tried to use you, Peri."

I can't stand it anymore. I need to be closer to her. I pull her into a hug, and she's gentle with her embrace, but it still hurts. I don't care. I don't want to let go.

"Whoa, what the fuck happened here?"

I look up from where my face is nestled into Peri's shoulder and see Vali, Sousa, and Karsten standing in the doorway. Both Vali and Sousa are in open-mouthed shock at the smoking destruction all around us. I honestly hadn't noticed until I saw their reaction. I've been a little distracted, you see.

Karsten, though, is looking at us with this satisfied grin.

"I can't wait to hear this story. Let's get you home so you can tell us everything."

Those are the second-best words I've heard tonight.

CHAPTER 31
ANAÏS MITCHELL – BRIGHT STAR

It's yet another relentlessly rainy spring day in the city, and Karsten's convinced me to go for a walk.
I recently started teaching them the basics of photography. Whenever we're both free, we get together and stroll around our Mount Vernon neighborhood, taking random photos. We try to shoot the same subjects, then we compare the results and explore what makes them different and why. It's a lot of fun, and we manage to find many distractions along the way, like wandering the vintage shops on Charles Street or ducking into the small art galleries in the area.

Today, we start off at the Frisky Bean because Vali's training Peri in the fine art of making espresso drinks. Peri's been complaining about not having any real-world skills, and Vali dared her to come pick up some shifts at the Bean. But really, I'm the winner because now I have two reasons to come and sit by the windows while I drink black coffee and work on editing photos.

Peri makes me take an oatmeal cookie latte, which evidently is made with oat milk and tastes just like advertised. It's not something I'd usually drink, but I'll admit that it's addictive. When I tell her I like it, her smile practically lights up the room.

So worth it.

We've been avoiding Mount Vernon Park for obvious reasons—namely that I'm not sure I'm ready to encounter the Nyxen yet. Instead, we stick to taking shots of architectural details that often get overlooked on some of the buildings in the neighborhood, like the little decorative stone carvings hidden in plain sight over our heads. Eventually, we're both rain-soaked and out of warm beverages.

"Perhaps we should head back to The Maithe, my friend. I believe that the rain is starting to come down harder." Even Karsten's snake-like hair is drooping and much less lively than usual.

It's a sensible suggestion, and I'm ready to agree when something catches my eye. It's a sandwich board sign with a rain-streaked chalk message urging us to visit the opening day of a new, exciting artist's show. The arrow on it points to a small gallery I haven't seen before. I can't spy a name for the space, either. I'm intrigued.

"Want to duck in here first? I'd love to see what it's like inside, and we could get out of the rain."

Karsten brightens at this thought. "I like this plan. I know you've been looking for places to show your latest work, so perhaps this will be a good choice."

Leave it to them to pick up on my unspoken thoughts.

We climb the stairs and push the dark metal and glass door open, which announces our presence with a soft chime. The gallery, despite the large front window, is darker than I expected, although the art is all carefully illuminated. It gives the feeling that each painting lives in its own bubble of light, one that will envelop the viewer while they stand before it. It's a really cool effect.

I grin at Karsten and see that they're looking around, confused.

"Where is everyone? It's so empty."

"It's a rainy weekday, so I wouldn't be surprised if we're some of the only people who visit today. The staff is probably in the back somewhere. They won't mind if we wander around and look at the art."

Karsten nods, but they still look uncomfortable. I get it because it does feel like we're the only ones here. It's so quiet. Even our damp shoes barely make a sound on the floorboards.

We drift over to the first painting, and my breath catches when I focus on it.

It's done in a style that feels familiar to me somehow, though I don't consciously recognize it. There's a field of soft blues and greens overlapping in many shades, from cerulean to a muted olive in an impressionistic blur. Overlaid on that is a movement of dots and swirls in more blues and greens, with a hint of purple and brown. I say movement because it truly feels like it's in motion, or it would be as soon as we look away.

I feel an uncomfortable itch in the back of my brain as I try to puzzle out what's happening in this piece of art, because it feels like I should know.

"Denny? You should come look at this."

I join Karsten, who is standing in front of a large canvas, mouth slightly agape. I'm glad I'm not the only one who is seeing this—but what we're seeing freaks me right the hell out.

They're Nyxen.

Each of the paintings are depictions of Nyxen. Some are more obvious than others, but they're like those magic paintings from the 90s, the ones that you'd have to look at the right way to see what's hidden in them. Once we've seen it, we can't not see it.

"What the hell?" I whisper, but it feels like my words echo in the gallery.

We drift from one capsule of light to the next, taking in the skillful, subtle depictions of beings that, until now, I thought were too secretive to allow themselves to be captured like this. I'll fully admit there's a tiny part of me that feels a little jealous, too. I guess I got used to the idea of being special to the capricious Elementals.

"Holy shit, that's Dorcha."

I stop in front of a triptych, two narrower panels that flank a larger one. It's obviously the crown of this exhibit, taking up the entire back wall of the gallery. I'm not even sure how we didn't notice it when we first walked in; it's so big and stunning, but nothing about this art show has felt normal.

The middle panel features Dorcha in all their brackish-water, seaweed-wrapped glory, a much more recognizable figure than any of the other paintings have had. It takes my eyes a moment to adjust to the rest of the composition, but slowly, the harbor, then the Broadway pier comes into focus for me. Dorcha looms terrifyingly large in the foreground, giving me the impression that I'm being judged for my misdeeds. The details are soft, but the effect is a nightmarish one.

I hear Karsten's sharp intake of breath, and I guess they're seeing it too, but I can't dwell on it too much. I've become too distracted by the smaller panels.

One is Bethany, recognizable to me even in this abstract style, falling backward into dark waters below her. There's a halo-like effect around her body, highlighting her helplessness as she falls.

The other is Joolie.

I take an involuntary step closer because, despite everything I've seen so far, this feels the most unbelievable. She's depicted on her knees, head lowered as if she's grieving or penitent, hands flat on the bricks. Where Bethany is surrounded by light, Joolie's form is confined by dark, glimmering mist.

It's got such intense energy that I feel a wave of guilt and nausea looking at it. There's no question in my mind that Joolie painted these, but how? And why is there an art show filled with her work?

"They're quite compelling, aren't they?"

I almost jump out of my skin at the voice behind me and whirl around to find myself face to face with a tall, thin woman with dark brown skin and silvery locs in a bobbed style. She's wearing a long kaftan-style dress in the same colors as Joolie's paintings, and if you told me that she'd stepped out of one of them, I wouldn't argue.

"Oh, I'm sorry to have startled you!" Her laugh is throaty and warm, and I feel my panic tick back just a little. I sense Karsten relax some, too, though I know without looking that they're still on guard.

"Um, it's okay. We were captivated." I gesture uselessly at the paintings behind us. "I hadn't heard anything about this show."

She nods like she expected me to say this.

"We just opened yesterday, but without the artist attending the reception, it made a much smaller splash than expected. No pun intended!" She laughs, and Karsten and I stand there awkwardly while I privately cringe at the joke.

"Can you tell us about the artist?" Karsten's low voice snaps the woman out of her amusement.

"Oh, it's all quite a mystery! I received an email with all the details about her paintings and not much else. I understand they've left behind a former body of work and don't want to be tied to it in any way, but you didn't hear that from me." She winks at me when she doesn't get a reaction from Karsten.

I'm not sure I give her the response she's looking for either because she raises an eyebrow and walks away from us at a clip, disappearing behind the wall that displays the triptych. She emerges a moment later with a small brochure in her hand and gives it to Karsten.

"Everything I know about the artist is here. As you can see, it's not much. If you're interested in any of these, let me know. Proceeds are being donated to several charities, so it's a write-off." The way she smiles after that tells me that she's practiced this patter on richer people than I'll ever be.

"Okay, thanks. We'll let you know if there's anything." I'm ready to get out of this awkward conversation, and that makes me ruder than I mean to be, but the woman takes it in stride. She's probably dealt with much less pleasant people.

She wanders back behind the wall, and Karsten opens the brochure that she'd found for us so we can both scan it. The front has one of the larger Nyxen paintings and the title "Whispers from the Water" in an italicized font, with the name J.L. Keyes in smaller print. It's obvious they've purposefully minimized the artist's name, which is so contrary to what I know about Joolie that, for a moment, I think maybe I'm mistaken.

The inside of the brochure is almost completely taken up by a photo of the triptych, with Dorcha's eyes boring into me like I'm disappointing them. Under that is a short paragraph mentioning that to honor the artist's inspirations, all proceeds from sales of the artwork will be divided between the Healthy Waterways Project and a scholarship program with the Art Institute.

"The scholarship is designed to offer support to at-risk and disadvantaged students in order for them to immerse themselves fully and freely in their studies without burden or distraction," I read aloud from the brochure.

"Like you were?" Karsten asks.

"A scholarship like this might have kept me from attaching myself to the Ants and Joolie. I would have had more money and freedom. She knows that's always been one of the reasons I stayed. She threw it in my face often."

For just a second, that buzzing feeling that had haunted me when we were fighting Joolie intrudes into my head, and I fight back the emotions that rush forward with it.

Maybe this is how I start to forgive her. Though I'll never be able to forget what she did to Peri in her quest to be something more than she was.

"I need to get out of here," I tell Karsten, my voice shaking just enough to betray that being here has gotten under my skin.

They don't even question it, moving immediately toward the door with one hand on my upper arm protectively. As soon as the glass door closes behind us, we're hit full-on by a thick wall of humidity. I feel like I'm suffocating.

I manage to get down the stairs, Karsten close behind me and keeping me upright until I find the cool stone wall of the building to press my back up against. Karsten doesn't ask any stupid questions like "Are you okay?" thankfully. They just watch me carefully, concern in their eyes.

"I just need to catch my breath—oh, come *on*."

I say it before I can censor myself as a Nyxen forms out of mist in front of us.

"Are you displeased to see me, Denny Myers?" From the twinkle in its eyes, I haven't managed to insult it, at least. I try to get my shit together before I respond.

"Just surprised. Overwhelmed. And aren't you worried that you'll be seen out here?"

"Oh, Denny." It laughs, obviously delighted by my ridiculous question. "Has that ever been a problem before? You know we have our ways to deal with mortals." It winks at me, and I get an uneasy feeling in my guts.

"Like you've dealt with Joolie?"

The Nyxen just smiles inscrutably and tilts its head like it's waiting for me to say more. So, recklessly, I do.

"Did you—did you hurt her? Punish her?"

"Ah, you mortals. Always looking for vengeance as an answer. Did we not allow her to paint? Does that seem like a punishment?" The Nyxen doesn't seem angry about my questions, just puzzled. And maybe a little disappointed.

"No, I don't want her to be punished. Not like you're thinking, anyway. I guess." I stop long enough to think about how I want to say what I'm feeling. The Nyxen waits more patiently than I might expect it to. "I mean, there's no way to make up for what she did. But, if there's a way she can become a better person? Fuck, I don't know. I don't think hurting her because she hurt someone else fixes anything, though."

I scuffle at the ground with one of my boots because I don't know what to say, even after all this time. It's been an open wound for both Peri and me that's only recently begun to scab over.

"Let me assure you, my dear mortal, that we have not hurt your former friend." I'm surprised by the softness of the Nyxen's words. "We used painting as a sort of therapy, you might say. She is directed to keep painting until she transforms the harm she caused into healing. We set the command on her, and she will paint until her charge is expunged. It is up to her to know when her ledger is wiped clean.

"She will continue under our protection until that time. Don't worry about her, little photographer. She is well-kept. Perhaps one day, we will arrange a visit."

It smiles again, and it's plain to see that it's quite pleased with itself. I can't decide how I feel about it. Before I can respond, it reaches out and puts a damp, barely formed finger under my chin.

"And you! We gave you a gift, and so did your muse. Yet you have done little with it but wander the streets and take photos of bricks. Get to living, Denny. You may argue that you've been doing that, but we both know you're meant to share the fruits of these gifts with others. Don't you think that now is the time?"

Before I can respond to agree or deny, the Nyxen dissolves into the rain as I watch.

Karsten and I stand there for a minute, dumbfounded by the whole exchange, while the rain continues to fall, soaking us thoroughly.

I finally ask, "Do you think I've been putting off living?"

"That's not something I can determine." There's a pause and then a grin. "I think a discussion over some very hot coffee is in order. Perhaps with some of our other friends."

"Peri won't say one way or the other. You know she's been so quiet about everything that's happened."

"I think you might be surprised, my friend. But why not ask her and see?"

When we get back to The Maithe, I go back to my room and find dry clothes. There's a warm towel waiting for me, too, courtesy of whatever magic The Maithe does that makes these kinds of things normal. Peri's not there, but I'm sure it'll be easy enough to find her. Ever since that night in Mount Vernon Park, we've been more in tune with each other than ever. Usually, if I think about her, my feet will just naturally take me to her, like a subtle magnetic pull.

What does it mean for me to get to living, as the Nyxen insisted that I do?

I do have an inkling. It scares me, but maybe my friends and my girlfriend will help me find my resolve.

Right on schedule, as soon as that thought crosses my mind, I feel that familiar tug that tells me where to find Peri. I let it take control and find myself a moment later walking into the library.

Of course. It's become our comfort place over the last couple of months.

"I knew you were on the way, so I poured you this." Peri, a big smile on her lovely face, waves me over with the familiar tardigrade mug in one hand. She pats the cushion next to her on the loveseat, a new addition to the library that she and I have basically commandeered as our usual spot.

"Wow, the gang's all here," I joke as I take the coffee from her. We'd made a casual circle out of the comfy seating in the library a while back. These days, most of the steady residents of the house come to claim a seat in the evening hours and read, talk, or show off what we're currently making. Pod jokingly calls it "Denny's Salon" because I was the first one to start inviting people to hang out with me there. The name has stuck, and I even heard Sousa once refer to it that way to some Eleriannan I don't know well.

I always make a point that anyone is welcome to join, but the usual group is me, Peri, Pod, Karsten, Sousa, and Vali. Often, we get Merrick, or Lucee and Cullen to join us, but not tonight.

"Karsten told us about your adventure today," Sousa says in a way of greeting. I expect him to look concerned or disapproving, but instead, he's got this air of "What can you do? It's Elementals" about him. It's hard for me to keep an amused look off of my face at his reaction, so I don't.

"You're surprisingly mellow about that."

"Think you proved to everyone that you can handle yourself." Unexpectedly, he winks at me. "Besides, I know the Nyxen like you. They've got a weird way of showing it, though."

"Yeah. Weird is the mildest way of putting it." I take a long drink of the coffee, then throw out what's been on my mind. "Did Karsten tell you that I was advised I needed to get a life? Evidently, I'm not living up to the expectations of my watery patrons."

"Hey! That's not how the Nyxen meant it," Karsten admonishes me. "Don't bring back that old Denny playbook."

"I was joking. Kind of. I mean, it did feel like a loving scolding." Karsten snorts at that, which was my plan. "Anyway, it was specific about one thing. It thinks I should be sharing the things I'm creating. And I guess it's right. Maybe it's time I did an art show of my own?"

My hesitant admission gets drowned out by cheers from Vali and Peri and a whoop from Pod.

"I was wondering when you'd finally decide about this," Pod exclaims. "It's been so long!"

"Y'know, Souz and I have been talking about it in anticipation of this day. We have ideas," Vali says. "If you're down, that is."

"Whaddya say to your photos, some pieces from Vali, and a set by The Drawback? Pod, too. It's not like we've got an entire ballroom or anything." Sousa's self-satisfied grin is almost too much. I can't help but laugh. He's so good at that.

"I-uh—"

"I'll help you with everything, you know." Peri slips her hand around my arm, reassuring me. "I'll be right here, by your side, for all of it."

I look around the circle at all of their faces. They've believed in me from the very beginning. How can I fail with them behind me?

"Okay." I pause, thinking about the last time I saw The Drawback play. "But let's try to keep the weirdness to a minimum?"

"Have you even seen us?" Sousa says, his face in mock offense. "That's our main draw! And like it or not, you're one of us now. You'd better get used to things being weird."

I don't say it aloud, but I wouldn't trade it for the world.

Made in the USA
Las Vegas, NV
21 May 2024